THE ADVENTURERS GUILD

TWILIGHT OF THE ELVES

THE ADVENTURERS GUILD

TWILIGHT OF THE ELVES

ZACK LORAN CLARK

AND

NICK ELIOPULOS

DISNEP • HYPERION

Los Angeles   New York

All rights reserved. Published by Disney • Hyperion, an imprint of Disney Book Group. No part of this book may be reproduced or transmitted in any form or by any means, electronic or mechanical, including photocopying, recording, or by any information storage and retrieval system, without written permission from the publisher. For information address Disney • Hyperion, 125 West End Avenue, New York, New York 10023.

First Hardcover Edition, November 2018
First Paperback Edition, October 2019
10 9 8 7 6 5 4 3 2 1
FAC-025438-19235
Printed in the United States of America

This book is set in FCarlsonTwelve/Monotype
Designed by Phil Caminiti and Mary Claire Cruz
Map art by Virginia Allyn

Library of Congress Cataloging-in-Publication Control Number
for Hardcover Edition: 2017058414
ISBN 978-1-368-00033-8

Visit www.DisneyBooks.com

SUSTAINABLE FORESTRY INITIATIVE

Certified Sourcing
www.sfiprogram.org
SFI-00993

Logo Applies to Text Stock Only

For Zack Lewis, a fantastic adventuring partner
—ZLC

For Andrew, who cast a spell on me
—NE

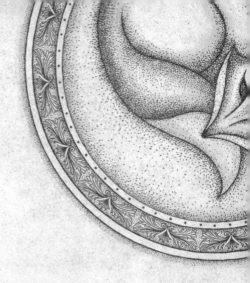

Chapter One

Zed

Zed crept through the snow-covered forest, shivering beneath his heavy cloak.

He moved quickly, cutting between the trees and following the footprints left by their leader. His friends trailed him in a staggered line, crunching noisily through the frost. Above them, the stars sparkled in a silent parade of their own.

They'd been hiking since sunup, and now, well after sundown, Zed was exhausted. His legs felt numb and ungainly, like he was walking on stilts. Ahead of him, their leader stopped midstride and raised a hand. Zed paused, huffing gratefully. His breath met the cold air as a plume of mist.

When a long moment passed and they still hadn't moved, Zed finally thought to search the woods.

"What is it?" he whispered. "A Danger?"

He quashed a kernel of panic before it had chance to take root. Still, Zed reached inward to draw upon his mana, in case he needed it. Soon he felt it there—a sensation like dipping his fingertips just below the surface of a pool of water.

Zed's *actual* fingers flickered with green pennants of flame. He was ready for anything.

But their leader turned instead, his eyes taking in the apprentices behind him.

And what a pair of eyes . . . So green and gemlike they practically glowed. The irises were huge, much larger and brighter than human eyes.

They belonged to an elf. And not just any elf: Callum was the leader of the rangers, Llethanyl's elite exploration force. He was a wood elf, the most common of the three sects. His skin was smooth and pale, with a tinge of green emerging from the hairline, and his auburn hair glistened in the moonlight like a dewy flower. Callum's ears were long and dagger thin; they made Zed's own pointed ears look practically round.

There was a crunch of snow as Brock sidled up behind him, followed by Liza, Micah, and Jett. All five of them wore deep-blue traveling cloaks.

The cloaks were new, and the fur that lined them was warm and soft. It was the finest piece of clothing that Zed had ever owned. In the last six weeks the Sea of Stars had made many friends in Freestone, friends who were excited to outfit its heroic young apprentices in luxurious, tailor-made gifts. Saving a city had that effect, Zed supposed. Recently smiths had been falling over themselves to provide the guild with the steepest discount; even Zed's mother had been given a tidy raise from her mistress.

"What's going on?" Brock flashed Zed a questioning look. "Are we there yet?"

Zed shrugged. "I'm not sure," he whispered. "Callum just—"

Behind them, Liza shushed for quiet.

"Keep moving!" Micah grunted impatiently. "It's colder than Frond's compliments out here."

Jett snorted. "Like you'd know."

"I know your mother's a—"

"*Shhhh!*" Liza hissed again, the noise buzzing through the trees.

The five were on their apprentice journey, an overnight scouting mission the guild ran to test their newest members' quest-worthiness. Any apprentices who passed would be able to join the guild on longer missions outside.

Zed knew they were headed toward some kind of shelter to bed down for the night. They had to be close now, with the sun so far beneath the trees. But he still didn't see anything resembling a man-made structure. Just mounds and mounds of white fluff.

The darker it grew, the more nervous Zed became. Most

Dangers hunted at night, and many in Freestone believed the horrors that had driven the elves from their home might follow them. Out in the quiet forest, it was hard not to imagine monsters lurking in every shadow.

The apprentice journey was usually made with a master adventurer as a chaperone, if not Guildmistress Frond herself. That Frond trusted Callum to lead her five young recruits said much about him, and about the bond that the human adventurers and elven rangers had formed over the years.

Zed only wished that the High Ranger wasn't so quiet and brooding. He had a thousand questions for Callum, only several hundred of which he'd been able to ask before the elf finally called for silence.

Jett spotted their goal. "There," he grunted. The dwarf hefted an iron maul in one hand, training it toward a particularly large snowbank.

Zed squinted at the pile that Jett was pointing to—and then suddenly he saw it. The snow parted over a tapered arch at the bottom of the mound. They weren't huddled near a snowdrift. They were standing at a doorway.

The six crept forward, congregating around the partially buried door. Liza began shoveling snow with her shield, and soon all the apprentices joined in, digging away at the pile. Callum neither helped nor commented. The elf merely watched, those bright eyes glinting in the moonlight.

Once they had dug away the pile, they saw the door itself was covered by a thick layer of ice: hoarfrost that had hardened over time. Zed could just make out a handle and lock buried under all that ice. The door appeared to be made of solid metal.

Jett pointed to his shiny new hammer, an excited gleam in his eyes. He'd been itching to use it on the mission but hadn't had a chance yet.

Micah and Liza both emphatically shook their heads no, their dark eyes and olive-skinned faces similarly grave. It was a rare moment of agreement between the twins.

Brock smirked, then raised his eyebrows at Zed. He wiggled his fingers toward the door.

"Right," Zed whispered. "Everyone stand back." He braced his feet and raised both palms toward the frozen doorway, linking his thumbs and closing his eyes. He could hear snow crunching as the other apprentices backed into a wide semicircle.

Zed glanced over his shoulder to make sure Callum was watching. The elf gave a little nod.

Silently, Zed called upon his mana.

The flames began as green ribbons snaking between his fingers, but soon they joined together and poured forth in a bright emerald torrent. In six weeks of training with Hexam, Zed had yet to match the power or precision from his first use of the spell—the blast that had destroyed the horrific monster threatening all of Freestone.

Still, anything caught within a six-foot cone in front of him would burn, and burn fast. The green flames seemed hungrier than normal fire . . . even other magical fire.

Zed opened his eyes to see that the ice was quickly boiling away. His friends' faces looked eerie, lit by the otherworldly glow. He quashed his mana with practiced care, lest it eat through the door entirely. The flames guttered out from his hands, revealing a steaming metal archway barely six feet tall.

Zed grinned, pleased with his work. After weeks of mishaps, this had been his finest spell-casting yet.

He glanced back again at Callum . . . and was dismayed to find that the elf had already turned away. Callum scraped at the ground, bringing a fistful of frozen earth to his nose. He sniffed it, his eyes narrowing as he sifted the particles between his fingers.

Brock moved forward, gingerly touching the iron padlock that was fastened to the door. Apparently satisfied it wouldn't broil his palm, he lifted it in one hand and peered into the keyhole. Then he produced a pick and torsion wrench with a quick flourish, as if he'd plucked them from the keyhole instead of his sleeve.

He curtsied theatrically to Liza, who snorted. Brock had been practicing that trick for weeks.

As Brock set to work picking the lock, Zed repressed a wave of almost delirious hunger. The strain of marching all these hours without a true meal suddenly tugged at his belly. Once inside, hopefully they could stop to eat something beyond travel oats and crumbs of cheese.

"Hey look," said Jett. "A raccoon."

Zed glanced up, following Jett's finger to where a squat catlike creature watched them curiously from the trees. Its reflective eyes shone behind a mask of black fur. Zed had learned the names of so many strange animals in the past several weeks—animals that lived only beyond the wall. Sometimes it was hard to remember which were natural and which were Dangers.

"Aren't you cold, little guy?" Jett called up.

The raccoon blinked, but was otherwise still. Zed didn't know much about such creatures, but this didn't look like a particularly healthy specimen. Its ribs jutted out, visible beneath patchy fur. A dark, unsettling wound had been clawed across its side.

In the moonlight, its shining eyes almost seemed to glow. They were a sickly shade of purple.

"Apprentices." Callum's voice was controlled, but there was an urgency behind it that sent all five of them jumping. "Inside. Now."

A low *click* followed. As he watched Brock unhook the lock from the door handle, Zed realized his jaw was clenched tight.

Liza pushed the door open, taking the lead. The hinges turned with a metallic shriek that echoed through the forest.

Micah hissed and rolled his eyes, but Liza wasn't around to see it. She'd already disappeared into the doorway.

The rest of them filed quickly inside, one after another, into the dark.

"What is this place?" Zed whispered, once the door had been closed and latched behind them. Now that they were out of the woods, his shoulders slowly relaxed.

The entrance opened to a wide staircase, which descended into the earth. Zed had no sense of how deep it went. He couldn't see farther down than a handful of steps.

The walls of the structure were made of carved stone, and surprisingly well-preserved. The air here was chilly—which was actually an improvement from outside.

"This is Halfling's Hollow, a wayshelter maintained by both the rangers and your guild." Callum's lilting accent drifted musically through the dark. Zed had yet to meet an elf who *didn't* have a lovely voice. "It's one of several that mark the path between Llethanyl and Freestone. Each is stocked with weapons and supplies. My people had to bypass this shelter on our way to Freestone. It hasn't been visited in six years. Reaching here was your first goal."

"Is it safe?" Jett asked. "The door was locked and frozen over. That means there are no Dangers here, right?"

The elf laughed, and the sound was as bitter as it was

beautiful. Zed could have sworn that Callum's echoes actually harmonized with his own voice. "Dangers have a way of breaching even the tightest seals," their guardian said. "There *are* no safe places in Terryn, dwarfson. As you all know from experience."

Zed glanced nervously down the staircase. "Who has the lamp?"

Micah snorted. "Who *needs* the lamp?"

Suddenly the air came alive with a gush of warm amber light. The radiance cascaded slowly over the walls, like waves of rippling honey. Zed turned to see Micah's left hand was raised, its outline glowing as if it had been sketched from pure light.

"Don't drain your anima," Liza scolded, though there wasn't much force behind the warning. Micah could keep this up for hours. The boy was annoyingly adept at the healers' arts—but, oh, did they all know it. Zed wondered if the Golden Way Temple had any idea what they'd lost when they let Mother Brenner turn their novice out onto the streets.

Callum watched Micah's glowing hand for a moment, then his eyes fell to the stairs. "Your mission is to gather what supplies you can and bring them back to Freestone. Lead the way, children."

Liza shuffled to the fore. Recently she'd graduated from leathers to chain-mail armor, wearing a hauberk commissioned from the Smiths Guild as a birthday gift from her father. (Micah had received a pair of socks.)

Zed truly had no idea how Liza could stand under all that metal, let alone march for hours. She might look like an average girl her age, but the noble's daughter was a force of nature.

Liza descended the stairs slowly, sword out and shield high. Micah and Brock followed just behind, with Zed and Jett behind them.

"How's your leg?" Zed whispered to the dwarf.

"Less sore than yours, I'm guessing," Jett cracked.

Zed grinned. "I think you're probably right."

Jett's left leg had been lost to a monster attack, during their very first night as apprentice adventurers. Beginning below his knee was a silvery prosthetic, a gift from the elven rangers. It was forged from a metal called mythril. "Elven steel," Jett had knowingly dubbed it. "Very impressive stuff.

"Though not as impressive as *dwarven* steel," he'd added.

The elves used mythril for all their prosthetics. It was springier than most metals, and tougher than wood. Jett's new leg ended in a long, elegantly bladed foot. With training, he had learned first to walk without a cane, and then even to run. Though he'd never been *especially* fond of running.

"If I'm honest," Jett said more seriously, "it tingles. I can still feel it there . . . literally an itch I can't scratch. And the stump aches like *Fie*."

"Micah can help with that," Zed whispered. "Once we settle in."

Jett rolled his eyes. "So it's a choice between a pain in the leg and a pain in the butt."

As they descended, Micah's light parted the curtains of darkness, revealing a second door, this one made of wood.

The door was ajar.

Zed glanced back at Callum, standing just behind him. The elf narrowed his eyes and raised his hand, hissing a short warning. The group stopped immediately.

Callum slid forward, gliding easily between the apprentices until he knelt at the open doorway.

He peered inside.

In the silence, Zed felt a single bead of sweat trailing down his back.

"You humans are sloppy," the elf said finally. He stood and pushed the door open, revealing a spare but clean barracks. "I'll have to remind Frond to shut the inner door next time."

A chorus of relieved sighs filled the stairway. Zed and the others entered the shelter. Cots had been stacked up into neat rows, enough for a dozen travelers. There was a wooden table in the center of the room, standing over a moldy brown rug—the room's only decoration.

There were also weapon racks and stands for armor, each of them bearing equipment, and a half-dozen chests containing Fey knew what.

"How are we supposed to carry all this?" Micah groused.

"Dutifully," Callum said, glancing back at the stairway. "I would also advise quietly. But that can wait until morning. You'll bed here for the night." The ranger adjusted his gloves, tugging on the buckles. "If you children can survive without me for a moment, I'll be stepping outside."

"*Now?*" Zed protested. "But it's dark out. Shouldn't we at least eat first?"

Callum shook his head, but his face softened. "You may eat without me. Magic is hungry work, I've heard."

"Callum," Liza said. "Is everything all right?"

The High Ranger frowned. "I'm just taking a look around." He unhooked his bow from his back. "I'll return soon. If I don't, do *not* come looking for me. Wait until daybreak, then head immediately for Freestone."

"Be careful," Liza said.

Callum nodded once, then slipped out the door and up the stairs.

Micah, Jett, and Brock each threw themselves into the lower-stacked cots, while Liza set to work lighting a single dirty lantern with smudged glass panes that was hanging from the wall.

"Everything hurts," Brock moaned. "This has got to earn us a day off from drills, right?"

"I'm pretty sure the Dolt doesn't *do* days off," Micah said, using his private name for Lotte, their quartermaster and drill instructor.

"Lotte *might*," Jett said. The young dwarf had rested his

hammer against the cot and was massaging his residual limb, just above the prosthetic's socket. "Frond? Definitely not. Unless one of you wants to volunteer to get bitten by the next monster."

"Let's not tempt fate." Lantern lit, Liza was now on the other side of the room, peering at the equipment. "Some of this stuff looks elven," she said. "Zed, there's a big wand over here. Or it might be a small staff. There's a crystal on top, anyway."

"Really?" Zed asked excitedly. He was tugging his boots off near the door. "I wonder if it's a scepter. They have a focus embedded on top to channel magic."

But Liza was already making her way down the line. "This armor looks serviceable, but we have better stuff at the guildhall."

Then she reached the chests. There were six in all. Five were the same size and make: simple wooden trunks with iron supports. The sixth looked slightly wonky. The proportions were all wrong, and it leaned almost at a tilt, as if the cooper who'd constructed it had been hitting the dwarven ale.

Liza knelt down, reaching out to open the first chest.

And then Zed saw the sixth chest, the strange chest, open its *own* lid. The inner walls of the chest transformed, its smooth wood exploding into hundreds of curling points. The interior bottom, upholstered in scarlet fabric, swelled into a fleshy, viscous blister. In the span of a moment, the chest was filled by rows of jagged teeth, leading down to an enormous dripping tongue.

"*Liza!*" Zed screamed.

The girl turned just as the tongue lashed out, gripping her

13

arm like a frog snagging a fly. Liza yelped as she was jerked toward the monstrous trunk. She tried to wrestle her hand out of the tongue's grip, but it held taut, dragging her across the floor to those awful teeth.

Zed rushed forward, his hands raised, summoning up his mana as quickly as he could.

"Don't! You'll burn her!" Brock's voice brought him up short. He was right—Liza was too close to the chest. She'd be caught within the flames.

The other three boys were fumbling for their weapons, but they were too slow and too far away to help. The Danger jerked its meaty tongue one more time and Liza was yanked from her feet. Her arm fell into the gaping mouth of the chest.

It snapped shut. Liza screamed as all those teeth closed down upon her arm.

Brock appeared behind the Danger as if from nowhere. He raised his two pointed daggers high above his head, then stabbed them into the lid of the transformed chest. It let out a series of distressed croaks and its body sagged, the boxy shape melting away. The monster was looking more like a giant frog by the moment.

"Aim for the tongue!" Liza shouted. "And *don't* stab my hand!"

"So many *rules*," Brock complained. "How am I supposed to remember them all?" He yanked the blades from the Danger's head and viscous, vivid yellow fluid oozed out of the twin wounds.

The chest's mouth drooped open as it croaked unhappily. Liza used the opportunity to jerk her arm from its maw, kicking her feet out and bracing each against the rims of the trunk. Her chain mail had protected her from the worst of the creature's bite, but healing would be needed soon.

The monster's tongue held fast, though, dripping not just with saliva, but the yellow muck. Zed rushed to Liza's side, joined by Micah, and they each grabbed her entangled arm to help pull against the creature's grip. Micah's glowing hand bounced around as they strained, casting a shadow play of the struggle across the shelter's walls.

Brock moved quickly, stabbing down on the tongue with both daggers. The monster's gloomy croaking turned immediately into a blood-curdling shriek, and the deformed chest began to lurch from side to side. As its grip slackened, Liza grabbed up more of the tongue, wrapping the cord around her arm like a coil of slimy rope. Sweat dripped down her face as she locked her legs, holding the seesawing chest in place.

"Any time now would be great!" Liza shouted.

That was when Zed saw Jett—his giant hammer already raised high. The dwarf let out a bellow that echoed off the stone walls as he plunged the maul down upon the Danger's head.

The shrieking abruptly cut off, punctuated by a loud, wet

crunch. The walls, equipment, and all five apprentices were splattered by a torrent of yellow muck.

There was a moment of quiet, broken only by Zed's and the others' labored breaths.

Then the wooden door flew open, and Callum burst into the room. Three quails hung from a loop of rope in his hand. The elf's eyes widened as he took in the scene.

"We should probably wash up before dinner," Brock huffed.

Freestone's walls rose high above the tree line the next evening, as Zed and the other apprentices trudged home. Zed didn't think he'd ever seen a sweeter sight in his life. Each of the apprentices carried a giant pack of equipment, and they'd taken turns dragging a makeshift sled bearing the recovered armor. Jett pulled it now, having insisted on doing his share.

Zed heard the gate horns blare, announcing their arrival. His grip tightened on the scepter in his hands. He intended to keep that particular trophy; not even Hexam could pry the magic implement from him.

The portcullis creaked open before they'd even made it through the wards, and Zed saw several figures standing within the archway.

Alabasel Frond loomed at the front, her arms crossed. Her scarred face was as still and serious as ever.

Behind the guildmistress, Lotte and Hexam looked a bit more taken aback. Zed realized he and the others must have made an interesting sight. The five apprentices were all covered in dried yellow crust, their once-beautiful blue cloaks now stained and grimy.

Only one of the younger guild members accompanied the three master adventurers to greet them. Jayna stood beside Hexam, nervously wringing her hands. The young wizard had passed her own apprentice journey the previous year, so she hadn't been allowed to accompany her friends on their trip.

A day before they left, Jayna had come about as close to Frond as Zed had ever seen her willingly go, intending to ask for special permission to join the expedition. The girl had summoned up her courage, sought Frond out in the guildhall, and approached her slowly, one step at a time. Then, just as Jayna was five feet away, Frond turned around.

Jayna had quickly scurried down a side hall.

Now, as the adventurers passed beyond the invisible boundary of the city's magic wards, Frond stepped forward to meet the party.

"How did my apprentices do, High Ranger?" she called to Callum. "Are any of them fit for questing?"

Callum quickly bypassed the five young adventurers, who were all showing the strain of their long trudge through the woods. He alone was clean of any yellow goo.

"You've trained a fine group of apprentices," Callum said, waving a hand to Zed and the others. "I would recommend all five as quest-worthy. But, Frond—"

Jayna squealed happily, interrupting the ranger. She dashed forward to hug Liza. The two girls clasped hands and danced around in a circle. With the rangers having crowded into the Adventurers Guild hall, private quarters were a thing of the past. The apprentices had all been paired with roommates—Jayna with Liza, and Brock with Jett—while Zed had been stuck with Micah even before the elves arrived.

Since moving in together, Jayna and Liza had become almost inseparable friends. Zed watched them for a moment, the sting of jealousy threatening to spoil his own excitement. He glanced at Brock, who was shucking off his heavy pack. It fell to the ground with a metallic rattle.

Once, Zed and Brock would have celebrated their accomplishment together. But things had changed in the last several weeks. Zed and his once-best friend had drifted. Now Brock's gaze passed briskly over Zed as he turned toward the city gate.

"It looks like you ran into a bit of trouble," Frond said, eyeing the apprentices.

"A Danger had infested the wayshelter," Callum said. "A shapechanger. I failed to spot it hidden among the equipment. Frond, we *must—*"

"Did you know there are monsters that can disguise themselves as chests?" Brock said. "Because that's just really not fair."

"But everyone's unhurt?" Lotte said, approaching the group. Her long blond curls had been tied back into a ponytail. The quartermaster lifted Brock's pack from the ground like it weighed nothing at all.

"Liza was bitten, but the healer tended to it," Callum said. "But Frond, we have *more urgent matters* to speak of. The Lich—" Callum cut himself off. His eyes flicked to the apprentices, then up toward the knights standing over the gate. He stepped closer to Frond before continuing in hushed tones.

Frond's eyes widened.

The Lich.

Nearly two months ago, an army of undead Dangers had risen from Llethanyl's own crypts, led by the mysterious conqueror. Zed didn't know much about him, except that he was once a high-ranking minister who'd defiled the elves' sacred traditions.

Because the undead had risen from within the city, Llethanyl found itself caught off guard by the attack. The elves fought back, of course, but those who fell to the horde all rose again, adding to the Lich's vile army.

In the end, all the survivors could do was flee. The elves lost their home, and Zed lost all hope of ever visiting his father's birthplace.

Hexam and Lotte joined the other two adults, the four of them speaking and gesturing animatedly.

"What's going on?" whispered Jayna. "What did you all see out there?"

"I . . . I don't know," Liza faltered. "Callum said it was nothing."

"Grown-ups lie," Micah said with a big stretch. "Or hadn't you figured that out yet, sis?"

Finally, Frond held up a hand. She turned and marched through the gates without another look at the apprentices. Callum grimaced, then followed closely at her heels.

Hexam glanced back at the others with a long sigh before departing. Zed noticed the wizard eyeing the scepter in his hands, and he clutched it closer to his chest.

"Leave the gear here," Lotte said as she returned to the apprentices. "I'll have Syd and Fife fetch it back to the guildhall."

"Lotte," Jett started, but the quartermaster just shook her head. She suddenly looked very tired.

"Later," she said. "A meal's been set, with plenty of ambrosia. I'd hurry, though—those scuds are more than happy to start a celebration without the guests of honor." Lotte smiled wearily over the apprentices, even Micah. There was enough pride in her eyes for both herself *and* Frond. "I'm sorry, kids. I'm sure this wasn't the congratulations you were hoping for. But, truly, well done."

Zed felt his ears flush. He turned to Brock with a grin. "At least we'll have a head start on Fife. You coming?"

"Mh," Brock grunted in reply. "Save a plate for me. I need to run into town." The boy unclasped his stained cloak, letting it fall to the ground, but he left his travel leathers on.

"Really?" Zed asked. "Right *now*? Where are you going?"

"Just a quick errand," Brock said. "I'll be back before last bell . . . or not too long after."

Zed frowned. "What should I tell the others if they ask about you?" he said. "Which animal cowl do you want to wear at the party?"

But Brock was already slipping away. Zed lost sight of his friend before he'd even cleared the gate.

Chapter Two

Brock

Freestone had changed since the elves had come.

Brock had spent nearly his entire life within the con-
fines of the city's walls, and in that time he'd walked
every street and alleyway, visited every plaza and market stall. He knew the best shortcuts, knew which benches
enjoyed the most sunlight on an autumn afternoon. Above all,
he had the great statues of the Champions of Freestone thoroughly committed to memory. These he could see with his eyes
closed: the paladin's grim face glaring from within his helm; the
enchantress's ornate staff raised high; the priestess with her arms
outstretched; and the assassin, Dox, staring impassively ahead,

22

his unblinking eyes forever upon the city he and his companions had saved so long ago.

Brock wondered what Dox would think of that city now.

Traveling intown, away from the wall, Brock skirted the large area that had once been the marketplace. Where craftsmen and merchants had once practiced their arts beneath a sea of brightly colored canvas, now there was a shantytown. Those same colorful tents had been repurposed to provide meager shelter to the thousands of elves who had survived the journey from the faraway city of Llethanyl.

The population of Freestone had exploded overnight. Not surprisingly, that had caused some problems.

Brock's eyes flitted among the elves, but he was really counting the human knights—the Stone Sons—among them. The Sons had always been responsible for keeping the peace in Freestone, but usually that amounted to standing guard outside important buildings, pacing the top of the wall, and breaking up the occasional tavern brawl. Brock had never seen so many of them stationed in the same area before the elves moved in.

There was no law keeping the elves within their shantytown. But the sheer number of armed men surely sent a message that this was where the elves belonged. And from what Brock had seen, they found little welcome elsewhere in Freestone. Their language, lyrical and strange, drew suspicious and even hostile looks when spoken in mixed company. Their alien features and manner of dress had become favorite subjects of mockery for Freestone's bards. Worst of all was the popular idea that the elves were somehow to blame for their own misery. As if their unfamiliar customs and talent for magic made Llethanyl's fall inevitable. As if that made it any less of a tragedy.

Brock sighed sadly and moved on.

Near the very center of town, just before the drawbridge that led to Castle Freestone, was a park—one of the city's few natural spaces. Ringing that park was a series of buildings, each large and very old and of an architectural style that spoke of a more affluent time, when stone and wood were less precious and could be molded in whimsical flourishes. Brock loved these buildings for their strangeness. Each time he visited, he attempted to find some small detail he'd missed before: some pattern or carving he'd previously overlooked.

The largest among them was the guildhall of the merchants. Brock had been coming here since childhood, and the building fairly towered in his memory. With its tall marble columns and oversize doors, it towered over him still.

The story went that Dox the Assassin had founded the Merchants Guild on the day after the Day of Dangers. His best friend and adventuring partner, Foster, had been the warlock responsible for tearing open the gateways between worlds, allowing monsters to pass over in such numbers they consumed all of Terryn. It had fallen to Dox to execute his friend, and in doing so, Dox had saved the world—or what was left of it.

Brock had always believed that Dox's establishment of the Merchants Guild was in some ways the more impressive achievement. The merchants oversaw everything. They ensured there was always enough food to eat, enough fresh water to drink, enough ore and timber for construction and repairs. There were lean seasons when everyone had to do without some luxury or other, but for the last two hundred years, the guild had provided. They had it down to a science. Or they used to, before the elves had come.

This night, however, all appeared to be business as usual within the guildhall. There was a banquet under way; three hundred candles lit the voluminous central room from a dozen chandeliers and four times as many sconces. Musicians played, servants circulated, and a lavish spread of food acted as the centerpiece for a lively gathering. Brock, in stained leathers still wet with snowmelt and his own sweat, looked severely out of place. He ducked quickly into a washroom, where the servants he'd befriended let him keep a spare set of clothes in their supply closet.

Face scrubbed clean, in a shirt and tunic smelling of lavender, Brock was less self-conscious upon his return to the grand hall. Whether or not he belonged here, he at least looked the part. He hadn't gone two steps before a servant lowered a plate of pastries before him.

His mouth watered. He took a sticky cake from the tray and brought it immediately to his mouth. It was so sweet it made his cheeks tingle. He finished it in two more bites, then licked his fingers unabashedly.

"Wow," he said to himself. "I thought we were supposed to be rationing."

"Well, elves don't eat cake, do they?" said a woman at his elbow.

"Not if they can't pay for it, they don't," a man answered, and they both chuckled.

Brock screwed up his face. Suddenly the treat seemed to have a bitter aftertaste.

He strode through the grand hall with renewed purpose. In a corner of the room, he approached a wall-mounted candelabra and, after licking his finger and thumb once more, he pinched out one of the flames.

It was only a matter of seconds before a servant appeared. "Allow me to relight that, Messere," he said.

"The light offends my eyes," Brock said. It was the secret phrase the servant was expecting, and when the man nodded and stepped away, Brock knew to follow.

As they walked along the edge of the great hall, Brock scanned the crowd for his father. He knew just where to look. These past few weeks, the elder Dunderfel had been the constant companion of Borace Quilby, guildmaster of the merchants.

Quilby stood in the very center of the room, ruddy-faced and jovial, sloshing wine from his cup as he regaled those around him with some story. Brock's father stood at his elbow and laughed on cue, his status with Quilby obviously undamaged by Brock's own troubled dealings with the man.

Brock was genuinely surprised to see who else stood at Quilby's side. Ser Brent, guildmaster of the knights, tugged at the collar of his formal white tunic and attempted a smile as Quilby droned on. The false smile didn't suit him. Ser Brent was handsome and bold, and he tended to be the focus of any room he was in. Now, though, standing among Quilby's bootlickers, he looked as comfortable as a kitten in a basket of kobolds.

Brock was deeply curious. In his experience, good things rarely resulted when the town's guildmasters got together. But it wasn't as if he could elbow his way into that conversation. Quilby hadn't so much as spared Brock a glance since last season's failed attempt to oust Alabasel Frond from the Adventurers Guild. That didn't usually bother Brock, though; he knew, now, who was really in charge here.

The servant led him out of the hall, through the kitchens, and to a nondescript wooden door, which he unbolted with a key and threw open. Brock stepped within, and the servant did not follow, instead shutting and latching the door.

Brock descended a spiral staircase and walked through a long low-ceilinged corridor lined with torches. The stone walls grew damp as he traveled beneath Castle Freestone's moat and into a space that had once been the castle's dungeon.

Freestone had no use for a dungeon now. Since the Day of Dangers, the city could spare no resources keeping criminals alive. Executions and exile had long been the norm.

And so the dungeon currently served a very different purpose. It was now the home of the Merchants Guild's Shadow, the heart of Freestone's black market—where everything had a price, and a heavy cost besides.

Before stepping through the final archway, Brock drew up his hood and pulled from his pocket a slender domino mask, a simple black figure eight, which he stuck to his face with practiced skill. As masks went, it didn't do much to conceal his identity. But it was a necessary formality—one of the few rules of the Lady Gray's court.

Brock emerged into a larger subterranean space, lit not by flame but by the incandescent orbs favored by mages. The room was carved of the same cold stone as the corridor outside, but here it had been softened by rugs and tapestries and piles of soft pillows for sitting; burning incense masked the smell of damp. Chimes softly tinkled in a pleasant arrangement from an ensorcelled cherrywood music box.

Scattered about the room were a half-dozen men and women. All of them wore masks. And though none of the murmured conversations missed a beat, Brock could feel every set of eyes registering his arrival. The large man tending bar at the far end of the space lifted a broad hand in greeting, and Brock set out across the room. He passed a woman in an elegant dress whose green-sequined mask shone with reflected light. "Apprentice," she said, inclining her head.

"Mistress Venom," he said, nodding in return. "Master Knife." He nodded to the man beside her, whose own ornate mask was shaped from steel.

"Apprentice," Master Knife replied.

The man at the bar greeted Brock more warmly. He smiled, reaching across the countertop to slap at Brock's shoulder. "Good to see you, lad," he said in a gravelly voice.

"Hey there, Gramit," Brock said.

Gramit was a rarity among the Shadows. Like everyone else, he had a title. He was known as the Facilitator, and he had a hand in everything the guild did. But he insisted on being called by name. He wore the simple domino mask of an apprentice, which did nothing to disguise his features. His bald scalp was lumpy, as was his once-broken nose, and his pale face bore a smattering of pockmarked scars. He reminded Brock of a bleached potato.

"And what have you brought us today?"

"Wealth that loses value in the telling," Brock said, and Gramit chuckled. It was a well-worn routine by now, and Brock enjoyed the comfortable banter and Gramit's easy laughter. Everyone else in the Lady Gray's circle was too serious by far.

"She's expecting you," Gramit said, waving him toward a door on the far side of the bar.

Brock nodded wearily. "Of course she is."

If he didn't know to look for her upon entering her office, he might have missed her completely. A plain-looking woman of indeterminate age who favored the dull gray tones of the Servants Guild, the Lady had a preternatural talent for fading into the background.

"Hello, apprentice," she said. "I hear the journey was a success."

"Right," Brock answered. "We did such a swell job of almost dying that we get to almost die more often now. And farther from home!" He shook his fists mockingly. "Yay."

The Lady smiled without a trace of amusement. "I was only making conversation."

"You can blackmail me into spying for you. Into stealing for you." He closed the door behind him. "Pleasant conversation wasn't part of the deal."

Without invitation, Brock stomped across the room to the far wall, where he removed a false panel to reveal a map. It was an old map, drafted before the time of Dangers, and therefore priceless . . . and also largely useless. It showed a hundred sites that simply did not exist anymore.

"To business, then," the Lady said, utterly unbothered. "The Smiths Guild recently received a shipment of ore that didn't come from the quarry district. Anything suspicious there?"

"No," Brock said, dipping a quill into ink. "That was us.

Lotte needed time at their forge to help the rangers with weapons upkeep. Frond authorized a trade."

"Very good," said the Lady. She made a note in her ledgers, and Brock made a face.

He loathed the woman for good reason. She knew, somehow, that Zed had flirted with magic that went beyond what was considered safe and appropriate. Their first day as apprentice adventurers, he'd used a staff to draw not on the plane of Fey as the Mages Guild did, but on the dark plane of Fie. And it hadn't stopped there; Brock knew that Zed kept a book on fiendish magic, and if Brock knew that, chances were good that the Lady Gray did as well. She seemed to have eyes and ears everywhere. And she had threatened to go public with what she knew about Zed if Brock refused to serve as her man inside the Adventurers Guild.

So far, however, her actual goals were hard to argue with. Someone, purposely or not, had brought into Freestone a monstrous parasite that had destroyed Mother Brenner. As the only individuals who ever left the safety of the wards, it was all but impossible to suspect anyone but the adventurers. And indeed, upon investigating the matter, the Lady Gray had determined that someone within the guild had been selling goods from outside the wall—everything from wildflowers to monster viscera had made its way to Freestone's black market.

That supply had entirely dried up, however. The person

responsible had disappeared. Not that the Lady had given up looking.

"You will mark the spot on the map? Where the ore came from, I mean."

Brock clenched his teeth. "Of course." He paused to consider the map before raising the quill to it. He hated marking up an artifact from before the Day of Dangers, but this was the job. At least he could do it carefully, and as neatly as possible.

The Lady tapped her ledger, a record of unapproved transactions—goods coming into or out of another guild's inventory without the Merchants Guild's authorization. While the anonymous smuggler had apparently retired, the adventurers themselves still bartered directly with people outside the guild—under Frond's supervision. It was how she kept the guild free from Quilby's meddling. But it also made it difficult for the Lady to know whether an unapproved transaction was an example of Frond's prudent, mostly legal dealings . . . or evidence that the smuggler was back in business. "The weavers recently received a large quantity of unidentified fabrics."

"Also us," Brock said. "We needed winter cloaks." He sighed heavily, remembering the current sorry state of those garments. "They were really nice cloaks."

He marked the path he had walked with his guildmates, noting as accurately as he could the location of the shelter they'd visited, as well as a grove of trees whose straw-like leaves had been full and green as if it were summer.

"Everything on my ledger is accounted for, then," she said. "Whoever our smuggler is, they've gone to ground."

"I think I've solved the mystery," Brock deadpanned. He pulled several small envelopes from his pocket. "These days, *I'm* the smuggler."

The Lady smiled silkily. "Ah, yes, but you're *my* smuggler. It's very different."

"Just so no one gets hurt," Brock said, and he handed over the envelopes. "There wasn't much alive out there, but I brought you some seeds. Everything's labeled. There's elfgrass, which is edible once it sprouts. A few brimstone berry pits."

"Not much, considering the length of the journey," the woman said, sorting through the envelopes.

Brock held his breath. She'd said it casually, lightly, but the threat was implicit. If he didn't keep her happy, if she thought he was shirking his end of their bargain, then she'd have no reason to keep Zed's secret. And with so much hostility being directed at the elves, it felt more important than ever that Brock quash any rumors that could hurt Zed.

"I'm trying," he said with forced calm. "We had a ranger with us the whole time, breathing down our necks. Plus, you know, the constant threat of death." He remembered how even Callum's unflappable demeanor had strained at the sighting of the raccoon. "Purple eyes," he said. "Shining purple eyes on an animal—a natural animal that looks sick, maybe. Have you ever heard of that?"

33

She tutted. "Doesn't sound particularly fearsome."

"The ranger seemed spooked by it," Brock said. "Then, when we got back, he and Frond had some kind of intense talk. Maybe Hexam's Danger handbook has—"

The Lady held out her hand in a gesture that brought him up short. At his confused look, she pointed to her ear.

Brock heard it, then. Distant and muted but unmistakable. It was the sound of bells tolling.

Bells rang for many purposes in Freestone. They marked the time. They signaled the start of festival days, and they rang uninterrupted for the better part of a day on the rare occasions when a royal was born.

But the series of low, monotonous notes that rang out now meant one thing only: Someone in Freestone had died.

Brock emerged into the guildhall in time to see Ser Brent beating a hasty retreat from the banquet. He followed, frowning as he noticed the chatter and laughter of the party had already resumed. As if the bells, and what they symbolized, were no more than a momentary nuisance, a fussing babe to be talked over.

A small regiment of knights joined Ser Brent as he descended the guildhall's steps, and Brock stifled the impulse to eavesdrop as he passed them. It was none of his business, and his bed was calling. He set out down Freestone's cobbled lanes, quiet at this hour until the racket of the Stone Sons' armor sounded at his back. He stepped aside to let them pass, initially annoyed that they should be going in the same direction—and then worried.

It had been different only two months ago. But these days, nearly everyone he cared about lived outtown.

Brock ran after the knights, keeping just far enough back not to be noticed. He became increasingly concerned as the houses grew smaller and more cramped, the windows grimier. They were definitely approaching the poorer district the adventurers called home.

But then the group made a sharp turn at the edge of outtown, and Brock followed around the corner—finally stopping cold as he realized where they were headed.

The knights didn't even slow down as they vaulted up the steps to the temple of the Golden Way.

Brock shuddered at the sight. Weapons were forbidden from the healers' temple, a rule that dated back to the guild's very founding, when Mother Aedra had decreed that matters of war, money, and politics were unwelcome in a place of healing. For two hundred years, that statement had gone unchallenged, and so the sight now of some dozen armed knights rushing the guildhall made Brock uneasy. Not least because he had been uncomfortable around the healers since their previous leader, Mother Brenner, was revealed to have used their temple as her feeding ground. Did Ser Brent's actions now have anything to do with that?

Curiosity won out over prudence and exhaustion, and Brock slipped inside.

The monks, nuns, and novices who called this place home kept few possessions, and so the temple's interior stood in marked contrast to the luxuries of the Merchants Guild—but for one major exception. Beyond the dimly lit entryway, ringing the large room that served as the heart of the temple, were five windows of intricately colored glass. Four of those windows depicted Freestone's Champions in action, while the fifth showed a plague of fangs and baleful eyes—Foster's own likeness having long been banned. Together the images told the story of the Day of Dangers in glittering polygons of blue and yellow and red.

Beneath those colorful scenes, the room was white: white stone walls, white tile floors, and row upon row of white fabric, strung up like curtains to provide some privacy to the healers' patients. There had to be dozens of them packed into this single room—Brock had never seen the space so crowded. The curtains rippled, parting here and there, and the curious faces of the sick and the elderly peered out. Brock saw a nun step briskly and silently through a side door, head down as if she were afraid to make eye contact with the knights.

The Stone Sons stood at attention in a tight cluster, halfway down the central aisle formed by the hanging fabric. Ser Brent stood just beyond the rest, looming before two women who blocked his way. They were *elves*, Brock realized, both with bright ocher eyes. One of them, auburn haired and brown skinned, had her shoulders thrown back in defiance. The other, with fair skin flushing pink and a green tint to her long blond hair, was curled into herself, gripping her elbows and biting her lip.

"It's time," Ser Brent said. "I've come for the child."

"We have no child," said the auburn-haired woman. She wore a simple blouse, frayed at the edges and covered with multi-colored patches. Brock thought it might look like a bird's view of the elven refugee camp with its mismatched tents.

The second woman uttered a small sob and hugged herself tighter.

"I'm sorry," said Brent. "But you must step aside. It is the law."

Brock's palms itched. He found himself poised on the balls of his feet. But he stayed put and bit his tongue. Whatever was going on, his few glimpses of Ser Brent over the years had given him the impression of a stern but fair man—the sort of person who'd be dreadfully dull at one of his parents' dinner parties, but no villain.

It was hard, though, not to feel a kinship with the elven woman, who looked the armed man in the face and said, "Your laws are nothing to us. They are as the mewling of a kitten committed to parchment. They are a candle flame in the bright sun of our honored traditions."

Brent sighed. "It's those 'honored traditions' that got you all into this mess, as I understand it. And I'll be thrice cursed before it happens here." There was a tense moment of silence before the knight continued. "Your son is dead. I am here for the body. If I must, I will take it by force."

"Hold!" cried a voice, and a man clad all in white entered from the side door through which the silent nun had retreated. "Ah, Ser Brent, hold just a moment, if you would."

Father Pollux, the new guildmaster of the Golden Way, wove a path through the maze of billowing fabric. Brock knew the man was an accomplished healer—he'd seen that firsthand when Pollux had helped save Jett's life only weeks before. But Brock had a hard time imagining Pollux equal to his new responsibilities as the head of one of Freestone's High Guilds. While his predecessor had emitted a sense of capable, confident purpose, Pollux . . . did not.

"Ser Brent, ah, how do you do?" Pollux said, finally drawing up to the other man. He stepped between him and the elven women. Brent was a head taller and looked flawless in the formal tunic he'd worn for the merchants' banquet, while Pollux gulped for air, wiped sweat from his brow, and attempted to straighten his robes.

"I know you're new to this, *Father*, but you're really not encouraged to interject in matters of Freestone's security."

"Right," Pollux said. "Each guild minds its own business. You're right."

"Then, if you'd please—"

"By the way, how was Quilby's fund-raiser tonight?" Pollux

asked with feigned innocence. "Did he raise the money you need for all your shiny new weapons?"

New weapons? thought Brock. Was that why Brent was rubbing elbows with Quilby?

Was Quilby throwing a fund-raiser for *weapons* when elves were hungry and freezing on their own city streets?

Ser Brent glowered at the healer. "And this is the best use of *your* resources, is it?" With a sweep of his hand he indicated the makeshift infirmary all around them. "It looks like the cursed Day of Dangers in here. How many humans have been turned away to make room for them?"

"None," Pollux answered without hesitation, but his voice was suddenly sad. "We turn no one away here, Ser Brent. Not ever." Brock looked about and saw several curious patients had emerged from their curtained cots. Nearly all of them were elves.

"I've spent time with our guests," Pollux continued. He stood a little bit straighter. "Every adherent to the Way has walked among them for weeks, and we've opened our doors to them here, as you noted. In the process we've learned a little bit about their customs. Perhaps we could work together, find a diplomatic solution to this matter. What do you say?"

Brent seethed. "There's no time for talk, Pol—*Luminous Father*," he said through clenched teeth. "You're more than welcome to share diplomatic words over the pyre, but we are burning that boy's corpse if I have to set fire to it myself."

"I've heard enough," said a voice, sharp with reprimand, at Brock's back. He moved instinctively aside to allow the speaker to pass. Every elf in view, even the grieving women, immediately touched two fingers to their lips, a sign of greeting and respect.

Elves, Brock had noticed, did not bow. Not even to their own queen.

The queen was a vision. Though she wore a simple dress of sheer green and a common hooded cape, with only an understated silver circlet about her head to mark her as ruler of the elves, she fairly radiated royalty. The elves might not bow, but it was all Brock could do not to drop to his knee in her presence.

And yet it was not only her regal beauty that drew his eye. There was unmistakably something dangerous in the way she moved. She was as much huntress as queen. Gliding past the assembled knights, her russet eyes seemed to scan Brent for weakness, even as she inclined her head in greeting to Pollux.

As if she were not intimidating enough, the queen did not travel alone. Half a pace behind her followed two female elves in glittering silver armor. They seemed to pay Brock no mind as they passed, yet he had the inescapable sense that if he made any sudden movements in their presence, it would be to his regret.

"Queen Me'Shala," Brent said, and he did give a small bow. "I am pleased to see you. My king bid me reiterate his invitation—"

"Thank your king kindly, Ser Brent," said the queen. "But I've no wish to enjoy his castle's luxuries when my people enjoy so few. My place is with them."

Brent seemed to hesitate, caught between king and queen. It was clearly not the answer King Freestone wished to hear. But in the end he said, "As you wish."

"But if you would be so kind," she said, "as to once more extend *my* invitation to your king."

"Which invitation is that, Majesty?"

"My invitation to join me in taking back Llethanyl, of course."

Brent was unable to mask a sour look. "I shall relay your invitation, Majesty. In the meantime, I fear I must remind you of the absolute sanctity of Freestone's laws. While your people are honored guests within our walls, we must insist—"

"Oh, I heard what you were insisting," said the queen. "The pyre, was it?"

Brent kept his eyes upon the queen. "It is our way," he said.

"It is barbaric," said the bolder of the elven women.

"If we could all just—" Pollux began.

The queen lifted her hand for silence. It was not an aggressive gesture, but it was heeded without question, by elf and human alike.

"You must understand, Ser Brent, that among our people there is no true death. When an elf is lost to us, lost to age or illness or Danger, this is a temporary state. A sort of slumber. Once, our honored ancestors were undying. Ancient lore says that when the elves have proven ourselves worthy, druids will once again walk the wooded paths of Llethanyl, and we will have earned back our immortality. To threaten this outcome—to *destroy* a lost elf, as you suggest—is considered a most serious offense."

"If you'll pardon my frankness, Majesty," Brent replied, "it's my understanding that Llethanyl's . . . *situation* . . . is a direct result of your practice of interring your dead. Just how many hours were you able to stand against your 'honored ancestors' once they began clawing their way out of their graves?"

The queen's warm eyes darkened, and a low wind cut through the interior of the temple, stirring the rows of fabric all around them. Brock quickly remembered that the queen was herself a formidable wizard.

Pollux took a step back. Brent did not.

"I don't believe I *will* pardon your frankness, swordsman," she said. The armored women beside her looked ready to draw their blades.

"I have my orders, Majesty," Ser Brent said. He put a hand to the hilt of his own sword.

"Wait!" Brock called. All present turned to consider him, including the full company of knights and the queen's guards. But it was the queen's gaze, still roiling with the threat of violence, that made him second-guess his decision to speak up.

The scorn in Ser Brent's eyes, however, brought him back to himself. Clearly the knight recognized Brock and didn't think too highly of him. Brock thrived on being underestimated.

"Majesty," he said, and he brought his fingers to his lips as he'd seen the elves do. He did not speak again until, after a moment's consideration, she nodded at him, her eyes light once more. "I've thought about your problem, and I think I might have a solution."

The queen laughed, a single earthy bark, and she turned toward Brent, her animosity blown away like a brief summer storm. "This youngling is one of yours?"

"Hardly," Brent answered.

"This is Brock Dunderfel," Pollux said, clearly happy for the distraction. "He's one of Alabasel Frond's newest charges."

"Alabasel Frond." The queen smiled broadly. "I was just wondering why she hasn't been by to see me yet."

"You know Frond?" Brock asked.

The queen nodded. "Alabasel is the only human to ever attempt to slap me."

Brock had to resist the urge to drop his face into his hands.

"And how would Alabasel's young charge solve so heady a problem as we now face?"

"Well, I was thinking," Brock began. "It's illegal to bury a . . . *lost* elf within Freestone. But the Adventurers Guild isn't bound by the city walls. What if we interred your lost one outside the city?"

The queen didn't even seem to consider it before turning to the mourning women. "Would this be acceptable to you?"

The elven women looked to each other, something passing unspoken between them. At last, they nodded.

The queen turned to Brent. "And you?"

"I'd ... have to check," he said. "I don't like the idea of opening the gates every five minutes, but as to the letter of the law, there's no issue with any of your people coming and going. Or Frond's, of course."

"Of course," the queen echoed. "I had almost forgotten not all humans follow the example of your *noble* king."

Brent stiffened, but said nothing.

The queen turned again toward Brock. "You have my thanks, young human. I've been so concerned with following the proper channels—I needed this reminder that a true leader must sometimes look for solutions in unexpected places." She turned so that her back was to Ser Brent and Pollux, lowering her voice to indicate that what she said next was for no human ears but Brock's. "I may require your counsel again very soon."

Brock smiled a beatific smile, but he panicked a little under her scrutiny. "Of course, Your Majesty," he said in a low voice. "But what could I—?"

"Tonight, I am needed here," the queen said, gazing at the scenes of battle laid out in the gleaming glass of the temple's windows. "But tomorrow, there shall be a council of war. Tomorrow, I will call on Alabasel Frond."

Chapter Three

Zed

Zed awoke early the next morning, still groggy from the night's celebrations. His teeth ached from too much ambrosia. Zed's mother would pop her kettle if she knew he'd fallen asleep without brushing again, but dental hygiene didn't factor high among his concerns these days. Just two nights ago his bedtime routine had involved tugging Liza's arm out of the jaws of a monster.

On Feydays Zed studied magic, but today's lesson didn't begin until later—if it happened at all. Hexam, Frond, Lotte, and Callum had all been conspicuously absent from the apprentices' celebratory meal the night before.

Zed would spend the early morning visiting with his mother

before her shift began. She worried constantly over how her timid son was fitting in with the rough-and-tumble adventurers, so Zed was excited to be able to share his recent accomplishment.

On the other side of the room, Micah snored loudly. That he was still asleep was a small blessing, at least. The two boys were awkward, distant roommates at the best of times. And at the worst? Micah was everything Zed had feared the former noble would be. Rude, arbitrary, and messy to a degree that Zed never would have believed if he weren't living in the middle of it.

Born the son of a servant, Zed had been taught to value cleanliness from a young age. But before six weeks ago, Micah had probably never picked up a dirty sock in his life. Glancing around at the many piles of soiled laundry that now covered Micah's side of the room, Zed couldn't say with certainty that Micah had picked one up *yet*, either.

Zed padded carefully from his bed, slipping into a doublet, jerkin, and clean trousers with practiced quiet. He opened his bedside drawer, where a wooden fox pendant lay, its bushy tail wrapped snug around its body. It hung from a glittering silvery chain.

Zed scooped the chain from his drawer, and fastened it around his neck so the fox charm hung over his chest.

In the six weeks since Zed had nearly died and experienced his strange dream—a dream of a witch who waited in the woods, offering him the power to save his friends and his city—he hadn't heard again from Old Makiva. No apparition had arrived from the shadows to collect on her promised payment. No odd smells or disturbing noises haunted Zed's sleep. (Not counting Micah.)

It was as if the dream had been just that: a hallucination, and nothing more.

But there was no denying the strange green flame he was now able to conjure. Flame that burned like nothing else, and that always seemed easier to cast when he wore the charm and chain Makiva had given him on the morning of his Guildculling.

Zed hadn't yet told anyone about the dream. Not even Brock. Every time he summoned up the courage, his friend seemed to disappear, vanishing into the city on his own. At first Zed hadn't thought much of his absences. After all, apprentices weren't tied to the guildhall when their duties were finished, and Brock had a family who worried over him, too.

But as time crept on, and Brock kept coming up with fresh excuses to steal away, suspicion had slowly dawned on Zed, as cold and inevitable as winter.

His best friend was avoiding him.

After everything Zed had been through the past six weeks, all the fear and hardship, *that* burden was the one he couldn't seem to shrug off.

"Yes, yes—it's a very pretty necklace," Micah grumbled, sending Zed spiraling around. He hadn't even noticed the snoring had stopped. "Now quit staring at it and *leave* already."

"Sorry," Zed whispered, feeling his ears flush. "I was trying to be quiet."

47

"Somehow that's worse," Micah said. "Knowing you're slinking around doing Fie knows what. Why can't you fart and knock into things in the morning, like a normal roommate?"

Zed scowled into the dark room. "Well, I was just leaving," he said.

"Good." Micah rolled over in his pallet, turning away from Zed. "And brush your teeth while you're out there—I can smell your rancid breath from here. Were you raised in a barn?"

Zed felt a sudden, intense urge to begin practicing his flame conjuring a bit early that day. Closing the bedside drawer with a *bang*, he grabbed his scepter and his old, threadbare cloak. Then he stomped noisily out of the room.

The recent snow had left outtown veiled in white. Zed pulled his cloak tightly around him as he exited the guildhall, turning westward. The city's enormous wall towered to his left, casting a brooding shadow over nearly the whole district.

The streets were quiet this morning, but far from empty. Knights marched across the icy cobbles, keeping regular patrols even in outtown. Before the elves arrived, Zed had never seen the Stone Sons so vigilant. The destruction of Llethanyl had put the city on edge.

But who could say that the Lich *wouldn't* follow the elves to Freestone? And after what happened with Mother Brenner, could the wards truly be trusted to keep him out?

Nothing felt safe anymore. Freestone seemed perpetually on the verge of war.

As Zed curved northward along the avenue that led home, he heard a hard voice cut through the quiet.

"Freestone first!"

The brawny man who'd shouted this was dressed too sparsely for the weather, Zed thought. But if the cold bothered him, it didn't show. The man's face was red with anger, and his posture was wide and challenging. Zed recognized him as Dimas Orlov, a mason in the Works Guild and a longtime neighbor.

For as far back as Zed could remember, Dimas had been a wastrel and a bully—often calling Zed *goblin* or *fairy boy* as he passed by. Once, he'd told Zed's mother that she should dump her "changeling" over the wall so he could give her a real son, all while Zed was standing well within earshot.

Zed's mom told him to avoid Dimas, but that wasn't always easy. Hatred, like any disease, needed fresh victims to thrive. And people like Dimas were always happy to spread it.

"These *elves*"—Dimas said the word like he was discussing a particularly loathsome strain of cockroach—"destroyed their own city. And now they mean to destroy ours. Their sins will follow them here, so help me. If we don't do something, the dead will be scratching at our gates before winter's end!"

"Pipe down, Orlov!" a man called out. "It's too early for this." Zed glanced around to find that other outtowners had paused to gawk at the commotion. A small crowd was forming.

"Better too early than too late!" Dimas called back. "Send them home. *Elves* should deal with *elven* problems." Again, the word sounded poisonous coming from Dimas's lips. Zed found himself cringing from it. Several grunts and "Hear, hears!" rang out from the crowd.

"They just want peace!" a woman called. "There's good folk among the elves. I know some!"

"And what of the bad ones?" Dimas snarled. "I've seen how they treat their own. How they hate our ways. Freestone first!"

"Freestone first!" a second woman screeched in echo.

"It's an elven trick! They're waiting for their moment to attack!"

"They're half monsters themselves!"

Zed searched around, but there were no Stone Sons in sight. Now was probably a good moment to hurry on. He turned on his heel, making for the side street that led to his mother's home. But before he could weave through the crowd, Dimas's voice brought him up short.

"Where do you think you're going, goblin?"

Zed froze in place. He wanted to just keep walking, but it felt less safe to have Dimas at his back. Slowly, he turned around and narrowed his eyes at the mason.

"Been a while since we've seen your pointy ears around here. I suppose you're palling around with your elven buddies now, eh? No time for humans while you're casting little spells and weaving pansies in your hair?"

Zed said nothing, just continued glaring. He didn't trust himself to speak. Beneath his cloak, his hands trembled.

"What's wrong, goblin?" Dimas growled. His lips parted into a predator's grin. "Too scared to answer? Maybe you've finally gone fey-brained after all." The man took a lumbering step forward.

What stung most was that Dimas was right. Zed *was* too scared to respond. If Brock had been here, he'd have a sharp reply ready to cut the man down to size. But Zed was alone within a mob—and he was paralyzed by his fear.

Dimas took another step. His wolfish grin widened.

And yet Zed *wasn't* defenseless. Far from it.

He reached inward, drawing upon his mana, and with it came a sudden flood of confidence and vitality. Beneath his cloak, Zed's fingertips began to tingle, the air between them growing warm . . . then hot. Zed lifted his hand, parting his cloak.

"Dimas Orlov, you shut your mouth!"

Zed quickly hid his hand again. A small elderly woman stepped out from the crowd, pointing a crooked finger at the mason. "That boy saved this city. He's a hero. You owe him your life, you ungrateful goon. Go on! You've said enough for today."

And just like that, the crowd turned against Dimas. Shouts of agreement rang out from behind the woman.

"Get to your job, you shiftless lout!"

"*Still* too early for this nonsense."

Dimas scowled, retreating a step, the snow crunching under

his boots. His eyes slid resentfully away from Zed. "You're all fools," he muttered. But as the crowd dispersed, like a misty breath fading in the cold, Dimas went with it. Before Zed knew it, he was standing alone in the street.

Zed dawdled for a moment in the quiet, sniffing and rubbing at his frost-nipped nose. Then he blinked several times in confusion and held out his hand.

Smoke trailed from his fingertips. Five tiny accusations, which thrashed away into the morning air.

"You're late!" Zed's mother called as he slipped inside the cramped tenement building. The scents of home, of familiar things, washed over Zed in a rush. The place smelled like safety, and of his mother's delicious pottage. The dwindling embers of a fire glowed in the hearth—pleasantly orange, rather than green.

"Sorry, Mom," he said. "I got held up."

"Oh, did King Freestone stop by again?"

Zed had encountered the king all of twice—and one of those times had resulted in the imprisonment of Zed's whole guild in their own hall—but his mother still loved to pretend he was on speaking terms with the royals.

"He sends his love," Zed said, falling into a chair and kicking off his boots. "But listen, I've got good news. I passed my apprentice journey. I'm officially quest-worthy."

"Oh! That's . . . How great!" Zed's mother emerged from

her room, pinning her hair into the bun she wore during her shift as a noble lady's servant. Like Zed, she had dark hair and fawn-colored skin, with small features that belied her expressive brown eyes. Unlike Zed, her ears were round and totally human. "So you'll be out *there*? More often?"

Zed nodded. "Not without a master adventurer. I was hoping you'd be proud of me."

His mother smiled incredulously. "I *am* proud; you know that. And I realize that this is your life now. My son, the hero! It's just . . . hard." She looked around the room. "No Brock today?"

Zed tried to keep his expression casual. "Not today."

"It's been a while since he's visited. Before you two joined the guild, I swear I saw him over here more often than I saw you. Is everything all right?"

No. I don't know. I made a pact with a witch, and my best friend is avoiding me. I'm roommates with a bully, and I nearly just set fire to our neighbor.

"Yeah, everything's great." Zed tried out a smile, but his mother was already turning back to her room, searching for her smock.

"Well, you two take care of each other while you're out there *adventuring*. I know you will, but after what happened to your friend Jett . . . and with that horrible Mother Brenner."

"It wasn't Brenner's fault, Mom," Zed said. "She'd been transformed into a monster."

"Oh, that's very comforting," his mom called back, "knowing

53

that's a thing that can happen. Let's just hope Father Pollux doesn't follow in his predecessor's footsteps."

Zed's mom reentered the room, smoothing out her smock. She stood there a long moment, just leaning against the doorway and silently watching her son. "So who took you out on this journey of yours? Was it Frond?"

Zed's mother had never had much fondness for the guildmistress of the adventurers. She found the idea of a woman warrior unseemly. But in recent weeks, her views on the subject had softened a little. Zed supposed that Liza—who his mother adored—probably had more to do with it than Frond herself.

The elves, too, allowed women to serve as soldiers. Rumor had it that Queen Me'Shala kept these so-called sword sisters on hand as elite bodyguards.

"Not Frond," Zed said. "It was one of the rangers, actually. The *High* Ranger."

"Oh . . . an elf." His mother paused, wearing a careful expression he couldn't quite read. "That must be so nice for you, getting to know the other side of your heritage."

Zed nodded, feeling the exact opposite was true. When the elves had first arrived in Freestone, Zed had nearly unspooled in his excitement. Though his own father had been an elf, Zed knew almost nothing about their culture.

So he'd wasted little time before making a nuisance of himself. Zed had followed the rangers around for days, peppering them with questions about their customs and history and magic.

To his great frustration, however, the rangers proved to be stingy teachers. And they were the *least* standoffish of the elves.

"You could come by," he said, "if you want. To say hello."

Zed's mother smiled, but she was already shaking her head. "You're such a sweet boy. I only knew your father for two weeks," she said a little wistfully. "And while they were among the happiest of my life, I can barely remember any of the other elves Zerend introduced me to. They certainly wouldn't remember some lowly servant girl barely out of her apprenticehood."

Zed frowned at his feet.

"I should get going, anyway," she added. "I'm running late." A shadow fell over Zed's feet as his mother approached, and then her fingers were touching his chin, lifting his eyes to meet hers. "I *am* proud of you, Zed," she said. "I hope you know that. I don't think I could be any more pleased with the young man you've become. The king didn't say so, but everyone knows you and your friends saved this city. And those that don't tend to get an earful from me."

"*Mom*," Zed groaned, but a smile had stolen onto his face while he wasn't paying attention.

His mother grinned, too. "Tell Brock I want to see him over here soon." She winked. "Or I'm going to start taking it personally."

"I'll let him know."

"Well, walk me out, then," she said, pulling her cloak from its peg. "Things have been a little tense in the neighborhood lately. I could use my son the mage beside me, to scare off the zealots."

Zed cast a glance to the door, thinking again of Dimas and his cruel grin. What might he have done to the mason if that woman hadn't stepped in?

"Don't worry, Mom," he said. "I can protect you."

Zed stood outside the marketplace, hovering at its entrance.

His mother had left him here and traveled up the narrow stretch toward intown. When she was finally out of sight, Zed pulled on his hood and—rather than heading back to the guildhall—sidled into a quiet corner. He glanced around anxiously for any familiar faces.

Besides the armored knights, most Freestoners avoided lingering near what had once been the market. Zed watched as the odd servant or page hurried past, but they were always careful not to stray beyond the throughway. None spared Zed a second look.

The new elven quarter was a place removed, as if a whole section of the city had disappeared altogether.

"Zed, is that you? Why is your hood up? Are you hiding from someone?"

Zed shrieked out a noise that was somewhere between startled boy and rusty door hinge. He spun around and found a young elf standing behind him. Her skin was dark as sable and her eyes flashed a lovely blue. Not the pale blue that some fair-skinned humans and dwarves had. Fel's eyes were a rich, dark cobalt. The color of sapphires.

"*Fel,*" Zed breathed. "You nearly scared the ambrosia out of me. I'm trying to be incognito."

Fel was a ranger—the youngest of them, in fact. An orphan whose parents had died years ago in a monster attack, she'd been raised by the rangers ever since she was a little girl. While she was still technically too young to join the order, she was unofficially acknowledged as one of them, and she stayed with the others in the Adventurers Guild hall.

For Zed, she was an invaluable font of information about the elves. While most were aloof around humans, Fel was almost relentlessly friendly. She'd quickly fallen in with the apprentices over the last few weeks, and even guided Zed through weekly trips to the elven shantytown.

Fel put a finger to her lips, studying his cloak. "*Incognito . . .* I'm not familiar with that word. Does it mean 'sloppy'?"

"No," Zed said defensively.

"'Suspicious'?"

"It *means* I'm trying to blend in," he puffed. "The elves always stare when I'm around. How am I supposed to learn more about them if my presence puts them on edge?"

Fel nodded sagely. "Zed, my people can be slow to trust, but after what happened at Llethanyl you can't blame them." She shook her head. "It might take a while, but sneaking will only hurt your cause."

The girl stood up straight and squared her shoulders. "Just follow my example. Put on a smile and *show* them that you're *worthy* of their respect." Fel grinned at Zed, an expression so bright it made his face hurt just looking at it.

"That's easy for you to say," Zed grumbled. "You're a full elf, so they already respect you. I'm an outsider to both Freestone *and* the elves."

Fel sighed and bit her lip. She looked like she might say more, but at that moment a shadow leaped down from the balcony above, landing right between them. Zed shrieked for the second time that morning, spilling backward into the snow.

Before him stood a creature so scarred and misshapen, so horribly ugly, that it had somehow ventured into . . . cute. This was Fel's cat, a half-feral tabby whose unpronounceable elven name translated to something like "the bane of all things small and simple." The apprentices just called her Mousebane.

"Mousebane, you scared me!" Zed reached out to give the cat a tentative pat, but she shrilled at him, bolting behind Fel's ankles.

Fel's eyes were wide as she helped Zed to his feet. "I think she's warming up to you! She didn't scratch or bite you at all this time."

"I'll win her over yet," Zed said, wiping snow from his cloak. The cat had taken an instant disliking to him, but he remained determined.

Fel turned toward the market entrance. Beyond, the tents and stalls stood in their usual colorful stacks, though they'd been emptied of merchants.

"Shall we?"

As soon as they entered the market, every eye turned toward the young visitors. Murmurs of conversation faded, as if muffled by magic. Fel ignored the looks, smiling broadly and standing straight as she strolled, but Zed felt his ears growing hot already. He pulled his hood on more tightly.

It was still strange to see the market teeming with elves instead of humans. It felt a bit like when Zed discovered his old outtown friends had shot up three inches since the Guildculling, or that their voices now swam in the deep tones of adulthood.

Everything familiar seemed to be changing, and while Zed would never side with scuds like Dimas, he felt a twinge of sadness at the thought that maybe *some* things had changed forever.

Zed spotted an elven family gazing toward him and Fel. The ruby-eyed toddler clung to her mother as she watched them pass. Both mother and daughter were tan skinned, with rich, dark hair that was streaked with glittering strands of green.

The toddler was smiling, but when she reached an arm toward them, her mother quickly snatched it back. The girl began to squall, and the mother retreated with her into a nearby tent. The flaps fell closed to reveal an intricate tree pattern painted onto the front.

Wood elves, Zed thought. It had taken Zed weeks to remember the elven names for all three sects: *cel'shea*, *ain'shea*, and *dro'shea*.

Wood, sun, and night elves, in the trade tongue. Once there had been more, back before the world ended.

All elves looked different to Zed, but even within a sect there could be wide varieties of color. The wood elves' skin ranged from fair pink to deep umber, and their hair and eyes were tinged by greens, reds, and browns. But they all seemed to share a sort of woodland palate, as if their sect had grown from the forest itself.

Wood elves were by far the most common of the three sects. Fel said they were the founders of Llethanyl. The other two had come later.

Up ahead, Zed spotted a group of elderly sun elves playing a complicated-looking game with multicolored stones. The men's skin ranged from pale to dark amber, and their hair and eyes glittered with gold, yellow, and white. Fel and Zed stooped to peer over one elder's shoulder, but the elf huffed and quickly turned to block their view.

"*El sal fal'en!*" Fel called as she continued on. She turned back to Zed. "That means 'May your match entertain the watching sky.' It's a sun elf thing."

Sun elves, Zed knew, had arrived in Llethanyl long ago from somewhere far to the north, a dark place of almost perpetual winter. As such, the *ain'shea* loved daylight and the sky. Birds permeated their designs.

"All right, Zed," Fel chirped as they walked. "Where would you like to go today?"

Zed inhaled deeply, taking in the strange scents of the elven encampment. Even their smells were different—suffused with the minty essence of magic.

"Well," Zed started. "I was actually hoping you could show me where the night elves are camped. I've seen plenty of sun and wood elves around. Where do *your* people stay?"

The *dro'shea* seemed to be the rarest and most mysterious of the three sects. Their skin tones contained both the palest and darkest shades among the elves, and were often tinted gray. But their eyes and hair held flashes of color, touched by blues, violets, and glittering silver.

Zed nearly crashed into Fel as she stopped suddenly. Mousebane hissed a warning at him, weaving protectively between the girl's legs.

"It's actually pretty far from here," Fel said. "I don't think we'll have time before your lesson with Hexam."

Zed sighed. He'd nearly forgotten. How long had it been since second bell? Maybe they should simply do a quick loop and head back around.

He glanced to his left and sucked in a sudden gulp of air.

A huge black smear lay ominously across the stones, encircled by a painted red ring and filled with an X.

It was the spot where Old Makiva's tent had once stood, until it mysteriously burned to the ground on the night the mystic disappeared.

No one had seen Makiva since—not counting Zed's strange dream—and all sorts of rumors flourished of what had really become of her. In the intervening weeks, the city magistrates had declared Makiva a fugitive and a witch. A hefty reward was offered to anyone who brought her into the Stone Sons' custody. Dead *or* alive.

It seemed the elves, too, had gotten word of her. Or else they instinctively sensed the spot had been corrupted. Though the shantytown was packed full, the foreboding circle was given a wide berth.

For six weeks Zed had somehow managed to avoid this place. Until today.

It burns, Zed.

Zed took an involuntary step backward. An unpleasant smell wafted in the breeze, gone before he could place it. Suddenly he didn't want to be here.

Fel glanced toward the circle, then back up at Zed. "Are you all right? You look pale."

"I'm fine," Zed said. "I just . . . I just remembered I should probably—"

He was interrupted by the clanging of bells, echoing from the nearby Golden Way Temple. At first Zed thought that third bell had come already, but as the ringing continued—a high, shrieking bell that was reserved for fires and other emergencies—he realized something was very wrong.

All around them, elves began jostling and shouting. Zed heard a voice scream from far off.

"We should go," he said.

Fel nodded, gazing worriedly across the market.

They squeezed between figures, with Fel leading the way to the outtown exit. The closer they came to the edge of the shantytown, the thicker the crowd became. Above the tumult, the Golden Way's emergency bell was still sounding, shrill and panicked.

Zed caught glimpses of gleaming metal between the bodies. *What's happening?*

Finally he and Fel arrived at the market exit, where they were met by a wall of steel.

Stone Sons—a whole blockade of them—stood in a tight line surrounding the shantytown, led by Ser Brent. Zed watched as the guildmaster bellowed an order and the knights suddenly marched forward as one, pushing the elves farther back into their pen.

Voices shouted in protest, but the elves retreated. They were being herded.

"Ser Brent!" Zed shouted. "Wait, *please!*"

The knight-captain glanced Zed's way, then made an ill-tempered noise as he caught sight of him. "For the love of . . . must *one* of you always be getting into trouble?"

"What's going on?" Zed asked.

Ser Brent's mouth clenched into a grimace. "This morning *your guildmistress* revealed that an undead creature was spotted near Freestone. Some sort of wild animal. The elves are being confined to the market while the king decides the best course of action." Zed opened his mouth to object, but the knight had already raised his shiny gauntlet to cut him off. "Yes, there will be exceptions, on a case-by-case basis."

He turned to one of the knights. "Let the boy through, but no one else."

Zed gripped Fel's hand. "She's with me! Fel is one of the rangers."

Brent's eyes narrowed as they traveled from Zed to the young elf beside him. His grimace tightened. "Fine," he said. "Go now."

Zed pulled Fel through a gap between the knights, but the ranger turned back momentarily, her eyes wide with shock. As soon as they'd passed, the Sons closed ranks.

The anguished faces of the elves disappeared behind a barrier of steel.

Chapter Four

Brock

"Hit me," Brock said, and for a moment he worried the burly, bearded man glaring at him from across the table might do just that.

But the man only slapped a card down on the table, which Brock slid into his hand. "Ooh," he said when he saw it. "Four of dragons. Just what I needed."

It wasn't. Brock had a horrible hand of cards. Four of dragons, eight of griffins, and a wild unicorn—it was hard to imagine a worse spread. But the point of this game was to bluff, and that was something he could do. The people sitting around the table were evidence of that—one by one, they'd all folded, convinced Brock held better cards than he truly did.

All six were journey-rank members of the Sea of Stars, the middle position in the guild's hierarchy. While they weren't masters like Hexam, Lotte, or Frond, all had passed—and survived—their apprenticeships. It was a badge of honor that Brock had come to realize was depressingly rare.

But as far as he was concerned, they'd all started out as suspects. At the Lady Gray's insistence, he'd spent his first month and a half as an adventurer talking to every one of his guild-mates, making conversation and sifting through their stories for clues as to who among them might have the means and the motive to steal from the guild.

Brock had expected to find a guild full of resentful draft-ees, all chafing under Frond's tyrannical yoke. He'd anticipated meeting dozens of kindred spirits as eager to break away from her as he was. But as he talked to one adventurer after another, he found quite the opposite to be true.

To his left were a pair of men, Raif and Damen, who had been guildless before joining the adventurers. Guildlessness was exceedingly rare—few guilds had enough members to turn anyone away lightly—which suggested the men had committed crimes their former guilds had found inexcusable.

To the contrary, Brock learned that the smiths had unjustly cast Damen aside when a workplace injury left him unable to tend the forge at the pace they required. A rival within the Scribes Guild had framed Raif for theft, following a heated disagreement about apostrophes. The two men were deeply grateful to have escaped guildlessness with the adventurers; Brock couldn't see them doing anything to jeopardize their standing.

There were several former Stone Sons in the guild's ranks, including the men to Brock's right: Adem Foci, who credited Frond with saving him from Ser Brent's despotism, and a young man named Tym Oh, whose strange fascination with fire could never have been satisfied among the knights. Tym would remain loyal to Frond so long as she allowed him to shoot flaming arrows at Dangers—and she showed no signs of changing her mind about that particular strategy.

Another fearsome warrior, a woman named Preet who was known for her expert use of a light saber, held no grudge for having been recruited at her Guildculling two decades ago. Based on her grumbling and glaring from across the table, she reserved her grudges for those who beat her at cards.

There were dozens of men and women in the guild, each with their own story about how they got there. And the one thing they all seemed to have in common was an absolute and unshakable faith in their leader, Alabasel Frond. Brock found it hard to imagine any of them going behind her back to make an extra copper or two on the black market.

His remaining opponent went exclusively by his nickname, the Clobbler, which the adventurers seemed to think was a hilariously clever play on words. Before Frond had selected him on the day of his Guildculling, he'd been apprenticed to a cobbler. Now, he liked to clobber Dangers with a large club. Hence, *Clobbler*.

It was what passed for humor in the Sea of Stars.

Just as Brock was sure his opponent was about to fold—the man's scars flushed pink whenever he lost—the door to the guild-hall burst open, and Brock turned to see Zed step through with unusual purpose. "Where's Frond?" he demanded to the room before he'd even registered Brock's presence there. He was followed by the young ranger Fel and an icy winter wind.

It wasn't the wind that gave Brock a chill. One look at his friend's face told him something bad had happened.

Brock dropped his cards and got to his feet. "She's out. What's wrong?"

Zed scanned the assembled faces, dismissing them each in turn, likely not recognizing any of them. While Brock had made his way through the guild's ranks, Zed had for the most part been content to stick by the other apprentices at meals and celebrations and in the training yard. The older adventurers had shown little interest in getting to know Zed, either, but at least they saw his sorcerous abilities as an asset. They didn't avoid him out of scorn, but because, as Preet had once admitted when Brock pressed her on the issue, "You young ones don't always last very long."

Still, Brock wished Zed would make an effort. If they were really stuck here, better to be among allies than acquaintances.

"I need to talk to Hexam or Lotte," Zed said. "Even Callum."

"We're in the middle of a game!" the Clobbler complained.

Brock tossed his cards down on the table. "I fold," he said. "You win, Clobbler."

"*That* was your hand?" the man roared, but Brock had already turned his back.

While Zed tugged at his cloak, nearly strangling himself in his haste to remove it, Fel met Brock's eyes. "Word has spread," she said softly. "About the creature you saw beyond the wall."

"The raccoon?"

"Not just a raccoon," Fel said in a hushed voice. She rubbed her arms as if suddenly cold. "Zed described it to me just now. That poor animal was defiled. It was in the thrall of the Lich."

The conversation at the table behind Brock grew silent. He heard the shuffling of cards, but knew they had an audience now.

"Ser Brent called it *undead*," Zed added. "He said Frond told the king about it. Now the Stone Sons are putting the market on lockdown. The elves are *terrified*."

"Our people will survive this," Fel said, and she put a hand to Zed's shoulder. The familiarity of the gesture surprised Brock. He hadn't realized the two knew each other that well.

Also: *our* people?

"Zed, what were you even doing in the shantytown?" he asked.

"*That's* what you're curious about?" Zed shot back. "I want to know why the *knights* were there. The elves don't have anything to do with the Lich! The Lich is their *enemy*. They came here for help!"

"*We* know that," Brock answered. "We've been living with

the rangers for weeks. But what does the rest of the town really know about them?"

Zed flinched. "Are you saying you agree with the king?"

"Absolutely not," Brock said without hesitation. "I'm saying his actions are understandable, given the information he has and the information he *doesn't* have." Brock thought about information, and the woman who tended to have more of it than anyone. "I've got to go."

"What? Where?" Zed asked.

"Guys, deal Zed in," he said to the table, then turned back to his friend. "Listen, knowing Frond, she flubbed the delivery of some bad news about a moderately suspicious Danger and the king overreacted. She's not back yet, which means she's probably trying to smooth things over."

Fel smiled. "Thank you, Brock. That's reassuring."

"It's not really," Brock said. "Frond is terrible at diplomacy. But I know some people who are good at it. I'm just going to check in with them. Okay?"

He didn't wait for an answer, leaning past his friend to pull a cloak from a rack by the door. "I'll be back before the game's over."

Brock stepped outside, pausing on the footpath to throw his cloak over his shoulders. It was then he heard a small voice at his back.

"Please don't go."

Brock turned, and the sight of his friend shivering there

cloakless in the light dusting of snow nearly broke his resolve. Zed's experience at the shantytown had clearly left him shaken.

But there was more at stake here than Zed's feelings.

"Hey, you're fine, right? You're okay." He put his hands on Zed's shoulders. "Tell Lotte what you saw. Tell Frond when she gets back. Get the full story, and if it's not all figured out by then, we'll figure it out together."

"But what are *you* doing? Can't I go with you?"

Brock sighed, drawing it out just long enough to formulate a lie. "No, I . . . I'm just going to see my parents. They have some influence, and . . . Well, I know how uncomfortable intown can be for you."

Zed opened his mouth to speak, but Brock spoke first. "I'm going to find a way to fix things. Just . . . don't get yourself into any trouble in the meantime, all right? *Don't* go anywhere near the shantytown. Stay here where it's safe."

"I don't think it *is* safe here," Zed said sadly.

"I'm going to fix that, too." Brock turned on his heel, snapping his cloak as he strode away and called over his shoulder, "I'm going to fix everything!"

By the time Brock had made his way to the Shadows' warrens, his confidence was flagging. He'd steered clear of the shantytown for fear of somehow getting involved, but he'd expected to *hear* it—to hear the sounds of protest, the commanding voice of

Ser Brent, the clamor of shields linking to form a wall against the press of bodies.

There was utter silence. The elves, for now, were not resisting. And if that changed? How many natural spell-casters were among them? How many could stand against swords and spears?

Brock hurried, and the silence kept pace with him. Throughout Freestone, the streets were empty and the shutters were drawn. People knew something was happening, and they chose to stay well clear of it.

Brock just didn't understand that impulse.

Gramit held up a hand, half welcome and half warning, as Brock entered the antechamber to the Lady's office.

"She's busy," Gramit said.

"I don't care," Brock said, and he pushed open the door to her office. It was empty.

He turned to Gramit and saw the man shrug. "I didn't say she was busy *here*. And you forgot your mask."

Brock rolled his eyes, but he affixed the mask to his face. "You're supposed to be 'the Facilitator,' Gramit. Facilitate a meeting for me!"

"Concerning?"

"Concerning the undead animal sighted a day's march from Freestone, the king's decision to bully the elven refugees when he found out about it, and the fact that their queen seemed *pretty ready* to throw lightning at him even before that."

Gramit tapped his chin. "That does sound relevant," he said.

"Yes!" Brock said. "It's extremely relevant, Gramit! To everything ever!"

The man stood from his stool. "Follow me, then. And watch your manners around Master Curse."

"Master . . . Curse?"

"Yeah. He didn't get that name for using foul language, if you're wondering."

Brock followed him past a curtain, exiting the masters' quarters and entering the long corridor that served as the market floor. The stone here showed none of the upkeep of the previous room. Decades-old mildew grew in the crevices. The hall was lined with dark, recessed hollows—spaces that had once been cells—and standing before each hollow was a seller's stall, which in most cases simply meant wooden boards propped up on stools. The stalls were closed for the daylight hours, sheets thrown over their wares, but Brock knew the nights had been busy. While Freestone's larger economy strained beneath the burden of the elven refugees, the black market was booming.

Brock eyed each stall as he passed, knowing that most of what was sold here was completely harmless, if hard to come by. One vendor sold precious oil for an outdated style of lamp. Another sold chicken feed with twice as much protein as the strictly regulated feed available through legal channels. The vendor didn't specify, but Brock suspected that the source of the protein was most likely rat meat. This was what passed for luxury in a city completely strapped for resources.

Some of the goods here were stolen, Brock knew. And there were darker items available: boots and bracelets with concealed blades, poisons of sinister effect, and counterfeit stamps bearing the sigils of noble houses. Nothing purchased here was cataloged or tracked in any way, and no Stone Son walked these corridors—at least, not in any official capacity. Black market customers were guaranteed their privacy, and they paid well for the privilege.

Gramit led the way to a small room situated between two former cells. It would have been a guard's quarters back in the day. Now it held a desk, a few well-worn tomes, and a scattering of strange artifacts—Brock saw a flute apparently carved from bone, and he didn't look too closely after that.

The Lady Gray was there, and two men—one in a simple domino mask like Brock's, and one in a mask of gleaming silver that obscured the top half of his face, arcing downward from his hood in the shape of a crescent moon.

"Ah, apprentice, what a pleasant surprise," said the Lady. But she didn't seem particularly surprised. Or pleased, for that matter.

Brock's eyes were drawn, however, to the hooded man. He couldn't smell magic like Zed could, but this man reeked of it, figuratively speaking. His mantled cloak looked like a darker, bloodred version of the one worn in public ceremonies by Freestone's most celebrated wizard, Archmagus Grima. And the mask was a sign, too, for the moon was known citywide as the symbol of the Mages Guild. Did the Shadows actually have a magus in their employ? If so, that was quite a coup. Wizards were rare and reclusive. Brock had seen no more than a few in all his life, and that was counting Hexam, who was no longer recognized as a magus by his former guild.

The door closed, and Brock turned to see Gramit had left.

"This is the one?" Curse said. There was a sneer in his voice. "He's awfully small."

"He is young," the Lady said. "But you can't argue with how well he's done. Apprentice, this is Master Curse. He is the final recipient of all the gifts you've brought me these past weeks."

Brock didn't understand, and the confusion must have been evident on his features. Unlike Curse's mask, Brock's hid very little of his face.

"The flora and fauna from beyond the wall," Curse clarified. "It's my job to ensure it's safe—not harboring any pests."

Brock nodded. He knew that there was a simple spell to ensure the parasite that had infected Mother Brenner was not present in any of the goods the adventurers brought into Freestone. It was only after Hexam had inspected each item, whether flower or wood or foodstuff or animal skin, that Frond would approve its use for bartering. The Lady Gray had assured Brock that anything he smuggled himself would be similarly examined before making its way to the black market floor.

"A dreary necessity, that," Curse continued. "But once I've done it, I am free to experiment."

"Experiment?" Brock echoed. He looked from the master to the Lady. "What kind of experiment?"

The Lady gestured at the other man, the one wearing a mask identical to Brock's, which marked him as another apprentice—though he was a full-grown man a head taller than Brock.

"Uh, well." He cleared his throat. "One example: You remember those little red rodents?"

"Pitmunks," Brock said, remembering the fiendish, razor-clawed creatures that roamed the woods. They were red as ripe tomatoes and not much larger, with sharp black quills running along their backs.

He also remembered the satisfying *squelch* when he'd dropped a sack of them on the Lady's desk the previous week. That had almost gotten a rise out of her, he was sure of it.

"Yeah, their meat is inedible," Brock said. "Hexam says it's because their sweat glands produce some kind of toxin. I was hoping the Shadows might find a way to fix that. It'd mean a new source of food. . . ."

"That is *not* the direction our experimentation took," Curse said, chuckling as if Brock were a fool to suggest it.

The apprentice waited until the master indicated he should continue. "My talents are in olfaction—in *scents*. I study how a smell affects the brain, how it triggers memory and emotion. Master Curse wisely suggested that the pitmunk's toxic sweat might be distilled and—"

"You're the perfumer," Brock said. "From the marketplace. You mixed scents to make people smell nice."

The man blushed beneath his slight mask. "Uh, I can't confirm or deny—the condition of anonymity is, ah—"

"Relax, Master Stink," Brock said. "Your secret's safe with me." He turned to the Lady. "But I'm not here because of—whatever in Fie these guys are going on about. There's a situation with the elves. The king's making a huge mistake. I know you have access to him."

The Lady nodded slightly. "I'm aware of the situation."

Brock glared at her. "Then you know it sounds dangerous. The more the king and his knights push the elves, the more danger we're *all* in. I know for a fact their queen is unhappy. What happens if they push back?"

Master Curse shrugged. "Fewer mouths to feed."

Brock ignored the heartless comment. He kept his focus on the Lady. "I know you don't think that way. Think of all the knowledge those elves have. All the *secrets*."

He saw it then, he was sure of it. Just the slightest gleam of interest in her eyes. She blinked, and it was gone, her placid smirk unmoved from her lips.

"As a matter of fact," she said, "I've a keen interest in what the elves have to say. I've been listening to their stories. Including the ones about that particular red rodent."

"Pitmunks? What's there to say about them?"

"The elves call them *gish'aelneu*," she said. "Despite the fact that they are Dangers and quite deadly in large numbers, spotting one in the wild is considered a good omen to the rangers of Llethanyl. Did you know that?"

"It never came up."

"*Gish'aelneu* translates, roughly, to 'fearsome rodent whose lack of grace alienates all potential friends.' See, the reason the *gish'aelneu* are considered good luck is because whenever they nest in an area, larger predators are said to flee. If there's any truth to the stories—and most stories have a nugget of truth *somewhere*—these things somehow scare off monsters ten times their size. We thought that was worth looking into."

"That's where we came in," Curse's apprentice said. "Master Curse asked me to extract the active chemicals in the pitmunk sweat and make a concentrated oil. And, uh, so I did that."

Brock scratched at the back of his head, thinking through the implications of what they were telling him. "You think their sweat has some quality or . . . or power. The toxin they secrete. It's, what, a Danger repellent?"

"It's certainly an interesting theory," Curse answered. "We do, however, need it to be field-tested."

Brock nodded sagely before he realized what Curse was implying. "Wait. Me? You want me to start wearing monster perfume? What if the smell alienates all *my* potential friends? What if it doesn't work at all?"

"That *would* be helpful to know," answered Curse.

"You're the only one with access, apprentice," the Lady cooed. "Aren't you glad you're quest-worthy?"

Brock groaned. "I just wanted to find a way to feed people. Next you'll tell me you've turned those elfgrass seeds into pellets for a magically ensorcelled blowpipe."

"*Magically ensorcelled* is redundant," Curse said sharply. "But the idea has some merit."

"It really doesn't," Brock replied. "And what about helping the elves?"

"So many defenders, those elves." The Lady steepled her fingers. "Between you and Pollux and that queen of theirs."

"'That queen of theirs' looked ready to tear through a dozen of Ser Brent's finest last night," Brock snapped. "She told me that she wants to have some kind of a *war council* with Frond."

The Lady gave him a strange look, as if she didn't understand what he was saying. It was unusual enough that Brock came up short.

"What is it?" he asked.

She pivoted to address Curse. "If you'd give us the room, please."

Curse opened his mouth, ready to protest—this was clearly *his* space—but thought better of it. He ushered the perfumer out and shut the door behind them.

As soon as they were alone, the Lady asked, "You met the queen?"

It was a simple question, but it sent Brock reeling. "You . . . didn't know that?" he said. A smile broke out across his face. "You didn't know that."

The Lady appeared mostly unbothered, but Brock could see the sudden tension in her shoulders, the tightness around her mouth. "Queen Me'Shala has proven . . . resistant to my attempts at . . . friendship."

"You mean your spies can't get near her," Brock said. "And you don't have anything you can hold over her head." He tapped his chin. "Well, she seemed to like me. Said she might need my brilliant advice again soon. Did you offer to braid her hair? That might work."

"Droll as ever," she said, and Brock felt a little thrill at her frustration. "But!" she said lightly, her hateful smirk returning. "It appears *one* of my spies has access, after all. . . ."

"Nuh-uh," Brock said. "No way."

But the tension was already gone from her shoulders. She slunk around the room like a predatory cat. "I told you I've been listening to stories the elves tell. And so many of those stories mention the wealth of the queen. Her glittering treasury, with riches so extraordinary and strange they must have come from the fairy plane."

"That's great," Brock said. "Do those stories mention anything about the queen's temper? Maybe the specific spells she'd use against someone who crossed her?"

"The elves left Llethanyl in a hurry," the Lady said. "They

took only what they could carry. If that included anything from the queen's treasury, I've been unable to learn where those treasures are now. They do not appear to have brought anything of true value to Freestone."

"So maybe they left it all behind. If it was a choice between their lives or their wealth—"

"It's a rare ruler who would choose the former," the Lady said coldly. "Perhaps the riches of the elves are hidden away in one of Frond's wayshelters. Perhaps they've been buried beneath a tree. If you could find out . . . If you could get your hands on just one of those treasures . . ."

Brock shook his head. Steal from the elves—from their beautiful, utterly terrifying queen? The Lady kept asking for more; he had to put his foot down while he still could. "It's too dangerous," he said. "And it's *not* what we agreed to. I'm honoring our agreement, but you can't keep changing it."

She narrowed her eyes, regarding him in silence for a moment. "Fair enough," she said at last. "Our smuggler friend seems to have thought twice about their actions, anyway, and you've learned what you could. So . . ." She paused once more, either to consider her words or else to keep Brock hanging on them. "Do this thing for me, and Zed's secret shall never cross my lips. Any evidence I have, I shall destroy. On that, I'll swear."

Brock's heart leaped in his chest, but his distrust fought with his excitement. While his feelings roiled, he mastered his expression, showing only skepticism.

"Just like that?" he said. "One elven treasure, and you'd let me off the hook?"

"I hear the doubt in your voice, Brock, but above all else I am a woman of my word." She shrugged. "You know this."

"Yeah, funny thing about blackmailers," he said. "So *trustworthy*."

"My threats only work if they're credible. Promises work much the same. If I didn't honor them, I'd have far, *far* fewer eyes and ears across this town."

Brock bit his lip. Could he dare to hope? Could he actually have a way out of this awful situation? Could it be that easy?

And then he remembered what she'd asked of him. It was a far cry from "easy."

"I'll think about it," he said, as if he could still say no. But she knew she had him.

She knew exactly what kind of hand he had. Four of dragons, eight of griffins, and a useless unicorn.

Chapter Five

Zed

Twice a week, Zed and Jayna met in the master archivist's office for lessons.

Feydays were supposed to be reserved for magical theory and Noxdays for actual spell-casting, but in practice Hexam just taught whatever felt interesting in the moment. The seminars were a hash of aimless lectures, arcane exercises, and digressions into Hexam's other great passion: the Dangers.

During less stressful times, Zed found it all fascinating. Hexam's unpredictable teaching style kept him on his toes. Today, for instance, a decanter full of black, oily scum waited on the wizard's desk as Zed arrived.

But Zed was in no mood for silliness. Just moments after Brock left, Frond had stormed into the guildhall like a winter squall. Her gray eyes were cold and furious as the sky outside.

Zed had tried to talk to her—pleading with Frond to help the elves—but the guildmistress just kept moving, stomping up the stairs to her personal quarters. The whole hall shook when she slammed the door closed.

Zed himself now stomped across Hexam's office, throwing himself into his usual chair. Jayna quirked an eyebrow from the seat next to his.

Near the back of the room, Hexam was stooped over and trying very carefully to liberate a book from the bottom of a lopsided stack of manuals, presumably without toppling the entire structure.

Zed cleared his throat, fussing in his chair.

Hexam ignored him. The wizard pulled at the load-bearing book, and the structure wobbled alarmingly. He winced, then slowly, *gently* began sliding the tome free from the pile. The book shifted by minuscule degrees—one inch, two, three—until only a corner was left confined.

"What's this black stuff?" Zed blurted.

The tower fell, and books toppled all around Hexam like a castle under siege. When the dust had finally settled, the archivist stood up straight with a groan, surrounded by literary wreckage. He carried the single book back to his desk.

"That," he said tightly as he sat, "is the excretion of a *stalking shadow*. It's a blessedly rare Danger that hunts by attaching itself to the *true* shadows of its prey. So far, the only means we've discovered to safely disentangle one is for a blood relative to speak the victim's name aloud three times."

Hexam shook his head. "Don't ask me *why* that works, though. I'm still puzzling it out." He opened up a cavernous drawer in the desk and smuggled the bottle inside.

"Maybe the elves know," said Zed. "We could send for some elven mages to be let out of the market. Do an exchange of information." He perked up, crawling up straight in his chair for the first time. "Actually, that would be amazing! There have got to be more sorcerers like my dad among the elves, right? Ones who could finally teach me how to use *my* magic!"

The archivist frowned. "Zed, believe me when I tell you that none of us are happy with the king's decision. It wasn't so long ago that he imprisoned *us* with false accusations. But Frond is the only reason the rangers haven't been confined with the rest of their people. I don't know how much further she can push it."

"So what *do* you know?" Zed mumbled.

The archivist sighed, his dark eyes falling to his hands. "I know I'm sorry," Hexam said. "Sorry that this is happening and sorry that I'm not a better teacher for you. But in this guild, we're forced to make do with what we have."

A long stretch of awkward silence passed, as Hexam began searching his desk for some clue or inspiration for the day's lesson. Jayna squirmed uncomfortably in the quiet, her pale skin and ginger hair shining blue beneath the room's multicolored orbs.

"Magus Hexam," she began, "last week you mentioned we might finally discuss broadening my portfolio of battle magic. I only really know the—"

"Once again, Jayna," Hexam interrupted tersely, "I'm not a magus anymore. That title was stripped from me when I left the Mages Guild." Then he glanced up. "Remind me, what was the last spell I asked you to learn?"

Jayna's face brightened at this opportunity. Though they were both wizards, Hexam was surprisingly stingy when it came to teaching the girl actual spells for the field.

Zed didn't learn his magic the same way Jayna did. While both were considered mages, Jayna was a wizard and Zed a sorcerer.

The way Hexam described it, sorcerous magic was less intellectual and more intuitive; a sorcerer's abilities appeared as the young mage grew, and then had to be practiced for control. Zed's few experiments in replicating wizard magic over the last several weeks had all ended explosively. After he accidentally shattered several first-floor windows while trying to cast a standard Wizard's Shield, Frond finally forbade him from any more attempts.

Jayna, however, was brilliant at the stuff.

"My last assignment was Eldritch Darts," she said brightly. "I believe I have it properly memorized, Ma—uh, *Master* Hexam."

Zed's eyes widened. "Didn't you say that was a second-level spell?"

Jayna turned and beamed at him. "My first one, yes."

The archivist nodded slowly, running a hand over the beard that framed his thin, dusky face. "Then I'd like to see you perform it, please."

Jayna and Zed stood from their chairs and began turning toward the door. Usually, the more dangerous exercises required that they head out into the training yard, away from any fragile equipment.

Usually. When they realized that Hexam hadn't risen to follow them, the two apprentices looked back uncertainly.

Hexam cleared his throat. "I would like you to perform the spell in *here*, apprentice," he clarified. He extended his hand to a small sphere that had been set on a pedestal near the far wall of the room, molded from silvery metal.

Zed recognized the sphere. It had been among the equipment they brought back from the wayshelter. It was decorated with looping shapes and elven sigils arranged in a series of overlapping circles.

The confidence fell from Jayna's face like Zed fell from a chin-up attempt—quickly and without composure.

"Um, Master Hexam," she began. "This room is very small, and the darts—"

"The darts," Hexam said with a small smile, "will follow whatever target they are cast at when the spell is performed correctly." The elder wizard's smile tightened, and his eyebrow quirked. "Of course, if you only *believe* that you have it properly memorized, perhaps we should wait until you're sure."

Jayna narrowed her eyes. In the last month and a half, Zed had discovered that there were two surefire ways of riling up the apprentice wizard, and Hexam was very fond of both. The first was talking about dark magic.

The second, far more dangerous way was to suggest that she had come unprepared.

Jayna made a sort of dignified squeak and strode to the opposite side of the room from the sphere. She held her hands up, fingers wriggling in the air. Zed stood back, pressing against the office door and hugging his scepter to his chest. He was ready to elf-step out of the room if need be.

Though Zed wasn't himself a wizard, he knew that wizard spells required three basic components: formulas, signs, and mana. After memorizing a complicated magical formula, a wizard could express it by weaving arcane signs—words, gestures, symbols, or magically conductible ingredients—into a spell. The more familiar a wizard was with the formula, the less complicated the sign necessary to cast it. Most master wizards like Hexam could conjure powerful spells with a simple flick of the wrist.

Jayna's fingers traced through the air, the movements slow and precise. This being a second-level spell, the gestures necessary were more complex than her usual Wizard's Shield.

She performed it perfectly. No sooner had Jayna spread her hands than three fizzing blue motes appeared in the air around her. The lights streaked forward like buzzing wasps, heading straight for the small sphere.

Jayna grinned, looking spent but pleased . . . until the sphere came alive.

A high pealing noise, like the ringing of a bell, filled the room as the darts neared the orb. Suddenly, three lashes of white light struck out, whipping into Jayna's missiles with a loud *crack, crack, crack!* Every one of the darts shattered and dissipated before finding their target.

Jayna looked like she herself had been lashed. "That . . ." she said, her eyes wide. "But I—"

Hexam finally stood from his desk, moving to inspect the sphere. "Well done, Jayna!" he said. "I wanted to test the enchantment on an unsuspecting mage." The archivist ran his fingers over the pristine surface of the orb. "Mythril is *remarkable* at holding enchantments," he breathed. "This one is years old, but with just a bit of mana added to it, the countercurse worked perfectly."

Hexam turned back to the apprentices. "Thank you for humoring me," he said. "This, and Zed's new scepter, were the only two items of any magical value recovered from the wayshelter."

Zed's ears twitched. He realized he was gripping the scepter maybe a bit tightly. "*My* scepter?" he asked. "I can keep it, then?"

"As long you learn how to use it safely," the archivist said. He walked back to his desk and sat down behind it, gesturing for Zed and Jayna to return to their chairs.

"Arcane implements can be a great help for any spell-caster," Hexam said, as they took their seats. "Jayna, I'll have Lotte find you a wand from the armory, and we can begin the principles for how to use them in our next lesson." He paused. "If you ever do find yourselves facing an undead enemy, then you'll need every advantage you can muster. They are relentless foes. Unlike other Dangers, they don't experience fear or pain."

"Why?" Zed asked. "What makes them special?" Beside him, Jayna leaned forward in her chair.

Hexam sat up a bit straighter as well. The wizard's mood had improved. "As you both know by now, the Dangers came to our world when Foster Pendleton opened the gates between the seven planes. Terryn, our home, was overrun by creatures from the other six. Fey, the fairy plane, and Fie, the infernal plane, are closest to ours—the inner planes. These are where most magic comes from. Jayna, can you name the four outer planes?"

Jayna nodded, her red curls bouncing. "There's Nox, the plane of chaos, luck, and shadows; Lux, the plane of order, logic, and light; Astra, the plane of the mind; and Mort—"

"—the plane of the dead," Hexam finished with a nod. "Very little is known of it, and no creature has ever emerged directly from the plane. Instead, the power that spills from Mort causes the dead in Terryn to rise. These Dangers are what we call *undead*. Once, necromancers were able to harness this power to raise undead armies—but at a terrible cost to themselves. Exposed to Mort's energies, many of them festered, becoming moldering creatures known as liches."

Zed's eyes shot up. "The *Lich*! That's the minister who took over Llethanyl. He's some kind of . . . death mage?"

Hexam shook his head. "To be honest, he's less like a mage and more like a focus. The outer planes don't provide mana, but at one time they *did* offer otherworldly abilities for those who were able—and willing—to access them. Necromancy was thought to be a lost art, like so many others from before the Day of Dangers. Apparently, we were wrong. One of Llethanyl's ministers, an elf named Galvino, rediscovered the art in secret. And due to the elves' long-standing tradition of burying their dead, he had plenty of material with which to practice."

Zed grimaced at this. From what he could tell, death was a taboo subject for the elves—a topic of extremely guarded reverence. So much so that they referred to their dead as simply *the lost*. Many still seemed baffled that such a violation had occurred at all.

A tentative knock sounded from the other side of the door.

"Enter," Hexam called.

The door creaked open and Fel's face poked through. She began to speak, but her eyes lit up as the office shifted from red to turquoise. The young elf's gaze traveled across the space, flitting from wonder to wonder.

"*Ast'la ven!*" Fel said. "What beautiful lights. And are those *skeletons?* . . . From *Dangers?* I thought that humans weren't supposed to keep large bones around."

Hexam coughed uneasily. "There are a *few* exceptions. Though I don't see the need to mention these to anyone outside the guild. Is there something the rangers need, Fel?"

The elf's face became suddenly serious, wonder transforming into graveness in a blink. "Frond asked for you," she said. "Something important is happening."

"Important?" Hexam said, rising from his chair. "Well, for Fie's sake, spit it out then."

"Queen Me'Shala is here," Fel answered, her eyes falling to the floor at the mere mention of the elven monarch. "She wants the adventurers to take back our city."

Hexam and Jayna walked up front, leading the way to the main hall, while Zed and Fel trailed behind. Zed glanced at the young elf beside him. "Do you think it's really possible?" he whispered. "To save Llethanyl?"

Fel's smile was cautious. "I don't know," she admitted. "But the queen doesn't ask things lightly. And I've heard that she's *very* hard to refuse."

For the first time in weeks, Zed allowed himself to truly imagine visiting the city of his father. Perhaps he'd find more answers there about the mysterious Zerend. Fel was too young to know anything about him, but Zed had tried asking the High Ranger—he'd asked every elf who would deign to speak to him, in fact.

He'd learned that Zerend was a wood elf and a sorcerer, like Zed himself. Zed knew his father was "lost" on the trip back to Llethanyl twelve years ago, and Callum had called him "a good elf."

That was all.

Zed had hoped that with time, Callum might open up and offer more. But each passing week had slowly snuffed out that hope. The elves were tight-lipped about their dead.

"You must be anxious to get home," Zed said. "Away from all the prejudice. I'm so sorry Freestoners are like this. It's not fair to you or your people."

Fel's smile faltered, and then quickly brightened again. "Yes . . . well," she said. "Every place has its problems!" She glanced away. "Here we are."

In his six weeks as an apprentice, Zed had celebrated half a dozen parties with the Sea of Stars. A life of constant danger meant that every day alive was a new victory—and victory, Zed had learned, meant revelry. Though food and drink were leaner than ever, the guild made the most of their meager larders, whipping elaborate feasts out of basic staples, plus whatever herbs still grew outside the city walls.

The remains of just such a feast were now strewn around the main hall.

Guildmembers stood in awkward clumps, for once keenly aware of the state of their greeting room. The floor was sticky underfoot, and there didn't appear to be six inches of continuous wall space that wasn't splattered with *some* kind of food or drink.

Only a statue near the back of the room was distinctly unscathed. A stone boy reached out one arm, his eyes wide with shock. This, Zed had learned on his first day with the guild, was no carving. It was an unfortunate apprentice, only a couple years older than himself. The poor boy had been petrified by the gaze of a basilisk, the very monster from which flinty-eyed Frond had earned her nickname.

Just as many elven rangers were also present in the room, and by the anxious expressions they were casting at Frond's office, it was clear where their queen had retreated to.

Hexam didn't dally. Zed had just enough time to realize he'd never actually *seen* the interior of Frond's office when he, Jayna, and Fel were all rushed up the stairs and through the forbidding door.

Beyond it, a steep climb zigzagged up at least two ramshackle stories, the old wood complaining with each step. Zed sympathized. Finally they reached a second door, which Hexam threw open without a knock.

The room was tidier than Zed would have expected. Unlike many adventurers, Frond kept no trophies of the Dangers she'd slain. Her bed—a neatly made four-poster—stood directly beside an enormous bay window with clean white curtains. The guildmistress's room was the highest point in the entire rickety hall—and certainly the highest in the neighborhood. Zed realized with a thrill that her window was set *over* Freestone's wall, offering a clear view of the forest line.

Perhaps Frond had watched them from here, when he, Brock, Liza, and Jett lingered glumly outside during their initiation.

The guildmistress now waited behind a large desk fashioned from lustrous wood. The legs had been carved into a set of four creatures Zed had never seen before. And judging by the many lovingly detailed teeth carved into each of the beasts' open jaws, he didn't want to. Their guild's blue flag, sprinkled with five stars, hung on the wall behind Frond.

And seated directly in front of the desk was Me'Shala, the queen of the elves.

"There you are," Frond grunted accusingly. By the way she hastily stood to greet Hexam, Zed suspected they had been sitting in awkward silence for some time.

Hexam ignored her tone, turning instead to the elven queen. Rather than bowing, the archivist brought two fingers to his lips. "Welcome, Your Majesty," he said.

Me'Shala smiled at the gesture, and the room seemed to grow brighter for it.

Zed had seen the queen only a few times. Though she lived with her people in the market camp, she was well insulated from outsiders. Even now, two elven women wearing glittering silver armor hung by the doors, casting wary looks at Hexam and the others as they entered.

The queen had brown skin and eyes like fire opals. Her dress was decorated with looping, leafy branches.

Callum stood in the room's far corner wearing a blank expression, his arms crossed. Two more elves, dressed much more fussily than their queen, were seated on a dreary sofa that had been pulled up to the desk. Both were sun elves—*ain'shea*. The male's hair was golden and his skin was fair, while the female's bronze skin was veiled by lustrous white locks. Both wore circlets adorned with the shapes of birds in flight.

And then there was Brock. The boy stood right beside the queen, as if he were her page. Zed's eyebrows shot up when he caught sight of his friend. How had he already managed to insinuate himself into this?

The female sun elf scrunched her nose as they arrived. She pointed a long elegant finger straight at Fel. Whereas Hexam, Zed, and Jayna had all stepped fully into the room, the young elf hung back, her eyes lowered.

"No," the sun elf said. She pursed her mouth into a pretty frown. "Not her. Too much is at stake here."

The two armored elves at the door stepped forward, each grabbing Fel by one of her arms. Llethanyl's city crest was molded into their identical suits of armor: a great tree wreathed by a halo of birds. Zed realized that these must be two of Me'Shala's illustrious sword sisters. Fel didn't resist their grasps, or even lift her eyes.

Zed's jaw fell open. What was happening?

"Wait!" he said, snapping back around to face the queen. "Why can't Fel stay? She's one of your people. She's a ranger!"

The female sun elf glared at him. "Are all human children so impertinent?"

Zed's ears grew red hot. He balled his hands into fists. "I'm *half* elf," he muttered.

The woman's lovely eyebrows lifted like birds taking flight. "There are no *half elves*, my ignorant little friend," she said. "There are elves . . . and then there is everything else. In any case, it's plain from your question that you lack even a basic understanding of how our society works."

Zed watched as Brock's face screwed into a scowl. He opened his mouth to say something, but was beaten to the punch.

"Threya," the male elf beside her chided. "Must you be so boorish in front of our hosts?" He rolled his eyes and shrugged, as if dealing with an eccentric aunt. "I say we let the night elf stay. What we discuss here affects all our people. That includes the *dro'shea.*"

Unlike most elves, even the men, this one wore his hair short, in a cut not dissimilar to many human nobles. As elves went, it was a brazen, modern style.

Threya cast an unhappy look at her companion. "Spare us your reformist blather, Selby. We cannot involve the deathlings in this. The Lich was one of theirs."

"You can't judge an *entire population* based on one unfortunate example," Selby snapped back. "Isn't that exactly what the humans are doing to us?"

"The Lich is not an *unfortunate example*. He is the destroyer of our people!"

"My friends." The queen's voice cut through the rising pitch of the argument like water through a parched throat. "Please remember that we're guests here, pleading for aid. We come in humility."

The two elves deflated back into their seats, though only Selby had the grace to look embarrassed. Threya stared forward, unwilling to even glance in Fel's direction.

"You must excuse us," Me'Shala said, turning to Frond. "But the truth is that I *rely* on this caution and passion from my ministers. The elves haven't always been a unified people. Before the *lleth'dia*—the Day of Dangers—our kind were engaged in a seemingly endless struggle. To call it a war would be too simple, for it impacted every part of the lives and worldviews of our ancestors. Many old angers still fester."

She sighed and her eyes landed on Fel, who stood silently at the entrance. The girl's arms were still gripped by sword sisters.

"Galvino claimed he wanted to help heal our broken peoples," the queen said. At the sound of the name, the ministers both flinched. Zed noticed that even Callum's arms crossed a bit more tightly.

"He was the first night-elf minister Llethanyl had ever seen," Me'Shala continued. "And he was brilliant: an eloquent diplomat and a wizard far more accomplished than myself. His betrayal—his use of our lost against us—was more than just mutiny. It was a message. We can never escape our past. It will always, *always* rise again."

"Your Majesty . . ." Callum spoke from the corner. Though he leaned casually against the wall, his voice was tentative.

Zed was struck by how tenderly the elven queen was treated by her subjects. Compared to King Freestone, Me'Shala didn't command the respect of her advisors so much as she enjoyed their love. She seemed as much a mother as a monarch.

She nodded for Callum to continue.

"This girl is named Felasege. Her parents were both rangers who gave their lives protecting our city," he said. "They were my friends, and I trusted them without reservation. They would settle for nothing less than a peaceful future for our people . . . and for their daughter."

Now Fel's gaze finally rose from the floor. Her cobalt eyes widened as she looked at Callum.

Threya scoffed. "This isn't the time for weepy sentiments. The deathlings have always been obsessed with mortality. It's why we went to war with them in the first place. How can we be sure this girl won't turn against us? That any of them won't?"

"Fel's parents are among our lost," the ranger responded sharply. "The Lich did not discern between sects when he profaned them." He returned his gaze to the queen. "Fel is one of us. I would ask that you let her stay."

The queen smiled appreciatively at Callum. "Thank you, High Ranger. Indeed, we're all one people, and we have all been betrayed—the night elves perhaps most of all."

She cast a glance to the sword sisters, who released Fel's arms without another word.

Frond, who had watched this little drama unfold with uncharacteristic patience, now rapped her fingers against the top of the desk.

"Queen Me'Shala," she said. "Involving the question at hand . . . I'm afraid that King Freestone still hasn't ordered a siege. But I am *imploring* him to show compassion for—"

"The spring that feeds your king's compassion has run dry," the queen said. "My people are no longer refugees here; they're prisoners. Which is why I've come to you, my old friend." A mischievous sparkle shone in Me'Shala's eyes. "We were close once, Alabasel. I implore *you* for compassion. You always favored action over talk."

Frond cleared her throat, unable to mask her flustered expression. "Be that as it may, the Adventurers Guild is only a small force. We don't have the numbers or the training for a full siege. Without the knights, mages, and healers beside us, what you're asking for is suicide."

"What use are all these knights, mages, and healers?" Threya grumbled. "Birds, who never leave the safety of their nest. It's appalling that the burden of actually protecting your city falls on the shoulders of a small band of miscreants."

"Miscreants *and* children," Brock piped up from beside the queen. "Thank you very much."

Frond sighed, running a hand through her cropped gray hair. "Our peoples have survived in their own ways," she said. "Regardless, my point remains the same. If my guild went up against an undead army on our own, we would lose. And Freestone would lose its sole agents to the outside world."

Me'Shala inclined her head. "I agree. Which is why we're proposing something a bit different. A bit subtler."

Frond leaned back from the desk, steepling her fingers. Zed wasn't sure he liked the intrigued expression on her face.

Selby scooted forward on Frond's shabby sofa. "Undead Dangers are usually rare. By harnessing Mort's energies, however, the Lich has created an army of them, and can maintain his thralls from any distance—but only so long as *he* lives. . . ."

Frond's eyes flicked over to Hexam. The archivist nodded slowly, his face thoughtful. "Necromancy hasn't been practiced for hundreds of years," he said, "but the literature agrees. A lich uses its own body as a sort of focus for Mort's energies. I wouldn't call it *alive*, though. Not truly. The person beneath has become a kind of Danger themselves."

"But if we destroy the Lich . . ." Callum started, his eyes

blazing. The elf bounded forward from the corner, graceful as a deer. "This is it!" he said excitedly, slamming his hand down on Frond's desk. "Not an army—a *smaller* force could sneak in and destroy the Lich. Then this curse over our lost would disappear."

Hexam shook his head. "Slaying a lich is no easy task. Whole wars were once waged trying to accomplish such a feat. Like any focus, the energies he houses would make him incredibly difficult to injure. Maybe impossible. They are *not* like simple undead."

"Could Zed's flame do it?" Frond asked. Zed's eyes shot to the desk, where Frond sat with her hands clenched. The guildmistress met his gaze unflinchingly. "That green fire is more potent than regular flames, yes? It destroyed a fully transformed penanggalan."

The queen now watched Zed with new scrutiny, her expression thoughtful. "Then *this* is the young sorcerer I've heard so much about."

"How fascinating," Selby muttered. "*Green* fire, you say?"

Hexam considered Frond's question, scratching at his beard. "It might work," he said, with a note of resignation. "Maybe."

This . . . this was it. A plan to save the elves—and they needed *him*! Queen Me'Shala herself had heard of Zed, and she was watching him now with undisguised hope.

"Then I'll do it," Zed said, his voice catching with the honor of it all.

"Not a chance," Brock said at the same time, only louder.

Zed rounded on his friend, for once bristling under Brock's protective impulses. Brock had all but disappeared the last several weeks. Now he suddenly had an opinion on what Zed did and where he went?

"What do you care?" he snapped. Behind him, Zed heard Jayna actually gasp aloud—her first noise the entire conversation. "I earned my quest-worthiness, same as you! Or maybe you don't remember, since you *skipped* the celebration."

Ignoring Brock's grimace—and the supremely entertained expression of the elven minister Threya—Zed turned back to Frond. "Callum is right. This is the best way. And I'm the only one who can do it."

Threya coughed out a laugh. "Would you listen to him? You mean to tell me this *child* is the most powerful sorcerer in Freestone?" She shook her head incredulously and waved toward Me'Shala. "Our queen is a wizard of no small skill. Even Selby could probably rival your precious *Mages Guild*. We came to you seeking aid, and you offer this . . . infant!"

Hexam frowned at the minister, placing a hand on Zed's shoulder. "Sorcery isn't as simple as *most* or *least* powerful," he said. "The boy lacks finesse, but the fire he conjures is among the most destructive forces I've ever seen. It is perhaps the only weapon we have that's capable of eradicating a true lich."

Frond watched Zed for a long beat, her scarred face unreadable. "We'll see," she said finally.

"If he goes, I'm going, too," said Brock. "Don't you dare try to stop—"

"Stop, Brock," Frond interrupted.

Brock came up short, then cursed himself.

"The answer is no," Frond said, her slate-gray eyes boring into him. "*If* we risk this plan, going behind the king's back and imperiling the life of an apprentice in the process—*if* we make this journey, which is already fraught with its own hazards, to face an enemy who may very well be impossible to destroy—then we need to minimize our potential losses. The team sent to Llethanyl will be small. It will be specialized. It will be *elite*. And by my express order, it will *not* include Brock Dunderfel. Do I make myself clear, apprentice?"

Brock stared at Frond, chewing on the inside of his cheek, his hands opening and closing at his sides. Slowly, very slowly, the expression of pure rage on his face quieted into something like acceptance—or at least a dull enmity.

"Crystal," he said.

Chapter Six

Brock

Brock yawned, loud and leisurely. It was a chill winter day, but he was wrapped in a blanket with a hot water bottle at his feet, reclining on a makeshift hammock he'd assembled from an old, torn tent. He turned the page of the book he had propped up against his knees.

"Oh, here's a nasty one," he said. "Lamprey bats."

"That doesn't sound so bad," Fel said, straining at the string of her bow, lining up a shot. "Bats are cute."

"These aren't real bats though," Brock said. "More like . . . hairy worms. With wings. And look at these teeth."

Fel took a peek at the page. "Okay," she said. "Not so cute."

"Brock!" Liza called from across the training ground. "Would you please stop distracting my sparring partner?"

Brock stuck out his tongue, but Fel snapped to attention. "Sorry!" she said, and she let her arrow fly. It ricocheted off Liza's shield.

"Apologizing while you shoot her," Brock said. "You fit riiiight in."

They were in the training yard, a dusty patch of ground in the shadow of the lopsided guildhall. Within the building, preparations had begun for the most ambitious and dangerous mission the adventurers had ever undertaken.

Brock had been told to stay out of the way.

"You're missing a great opportunity to practice against projectiles," Liza said, walking over to return Fel's arrow—really more of a bolt: a thick, blunt wooden cylinder that could bruise but wouldn't pierce. Liza, who had a talent for woodworking, had made it herself.

"You're missing a great opportunity to relax," Brock countered. "After all, didn't you hear? *We're* not essential to the success of the mission." He meant to sound flippant, but it came out sounding bitter.

"So?" Liza said. "What's your plan?"

Brock leisurely turned the page of Hexam's homemade Danger handbook, revealing another highly detailed horror. This one was an insect the size of a human hand, with fish-scale wings and a savage-looking barbed proboscis. "My plan?"

"You're telling me you *don't* have a plan for undermining Frond and getting us on the mission?"

"I've got nothing of the sort," he said. "I'm perfectly content to sit here and consider all the terrible monsters that definitely won't be eating me tomorrow. Ew, you wouldn't believe where the fiendfly lays its eggs—"

"What about Zed? You've given up on trying to keep him safe, have you?"

Liza's question was punctuated by a pitiful *meow*, and Brock saw Mousebane weaving between the girl's legs. He frowned at the sight of her—wild and bedraggled, with a notch missing from one ear, she was a far cry from the pretty, docile house cats of the merchant quarter. Her snaggletooth, the sharp canine projecting from her lower jaw that the others insisted was cute, made her look to him as if she were perpetually annoyed.

If Alabasel Frond had been born a cat, he decided, she would look something like Mousebane.

Liza bent over to run a hand along the cat's mangy tail.

Brock turned another page—sharply this time. "Keeping Zed safe is a losing proposition. To coin a phrase, you can lead a horse from water, but you can't stop it from hurling itself off the next cliff."

Fel wrinkled her brow as if puzzling out his meaning. "Humans do such . . . unusual things with language," she said.

"What can I say? I've got the soul of a poet."

"Sure you do," Liza grumbled. "Trapped in a cursed gem under your bed, maybe."

Brock watched as Mousebane's ears perked up; the cat's entire body went taut in response to some sound or movement across the yard. She took off like a bolt from Fel's bow, disappearing from his line of sight. "Listen, you've said it a hundred times: Zed can take care of himself. And he can make his own decisions. His own terrible, utterly senseless decisions."

"Liza!" someone shouted from an upstairs window.

"What!" she shouted back.

"Have you seen my traveling cloak?" It was Micah, leaning out dangerously far.

"I'm not going to have a shouted conversation with you from the yard, Micah!" she yelled. Then she turned casually to Fel. "What about you? Is Callum's decision to leave you behind final?"

Fel nodded. "It makes sense. We can't *all* go. And I . . . my presence . . ." She looked lost for a moment, sad, and Brock realized he'd rarely seen the girl without a smile on her face. "It's complicated." She flashed her smile again. "But their plan is a good one. I'm happy to know I'll get home eventually."

Home—Brock felt a little pang at that. It was easy to forget that, to some, Freestone wasn't synonymous with home. There was a whole other city out there, one he might never see for himself.

Even under the circumstances, Zed must be beside himself with excitement to see Llethanyl. Was he thinking of it as a sort of homecoming?

He *would* come back, right?

"What is that?" Liza said, peering down at the book.

"Ah, yes," Brock said. "'Shambling Slime, the Ooze that Walks Like a Man.' Apparently its weaknesses include fire and sharp weapons. So I guess we have *that* in common."

"'Walks like a man'?" Liza complained. "Shouldn't it be 'walks like a person'?"

"Really?" Brock said. "That's the part that disturbs you?"

"Liza!" Micah shouted as he entered the yard.

"What!" she shouted back.

Fel took a small step away, her smile faltering again. She still wasn't used to the Guerra sibling dynamic. Possibly, elven siblings tended to be less outwardly murderous toward each other.

"Have you seen my traveling cloak?" he asked again.

"No," she said.

Micah growled. "You couldn't have said that before I came all the way down here?"

"First of all," Liza said, "your cloak looks exactly the same as everybody else's! Second—"

"Oh, no," Brock said, a realization settling upon him a split second before it did Liza.

"Micah," she said darkly. "Why do you need your traveling cloak?"

A self-satisfied smirk broke across Micah's face. That was what he'd wanted her to ask from the start. "Didn't you hear?" he said. "Frond and the queen of the elves need a healer for their quest to liberate Lefanol. And I'm the best they've got."

Fel winced, presumably at his pronunciation of *Llethanyl*. Liza flinched, too, but Brock guessed it was for other reasons.

"You're also the *only* healer they've got," he said, hoping to lighten the mood.

It didn't work. "*You're* on the mission?" Liza demanded.

"Of course I'm on the mission," Micah said, smiling widely now. "Brock, I tried to get you on the team, too. You know, in case we run into any locked doors?" Here he drew his sleeves back and flexed his biceps. "But Frond called these her 'skeleton keys.' Said they should be able to open just about anything."

Brock and Liza rolled their eyes at the obvious lie, but Fel perked up. "I knew Frond was kind. She keeps her heart warded, but carries within it the seeds to a magnificent tree."

Micah faltered midflex. "She what?" he asked. Fel took a deep breath, preparing to launch into an explanation, but he spoke over her. "No, you know what? Elves are weird, and I've got packing to do, and that's that." He winked at Liza and flicked his chin at Brock. "Wish I could heal your bruised egos. But even I'm not that good."

Liza stared after her brother in disbelief as he strutted back across the yard.

"Well, I think we'll all breathe a little easier these next few weeks," Brock said lightly. "Assuming he remembers to pack his—"

In a single fluid motion, Liza gripped the end of Brock's hammock and flipped it, dumping him out onto the ground. Then she leaned in and gripped the fabric of his shirt.

"You!" she spat. "Plan!"

"—socks," Brock said.

"I want us on that mission, Brock," she stated, a vicious gleam in her eyes. "Make it happen."

She stalked away, leaving Brock dazed upon the ground. Before he could gather his wits, Mousebane sauntered up, dropping a dead rat beside him.

Brock recoiled, scooting swiftly away, and he brought his backside down on something squishy—the hot water bottle had fallen with him from the hammock, and now wetness saturated his pants as it burst beneath his weight.

"Perfect," he muttered.

Fel was practically bouncing in place. "It's just so *sweet*!" she said.

"Sweet?!"

"It means she likes you, silly."

She patted Brock on the head and skipped off.

"You mean the cat, right?" he called after her. "You're talking about the cat?"

They gathered for a funeral before dawn. The entire guild and all the elven rangers were there at the edge of the forest as the sky began to lighten by degrees above the endless trees and Broken Roads that stood between Freestone and Llethanyl.

For all the talk of the adventurers' steep mortality rate, none of Brock's guildmates had died since the Guildculling, and for that, he was grateful. But he was no stranger to funerals. His last remaining grandparent had passed peacefully in her sleep just a year ago, and Brock had held his mother's hand from the moment the funeral pyre was lit until the fire burned out and all that was left was ash.

An elven funeral, however, was an altogether different affair—and despite the cold, the elves showed no interest in rushing through the ritual, which involved a series of speeches that Brock, of course, couldn't understand. The hole, at least, had been prepared the night before; a rectangle of pure black against the white snow.

"I still can't believe they're going to *bury* him in the ground," Brock whispered to Jett. They stood apart with the rest of the adventurers, on guard for any threat from the woods. But Brock's eyes kept drifting over to the clutch of elves and the dark pit they encircled. "It's too weird."

The dwarven boy nodded slightly. "It's all weird, though. The things people do. You don't see it when you're steeped in it. But from the outside looking in . . ." He rubbed his shaven chin, which was chafed pink in the cold. "You know my people put the ashes of our dead into molten metal? We forge things with them. Weapons and shields. Boots, for all I know!"

"I think I read that somewhere," Brock said. "Not the boots part."

"I'm just guessin'," said Jett. "I'm a dwarf, but I'm also a Freestoner from birth. Sometimes the two things fit together, and sometimes they don't. I try not to judge any of it." He clucked his tongue sadly as four rangers brought forth a small pinewood box—the vessel that held the child elf's body. "Shame about this boy, though. Do you know what happened?"

"I heard he was sick," Brock answered. "Born sick, and the voyage was too much of a strain. He never recovered." Brock looked from the box to the top of Freestone's wall, where the mourning women he'd first seen in the temple stood among a small group of elves—and a larger group of knights. Only the rangers, the queen, and her retinue had been allowed through the gates. Anyone else who wished to attend the funeral had to do so at a distance, and at swordpoint.

The sight hurt Brock's heart, but even at this remove he could see that the rage and the grief were gone from the women's faces. It was clear they found peace in the idea of burial, whatever Brock thought about it. Every elf in sight was a picture of tranquility, Fel included.

Zed, on the other hand, was a mess. Tears streamed freely down his face, and he pressed his lips together tightly to avoid making any sound. Brock wanted to go to him, to sidle up and whisper a joke, but Zed had positioned himself in a tight cluster of those chosen for the mission to Llethanyl. There was no way for Brock to reach him without making a commotion. Then Zed saw Brock looking, and hastily wiped the tears away.

One elf was doing most of the talking. Brock recognized him as Selby, one of the queen's two remaining ministers. As Brock had pieced it together, the ministers provided counsel to the queen. The position obviously held some sort of cultural significance, too, for Selby to be conducting this ceremony now. He wore an elaborate headdress of gleaming bronze, with projections radiating outward like a child's drawing of the rays of the sun. His voice was musical, rising and falling and rising again, and Brock felt for a moment as if he were drifting upon it, the way people in stories drifted on the sea, an expanse of water said to be so huge you couldn't see the end of it.

Then there was a creaking of branches, and Brock's eyes cut back to the trees, his heart in his throat. It was just the wind. This time.

He focused his attention on the woods after that.

Eventually Selby's voice came to a halt, and Brock risked another glance at the funeral. Selby had opened a small window in the pinewood vessel's lid. He placed within it a wooden flute and a tarnished gray dagger.

"What is that about?" whispered Brock.

"It's for the little lost one," Fel whispered in response. "Now he will have what he needs on his return, whether it is a time of peace or . . . not."

Brock couldn't help but think that, given the current circumstances, burying the dead with a weapon was an especially bad idea.

As the rangers who held the box slowly lowered their burden into the hole, Selby produced a sphere of bronze. It was about the size of a cannonball, but hollow. Brock could see clear through it where the bronze had been worked into elegant swirling patterns that left gaps in its surface. As the others took up spades and began shoveling icy dirt atop the coffin, the minister chanted, and smoke poured from the sphere in his hands. It drifted in the breeze, finding its way to Brock's nose.

"That's myrrh," Fel explained. "It will keep this lost one safe, ensuring a peaceful slumber and warding off evil."

"Let's hope." Brock shuddered, turning his head to watch the forest again. The space between the trees was as dark and forbidding as that hole in the ground.

Jett's gaze was not on the forest, but on the wall at their backs, where the elven witnesses were being escorted away under heavy guard, leaving only a few remaining Stone Sons as sentries. "Isn't this all a bit obvious?" Jett said. "As secret missions go, I mean."

Brock considered the adventurers and the rangers gathering at the forest's edge. The queen herself was there, though dressed as a common ranger, longsword at her hip and longbow at her back, her hair in a tight plait. He'd been raised with stories about the warrior kings of Freestone's past, but the current reality of royal life in the human city kept the king and his family cloistered far from any danger. The elves clearly lived by a different philosophy. If he hadn't met the queen only days before, he never would have recognized her. Certainly not from the top of the wall.

"It's a good plan, actually," Brock conceded. "A big party goes out, practically the entire guild, all at once—and then most of them come back the next day. Overnight excursions into the forest aren't that rare, and the knights aren't counting heads—especially with a funeral to distract them. So they'll never know a small party is still out there."

A good plan, yes; but it would also be quite easy to sabotage, Brock knew. He'd even considered doing it: going to the king, telling him what Frond and Me'Shala had planned without his consent. The king had been quick to arrest Frond for her insubordination when the wards had been corrupted. It wasn't difficult to imagine the fury her current actions would incite. At the very least, the mission would be shut down, Frond reprimanded, and Zed kept safe.

But fury was like fire: easy to stoke and hard to control. The king might not be content with blaming Frond. The whole guild could be punished, and the elves, too. And Queen Me'Shala seemed the type to meet fury head-on. If the tension between the two royals bubbled over . . .

More suffering. That was all Brock could imagine as a result of stopping this mission now. And despite his misgivings—and he had *serious* misgivings—he didn't want to stop the mission, not really.

If there was even a chance the elves could take back their city, he wouldn't be the one to stand in their way.

Brock noticed Liza glaring at him, but if that made him doubt his decision, the sight of Zed trembling with excitement squashed those doubts in an instant.

"Come on," Fel said. "All that's left is to cover the coffin, and then we will be expected to return to the guildhall. It's time."

She led Brock and Jett to where the rest of their friends had gathered. Liza had turned her fierce gaze away from Brock to address Zed and Micah and Jayna. "You three look out for one another, you understand? Whatever else you have to do, you need to have one another's backs."

Zed nodded solemnly, Micah picked at his teeth, and Jayna stepped forward, her eyes brimming with tears. "We'll be okay," she said, smiling bravely.

"I know you will," Liza said, and she embraced the other girl. "You guys are the best. And you're going to save Llethanyl." She pulled back, but kept her hands on Jayna's arms. "Think of how much magic you'll learn along the way!"

Jayna's eyes cut over to Hexam, who was pawing through his supplies for one last check. With himself and Zed both potentially crucial to the mission, the archivist had insisted on bringing Jayna along as well. It seemed he put more stock in her magical education than she'd thought, and that revelation had been exciting enough to undercut her anxieties.

The wavering tears in her eyes were gone now, replaced with the spark of that excitement. She hugged Liza once more.

Brock couldn't help being impressed. He'd initially resisted the idea of Liza as their leader, and now he wondered how he ever could have imagined it going another way. Liza didn't shoot mystical darts or heal with a touch, but it was obvious why the others looked up to her.

Even Micah. She embraced him next, and though he affected annoyance, he leaned into it.

"I'll admit it, I'm jealous," Jett said to Zed. "Do you know what I'd give to see a dwarven city?"

Zed frowned. "Yeah, but Llethanyl is overrun by the undead. Not quite how I've imagined it."

Jett shrugged as if it were a minor inconvenience. "So waggle your fingers at 'em." He waggled his own. "Set 'em ablaze. See the sights. Then you come back to us." He leveled his steely gaze at Zed, the one that made him seem taller than Brock, taller than Frond. "You come back to us, Zed, all your parts intact. Do you hear me?"

Zed's ears flushed pink in the dawn light, and he smiled. "I promise."

"Good," Jett said, the hardness gone from his eyes in a blink. "And bring us back some elven sweets, or we won't be opening that door for your half-lazy half butt, you hear me?"

Zed giggled, and the sound of it broke Brock's heart a little. He hadn't heard his friend laugh like that in some time. But he couldn't say whether that was because Zed hadn't been laughing, or if Brock simply hadn't been around to hear it.

"I'll miss you," he said, pulling his friend into a hug. The fox charm Zed wore beneath his shirt felt sharp, but he didn't pull away.

"Are you sure you'll even notice I'm gone?" Zed said.

Now Brock pulled away.

The dawn was making slow progress, and with Zed's back to the forest, Brock couldn't make out his expression.

"Zed, I'm sorry I haven't been around much. It's . . . complicated, and—"

"I'm teasing, Brock," Zed said. He slapped his friend's shoulder. "I just mean I'll be back before you know it. I won't even *need* to 'waggle my fingers' once I get the hang of this." Smiling, he held up the jeweled rod he'd been carrying around almost nonstop since their night in Halfling's Hollow.

Brock felt a new worry bloom in his chest. "Zed, that thing isn't . . . like the staff you used that time, is it?"

The smile dropped from Zed's face. "What do you mean?" he asked.

"You know," Brock said, lowering his voice. "It's not . . . tainted? Not *dark* magic, right?"

Zed's eyes went stony. "It's just an implement, Brock. It's no more tainted than the mage who uses it."

"Oh. That's—that's good."

"I thought it didn't matter," he said, his voice straining a little. "I thought you didn't care, that Hexam was right, that magic was magic."

"I *don't* care," Brock said, looking around cagily. Jett had taken a step back, retreating from the argument, but they were well within earshot of a dozen adventurers. "I don't," Brock repeated, whispering. "It's just that *some* people would."

"What are you trying to say? Just say it!" Zed's voice cracked, and Brock knew for certain they had an audience now.

And isn't this typical, he thought bitterly. The Lady Gray had Brock tied around her pinky because of Zed's mistakes. And Zed was mad at *him*?

"I'm just saying don't be reckless out there," Brock said, grinding his molars to keep his voice down, to force the appearance of calm. It made his words come out sharp. "There are people here who care about you, who *worry*."

"Well, if you see any of those people, tell them I'm just fine," Zed snapped. "Tell them I know how to take care of myself." He turned and walked away, stomping into the throng of guildmates.

The worry in Brock's chest flared white-hot, consumed by anger. Zed was the last person he expected to talk to him that way. The last person who had a *right* to.

Through the haze of his anger, he was dimly aware of the good-byes all around him. He swept the crowd, unseeing, until his eyes landed on Frond.

The guildmistress was leaving final instructions with Lotte. She showed no emotion whatsoever, all flint and steel against the backdrop of the chattering, anxious guild around her. She, and the austere queen beside her, seemed to be the only ones who registered the true gravity of this mission.

It wasn't an exciting opportunity to see a foreign city. Or an expedition into the unknown.

They had one real purpose: to kill the creature that had taken Llethanyl.

It was an assassination. Frond was the killer, and Zed was her weapon.

Chapter Seven

Zed

The Broken Roads from Freestone to Llethanyl were just that: wide avenues of cracked stone bricks, now smuggled by green fingers of ivy beneath a cloak of frost.

Zed and the small party had woken early that morning, after a tense night of camp. The rangers had stood guard in shifts, allowing the main party as much rest as they could claim from the cold.

But Zed had slept fitfully. His dreams troubled him.

He dreamed he was kneeling in a smoke-filled forest, tugging desperately at the mythril chain around his neck. The chain had become molten and hot, and though Zed scrabbled to pull it off, his worrying fingers couldn't find the clasp. It had melted away. In his nightmare, the edges of his fox charm were blackened and burned, smoldering with eerie green embers.

Then, at the very end of the dream, he'd discovered that he was being watched.

A ghostly figure observed his struggle from the edge of the trees, an animal that was just barely visible against the haze that surrounded them both.

It was a fox. Zed realized it with the eerie certainty that sometimes came in dreams, before he'd even gotten a good look at its bushy tail. The fox, too, burned. Its slitted eyes flickered with the same ghastly green light that wreathed Zed's throat.

Those eyes stayed with Zed long after he'd jolted awake. He slept uneasily the rest of the night.

Micah's snoring had not helped in that regard.

"Your bunkmate," Callum said now to Zed, drawing him out of his thoughts and back to the hike. "Is he always such an . . . enthusiastic sleeper?"

"It's worse when the air is dry," Zed lamented. "Or when he sleeps on his back. Sometimes when he's eaten a lot. And on Luxdays, weirdly."

Zed couldn't tell whether the elf's expression flashed with amusement or pity.

Their team was treading carefully along the trail. Even knowing the plan required it, their party still looked too small to save a city. When the rest of the elves and adventurers had split off, Zed's stomach quailed at the sight of the scant company left behind.

Frond had wanted to minimize their possible losses, but when Queen Me'Shala and her two remaining ministers insisted on joining, she didn't put up much of a fight. Besides these retainers, the queen was flanked by her two sword sisters, and a team of elite rangers scouted their path.

Of the elves, only Callum seemed willing to part from the queen. Zed had been surprised when the High Ranger fell into step beside him, but he was glad for his presence. Callum watched their surroundings like a bird of prey.

"There aren't any night elves on the mission," Zed said quietly, hoping only Callum could hear him. When he glanced to the others, Zed found Threya was scowling, but scowling seemed to be the minister's resting state.

Callum nodded slowly, keeping his gaze on the trees. "As the queen said, there is mistrust among our kind. And the Lich himself is *dro'shea*."

Zed frowned. "But there *are* night elf rangers. Fel, for one."

"Felasege is young," Callum said.

"Well, then prepare to have your world turned upside down, because"—Zed passed a hand over his face, lifting an imaginary curtain—"*I'm* young," he revealed.

The High Ranger's eyes flicked down at him. They were back on the forest just as quickly. "Yes," he said. "You are. And bringing you was Frond's decision to make."

Callum looked thoughtful for a moment. When he slowly exhaled, the pensiveness went with it, a doubt resolving into mist. "The night elves who survived the Day of Dangers were all captives," he murmured. "Prisoners of a long and brutal war. Eventually, their descendants were freed, but it took nearly two centuries for all elves to be declared equal in Llethanyl. Two hundred years of lawful oppression."

"Oh," Zed breathed. "Fel never mentioned."

"It's not a happy subject for her." Callum shook his head. "And as you've seen, *declarations* of equality mean only so much. Some say the ancient night elves lived in darkness and worshipped death, a concept our culture doesn't officially believe in."

Zed frowned. "Didn't we just attend a funeral?"

Callum nodded slowly. "It was more of a . . . farewell. According to our sagas, the elves were once immortal, with fathomless life spans spent in quiet contemplation. Wood and sun elf traditions claim that druids still guard the secrets to our endless life. Thus our 'dead' are merely *lost*, until we prove ourselves worthy of eternity again."

Zed stared at the long path ahead, tracking it into the horizon. He thought of the elven shrine he'd discovered several weeks ago, the druids inside all collected in a hill of bones.

"But we'll never truly know what the night elves believed about death," the High Ranger continued. "Their old traditions are gone now."

"Gone?" Zed asked.

"Erased. The surviving *dro'shea* were converted to our sagas." The ranger paused. His cheeks colored in what might have been shame. "Many of the *dro'shea* are angry at the theft of their culture. They're right to be. The night elves lived in a small, isolated district. As rangers, Fel's parents fought for a city that might one day be worthy of their daughter. I, too, wish for such a city. She's a good elf, and she deserves a better world. But for that dream to be realized, there must still be a Llethanyl. And a Fel."

"A good elf," Zed mumbled. "You said the same thing about my father once."

Behind them, Jayna shrieked as Micah stuffed a clod of frozen earth down the back of her cloak. Zed grunted in annoyance. He glanced back upward, hoping Callum would continue the thread, but the elf's attention had drifted.

"I'd always thought healers were a compassionate sort," the High Ranger said mildly. His eyes stayed focused on something far away.

Zed snorted. "The nicest thing Micah's ever done is fart downwind of me. *Once.*"

Callum laughed, an extraordinary sound, and Zed found himself grinning as well. Then Frond barked for quiet, and the group fell again into silence.

They paused for lunch beside a jumble of enormous gray rocks dusted by flecks of snow. As far as Zed was concerned, the whole configuration looked unnervingly like King Freestone, and he privately dubbed the spot the Kingrock.

He wondered if King Freestone had discovered the queen's disappearance yet. Not that he could stop them at this point.

While Zed and the others watched the trail, Me'Shala's two sword sisters swept the Kingrock for Dangers. Both were wood elves, though that was where their similarities ended. One was tall and reedy, her tawny skin almost green against the pallid white of their surroundings. She moved in sharp, precise jabs.

The other was stocky—or at least as stocky as elves got—and there was no other way to describe her complexion but *pink*. She always seemed to be smiling serenely. Once, she'd winked at Zed when she caught him staring.

Zed hadn't learned their names yet. They didn't appear to speak the trade tongue at all, and Callum had warned him to steer clear while they guarded the queen. For now he just thought of them as Thorn and Petal.

After a few moments of searching, Thorn caught sight of something hidden within the rocks. She stabbed her longsword into a crevasse, then revealed a diminutive Danger impaled on the blade.

It appeared to be a strange cross between a clock and a bird. Four levered mechanical arms scrabbled at the sword, while a pair of colorful wings beat futilely against the air. The creature had no head to speak of, though a single large eye spun wildly inside its brass abdomen.

"I believe that's a cherubet," Hexam called. "Lux origin. They're among the weakest class of celestials. Perfectly harmless."

Thorn bashed it against the stone anyway. After a mechanical-sounding *crunch*, the cherubet went still.

When the Kingrock was finally deemed safe, the party sat down to lunch. Though they'd been walking for hours, Zed found his feet didn't yet hurt. Which was only a relief until he wiggled his toes and discovered he couldn't feel them at all.

After Frond passed around their lunchtime rations—twice-baked bread that had been soaked in oil, and two small morsels of cheese—Zed removed his boots. He held a cupped hand just in front of his feet and called forth a small gulp of mana.

Above his hand, a fork of green fire untwined. Zed warmed his toes like this for a while, careful not to let the flame touch his socks.

"No magic," Frond finally ordered. She gnawed at her loaf, ripping a piece away in a manner that reminded Zed of dogs destroying upholstery. "Sarve wur marna," she added, her half-chewed food on full display.

Zed sighed, quashing his *marna* and the warmth with it.

The queen, her ministers, and the sword sisters all sat in a separate group from the adventurers, closing themselves off into a forbidding circle. The rangers hung around more loosely, their eyes ever on the trees.

"Perhaps we could sing to pass the time," Jayna suggested between nibbles of cheese. "Adventurers enjoy ... bawdy stories, right? Fife certainly knows plenty. In the Silverglows, I once heard a very *naughty* song about an apprentice who accidentally sends her instructor's robes billowing up during—"

"No singing, either," Frond said.

So they ate in silence. Or as close to silence as Frond's chewing allowed. Zed couldn't help but notice Selby, the queen's minister, start a small fire in the center of *their* circle with a flick of magic.

Zed only repressed another woeful sigh by imagining Frond's voice barking, *No sighing!*

Dear Brock, I'm sorry.

Zed crossed out the line with a grunt.

Dear Brock, he wrote. *I'm scared.*

He dipped a small wooden pencil into a phial of ink. Technically, the writing tools were supposed to be for his lessons with Hexam, but since Zed didn't record the same magical formulas Jayna did, he decided he'd put them to more practical use.

Well, if you see any of those people, tell them I'm just fine.

Zed grimaced, remembering his last harsh words to Brock. In truth, he wasn't fine at all. The weight of the task he'd undertaken lay heavily across his shoulders. After several more hours of trudging—so much *trudging*!—the group had stopped again to take a brief rest.

But Zed's mind was whirring.

Why, with everything that was happening, had he ever agreed to this? Kill the Lich? *Him?* Zed could only barely control the green fire he summoned. Worse yet, he'd lied about its origin.

A whole city full of elves relied on his mastery of *sorcery*, but Zed knew the truth. The fire Makiva had given him was something else entirely. Something darker. Brock had been right all along.

I should probably start at the beginning, Zed wrote, *when things first went wrong.*

"Ah, there you are!"

Zed glanced up to find Selby, Queen Me'Shala's minister, grinning over him.

"Oh!" Zed cried. He quickly folded the note in half, then leaped to his feet. "Um. Wow. Hello!"

"Continuing your studies even in the midst of our journey?" the minister said. He flashed a handsome elven smile. "That's *wonderful* to see. Your industriousness does you credit."

"Th-thank you!" Zed replied far too loudly.

"It must be difficult to be a sorcerer among humans," Selby said. "I suppose they don't quite know what to do with you. Sorcery is more common among our people, you know. There are few families who don't have one or two examples."

"Are you one, Messere—I mean, Lord . . . ? Um. What *should* I call you?"

"Call me Selby," the elf said with a wink. "You might have noticed, but I'm less formal than my fellow minister. To her endless annoyance." Selby shrugged sheepishly. "As to your question, no, I wasn't blessed with natural magic. I did have an aunt who could conjure cold when she was feeling depressed. She made these delicious chilled drinks, but it took a toll on her mental health."

The minister began rummaging through a satchel at his side covered in luscious white fur. "Every sorcerer is different, however, even within bloodlines permeated by magic. It makes you hard to teach, but . . . ah!"

Selby retrieved something from the bag. It was a small, beautiful book. The leather that bound it was pure white, and its latch was made of glittering mythril. The minister held the book out, but it took Zed a few stunned moments to realize that *he* was meant to take it.

He retrieved the tome with shaking hands. "What is it?" he asked.

"A codex of arcane exercises for sorcerers, developed over generations. It's been translated into the humans' trade tongue, don't worry. Queen Me'Shala thought perhaps it could be useful."

Zed pressed the book to his chest. The world spun around him. "You'd really give this to *me*?"

"It's a small thing," Selby said, "compared to the incredible risk you're undertaking."

"Oh, it's . . . I mean—"

"Now, don't be modest," the minister said with a smile. "We all know how dangerous the mission is. Why, the undead could be watching us this very moment. You'll need every tool at your disposal."

Zed nodded slowly, his elation giving way to dread once more. He caught a strange scent on the air, clinging to Selby's clothes. It was sweet—almost edible smelling—but also had a gamy quality, like leather. Then he remembered: Fel had called it myrrh.

"That was a beautiful ceremony you gave," Zed ventured. "For the babe."

Selby chuckled bashfully, rubbing the back of his neck. "Thank you, but if I'm being perfectly honest, Zed, I felt a bit ridiculous. I'm glad it brought the mother some comfort—truly— but from my vantage point, I could see the expressions on your Stone Sons' faces. *They* weren't comforted."

Zed frowned. "Aren't those traditions important to you, though?"

"Oh, certainly, to many of us," Selby said. "But tradition can also be a yoke. I encourage Queen Me'Shala to be more . . . forward-thinking. So many elves are obsessed with the druids bringing us back our immortality." He held out his arms, waving across the fallow landscape. "If the druids had really held such power, don't you think they would have used it well before they were wiped out?"

"It's a nice idea, though," Zed said softly. "That our loved ones could return to us."

Selby opened his mouth, then paused. He nodded, smiling wistfully. "Yes," he said. "It certainly is." The elf patted Zed on the shoulder. "Happy reading."

As the minister crunched through the frost heading back to the elves, Zed turned the sorcerous codex over in his hands.

On the back cover, a tree had been imprinted into the leather, wreathed by a flock of birds.

Chapter Eight
Brock

Brock was fretting and pacing before the wall of mounted monster trophies when Syd and Fife returned late in the day.

It had been unusually—and uncomfortably—quiet in the guildhall since the mission to liberate Llethanyl had begun the day before. Lotte had insisted on business as usual for the remaining apprentices, and she pushed them hard through the regular battery of sparring and drills. But even she could keep them occupied for only so many hours in a day, and with the packed-to-bursting building suddenly all but empty, those left behind found themselves with time to burn.

Brock spent that time revisiting old conversations and wondering what he might have done differently. And not just the conversations with Zed. The Lady Gray had charged him with stealing from the queen's own treasury, and he was unlikely to have a better opportunity than would have been provided by a quest to Llethanyl itself. He didn't look forward to facing her disappointment at the fact he'd been excluded from that quest.

On the other hand—what if Zed pulled it off? What if he returned as the hero who single-handedly stopped the greatest threat to Terryn in two hundred years? Zed wouldn't need Brock's protection then. What harm could the Lady's accusations of forbidden magic do to a hero of two cities?

These were the thoughts occupying Brock's mind when Syd poked his head into the guildhall basement. Only a few years older than Brock, Syd and his best friend, Fife, were among the more sociable members of the guild. They'd left with Frond and the others the previous morning, as part of the larger decoy party, and weren't due back for another day or two.

"You're the one who isn't squeamish, right?" Syd asked. He wore both a helmet with three horns and a perpetually sleepy expression. "I could use your help."

Brock followed the older boy back to Hexam's work chamber, a subterranean room, warded with cold, where the man performed his most important duties as archivist, stripping valuable organs and fluids from the monsters defeated beyond the wall. Evidence of his grim harvest was preserved in jars and vials all around the room. Evidence of Fife's weak stomach had been splashed against the far corner.

"I'll . . . just get a mop, shall I?" Fife said, wiping his mouth with the back of his hand on his way out.

"It attacked us after Frond's party split off. They had me and Fife drag it back so it wouldn't spoil, while the rest of them flush out this one's nest," Syd explained, seemingly unconcerned with his friend's departure. In truth, Brock himself found it difficult to focus on anything but the table at the center of the room, shrouded as it was with a heavy white sheet. Whatever lay beneath that sheet was vaguely humanoid . . . but just vaguely. "I've been working with Hexam," Syd added. "Not the mage stuff, but the monster stuff. He asked me to fill in while he's away. Starting with this."

Syd drew back the sheet, revealing a beast that appeared as much salamander and insect as human. Its flesh was waxy and wet but covered in large patches of hard shell like natural plate mail. Its humanoid chest ended in a long plated abdomen, hanging from which were a half-dozen segmented insect legs. Its two dead eyes were affixed to the ends of long stalks, and its toothless mouth hung open like a craggy gash between razor-sharp plates of exoskeleton.

"Gross," Brock said.

"Yeah, that's what they all say," Syd responded. "But you should see what Lotte can do with locustrix chitin."

"Locustrix?" Brock said. "I read about it in . . ." He gestured at the empty platform that usually held Hexam's monster book. "Oh. Do you need the book?"

Syd nodded. "Probably. I need to get the plates off without breaking anything. And I'm not sure if the eyes have any use. . . ."

"I'll get it," Brock said, and he stepped into the relative warmth of the hallway, leaving the door to Hexam's workroom ajar. Rather than heading immediately upstairs, he snuck a peek back inside the room. Syd was lining up the tools he would need for the autopsy, as if the hulking beast laid out before him were no more intimidating than a jigsaw puzzle.

How long had Syd been working with Hexam?

And when had the guild's smuggling problems begun . . . ?

Brock shook his head. Now wasn't the time. Even if there was a smuggler still at work, they all had a common enemy in the Lich. Everything else could wait until word came back that Llethanyl was free, the elves were saved, and Zed was returning to Freestone a hero to two peoples.

He hurried down the hall, past the trophies, and up the stairs. Liza was in the dining room, carving up the central table with a dull cutlery knife, seemingly lost in thought.

"Syd and Fife are back early," Brock said.

"Great," she said absently.

He turned to continue up the stairs to his bedroom, but she called him back.

"Brock, listen. I thought you might want to talk."

"Yeah, okay," he said, stepping fully into the room.

"Great," she said. Then she sat there in silence, looking at him.

"Uh, go ahead?" Brock said.

"I mean I thought you might want to talk about your feelings."

"My feelings?" Brock said, cringing. "I thought you were going to apologize."

"*Apologize?*" Liza said. "To who? To *you?*"

Brock took a step back. "I'm . . . thinking . . . no?"

"Exactly what should I apologize for?"

"I just . . . nothing, but . . . out in the yard, the other day? You can be a little, you know, intense. . . ."

Liza's expression darkened, and the words failed Brock. They just evaporated beneath the heat of her regard, leaving him wondering what he ever thought he might have to say on the subject, or any subject, ever. Were there words he could speak now that wouldn't lead to him getting clobbered?

A plaintive *meow* sounded in the silence of the dining hall.

Brock smiled. "Oh, the cat!" he said. "I love the cat. Don't you?"

Liza scowled.

"Here, cat!" he cried, taking another step into the room.

There was a scuffling sound from beneath a far table, then the pattering of feet, and Mousebane appeared. In her mouth she held another rat, lifeless and bloody.

"Gross! Ugh, where is she finding those things?" Brock said.

And then, with a sudden seizure of movement, the rat writhed free from the cat's jaws. It fell to the ground with a wet red *plop*.

Mousebane hissed at the mangled rat.

And the rat hissed back.

"How is it still alive?" Brock asked in horror.

Liza's grip on her butter knife tightened. "Brock," she said, so calmly it gave him chills. "Listen . . . I need you to step back now, very slowly. . . ."

"What?" Brock asked. "Why? I don't—"

She shoved him aside with a firm hand to his chest, and with her other hand lobbed the knife across the room. It flew true, finding its mark, sinking into the rat's side. Brock figured it must have cut right through the animal's heart and lungs and many other organs, too.

It remained on its feet. It fixed Liza with its eyes, flashing strangely purple in the low light, and it skittered forward, the knife still lodged in its side.

Brock screamed. He pulled Liza back with him, retreating as the rat advanced.

"It's little," she said. "It can't hurt us, right?"

"I don't know!" he shouted, tipping over chairs, trying to block its path however he could. "Let's just not ever touch it or look at it ever again!"

The door to the training yard burst open, and the door to the kitchen, Lotte and Jett and Fel all rushing into the room. "What in Fie is happening?" Lotte demanded.

"Undead rat!" Liza cried, pointing. "Undead rat!"

Jett and Fel both stopped short, but Lotte darted forward, grabbing the warhammer from Jett's hands and making a tremendous overhead swing.

Brock's view was blocked by furniture, but he heard the splat.

"*Dead* rat," Lotte said, handing back the hammer. Jett grimaced at the mess on it.

There was a loud creak from the floorboards upstairs.

"Who else is here?" Lotte asked sharply. "Is the decoy party back already?"

"Just Syd and Fife," Brock said. "But I think they're downstairs."

Lotte nodded grimly. "Of course. An undead rat isn't much of a threat, but it's a great distraction."

"To distract us from what, exactly?" Liza asked.

"If Hexam were here, he'd have a theory," Lotte said. "All I have is a bad feeling in my gut and a burning desire to stab somebody. Follow me. Stay close."

They crept upstairs, Lotte at the head with her sword drawn, Jett bringing up the rear with his hammer. Fel nocked an arrow in her bow; the two of them must have been training in the yard. Brock's only weapon was a spoon he didn't remember grabbing. The hallway was lined with doors, and they checked behind each one, making as little noise as possible. Lotte blocked each doorway in turn while Fel readied an arrow over the quartermaster's shoulder. One after the other, the dorm rooms proved empty.

They were running out of doors when they heard a shuffling sound.

"They're two doors down," Lotte whispered. "Fel, with me. The rest of you, hang back. Don't let anyone past you."

Lotte and Fel crept to the closed door. Brock's stomach clenched with anticipation, and he took a step away from Jett. He didn't want to be in the dwarf's way if he needed to swing that hammer.

Lotte kicked the door open and dashed inside, shouting a battle cry—which abruptly cut off.

Fel lowered her bow. "It's just Fife," she said.

Brock and Jett exchanged a look, chuckling with momentary relief. And then a door exploded at their backs.

Brock stumbled forward, and Jett flew back. He turned in time to see the dwarf was stuck in the grip of some monstrous claw. It had clamped around his arm and an instant later had pulled him into the darkness beyond the shattered door.

"Jett!" Liza bellowed, and she took up his fallen hammer and followed him. Brock scrabbled after her, only fully regaining his feet in time to step over the broken door frame.

Inside was the creature Brock had seen downstairs. It had been dead then, he was sure of it—but here it was, standing on its eight segmented insectoid legs, gnashing its jagged maw and holding Jett aloft in one clawed hand. The dwarf battered it about the head with his free hand and kicked at its body with his dangling foot, but it seemed totally unconcerned with him, turning its tentacle-like eye stalks upon the new arrivals.

Like the rat's, its eyes glowed purple.

The air whizzed all about Brock's head, and he and Liza instinctively ducked aside as Fel peppered the beast with arrows, one after another. Where arrows struck chitin, they bounced harmlessly away. Where they struck flesh, their effect was equally harmless; the creature had no reaction to its skin being pierced, and soon, Fel had no more arrows.

Liza swung Jett's hammer, and that got a reaction; the locustrix skittered sideways, out of the hammer's range. But Liza had put all her weight into the swing, and she couldn't change her trajectory now. The hammer slammed into empty ground, shattering floorboards and leaving the girl open to a sweeping backhanded blow. Liza went flying, smashed into the wall, and crumpled to the ground.

Brock cast about the cramped room for a weapon. The only object within reach was a silvery sphere set against the wall. He took it, intending to lob it at their adversary, when suddenly Lotte came charging into the room, rushing past him and severing the arm that held Jett with a single overhead swing of her sword. Brock lunged forward to break Jett's fall. Black blood oozed from the monster's severed limb, and when it opened its maw, Brock thought it must be about to scream—it must have finally *felt* that attack.

But it hadn't opened its mouth to scream. Brock watched in horror as the beast's black gullet crackled with purple lightning.

It was casting a spell, and he was helpless to stop it.

Lightning arced from the creature's mouth, a brilliant flash of brutal light that Brock knew would end them. Before he could blink, however, the bolt of purple had struck—not him, not Jett, but the silver orb he'd forgotten he still held.

The orb flared white, the unfamiliar sigils on its surface glowing for an instant before a sharp *crack* sounded and the sphere broke down the middle. The two halves fell from Brock's hand as he blinked furiously to clear his vision.

"Get back!" Jett said, and he pushed Brock out of the path of Lotte's sword. In those horrible, endless seconds in which the locustrix had turned its attention on them, the quartermaster had wound up for another blow, and this time aimed her blade at the thin segmented legs on which it stood. The locustrix collapsed, its legs sliced out from under it, and Lotte bore down, hacking away ferociously until the creature was still at last. Then she hacked away some more.

"It's dead, Lotte," Jett said gently.

"Yes, it is," she said. "That's what worries me."

She drove the sword through its now-limbless torso, pinning it to the ground.

The monster had blindsided Syd; they found him on the floor of the warded room, cold to the touch, concussed but alive. From there, the creature had crept upstairs. That was where Fife had stumbled upon it. When he'd barricaded himself away from it, he'd unwittingly become the bait for the creature's ambush of Jett.

"But what was it *doing* up there?" Liza asked, rubbing the swollen knot on her forehead.

After retrieving Syd, they returned upstairs, to the room the thing had burst from when it had attacked. It was Hexam's room, and Brock's heart sank at the realization. The archivist's personal effects had been smashed to bits in the skirmish. The floor was a mess of splintered wood, shards of bone, and the strange glasslike material of shattered magelight spheres.

The only item remaining on his desk was a map. It showed the route to Llethanyl, the very path Zed was walking at this moment. Every wayshelter was clearly marked, as was the precise entrance Frond had targeted.

"Uh," said Jett. "It wasn't . . . looking at this map, was it?"

Syd shook his head. "It's got to be a coincidence. These things are just dumb animals. I was there when they killed it." He scratched his chin, considering the mutilated corpse nearby. "The first time, I mean."

"There was something in its eyes," Liza said. "Some intelligence. It looked at me like it knew me. Like it *hated* me."

"You're right," Brock said. "It *does* sound intelligent."

She glared at him, black blood in her hair. "You really just can't help yourself, can you?"

"And you're *sure* it was dead, Syd?" Lotte asked.

"Definitely. We carried it back the whole way, and it never stirred."

"Not even when we dropped it once or twice," Fife added.

"Somehow we only ever seemed to drop the end Fife was holding," said Syd.

Lotte clamped her hand over her eyes. "We all know what this means, don't we? I don't want it to be true, but there's no other explanation."

"Its eyes were purple," Liza said. "Like the raccoon we saw. The one they all said was under the Lich's sway."

"But the Lich is in *Llethanyl*," Jett said. "How . . . how can his power possibly reach all the way here?"

"Again, Hexam would have a theory," Lotte answered. "But Hexam isn't here."

"No, Hexam is *here*," Brock said, stabbing the map with his finger. The very map the Danger had apparently been poring over. "Can the Lich see through that thing's eyes? If it can, then it knows Frond and the others are coming. It knows the exact route they're taking into the city!"

"Oh. That's bad," Syd said.

"Pretty bad, yeah!" said Brock. "We have to go after them. We have to warn them!"

"I agree," Lotte said. "But our first duty is to Freestone. Ser Brent has to know that anyone—any*thing* that dies can be corrupted, even on this side of the wards."

"No!" Fel said sharply. She'd been so quiet, Brock had forgotten she was there. He turned to see her standing in the corner, cradling Mousebane to her chest. She seemed to shrink a little bit at the sudden attention.

"No?" Lotte echoed.

"I mean . . ." Fel faltered. She bit her lip. "I mean, maybe we shouldn't tell him?"

"You're afraid he'll take it out on the refugees," Liza said, and Fel nodded.

"I'm sympathetic," Lotte said. "But it would be irresponsible to keep this to ourselves."

"It would be irresponsible to start a panic over this," Jett argued. "People could get hurt."

"Or killed," Liza put in. "And then we're in *real* trouble."

"You could tell Father Pollux," Brock said. "He's trustworthy, I think. And if anyone . . . *passes away*, it's likely to happen in the temple, isn't it?"

Lotte narrowed her eyes. She looked from one apprentice to the next. "All right." She sighed. "I'll talk to Pollux, then at daybreak I'll go after Frond."

"We'll be packed and ready by the time you're back from the temple," Liza said.

"You . . . ?" Lotte said. "You won't be coming."

"Yes, we will!" Liza countered. "It's against the rules to go out alone—"

"You'll need help—" Brock began.

"Made the journey once—" said Fel.

"Plenty of other Dangers—" Jett started.

"Happy to stay here and watch the guildhall!" said Fife.

The apprentices turned to glare at him.

Fife shrugged. "What? Someone will need to be here to cover for you. And I'm pretty sure my best friend has a concussion."

He hooked his thumb toward Syd, who appeared dazed and unsteady as he slumped against the wall.

"Well, Frond's certainly raised a willful batch this time, hasn't she?" Lotte said humorlessly. "Fine. You," she said, pointing at Fife, "will hold down the fort and stall anyone who comes looking for us. I'll take Syd to the healers, which will provide me an opportunity to talk to our Luminous Father while, as a bonus, making sure Syd isn't permanently broken. The rest of you—be ready to go at dawn, or else you stay behind." She swept her eyes over the group. "And you'll do as I say, without question, starting now."

"Understood," Liza said, nodding sharply.

"We will catch up to Frond, warn her that the plan is compromised, and then come right back," Lotte continued. "Which means we'll be moving fast over hard terrain. So get some rest once you're packed." She directed Fife to help her walk Syd from the room, leaving Brock, Fel, Liza, and Jett alone with the fallen, mauled Danger.

"She expects us to be able to sleep?" Jett said, eyeing the corpse. "Up here?"

"Not me," Brock said. "I'm going out, too. I'll be back before dawn."

Liza sat heavily on the shattered desk. "Don't you think you should at least try to sleep? Tomorrow's not going to be easy."

"I'll sleep when I'm dead." He shuddered on his way out the door, casting a final look at the beast that was still pinned to the floor. "And maybe not even then."

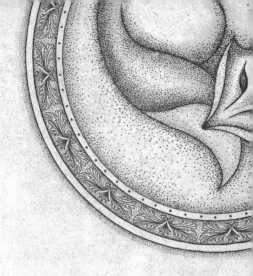

Chapter Nine

Zed

"Tell me more about the elves," Zed said.

Their party was on the move again, marching through the frost. Zed had tried to keep quiet. Fie, he'd even managed it for a while. But the cold had wormed its way into his bones like some invasive Danger. He needed a distraction from his misery—and the thoughts of home, and his mother, and the other warm things he'd left behind.

Callum didn't seem to mind the question, at least. "What would you like to know?"

Zed couldn't quite believe the opportunity. Outside of Fel, none of the elves had ever asked him this. It was like King

Freestone had told Zed he could take anything he wanted from the castle treasury.

"Everything!" Zed demanded.

Callum chuckled. "Then perhaps we'll begin our discussion of *everything* with Llethanyl itself."

Zed nodded enthusiastically.

"The city is"—Callum looked thoughtful—"tall."

"I'm going to need more than that," Zed muttered.

"I mean that it's exaggerated. A legend that is more embellished with every telling. To hear some elves describe it, you'd think the place had burst fully formed from the ground in a great act of magic."

"So it . . . didn't, then?"

Callum shook his head. "No matter how grand it *becomes*, a city is just a place where people come together to build their lives. In that way, it's made by many little acts of magic, I suppose. For the elves, Llethanyl is a place to return to. It gets its name from a common elven exchange. The greeter says, *lleth elan*, or 'Welcome home.' And the greeted replies, *lleth anyl . . .*" The ranger's voice constricted. "'I'm home.'"

Zed watched Callum solemnly. The High Ranger cleared his throat, not meeting his eye.

"But you probably want to hear about the sights," Callum said. "Llethanyl is built around a great tree, one my people have nurtured for nearly a thousand years. I'll take you around the base once we've defeated the Lich. In the summer, the tree is home to hundreds of birds from all over Terryn—with feathers of every color you could imagine. Maybe a few you couldn't."

"That sounds messy," said Zed, thinking of the many times he'd scrubbed pigeon dung from the stone steps of the training yard.

Callum smirked. "The *ain'shea* clean up after the birds. The sun elves consider it a sacred duty."

When Zed burst out laughing, the ranger looked down at him quizzically.

"Sacred *doodie?*" Zed asked.

"Did I . . . say that wrong?"

Zed shook his head, wishing with a pang that Brock was around. "No, never mind. Keep going."

"Well, there are several magical academies, of course, and even a specialized school for sorcerers."

Zed's eyes lit up. "Did my father go there? You know my real name is Zerend, right? Zed's just what everyone calls me. Mom named me after him, and then I became a sorcerer, too. Does that happen a lot with our people?"

Callum stiffened, the warmth in his eyes going cold. The High Ranger glanced back at the other elves. "Zed, I'm sorry, but I should be keeping watch. Maybe we can talk more another time."

"Sure," Zed said uncertainly. "How about tonight? I could come sit with the elves for a while, if that's all right."

"That . . ." Callum swallowed hard, the lump bobbing in his throat. "Perhaps."

And then the ranger was gone. Zed had never seen anyone move so swiftly. It took only two long strides for Callum to flee from Zed and his pestering questions.

"Stupid," Zed berated himself. He'd had a chance and he'd blown it. In the elf's retreating form, Zed was reminded of yet another back he'd been seeing a lot of recently.

He marched alone for the rest of the day, the cold gouging deeper into his bones.

They made camp as the light began to wane. Zed had expected Queen Me'Shala to tire easily, but none of the elves seemed especially taxed by the journey. Even the two sun elf ministers appeared perfectly at ease in the wilderness, their fine silvery coats gleaming in the half-light. Threya immediately began barking orders at Thorn and Petal. Selby paused to take in the view, shielding his eyes as he gazed toward a lonely mountain in the distance.

Frond started a small fire for the humans, while Hexam pulled Zed and Jayna aside for their lesson on arcane implements. Micah sat languidly against a tree, pretending not to listen, though Zed was certain he could feel him smirking.

"Wands, staves, and rods are the most common examples," Hexam said. "Though I've seen orbs, jewelry, and even books used, as ridiculous as it sounds. The principles are generally the same as any focus. A spell is folded into the material. Add mana, and presto."

"Just like that evil staff that Zed used during his initiation," Jayna said helpfully.

"Exactly so," Hexam agreed, as Zed's ears began to burn. "That particular piece had been sitting on our wall for years, something the guild discovered decades ago in an old ruin. Actually, I had no idea it was a warlock's implement until you accidentally set it off, Zed. But it illustrated another important principle where foci are concerned: Materials matter. Do you remember what happened to the staff when you used it?"

"It . . . broke in half," Zed answered. He recalled the way the ends had been singed black, though Zed himself was unharmed by the spell.

"That staff was made from silver maple," Hexam explained. "A brittle wood, ill suited for spellwrights. Not all components are enchanted equally, I'm afraid. Iron is among the worst materials for magical work, though steel is a bit better, thanks to the carbon. Highly structured crystals are some of the best."

"What about mythril?" Zed asked.

"Yes!" Hexam exclaimed. "Very good. Like the orb we tested in my office, mythril is exceptional in that regard. No surprise that the metal was developed by the elves."

Zed glanced away. He hadn't been thinking about the orb when he'd asked the question. Instead, his mind had gone immediately to the chain around his throat. Makiva's chain.

"Tomorrow night we'll work on some actual enchantments," the archivist continued. "Jayna, I'd like you to prepare Eldritch Darts for imbuement with your new wand. You're already familiar with the principles of handling a focus. Zed, I'm . . . less knowledgeable on sorcerous approaches, but let's see if we can't give it a try with that gorgeous green fire of yours. A working scepter could make our coming task that much easier."

Easier sounded good to Zed, because from what Hexam had said, it didn't seem like killing the Lich would be easy at all. Not for the first time, he wondered what exactly he'd gotten himself into.

Hexam rose to join the others, and Jayna followed him, peppering the elder wizard with additional questions that Zed barely heard. His fingers brushed the mythril chain beneath his shirt. Was it a focus of some kind? Was that why the fire was always easier to cast when he wore it? Was the chain a part of . . . a part of his *pact*?

It was a word Zed had avoided even thinking about. In the weeks of quiet that had followed his vision of Makiva, he'd almost been able to pretend that it hadn't happened—that he hadn't made a bargain with a witch.

But last night's dream scared Zed. It had felt so real, and the fox that watched him struggling against the chain was still burned in his memory, as if it observed him even now.

He wished that Brock was there on the journey with him. Why did everything feel so complicated between them?

Zed pulled the sorcerous codex out from his pack. He opened the latch and removed his note to Brock, carefully unfolding the vellum.

Dear Brock,
　　I'm scared.
　　I should probably start at the beginning, when things first went wrong. It all begins with Makiva.

Zed gazed anxiously at the sheet, considering what to write next. Or whether to continue at all. If this ended up in the wrong hands, it would be his confession.

"If you're looking for your wit's end," Micah called from behind him, "I'm pretty sure we passed it a long time ago."

Zed scowled, whipping around. "You've got a whole forest of personal space," he said. "Why are you *still* bothering me?"

Micah shrugged. "You're easy to rile. I swear I can actually see your little mind tying itself into knots over there."

Zed glanced to the others and hurriedly folded the note back into the book. Frond had stoked a healthy fire and was now standing over it, rehashing strategy with the queen and her ministers. The rangers had spread out to form a thin perimeter around the camp, keeping their watchful eyes on the landscape.

Twilight brought an increased risk of Dangers, and before their journey, Frond had warned that the undead were especially active after dark.

Beyond the leafless trees, the sky was a burning scrim, filling the forest with skeletal shadows. Far in the distance, a black mountain loomed. Zed could feel the already frigid temperature falling with the sun, and he hugged his cloak tighter to himself.

He'd stupidly volunteered to do something he wasn't even sure was possible, using a power that the city would execute him for if they knew its source. Zed was out of his depth. He was cold, and lonely, and very afraid.

"Please," he rasped. "Please just leave me alone."

Micah's smirk faltered. He opened his mouth, then closed it and cleared his throat. "Listen," he said finally. "You're going to be all right. I've seen that moldy fireball of yours take out worse than a few mummified elves. And that was *without* Frond babysitting you."

Zed was silent. He pulled his knees to his chest, keeping his eyes on the shape of the faraway mountain.

Micah groaned and pushed himself up from the tree. He took a few steps toward Zed, bracing his fists against his hips. It was a pose Zed had seen Liza strike dozens of times, just before she gave one of her inspirational talks.

"You," Micah said, "are a skinny, weird little sissy."

Apparently the Guerra siblings offered different sorts of encouragement.

"I thought so the first day we met," Micah continued, "and since then, you've only proven me to be an astute judge of character. But that's exactly why Frond brought me on this mission. Not only am I insightful and hilarious, I'm also uniquely gifted at fixing skinny, weird little sissies when they've gotten themselves hurt."

Micah held out a hand to Zed, the edges of which began to sparkle with golden light.

"I'll back off for a while," Micah added. "At least until Liza's around to defend your scrawny butt. In return, you have to stop looking so pathetic all the time. You're going to Elf-ville, woo-hoo!" Micah waved the glowing hand around theatrically, trailing a comet's tail of radiance. "It's your pointy-eared dream!"

Zed was quiet for a moment. "All right," he said finally. "Deal." Then he took Micah's hand and pulled himself to his feet.

The shouting began almost as soon as he'd stood.

The rangers who had been standing guard burst back into camp, surrounding Me'Shala and pointing into the distance. Frond drew her sword and Callum flew off into the trees, his face panicked. Zed followed their gestures toward the shadow of the mountain, but he couldn't see what had them so alarmed.

Then the mountaintop began to uncoil.

Two appendages peeled themselves away from the mass, revealing a pair of enormous wings silhouetted against the bloody sky. The mountain's peak had been a gigantic pair of wings the entire time, encircling the summit like a tent. Zed's mind came unanchored just trying to comprehend the sheer scale of such a creature. A goliath figure unfolded in the distance, though its details were impossible to make out against the setting sun. Slowly, without a sound, the Danger rose into the air, its two great wings beating lazily.

In a moment it was gone, disappearing over the horizon. In the next moment, the sound of its ascent finally reached them. Each wingbeat was a drum of thunder that Zed felt in his teeth.

He and Micah stood side by side, staring dazedly into the distance. Whatever they had just seen, it had flown in the same direction they were traveling.

Straight toward Llethanyl.

Chapter Ten

Brock

"And *that's* why elves have no word for 'surprise,'" Fel said brightly. "Isn't that interesting?"

Brock realized he hadn't been listening for some time, but he made a thoughtful *hmm* sound. They were walking down a broad, icy path through the forest, and he was concentrating on where he put his feet.

"I don't get it," Liza said. "I've *seen* surprise on your face, Fel. Wasn't everyone in the city surprised by the Lich's actions?"

"You could say that," Fel answered, "but *we* would not. When the unexpected happens, we *mae vahrel*, which translates to 'alight upon a hidden truth.'"

"I guess I don't see the difference," Liza said. "Whatever you call it, a surprise is a surprise. A rock is a rock."

Brock knew what she was too polite to say: *death is death.* Even if you called it "lost." Even if you imagined it was temporary.

"But a rock *isn't* just a rock," Jett put in. "Dwarves have thirty-two words for 'rock.' Just because humans are blind to the differences between *drostoff* and *mektin* doesn't mean they aren't there. Language shapes the world around us—shapes how we *see* it." He clucked his tongue. "That's why translations of dwarven poetry are so terrible. You really lose the effect when every other word is 'rock.'"

"Sure," Brock said absently. "*That's* why dwarven poetry is terrible."

Liza elbowed him.

"Seriously, though," Brock said. "If we all just spoke the trade tongue, maybe we wouldn't focus on our differences so much. Maybe that would be good for everybody."

"Easy for you to say, *human*," Jett groused. "The trade tongue is a human language."

"Okay, so everyone should speak dwarven, then," Brock said. "My point's the same."

"Respectfully, I think maybe the opposite is true," Fel said. "We should all learn *more* languages. I want to learn enough dwarven to read Jett's poetry!"

"Hold on," Jett said, instantly blushing. "I never said *I* wrote poetry."

She giggled. "You never said you didn't."

Brock couldn't help smiling. Fel was so positive, so . . . cheerful. More than that, she was utterly at ease in the wild. It was something he'd never seen before, not even from Frond. He couldn't imagine he'd ever manage to relax in the realm of Dangers.

Yet despite his fears, Brock's boots had a good grip, his cloak was warm, and the sun was bright overhead. The trees were spaced far enough apart that it would be difficult for anything to sneak up on them. Maybe their luck would hold out.

Then again, Brock liked to say that he made his own luck. He kept one hand in his pocket, wrapped around the vial of pungent orange liquid he had hidden there. It was the pitmunk toxin he'd retrieved from Master Curse and the perfumer last night when he *should* have been sleeping. But he'd known he couldn't afford to leave a potential advantage behind.

Every once in a while, he drifted to the back of the party and pushed the stopper aside with his thumb, letting out the vial's fumes. Maybe *that* had something to do with the absence of Dangers so far.

"It's been quiet," Liza said, echoing his thoughts. "I wonder if the others already chased off everything that was in this area."

"That could be it," Lotte said. "But this season tends to be less active, generally. Many Dangers hibernate in the winter."

"'Hibernate'?" said Jett. "What's that?"

"Let's use context to figure it out," Brock suggested. "Does it mean . . . 'drool'? *Many Dangers drool blood from their horrible mouths in the winter.* That sounds right."

Jett chuckled.

"It means 'sleep,'" Liza put in, and Jett's chuckling stopped short.

"Right," said Lotte. "They sleep through the winter. Especially the cold-blooded ones . . . You won't see anything with scales lurking about until spring."

"Well, that's downright sensible of them," said Brock. "In fact, I don't see why we don't all just nap through the winter. All in favor?"

Nobody said anything.

Brock gave Jett a sideways look. "Nothing?"

Jett shrugged apologetically and snuck a glance at Liza, which made his allegiances clear.

Traitor. Zed would have played along.

Maybe.

"Elves also have no word for 'nap,'" Fel said instructively.

"I never wanted children," Lotte muttered to herself from her place at the front of their column. "I made a choice—adventures, not children. And yet here you are, Lotte, here you are."

Brock turned to the others, crossed his eyes, and stuck his tongue out the side of his mouth: *She's weird.*

Fel's eyes went wide and she gasped. Before Brock could ask why, the young ranger sprang forward, quick as a bolt, pushing him aside and rushing up behind Lotte. She shoved the woman in the small of her back, simultaneously looping her foot around to trip her. Lotte went sprawling forward into a snowbank.

"Fel!" Liza screamed. "What—"

"Whoa—!" said Brock.

Lotte rolled onto her back and glared murderously at Fel, but before she had found her voice, Fel splashed the contents of her waterskin across the quartermaster's face.

Everyone froze. Brock found himself holding his breath as he looked upon Lotte, her eyes closed and her mouth open in shock as the ice-cold water dripped off her chin.

The silence lasted for several long moments until finally Fel spoke.

"I ... think perhaps I made a mistake," she said meekly.

Lotte's eyes opened and they were furious.

And for some reason, they were fixed upon Brock.

"What, me?" he protested. "I'm as surprised as you are!"

"Fel," Lotte said, only just mastering the angry warble in her voice. "Who put you up to that?"

"I thought ... Brock indicated ..."

Now Lotte, Liza, and Jett were all eyeing him. Even Mousebane glared from her comfortable burrow within Fel's backpack. Fel's expression, at least, was contrite. "The face you made behind Lotte's back. Doesn't it mean one is infected with a psychic worm?"

Lotte rose stiffly to her feet. "Yes, Brock. Let's see this face you made behind my back."

Brock grimaced. "I, ah . . . I think maybe the nuance of my joke got . . . lost in translation?"

Lotte stepped slowly toward him, her boots crunching in the snow. "Your joke? Well. Perhaps you need a lesson in humor."

Brock liked Lotte well enough. Certainly she was more agreeable than Frond, and generally more reasonable. But she was fearsome, too, and a true taskmaster. During long days of physical training, when Brock thought he could endure no more, it was fear of provoking Lotte that motivated him as much as any desire for self-improvement.

He tried not to flinch as she stood close enough to throttle him. She smiled, but there was something evil in it. Then she lifted her own waterskin above him, tipping it so that its contents poured out upon his head.

It was freezing. Brock's lungs seized up and the muscles of his neck and back clenched painfully. He gasped.

"See? Now *that's* funny."

Fel laughed, and when she registered that she was the only one, she immediately stopped.

"Wait, is it funny or not?" she asked. "I'm *so* confused."

"Lotte," Liza said. "Lotte, you're not injured, are you?"

Lotte turned, looking herself up and down. "The snow broke my fall," she said. "I'm only wet."

"What's that, then?" Liza asked. And she pointed toward the snowbank where Lotte had fallen.

Only a few paces from that spot was a trail of bright red blood.

They followed the blood into the woods, fearing the worst. What if the party had been overwhelmed? What if Zed was bleeding out in the snow? Brock shivered with fear and with cold. His hair was stiff with ice.

They did not have to travel far from the path to find the source of the blood: a young deer, curled up at the base of a tree. It wasn't moving, but it was alive; Brock could see its breaths misting in the air about its muzzle. Blood ran from a wound on its rear leg.

"The poor thing," Fel said sadly.

"We have to do something," said Liza.

"What *can* we do?" asked Jett.

Brock frowned. "Should we . . . put it out of its misery?"

They all turned on him.

"Are you serious right now?"

"What is wrong with you?"

"It's just a flesh wound, Brock!"

Brock held up his hands in surrender. "Sorry! I thought it was dying. I was trying to help!"

Lotte put a hand on his shoulder. "That's all right. You won't have encountered this before. Fel, do you recognize the wound?"

Fel nodded, crouching down for a closer look. Brock noted the deer still did not move, though its eyes were alert. Panicked.

"It's a scourge spider bite," Fel answered. "They hunt alone. A spider drops from the trees, injects its paralyzing venom, and then retreats. Comes back to eat once its prey is totally defenseless."

Brock took a shuffling step back and eyed the barren branches above and all around them.

"That's right," Lotte said. "But relax, everybody. Scourge spiders don't like crowds. They're opportunistic. Total cowards."

Nevertheless, Brock kept his eyes on the trees.

"I can't believe I'm saying this," Liza said. "But I wish Micah were here. Maybe his healing could counteract the venom."

"The effect is temporary," Lotte explained. "We've probably saved her life just by stumbling across her. The spider will have scurried away."

"And what if it comes back?" Jett asked. "It . . . eats her? It eats her alive?"

Lotte frowned. "Yes, but . . . it's probably painless. . . ."

"We can't leave her!" Fel cried.

"We are on a vital mission," Lotte insisted. "Zed is—they're *all* in tremendous danger."

"We can save her *and* continue the mission," Liza said.

"Have mercy, Lotte," said Jett.

Brock, eager to be on the right side of things this time, pumped his fist enthusiastically. "Save the deer! Yes! Let's do it!"

"You realize this isn't up to a vote?" Lotte said. "I'm definitely in charge, yes? We all remember?"

"So we take the deer with us," Liza said. "We can carry her—"

"We can pull her!" Brock offered. "Our tents are tarred canvas. They can be pulled on the ground without tearing. It won't even slow us down."

Lotte clucked her tongue. "It's not the call I'd make on my own, but it's hard to argue with your problem solving. And I *like* seeing you work as a team." She nodded. "All right, then. Load her up and we'll take her with us until the venom's run its course."

Liza held out a hand to Brock.

"What?" he said.

"Hand me your tent," she said.

"What, mine?"

"It was your idea," she said.

"Yeah, I contributed the idea," he replied. He imagined his tent dripping with muddy ice and deer blood. "So someone else should contribute their tent." He reached for Fel's backpack, then pulled his hand back as Mousebane appeared hissing from within.

"No more fooling around, Brock," Lotte said. "I mean it. Last warning."

Jett, at least, volunteered to drag the deer, freeing Brock to sulk in relative comfort—aside from his aching feet, his freezing ears, and his nose, runny and rubbed raw.

His pride hurt most of all, though. He wasn't used to feeling like an outsider. But that was how he felt without Zed there.

How did *anybody* manage without a best friend?

He turned to Liza, who had no trouble keeping pace despite the weight of her chain mail. "Do you miss Jayna?" he asked her.

"Jayna?" Liza said. She was scanning the woods, alert for any danger. With her dark hair pulled back in a ponytail, he could see the yellow bruise blooming on her forehead, a souvenir from their fight in the guildhall. Lotte had tried to get her to stay behind with Fife, and Brock and Jett made no effort to disguise their relief when she'd refused. If the wound bothered her now, she gave no sign of it. "Why are you asking me about Jayna? What are you getting at?"

Brock sighed loudly. "Never mind."

"I just saw Jayna a few days ago," Liza said, still watching the trees. "I'm not totally codependent."

"Ugh, we get it! You're awesome!"

Now she turned to look at him. "Why are you being so hostile lately?"

"Uh, guys . . ." Jett said from behind them, still pulling the tarp. "Maybe not so loud?"

Brock let Liza walk ahead, waiting so that he could fall into step beside Jett. "She thinks *I'm* hostile," he muttered to Jett.

"You do seem a little . . . *tired* lately," Jett said, not unkindly. "You're always coming or going on your little errands. When do you sleep?"

Brock felt a buzz of panic. In the six weeks they'd been bunking together, Jett had politely ignored the fact that Brock snuck in and out of their room at all hours of the night. But of course he noticed.

For a moment, Brock thought about answering truthfully. Jett was trustworthy, levelheaded, and wiser than many adults. He might be able to see a way out that Brock had missed.

More likely he'd just get caught up in the Lady's web, too. Involving Jett was a violation of the Shadows' tenets, and keeping *anything* a secret from the Lady Gray felt next to impossible. He couldn't risk putting Jett in harm's way.

So he put a fake smile on his face and changed the subject.

"There's a lot going on," he said easily. "Even Zed's been busy. He was in the shantytown with Fel the other day. Did you catch that?"

Jett gave him a dubious look. "Yeah, Brock. Everybody knows about it. Fel's been showing him around, introducing him to folk. Zed frets about it every week for hours beforehand, and then buzzes about it for days afterward. Some days it's all he talks about."

"Oh," Brock said. "Yeah, I just—I wasn't sure he mentioned it to you, specifically."

They fell into silence for a spell after that. When Brock

couldn't stand his own thoughts any longer, he asked, "You don't think Zed would ever *leave*, do you?"

"Leave?" Jett echoed.

"It's just that he's so interested in the elf side of his heritage and . . . I know he's never exactly had an easy time in Freestone. He talks like he doesn't belong there. He's always felt that way. Imagine he pulls this off, imagine Zed saves Llethanyl and—"

Jett held up a hand for quiet. He moved in a slow circle, peering into the forest from every angle, while Brock looked frantically from side to side. "What is it?" he whispered.

Fel noticed they'd stopped and retraced her steps to join them. "What's wrong?" she asked.

"Heard something," Jett said. "Thought I did."

"I've felt eyes on us for some time," Fel said. "But I assume my imagination is . . . overactive after last night's surprises."

"Yours and mine both," Jett said. "Let's hope." He waved on Lotte and Liza, who'd paused up ahead to wait for them. "Let's catch up. Brock, you were saying?"

Brock sighed. "Nothing."

"You think Zed's going to leave Freestone? Live in Llethanyl, is that it?"

Brock shrugged sullenly. "I'm just saying it crossed my mind."

"Nonsense," Jett said. "Zed's not going anywhere."

"But if you had the opportunity—if you could live in Dragnacht, even just for a few years? You wouldn't be tempted?"

Jett answered, "No. Of course not."

But he hesitated before he said it. Just long enough to make Brock's fears seem reasonable.

"I'm sure Zed would be quite happy in Llethanyl," Fel said, trying to be helpful and missing the mark by a wide margin. "It's a wonderful place."

"Really?" Brock said. "Even for a night elf?"

The smile froze on Fel's face. "I don't know what you mean."

"I just mean I'd be a little angry if I were you. All that stuff the minister was saying about your people, about who's trustworthy and who's not. You don't have to put up with that. I used to tell Zed—"

"Llethanyl is changing for the better," Fel insisted.

"Sure, but it sounded to me like—"

"It wasn't always easy for my people, that much is true. But the city is a little better every day."

"Right," Brock said. He thought about that for a moment. "You mean before the undead thing, though," he said.

"Obviously, yes, before that," Fel said through her now very strained smile.

"What's wrong, Lotte?" Liza asked, as Brock's group rejoined them. "You seem worried."

"It's probably nothing," Lotte said. "But I thought we'd have found them by now."

"They had a good head start on us," Jett said.

Lotte shook her head, but kept moving and kept her eyes on

the trail she followed. "But only a small force was going all the way to Llethanyl, remember? The rest of the guild was supposed to turn back. Our paths should have crossed."

"Is it possible we missed them?" Liza asked.

"It's unlikely. We've been following their trail all day. I don't know why they wouldn't take the same path back."

Fel still bristled with annoyance over whatever Brock had said to upset her. He'd been trying to make her feel *better*—to say he was on her side. "Hey, listen," he said, reaching out to pat her on the back.

He forgot about the sleeping cat hitching a ride in her open pack.

Mousebane, screeching in surprise, leaped in the air, legs rigid, arcing toward Jett, whose dwarven stature put him directly in harm's path. Before he knew what was happening, he had a furious, hissing cat on his head.

Jett shrieked, reaching up to pry the cat from his hair, but he'd wrapped the tent's ropes around his forearms. At the sudden movement, the canvas billowed out like a sail. The deer caught air. Spurred on by its sudden startling predicament, it regained use of its legs, kicking madly as it soared past Brock. Its hoofs connected with a tree, and the snow upon the tree's boughs came loose, hurtling down at Brock's head.

He sidestepped just in time, and the snow fell harmlessly to the ground.

"That," Brock began, "could have been much wor—"

Suddenly the world was spinning. He'd been so quick to dodge the falling snow, he'd given no thought to where he put his feet, and now up was down and the ground was high above him and his arms and legs were all tangled.

Tangled, as if in a web.

"Spiders!" he screamed. "Scourge spiders! Fiendish spiders! *Undead spiders!* Someone help!"

"Calm down, Brock, you're all right," Lotte said from the ground. She smiled, but upside down it looked far from reassuring.

"Should we put him out of his misery?" Liza asked sweetly.

The blood was rushing to Brock's head. "Brace yourself," Lotte said. Then she drew her sword, and sunlight flashed upon it as she struck the tree trunk.

Brock came crashing to the ground, his landing softened by the pile of snow at the base of the tree. He leaped to his feet and pushed free of the tangled threads—not webbing, but some kind of rope, pliable and strong.

He'd been snared in a net.

"Some kind of hunter's trap?" Lotte mused. "Fel, make my day and tell me this is elven."

"Oh! Uh, it's not," Fel said, clearly dispirited at the lost opportunity to make Lotte's day.

"That . . . is very troubling news," the quartermaster said.

Brock's head was spinning. He saw Liza fussing over Jett's bleeding scalp. He saw Fel trying to coax Mousebane out from beneath a shrub. He saw the deer walking drunkenly away, not sparing a backward glance for her rescuers. And he saw Lotte, a shadow across her features as she contemplated the netting in her hands.

"We've been following the wrong trail," she said.

"We'll make up the time, Lotte," Fel said in the same soothing tone of voice she'd been directing at the cat. "It will be all right."

"No, wait," Liza said. "What do you mean the wrong trail?" She pointed at the net. "Who set that trap?"

"It wasn't elves," said Lotte. "And it wasn't our people, either. I've never even seen this material."

Brock tried to focus past his vertigo. "What does that mean?" he asked.

"It's impossible," Lotte said. "But it means someone else is out here. Someone we've never encountered before."

Chapter Eleven

Zed

"Answer me truthfully," Frond said. "Do you know what that thing was?"

"A complication," Queen Me'Shala replied. Her expression was a study in vagueness: lovely and exquisitely blank. Behind her, the queen's ministers were similarly beautiful and unreadable.

Their whole party—elves and humans, adults and children—were clustered around the beginnings of a fire, working through their evening rations. It had been a full night and day since they'd spotted *the thing*. A span of urgent whispers, unanswered questions, and still more snoring from Micah.

Frond crossed her arms, causing her belt of throwing stars

to tinkle like bells in the quiet. "We made this journey in good faith," she said, "with what we believed to be a complete understanding of the risks. If I think you're keeping something from me, Your Majesty, then I'll have to insist we retur—"

"*Complete understanding* is a children's fantasy," snapped the minister Threya. Her golden eyes narrowed on Frond. "Even you must know this, human. There is no certainty where the Dangers are concerned. They prey upon your *understanding*. They stalk it from the shadows while it sleeps, sure of its own safety. And then they drag it, crying and screaming, into the jaws of everything it doesn't know."

Silence fell over the camp.

"That," said Micah, "is the worst children's fantasy ever."

Queen Me'Shala sighed. "What Threya means is that situations can change without our knowing." She stared imploringly at Frond. "As you said, you entered into this quest in good faith, and I cannot convey the depth of my gratitude. The Adventurers Guild represents the very best aspects of your people. I would never knowingly jeopardize the friendship we share, even to reclaim my own city. I swear I've told you all I can. That creature . . . it may not even be related to the Lich."

Frond glanced to Hexam, who was brooding over the fire pit. "There's any number of giant flying Dangers out there," he murmured. "Dire rocs come to mind, as do winged nightmares and a baker's dozen of fiends. . . ."

"And dragons," Jayna said in a small voice. The girl was

seated on a log, her arms curled tightly around her stomach. Her eyes were focused on the wizard.

Hexam nodded slowly. "But a necromancer could reanimate any of those, in theory. The toll it would take, however—"

"—would be catastrophic," Selby finished for him. The second sun elf minister leaned against a tree; his face was screwed up in thought. "It would rot his body and mind. Even as he became a more powerful focus for Mort's energies, he would grow slower and weaker. And more insane. Difficult to destroy though they are, this has been the undoing of many a lich throughout history."

Frond contemplated all this, her fingers tapping rapidly against the pointed stars on her belt. Finally, she let out a misty breath. "Let's get some sleep. Tomorrow, we'll continue on to the Celadon Falls wayshelter." She frowned over the small group clustered together in the cold, then spat on the ground. "Everyone be on your guard. The closer we get, the more likely it is that we'll run into trouble."

Zed rose with the others, but his mind was far away, trying to imagine what sort of creature had earned the name *winged nightmare*.

There was a billow of green from the corner of his vision, and then Callum stood beside him, unfastening his moss-colored cloak. The ranger leaned in. "The queen would like to speak with you," he whispered.

Zed wasn't sure he'd heard that quite right. "The . . . the queen of . . . ?" His ears roasted.

A glimmer of amusement touched Callum's eyes. "Of the elves," he confirmed. Then the mirth vanished from his face as he cast a glance toward his monarch. "Zed, stay close to me the rest of the journey. The path from here becomes . . . complicated."

Zed frowned, but he nodded at the ranger. They walked together to a section of camp where Queen Me'Shala spoke in low tones with her two ministers. Behind them, Thorn and Petal were erecting a large tent made of shimmering fabric. Petal winked at Zed as he arrived.

The queen turned to him with a bright, inviting smile, and it was like a log had been added to the furnace heating Zed's ears. He thought belatedly to bring fingers to his lips, in the way Hexam had greeted her, but couldn't remember how many and so settled on all five. The queen's smile broadened at the gesture. Behind her, Threya rolled her eyes and Selby chuckled.

"How charming," Queen Me'Shala said. "And it seems that you're gifted in other ways, too. You conjured a miraculous fire that saved your very city. I hope you can do the same for mine."

Oh, Fie. How was he supposed to respond to that? Confidently? With humility? Laugh until he broke into tears? Zed mumbled, "So do I, Your Majesty."

"Callum tells me that you're something of a pioneer among the adventurers. The first to explore a shrine once occupied by elven druids. What an experience that must have been."

Zed glanced toward the High Ranger.

"That was weeks ago," he replied. "The rangers and adventurers have been back many times since then."

"Once, elven druids filled the wilds of Terryn," the queen said somberly. "They were revered among our people as sages and mentors. The druidic sagas are where our most sacred customs come from, along with our symbols."

She extended an ungloved hand, on which the crest of Llethanyl glittered atop a mythril ring—the great tree wreathed with birds.

"But though they counseled us," the queen said, smiling sadly down at the ring, "the druids avoided cities. They brought their students to the wilderness to learn, and kept no written records. And when the Day of Dangers struck, the druids were all lost. Their secrets, and their promises, were lost with them."

The queen dipped her hand into a fur-lined glove, glancing wistfully back up to Zed. "Thousands of years of culture and philosophy, gone. That is the crisis we now face again. It's a daunting responsibility, isn't it?"

Zed could only nod in agreement. But why was Queen Me'Shala telling him this?

"Perhaps you could do me a favor," she said brightly. "I'd like to see this green fire of yours firsthand."

Tiny hairs exploded along Zed's arms. *Oh, Nox's shadowy butt.* Cast the *fire*? In front of the *queen*?

"Your Majesty, I . . ." Zed faltered. "It's very dangerous, you see."

"Frond has put so much faith in you," Me'Shala said pointedly. "I'm sure you're up to the task." She held out her gloved hand, into which Thorn immediately placed a gray lump of metal. "Aim at this, if you'd be so kind." The queen tossed the lump a few yards away, where it landed heavily on the frozen earth.

Zed pivoted, his knees nearly buckling beneath him. He took a deep breath and turned his mind inward, reaching until it found what he was looking for.

His mana. He took a small sip, extending his palms.

The fire started slowly, like the first morning pumps from a well. But soon an emerald torrent flowed, bathing the camp in green. Zed aimed for the metal knot, concentrating with all his effort. Then, just as a bead of sweat fell from his nose, he snuffed out the mana, and the fire went with it.

Threya stomped to the spot where the queen had thrown the ore. She touched her fingers to the ground. Only a dark scorch mark remained.

"That's . . . *astounding*," Selby breathed. "That was dwarven orichalcum, the most magically resistant material in Terryn!"

"Astounding indeed." Me'Shala's eyes were practically glowing with excitement. She stepped toward Zed and gently pressed his ear tip between her gloved fingers. The material was softer than anything he'd ever felt. "Fate has cast you among the humans," she murmured. "But perhaps you'd always hoped for a chance to make your own decision, hmm? A real choice." She smiled warmly. "That choice could come soon. If you so decide, you'd be welcomed among my people, Zed." The queen hesitated, looking almost bashful. "*Our* people."

"I'm so sorry to interrupt," Selby interjected. "But I believe our human comrades may wish for their apprentice back." Indeed, on the other side of camp, Frond was actually tapping her foot with impatience. Her expression was dour.

The queen retreated a step, glancing from Zed to Callum. "This one is precious, High Ranger. Please watch him carefully. Though I know you will."

Callum nodded slowly, the edges of his mouth tilting into a frown. "Of course, Your Majesty."

Zed's thoughts were muddled as he joined the other adventurers to bed down for the night.

Frond had packed a large linen tent for all five of them to sleep beneath when it snowed, though most nights the party just pulled their bedrolls close to the fire. She and Hexam took turns keeping watch with the rangers, so there were always multiple eyes on the forest.

Tonight, Frond's watch was first. Hexam was already curled up in his bedroll, while Micah's wheezing foretold of another long, loud evening. Jayna lay on her stomach, reading by the firelight.

Frond grunted as Zed approached, now sitting on a log she'd

dragged to the fire pit. She polished the blade of her sword with an oily rag, running the cloth along the steel in long, languid motions.

"Have a nice chat with the queen?" she asked suspiciously. "I thought I told you to save your mana."

"Sorry," Zed whispered. "She asked me to demonstrate, and . . ." He trailed off, still basking in the high of Me'Shala's approval. Had the queen of the elves just truly called *him* astounding? "She's very nice, isn't she?"

Frond smirked. The firelight intensified her scars, making the expression look gruesome. "She's very good at getting people to think so."

Zed swallowed. What did *that* mean?

"How long have you known her?" he asked. He hovered over his own bedroll, not quite ready to crawl inside. His bladder was achingly full.

"I knew her when she was still *Princess* Me'Shala," Frond said, glancing back down at her blade. "She was less *nice* then, but more kind, I think. I was a young adventurer and she was beginning her mandatory tour with the rangers. We grew close." Frond cleared her throat. "Quite close."

Zed felt a sudden warmth burning in his cheeks that had little to do with the fire. Frond and the queen were . . . close?

The guildmistress smirked at his scandalized expression. "Yes, romantically. Back then Me'Shala had a wild streak," she continued, "which has since been ironed out by the burdens of rulership." Frond scrubbed at a spot of rust, clicking her tongue. "Still just as pretty, though. Not like me. I've only become more beautiful over the years."

Frond's gaze flicked up, an almost playful gleam in her eyes. Then her face was hard again as she set back to her work. "Me'Shala's charming, Zed," she grunted, "but she's cunning, too. Just be careful around her. And remember who your people are."

Zed bristled. As if anyone had given him a choice in his *people*.

"Sleep now," she said. "Both of you." She flicked her chin toward Jayna without looking. By the way the girl hurriedly closed her book, it was clear she'd been listening. Jayna dug into her bedroll.

"I need to make water," Zed said.

Frond nodded. "Don't go far."

The fire's warmth faded quickly as Zed crunched through the snow. Beyond their little encampment, the darkness was a wall every bit as thick and foreboding as Freestone's.

Zed tried not to think what might be just beyond, watching him from within that murk. He didn't dare stray more than a few timid yards from the fire, though modesty drove him to take cover behind a tree.

Zed glanced across the pale snow. With the fire far behind him, his shadow stretched out into inhuman lengths, craning deep into the trees. Its neck was swallowed by the darkness, giving the shadow a headless appearance. Zed thought of the executions that took place in the market square, and he shivered.

He did his business quickly and trudged back toward the fire.

For the first few steps, everything was fine.

Then, on his fourth, Zed's throat began to feel dry. He coughed softly, trying to clear it. A few steps more and his airway contracted. Zed wheezed, pausing midstep. He cleared his throat once, twice, but couldn't seem to draw enough breath in.

"Something . . ." Zed sucked in a gulp of air. "I think something's wro—"

He couldn't finish. Zed's throat had closed completely. His eyes bulged with panic, darting up toward the campfire, where Frond was squinting in concentration and scrubbing the blunt edge of her sword.

She hadn't heard him.

Zed stumbled forward, reaching toward Frond. A painful pressure was now squeezing his neck, but when he reached for it his fingers found nothing but his own throat.

Help! Zed thought wildly. But when he opened his mouth, no sound came out.

"Oh, Fie, Zed! What *is* that?" Jayna's voice pierced the quiet. The girl was sitting up in her bedroll, her wide eyes staring at something behind him.

Frond shot up just as Zed spun around to face whatever horror loomed there. His head was spinning and the edges of his vision were going strangely white, and all Zed could see was . . .

"Your—your shadow!" Jayna stammered.

Zed's shadow floated among the trees. Its misshapen limbs were impossibly long. *That's not right*, he thought deliriously. *Get back on the ground.*

Somehow the shade had unanchored itself. It curled upward from the forest floor like a roll of parchment billowing in the wind. One of those spindly arms was stretching toward Zed. Its fingers grasped his face, crawling across it like the legs of a scuttling insect, until they found his mouth.

Then they pushed inside.

Zed's throat filled with a cold, tingling rush. His legs gave out just as Frond bellowed, "Stalking shadow!"

There was an odd lurching sensation when, instead of crumpling to the ground, Zed felt himself being yanked into the air. The whiteness at the edges of his vision expanded.

Many voices began shouting then, though Zed couldn't understand everything they said. He thought he heard Hexam's voice yell, "No, don't touch him! Only a blood relative can remove it safely!"

"But we'll never get back to his mother in time!" Jayna cried.

Mother, Zed thought. He hoped she was warm. It was getting so cold.

Darkness filled his vision and the world tilted. Distantly, Zed felt himself being pulled downward.

"Tell me what to do." Callum's urgent voice pressed against his thoughts. The elf was so *loud*, and all Zed wanted was to sleep. He was very, very tired.

"Didn't you hear me?" Hexam snapped. "Only someone of his blood can—"

"Then just tell me what to do!" Callum barked.

There was a moment of silence that Zed swam in. The world was getting very quiet. The stars were growing very large. Very white.

"His full name. Three times."

"Zerend Kagari." At the sound of his own name, something changed. A great rushing noise filled Zed's ears, like the wind howling against Freestone's walls during a storm.

"Zerend Kagari." Now the pressure in his throat loosened. Sensation began flooding back into his limbs.

"Zerend Kagari." And all at once, Zed sucked in a gulp of air. His body began to seize violently, but someone was holding him tight, softening the convulsions.

Zed opened his eyes to witness a cloud of oily black spume pouring upward from his own mouth. The strange howling-wind noise now filled the encampment, baying out from the cloud.

It billowed through the air, its shapeless limbs thrashing like tentacles. One moment it seemed to try to escape, surging straight up toward the treetops. But the shadow had been weakened somehow. Or wounded. It wobbled heavily, then crashed to the ground as a torrent of ichor. There it bubbled against the snow, its smoky edges coagulating into thick sludge.

Frond slashed her sword through the mass, cleaving it in half. Both pieces dissolved into hissing puddles, and the howling went silent.

Everything was quiet as Zed caught his breath and his shaking slowly abated. The figures of humans and elves swam into focus: many eyes pointed at him. He discovered it was Callum who'd been holding him while he convulsed, who was still holding him now. Callum who'd spoken his name and—

Zed glanced up. The world tilted again. "You . . ." he croaked.

The High Ranger's face was grave.

"Are you my father?" Zed wheezed. A hot tear burned its way across his cheek.

Callum shook his head, his eyes wide with . . . shame?

"No, Zed," he said. "I'm the man who killed him. I'm your uncle."

"It's not possible," Brock said. "People? Living out here? We'd have encountered them before."

"Would we?" Jett asked, scanning their surroundings as he kept his palm on the handle of his maul. "I'd never seen a proper *tree* until six weeks ago."

"You know what I mean." Brock had his eyes on the space between the trees, too. "*Lotte* would have encountered them before. Or someone would. Adventurers have been scouting this forest for two hundred years!"

"And stumbling over new surprises every day, believe me," said Lotte. She clucked her tongue. "This doesn't change the mission, though. We keep moving. *What* is that smell?"

Lotte didn't wait for an answer. She hoisted her pack higher on her shoulders and trudged on, veering off the path they'd been following. Brock, however, froze in place, patting himself up and down. What *was* that smell . . . ?

His pants were wet, and not just with snow. The pitmunk toxin had spilled all over him when he'd been caught in the trap.

"Oh, man, those ropes stink," he said quickly, kicking snow onto the net, which Lotte had left behind on the ground. "I hope they didn't ruin my pants." He waved his hand across his nose.

Liza gave him a skeptical look, but she fell into step behind Lotte. Brock let the others go ahead of him, determined to stay downwind until his clothing had aired out a bit. But if the scent *was* keeping the Dangers away, then they'd certainly be safe for a while.

From Dangers, anyway.

"Are we very far off track?" Liza asked.

Lotte was consulting a compass as they walked. "We can't have strayed too far in a day. I think we're just a little north of the path Frond was taking. Fie, did they have to take *all* our mages with them?"

Brock saw Jett and Liza exchange a look. He wanted to ask what they were thinking, but he didn't have the breath. He realized Lotte had increased their pace considerably.

Lotte was worried.

"Do you really think there are people out here?" Brock huffed.

"Anything could be out here," Lotte answered. "But in the early days of the guild, we sent search parties to every city, town, and roadside inn within two hundred miles. We found Llethanyl still standing." She shook her head. "Nothing else."

"Is it possible . . ." Liza began. "Freestone does send its citizens out here sometimes. You know, the banished . . ."

Brock shuddered. Capital crimes in Freestone were punishable by execution . . . or by exile beyond the wall, which was really just a slower form of execution. By far, most condemned criminals preferred the certainty and swiftness of the executioner's ax.

"It's hard to imagine humans surviving out here for any length of time," Fel said.

"I'd love to take offense at that," Brock said. "But I agree."

"I'll bet a Danger made that trap," Jett said. "Kobolds wear clothing. Surely they could make a net."

Lotte shook her head again. "Some Dangers do use tools, but most are of the sharp-and-pointy variety. Traps are a little subtle for them."

"The thing Zed met in the old elven shrine was pretty subtle," Brock reminded her.

"Oh, no," Liza said. "You don't think . . . the people Mother Brenner infected . . ."

"What about them?" Jett asked.

"Remember?" Liza continued. "Once they were infected, she

cast them out. That way they couldn't give her away before she was ready—and *they'd* be ready to return when the wards fell. Some of them must still be out here."

"They're not people anymore," Lotte answered. Her voice was sad but certain. "They wouldn't make nets or leave boot-prints in the snow. The infection spreads too fast."

Silence descended on them then, and Brock thought back to the horrors of the previous season, when the town's most respected and trusted figure had been infected by a monstrous spore—and had infected others in turn. Under the influence of the penanggalan, Mother Brenner had targeted Freestone's most vulnerable, preying upon the guildless and the sick, and then casting them out of the city before their transformations took hold. In that way, she'd covered her tracks and made the Danger-infested wilderness that much deadlier than before.

Brock was brooding on such unwelcome thoughts when he caught a flash of movement from the corner of his eye.

"What was that?" he said, whirling around. The trees were empty.

"Over there," Liza said, pointing in another direction. "Did you see it?"

Whatever it was, it had vanished before Brock had caught a glimpse.

"Pitmunks," Fel whispered, pointing. "There's a bold one."

This time, Brock saw it. The creature stood upon a branch,

craning its head back and bobbing its snout as if sniffing the air. It reminded him somewhat of the squirrel he'd seen during his first official mission. But this animal was hairless, with wrinkled red skin, and its flaring bushy tail was composed of sharp black quills; the same quills that ran in a single row down its back and swayed slightly in the wind.

As the adventurers paused to watch it, the diminutive Danger was joined by a second pitmunk, and a third.

"That's weird," Fel said. "They normally aren't social outside of mating season."

"Mating season?" Brock asked, suddenly nervous.

Fel nodded enthusiastically. "They give off a pungent scent that attracts mates. But they're *very* competitive about it. You don't want to be caught anywhere near one of those frenzies." She shrugged. "The colors are pretty from a distance though. All that red . . ."

The wind shifted, so that it was at Brock's back.

The nearest pitmunk's spines quivered; its tail fluffed up.

"Oh, Fie, Fie, Fie . . ." he said.

Another pitmunk appeared on a nearby branch, while two more poked their heads from the hollow of a fallen tree. Twelve, twenty, thirty gleaming black eyes turned toward the party.

They were all focusing on Brock.

"We have to run!" he shouted. "Everybody run!"

He didn't wait to see if they listened. Brock turned and bolted as the trees ahead burst to life, the entire canopy shifting and creaking under the weight of dozens of tiny Dangers leaping into motion as one.

They were swarming Brock in seconds, climbing up his arms and across his back, quills cutting right through his leather tunic as if it were cloth. The chittering was almost deafening, and while each animal alone weighed almost nothing, their combined weight was quickly stacking up. Brock stumbled.

Something struck him from behind, and then he was down in the snow again. Liza had tackled him, sending his tiny passengers flying.

"Why are they after you?" she cried, covering him with her body. "OW!"

"Something on my clothes," he said. "My pants . . ."

"Fix it!" she said, leaping up and battering the swarm with her shield. Lotte and Fel and Jett were there, too, and the four of them formed a box around Brock, slashing and swiping and knocking the leaping Dangers right out of the sky. But there were too many to keep them all back.

"I can't believe this is happening," Brock muttered, pulling at the drawstring on his pants.

"If you have a plan, hurry!" Liza shouted, looking back at him.

"Don't look!" he shrilled. "Eyes on the murderous swarm, please!"

Brock disrobed quickly, cutting off his pants with a knife and hurling them as far as he could manage over Jett's head. The leathers fell into a heap at the base of a tree, and the entire swarm of pitmunks wheeled away from the adventurers to descend upon the pile in a chittering mass.

"Let's hurry," Lotte said, wiping sweat from her brow. "I want some distance in case they decide they liked the taste of us."

"If I could just get some pants from my pack . . ." Brock said. He stood shivering in his boots, pulling his tunic low to cover as much of his bare legs as possible. It was like wearing an extremely short dress. He looked ridiculous, and he knew it.

"Keep moving!" Lotte barked, and Brock didn't argue. He marched through the snow and past his tittering teammates, who he was sure caught a glimpse of his underclothes with every step.

Brock was shivering and miserable by the time Lotte was satisfied they'd put enough distance between them and the swarm. The light was fading, and a deeper chill was settling in for the night.

"Let's rest for a while," she said, peering at her compass in the low light. "Girls, gather some wood. Jett, get a fire going. Brock . . . pants would be good."

"Oh, thank you," he said, pulling off his pack.

Fel was somehow just as energetic as she'd been at the long day's start. By the time Brock had laced up his trousers, she had already dropped a small pile of branches at Jett's feet.

"Ah . . ." the dwarf said. "About *my* assignment . . ."

"Yes?" Lotte said curtly.

"Well, Zed normally does this bit. You know, with the . . ." He waggled his fingers at the pile of sticks.

Lotte huffed. "You kids rely entirely too much on magic. Fel, can you start the fire, please?"

"Yes! On it!" Fel said joyously, rushing back with another armful of branches. She set to work with flint she pulled from her belt.

"Why *aren't* there more mages in the guild?" Liza asked.

"Frond does recruit them," Lotte answered, dropping onto one of the small logs Liza had set in a circle around the pile of kindling. "But they tend not to last as long as the fighters."

"No kidding," Brock growled. He dabbed at his fresh cuts with a minty salve.

"It's the healers we've really coveted, though. To have an actual healer in our ranks, on journeys with us, instead of having to carry the wounded back to town—it's only been a month or two and Micah's been a huge boon already."

"What's that mean? *Boon?*" Fel asked, stoking her small fire.

Brock, Liza, and Jett all spoke over one another in their rush to answer.

"Half-wit!"

"Menace!"

"Rock eater!"

"It means he's been *helpful*," Lotte insisted. "Imagine if we had ten of him."

"There's no reason to be cruel," Brock said. He patted Liza's shoulder, and she pretended to pull her hair out.

"Anyway," Lotte said, passing around a small satchel of cured meat. "Maybe now that Pollux is in charge, we can use the draft to enlist more healers in the future. Even Frond didn't care to cross the Luminous Mother."

"Really?" Jett stroked his chin. "I didn't think Frond was afraid of anybody."

"I don't know that it was fear, precisely," Lotte said. "But Frond would do anything for the guild. Sometimes that means playing politics."

"Right," Brock said. "That Frond, so politically savvy."

"It's a fine art," Lotte said pointedly. "Pushing back *just* enough. Knowing the difference between a line you can cross and one you can't."

Jett leaned over to Brock. "I think she's talking about you," he whispered loudly.

"I'm sorry, but . . ." Brock glanced to his left and right, looking for support from his friends, some sign they were thinking what he was thinking. They only looked back curiously. "Is no one else going to say it? You're talking about the draft, about . . . *abducting* people from their lives. Frond isn't collecting painted pebbles; she's collecting cannon fodder."

"Some of us volunteered, Brock," Liza warned.

"Well, sure, but you're weird."

"'Some of us' includes you, idiot! You volunteered, too!"

"Oh, right," he said. *Sort of.*

"I volunteered," said Lotte.

"Really?" Brock was surprised. All he knew about Lotte's life outside of the guild was that she originally came from intown—Brock often saw her consulting an ancient timepiece, some treasured family heirloom worth a small fortune.

"I was in the Stewards Guild," she said. "And I was good at my job. A born administrator."

Fel wrinkled up her nose. "Administrator?"

"It means . . ." Brock paused. "Um . . ."

"An administrator is a person who . . . administrates," Liza said.

The fire crackled in the silence.

Jett shrugged. "Don't ask me."

"An administrator is a person who makes things happen," Lotte said. "The stewards keep Freestone running just as much as the merchants do, but with less posturing and fewer rewards. They coordinate the Guildculling, file important paperwork, schedule construction projects for the Works Guild; they're judges and chancellors and pages . . ."

Jett pretended to snore.

Lotte laughed. "Okay, you're not wrong. It's important work, but it's *boring.* Which is probably why I fell in love with Jak."

"Oooh," Fel said. "Lotte and Jak, why don't you plant a tree? Let it bask in your mutual affection as it does the light of the sun!" She giggled.

Brock gave Fel a confused look, and he wasn't the only one.

"I'm guessing you don't have that saying," she said bashfully.

"I recognize the sentiment." Lotte smiled to herself. "Jak was fearless and . . . rowdy. We were from different planes, as they say. The adventurer and the administrator. I wouldn't have even *met* him except that I'd had to fine him for making rude noises during Master Quilby's speech at a public ceremony."

"Love at first *cit*ation?" Brock said.

"Something like that. We began seeing each other. My parents were very unhappy about it. I was still living at home, and this was the first time I'd ever defied them. The first time I'd ever put my own needs first.

"One day, there was a knock at my door. It was Alabasel Frond, looking about as out of place intown as a dog in fancy dress. But there was nothing funny about her expression. I knew what had happened before she said a word—Jak was dead."

The humor around the campfire dried up in an instant. Fel uttered a little gasp; otherwise, it was silent until Lotte finally spoke again.

"My parents were . . . *pleased*. They didn't even try to hide it. I could finally get past my rebellious phase, is how they put it. They locked me inside my room to keep me from going to his funeral pyre." Lotte smirked. "First door I ever kicked down."

Fel clasped her hands together. "And you joined the Sea of Stars in Jak's memory?" she asked dreamily.

"I tried," Lotte answered. "But Frond said no."

"No?!" said Jett.

"She really turned you away?" Liza asked.

"She did," Lotte confirmed. "Told me that she couldn't accept my application unless she was certain I'd thought it through. Told me to come back in a week if I still felt the same. Seven days later, I was knocking on her door at the crack of dawn." Lotte frowned. "The whole guild slept until third bell that day, so it was a long and frustrating morning for me."

She fixed her gaze on Brock. "My point is, none of us is 'cannon fodder' to her, Brock. The rest of Freestone might take what we do—what we *sacrifice*—for granted. Frond assuredly does not."

Brock nodded, keeping to himself the fear that Zed or Jayna or even Micah might already number among those sacrifices.

Despite his worries, Brock slept easily and deeply beside the fire. It took a long moment to get his bearings as Lotte shook him awake.

He tried to ask if it was his turn to keep watch, but his words came out slurred with sleep.

Lotte shushed him. "Come with me," she whispered.

Brock kept his blanket around him as he stood and trudged in the snow, following Lotte a good thirty paces from their campsite. The cold was invigorating, and by the time Lotte came to a stop, he was fully awake.

"What is it?" he asked. "Did you see something out here?"

"Oh, I've seen something," Lotte said. "Empty your pockets."

"Uh, what?" Brock said.

"Do it now," she insisted.

Brock repositioned his blanket so that he could reach his trouser pockets, turning them inside out. He gave Lotte a look that said: *Satisfied?*

"This one," Lotte said, tapping a small pocket woven into his tunic.

Brock hesitated, but there was no getting out of it. He produced a folded sheet of waxed parchment. Lotte snatched it from him, unfolding it to reveal a clutch of cottony spheres, fuzzy tufts no larger than a walnut.

"Do you know what these are?" she demanded.

"No," Brock said, and at her hard look, he said, "No, Quartermaster. I thought maybe the material would be of use, though. I was going to ask you—"

"These are cocoons," Lotte said sharply. "Bladewort cocoons. You ever see a bladewort? They blend right in with the trees in the springtime. Look like leaves. Pretty little green butterflies."

"What's a butterfly?" Brock asked.

"Doesn't really matter; they're extinct by now for all I know. But the bladewort thrives out here. They're small and hard to capture or kill. Their wings are as sharp as Frond's throwing stars, and they use them to cut you open so they can lap at your blood. Sometimes they nick a minor artery. Sometimes they cut your throat right open. What do you think would happen if they hatched in your tunic?"

Brock dropped his gaze to the snow, chastened. "I'm sorry," he said. "I didn't know."

"And did you know what would happen with that . . . that pitmunk spit or shelled rat urine or whatever it is you had in your pocket today?"

Brock felt the color drain from his face. "It wasn't urine," he protested.

Lotte sighed. "Look at me, Brock." He lifted his eyes from the ground; Lotte looked serious, but not angry. "I've seen you poring over Hexam's monster manual. And I want to encourage your curiosity. But with Dangers, the smallest mistake could have disastrous consequences. Consequences that could kill you, or worse, kill somebody else and haunt you forever. So you have to run *everything* you do by me or Hexam, you understand?" She held his eyes, waiting for an answer.

Brock nodded. "Yes," he said.

"And no souvenirs without our consent, all right?"

"Yes, Quartermaster."

"Good," she said. "Now go toss these in the fire, and we'll rouse the others. It'll be light out soon."

They plodded back to camp, and Lotte watched as Brock approached the fire with his handful of cocoons. He hadn't known what they were, and it obviously wasn't a good idea to bring such a thing into Freestone. But his mind still swam with the possibilities. Wings like sharpened steel? A town with regular shortages of metal could use that. And the creature must somehow produce this silky cocoon. Could bladewort larvae be used to produce material for clothiers?

"Go on," Lotte said, and Brock realized he'd hesitated. He quickly dumped the cocoons into the fire. Only then did Lotte turn her back and begin waking the others.

Brock cursed himself silently. Lotte wasn't likely to take her eyes off him now. Which meant his work for the Lady Gray had gotten a lot more complicated. She wouldn't be happy if he came back empty-handed. And if she wasn't happy, Zed wasn't safe.

The cocoons popped and sizzled in the fire, marring the morning's crispness with the acrid smell of burning.

Chapter Thirteen

Zed

The morning after the stalking shadow's attack, Zed felt numb. He moved listlessly around the camp, packing his gear and tying his bedroll. His thoughts were thick as syrup.

I'm your uncle.

Callum's revelation throbbed like a headache, pulsing just behind Zed's eyes.

Last night a million questions had been at his tongue, a torrent beating against a dam. But the dam had held. The stalking shadow's attack had left Zed feeling poisonous and tired. His throat burned. Frond had immediately set Micah to work on him, shooing Callum and the rest of the elves away.

Zed tried to protest, but the guildmistress had placed her cool hand against his chest.

"Tomorrow," she said. "Right now you *must* heal."

So he'd healed, as Micah's glowing hands illuminated the night.

Now tomorrow had finally come, but Zed found his questions had all dried up, replaced by a not-unpleasant emptiness.

Micah, at least, was giving him a wide berth. If Zed didn't know any better, he'd say the boy looked almost pensive as he stared out into the muddy morning. Perhaps the long night of healing had finally exhausted his endless reserves of snark.

As Zed stooped to pick up his scepter, a lanky shadow passed across the snow, jolting him with panic. He snapped up to find Callum looming, those wide green eyes unreadable.

Zed felt a flare of irritation that disturbed his stupor. He frowned as he slid the scepter into its leather holster. The camp had suddenly cleared out. Glancing around, Zed discovered the adventurers had all joined the elves on their side.

Traitors. Brock would have backed him up.

Well, Zed wouldn't speak first.

He'd already asked his questions—had been asking them for weeks—and Callum had chosen to rebuff him over and over. Zed didn't owe the elf a single word more, and he was determined not to give him one until Callum begged for forgiveness.

"Why?" Zed asked.

He bit down on his own cheek.

Callum flinched softly at the word. "Is there any answer I could give that would satisfy you? That would absolve me?"

Zed's anger squalled again at that. He scowled at the elf. "No," he said. "But you don't get to do that to me now. I've been begging you for answers about my father, and all I've gotten are *lies*."

The High Ranger frowned. "I never lied to you, Zed."

"A lie by omission is still a lie!" Zed shouted. His voice echoed through the forest. Zed heard the startled cries of birds in the distance.

He knew he was being foolish. A tantrum now would just attract more Dangers. He should rush past Callum and rejoin the group, march glumly behind Micah while the boy attempted to scratch himself beneath layers of winter clothing, or listen in while Jayna snuck Hexam her clever questions.

Instead, Zed began to cry. This infuriated him even further. He spun around and wiped angrily at his eyes. The ache for familiar things—for his mother, and Brock, and the safety of the city—throbbed deeply in his chest.

"You think I've failed you," Callum said from behind him. He placed his hands on Zed's shoulders, turning him gently back around. "And you're right. But how could I tell you the true extent of it? That I've been failing you since before you were born?"

Callum kneeled, putting them at eye level. Zed found his gaze locked with the elf's, and he was unable to look away.

"My brother and I were together on that journey to Freestone," Callum said. "It was his first to the city of the humans. On the giddy night of our arrival, I watched as Zerend introduced himself to a pretty young servant girl who had been waving from the crowd, ignoring the strange looks he received from both humans and elves. I loudly toasted them when they thought they'd snuck a kiss at the tavern and listened to my brother's breathless professions of love as we left the city two weeks later. I physically restrained him when he tried to double back and return to her." Callum's mouth opened, closed, opened again. "We lost him on that very same journey. He was slayed before my eyes by a monster that *I missed*."

Zed stared, dumbfounded.

"Six years later, I learned from the Adventurers Guild that the pretty human servant had birthed a child with pointed ears. And do you know what I did, Zed?" Callum suddenly gripped Zed's arms, his eyes burning with a terrible intensity. "I did *nothing*," the elf rasped through gritted teeth. "I told them that Zerend was lost and sent them on their way. I took no responsibility for you, or the many things I owed you. How could I? You had a mother, so what claim could I make? I was the leader of the queen's rangers; I couldn't very well abandon my obligations to live among *humans*. To bring you the news that it was *my* fault your father . . ."

Callum's voice faltered, a lute string breaking midsong.

Slowly, the manic light died from his eyes, and his grip on Zed's arms loosened. "I left you and your mother alone, because of my shame."

The elf stood, ignoring the snow and dirt that now caked his trousers. "And then there you were. An adventurer, of all things. So different, and yet so like him. You've repaid my unkindness by risking your life to save us. You rescue a people who won't even claim you as one of their own." Callum's hands were clenched into fists at his side. "And we betray you even now. Even as I say this."

Creeping fingers began to scale Zed's spine. That didn't sound good. "'Betray'? What do you mean?"

"A lie by omission." Callum watched him for a long beat, his eyes large and sorrowful. "The queen is lying. To all of you."

Ripples of dread exploded along Zed's arms.

"I'm so sorry," Callum said. "I've brought you into terrible danger."

And at that moment, the Danger arrived.

Zed heard the screams before he saw anything.

Voices shouted from the other camp, the elven and trade tongues knotting in alarm.

Callum tilted his head to the side. "What—?"

Which was when the arrow found him. It plunged into his

shoulder as suddenly and quietly as a bird alighting on a branch, sending the High Ranger spinning into the dirt with a grunt.

"Callum!" Zed screamed. He fell to his knees by the elf's side.

Callum glanced down at the shaft. "I'm fine." He twisted the arrow with practiced skill, unhooking the beaklike head from his shoulder. "It's one of ours." Callum's wide eyes darted around the camp. "An ambush. They're here!"

Figures appeared along the edges of the clearing. Stark gray shapes that lumbered within the whiteness.

They had been elves once, Zed could see that much. But where living elves were beings of color and beauty and magic, these creatures blighted those qualities from the landscape with their very presence. Most were little more than skeletons, on which pustules of flesh and hair clung stubbornly, like toadstools to a dying tree.

The only color Zed could make out in all that deadness were the pinpricks of bright purple light that burned from within every skeleton's eye sockets.

They were led by a single stooped elf for whom death was more recent. Her skin was ashen, as if she were wearing thick layers of makeup, and her eyes were spoonfuls of cloudy milk. She moved in teetering steps, as if just on the verge of falling over. Beyond these strange, dancing strides, she made no other noise.

None of them did.

"Stay behind me," Callum whispered as he stood. Slowly, the High Ranger unhooked the longbow from his back, nocking it with fluid, almost casual motions.

Zed shook his head, though he didn't dare look away from the figures. They were forming a staggered line, separating Zed and Callum from the others. A few of the skeletons carried jagged, rusty weapons. The bent elf stood behind the line, wielding a bow just like Callum's. She wore the uniform of a ranger.

"Zed, *behind me*," Callum rasped. "I can't protect you and fight them at the same time."

Zed took a deep breath. He'd expected to feel afraid right now. He'd been in a near panic the entire journey so far. The fear was still there; Zed's heart beat in his chest like a dog scratching at a flea. But above it, insulating him from the worst of the terror, something else was growing. It was a restlessness, a yearning.

Zed wanted to burn.

"No." He pulled the crystal-topped scepter free of his belt. Zed narrowed his eyes, drawing carefully from his mana. "I've gotten this far without your protection," he said. "I don't need it now."

And as a nimbus of silver mist closed Zed off from the world around him, the last thing he saw was Callum's stricken face.

He reappeared several yards away, trotting out of a second cloud just behind the line of undead. This was elf-stepping, the first sorcerous ability he'd manifested. It allowed him to pass between distant locations in a blink, as long as he could see where he was going.

Zed raised the scepter, recalling Hexam's lesson. *Fold the magic into the material.* He summoned his mana and focused on the crystal, pointing at the back of the stooped undead ranger. He felt the magic thrumming through his hands like usual, felt the air around his fingers begin to boil, but he tamped it down. The current passed easily into the rod, as if it were an extension of his own arm. As the mana left him, the crystal at the top glowed vivid green.

A high, tinny noise rang out from the stone. The air around the undead elf shimmered with heat. But just as the power exploded from the scepter, the implement kicked back, throwing Zed's aim off course. Green fire discharged into a row of skeletons, incinerating them.

Zed had missed the archer. Her empty gaze flicked back at him, pinpricks of purple light widening slightly, like pupils dilating.

Three long strides and she was on him. The elf leaped into the air, pouncing upon Zed and sending the scepter pinwheeling away into the snow. The wind left Zed's lungs in a great rush as he crashed to the ground.

Whatever bluster had insulated him from his fear evaporated now. The ranger bent over Zed at an inhuman angle, pinning him to the ground with spindly limbs. This close he could see her face was ripped with a ragged, untreated wound. Behind the violet gleams, insect larvae swam in her milky eyes.

Zed tried to scream, but the elf grabbed his neck and squeezed hard. Her face was completely emotionless as she started crushing his throat.

Then, suddenly, she was gone. Zed heard Callum bellowing as the High Ranger ripped the undead elf off of him. A hoarse gasp later, and his lungs filled gratefully with cold air.

Zed was getting very tired of being strangled by Dangers.

He scrabbled up to his hands and knees to find Callum wrestling with the undead elf.

"Get to Frond!" Callum roared as he plunged a hunting knife into the creature.

This time Zed didn't argue. He snatched up the scepter from the ground and took a quick gulp of mana, casting his eyes to the other camp, where many more figures were blurring between the trees.

A skeleton lunged at him just as the silvery mist enfolded Zed. Its rictus grin disappeared into the clouds.

When the mist parted, Zed fell out of it and into a full-scale battle.

All around him, elves fought for their lives against a skeletal horde. The queen and her ministers stood together, buffered by Petal and Thorn, who whirled and slashed with their longswords whenever the creatures came too close.

Energy sparked from Queen Me'Shala's hands—Zed could feel the charge in his own hair—and then bright webs of lightning connected a whole line of the skeletons, burning them with a sudden flash. A loud *crack* followed the brightness, popping Zed's ears.

Selby was chanting under his breath, a spell that seemed to be generating a bright red aura around the elven forces. Threya brandished two large swords and used them to impale a Danger that had made it past Thorn's defensive line, right through the eyes. She removed the offending skeleton from her weapons with a spirited shove of her boot.

The queen's gaze landed on Zed, her expression brightening. "Zed!" she called, waving him over. "This way!"

The queen is lying.

I've brought you into terrible danger.

Zed took a step back, shaking his head. His hands clenched around the scepter's handle.

The queen watched him retreat and something in her face changed. For a moment she looked alarmed. Then her eyes narrowed.

Zed whirled around and ran. He searched the woods desperately for Frond, or any of the other adventurers, but he couldn't find a familiar face in the chaos.

A shadow fell across his path. Zed glanced up in time to see a skeleton plunging down toward him from the trees. He yelped, elf-stepping out of the way. Zed tumbled out of the silvery mist and slammed against a tree just as the skeleton hit the forest floor, exploding into a mess of bones.

He stood there for a moment, propped against the tree, just panting and willing his heart to be still.

That was when he saw Frond. The guildmistress was midleap, swinging her curved sword out in front of her. She unburdened a particularly stooped skeleton of its cumbersome head, then skidded into the body, sending it crashing away. Frond was back up immediately, her sharp eyes scanning for threats.

They landed on Zed. Frond raised her hand, her lips parting to say something, just as a scream filled the encampment.

A high, keening voice echoed from the forest. The sound was unearthly in its pitch and intensity, but somewhere inside it was the wail of a woman's voice. Zed grabbed his ears against the cry, searching the camp for the source. He gasped as the Dangers began to part, making way for something else to come through.

What emerged was no shambling corpse. A female elven figure floated several feet off the ground, shivering with ghastly purple radiance. Lank strands of hair encircled her head in a snarled corona. The dead woman—for she was surely dead; her mummified face was frozen in a sob—was almost transparent. She flickered in and out of sight, her form blurring one moment, and then focusing the next.

"*Ban'shea!*" Many elven voices began screaming the word, all of them sharp with panic.

An armored figure exploded toward the spirit, her sword carving looping patterns through the air.

It was Petal. The sword sister moved with languid grace. Her flowing slashes drew the *ban'shea*'s attention. Petal caught Zed watching her and spared him a cheerful wink. She stepped between Zed and the creature. She was protecting him.

The spirit turned toward her. The *ban'shea*'s sorrowful eyes brightened with desperate intensity.

Petal spun, expertly swiping her longsword into the Danger. But the blow passed right through it, leaving only a billowing trail of purple vapor. The sword sister tilted, caught off balance.

The *ban'shea* descended before she could recover. The purple light radiating from the Danger brightened, flooding the encampment. She took Petal's face in her hands and the echoing wail sharpened, rising to an almost unbearable pitch. Zed kept his hands pressed firmly over his ears, but he watched as Petal's face went slack. He saw her wide, lovely eyes unfocus as she stared up at the spirit. The sword sister's mouth fell open, and the pinkness drained from her skin, blanching to pale blue.

The *ban'shea*'s wail relented, but the silence that followed was almost as awful. She released Petal, and the elf's body fell to the ground.

Petal was dead.

Zed discovered he'd stopped breathing, and couldn't will himself to start again. In place of air, a liquid rush of horror flooded his chest. His hands were shaking uncontrollably.

Only the sheer force of Frond's order brought him back.

"Zed, *run!*"

Zed came to in time to discover that the *ban'shea*'s fervid eyes were now trained on *him*.

He ran.

He plunged into the trees without a thought for where he was headed. Behind him, the spirit's wail rose again, echoing miserably. Zed sucked in a gulp of mana and cast his gaze as far out into the forest as he could see. He passed through a tunnel of mist and arrived many yards away.

He curved right, into a thick stand of trees, panting and sobbing as he ran.

A shape leaped in front of him. Zed screamed, lifting his scepter and summoning his mana. It flooded into the crystal, the stone glaring green, just as recognition dawned.

He knew the person standing there.

It was Brock.

His friend's eyes widened as he saw the glowing scepter pointed right at him.

Zed's mouth fell open. "How—?"

The spell went off before he could stop it. A spray of green fire gushed from the crystal, splashing over Brock and exploding with blinding intensity.

Zed was blown off of his feet and landed in the snow with a hiss and a cloud of vapor. He pushed himself up in a panic, his eyes darting wildly to where he'd just annihilated his best friend.

Brock still stood there, totally unharmed. Though he looked a bit shaken.

Surrounding him was a glittering, semitransparent barrier. Then Zed saw Jayna standing just behind the boy, her arms raised. Her red curls were matted with sweat. Jayna lowered her hands and the shield dissolved into air, a bubble popping.

Zed and Brock said nothing for a long moment, both boys just huffing and staring at each other.

"Am I dreaming?" Zed finally asked.

"We came to warn you that the Lich knows your plan," Brock said. He waved weakly toward camp, where the sounds of battle still raged. "Brock to the rescue."

"'We'?"

Other figures stepped into view. Liza stood just a short distance away, with Jett beside her. Micah hung back, nervously scanning the forest, while Fel moved to help Zed to his feet.

"When the undead attacked, Frond ordered Micah and me to run." Jayna shook out her trembling hands. She looked even paler than usual. "We ran into Lotte and these guys just a few moments ago. *Zed, you nearly killed us!*"

Zed grabbed Fel's arm after she'd helped him up, his eyes searching the trees. "That doesn't matter right now. Where's Lotte?"

"She ran toward the battle," Liza said. "She made us promise to stay far away."

"Naturally, Liza ignored her," Brock said with a sigh.

The image of Petal's blue face pushed unbidden into Zed's mind. "We have to run!" he said. "There's something still chasing me. It *killed* a sword sister with just a scream. It—"

"*Ban'shea . . .*" Fel's voice wheezed in Zed's ear, so thick with fear it seemed to fog the air around them.

Zed turned just as the scream rose through the forest, high and despondent.

The *ban'shea* floated through the trees. Her anguished eyes were wide and wild. She reached pleadingly for Zed.

"*Run!*" he screamed.

They ran, tumbling backward into the woods. Trees flashed by Zed, and he heard shouts from the others, though he couldn't pick out any distinct voices. Behind them, the *ban'shea* wailed again, alarmingly near.

As he ran, he glanced above him into the bony branches of the trees. In the distance, Zed spotted what he hoped was a particularly sturdy one. He held his breath and leaped into the air. Mist exploded around him, and then the wind was knocked forcefully out of Zed's chest as he slammed into the branch. He latched on to it with his arms and legs and just hung there a moment, willing himself to breathe until he finally could.

Zed crawled carefully on top of the bough, acutely aware of the sound of creaking wood. He glanced down. His friends were still running, some in wildly different directions. Beyond them, the sickly purple light of the *ban'shea* flitted between the trees. If he could just get close enough to hit her with his flame, before she caught him like she had poor Petal . . .

There was a *crack*, and a sharp dip. Zed shrieked as the branch buckled. He sucked in a breath and fell through fog—

—then landed in a heap on the ground. Zed scrambled to his feet, raising his scepter, which was illuminated by a strange purple glare. He looked up.

The *ban'shea* floated just above, watching him with her dolorous gaze. The Danger's face blurred, her features swimming, and when they reformed Zed was surprised to see a normal elven face staring back at him.

This woman was beautiful. She had kind, wet eyes, which reminded Zed of his own mother's. Her expression was soft and sorrowful. She reached a hand down toward Zed, seeming just on the verge of telling him something. Some tragic and wonderful secret.

No, Zed. This isn't a secret you wish to know.

Something called him back to himself. Zed raised the scepter high, toward the *ban'shea*'s outstretched hand, and summoned every last bit of mana he had.

The fire erupted as a great green sphere, enveloping the Danger in a swirling orb. It churned like a miniature sun in the desolate forest.

Zed's stomach quailed as the last of his magic was used up. His legs buckled beneath him, sending him sprawling into the snow. He panted, closing his eyes as the heat of the flames swept over him.

He was alive. He was alive, and he'd rescued his friends.

Eventually the blaze faded, the warmth giving way back to crisp, cold winter. Zed opened his eyes.

The *ban'shea* still floated above him. Somehow the green flames, which burned anything they touched, *hadn't* touched her.

Oh, no, Zed thought exhaustedly. *There's a flaw in the plan.*

The spirit's beautiful face liquefied, contorting into a wide, starving smile. Zed screamed, crawling backward. The *ban'shea* sailed slowly closer. Her ragged locks of hair reached toward him like fingers. Her torn lips opened wider and wider.

The trees around them began to glow with honey-colored light, illuminating the forest in sunny radiance. Zed wondered if he was dying already, if this was part of the *ban'shea's* deadly scream. But this light seemed wholly different. It reminded Zed of Micah's healing hands, but instead of coming from a person, it rippled out from the forest itself, billowing from the leafless trees.

The *ban'shea* recoiled from the light, shielding her eyes. Zed noticed that several figures had joined them, emerging from within the foliage.

Brock? he wondered. *Liza? Micah?* No, these shapes were too tall. The figures stood in a tight circle, positioned behind the sudden glare, shrouded in shadow. And they were all chanting something in a language Zed didn't recognize.

Above him, the *ban'shea* shriveled beneath the amber light. She fractured and folded in upon herself, until she was nothing but a curl of violet smoke. Then the smoke vanished; the warm light dimmed, and Zed dimmed, too, falling into unconsciousness.

Chapter Fourteen

Brock

"Zed!" Brock shouted. "Zed!"

The forest mocked him with its silence.

It was awful, that silence. Unnatural. No matter how far he hurled his voice, the snow seemed to swallow it up. The sounds of battle had been so loud, a fearsome din of clashing steel and shouted curses. And that dreadful *wail*. But now, utter silence. Just how far had they run?

And at what point had Zed fallen behind?

"Zed!" he screamed, and even though his voice, high with panic, fell flat among the drifts and barren trees, still there was an echo of a sort as Micah took up the call, and Jayna, and Jett with his tenor sounding out like a foghorn.

And then Fel's voice cried: "Over here!"

Brock scrambled through the snow, arriving at the base of a tree where Fel squatted, examining the ground. But he saw only more snow.

Liza's breath was visible in little clouds. "What are we looking at, Fel?"

"Here." Fel gestured at a spot where the snow was disturbed, as if pushed aside. She picked up a broken branch, gazed up at the tree. "He fell. He scrabbled about. And here . . ." She took a few steps forward, to where the snow remained unmarred, and placed a hand upon a patch of ice. Brock noticed the area shimmered in the sunlight like glass. "The top layer of snow was melted and then froze again. As if exposed to a brief burst of extreme heat."

"His fire," Jayna said.

Micah tucked his mace under his armpit so that he could rub his frozen fingers together. "Fire, right. So there *is* a good reason to find him."

"But where is he?" Brock asked, scanning the trees.

Fel pointed off to the side. "Footprints."

"So he's okay?" Brock prompted. "He got up and walked away?"

"I'm sorry, Brock," she said. "I don't think they're *his* footprints."

"What does that mean?" Liza asked. "Someone took him?"

Fel showed her palms. "This is good news. There's no . . . Forgive me, but there's no blood. And a *ban'shea* would leave no prints, so . . . I think he's okay. But I think he was taken."

"ZED!" Brock shouted into the distance. He moved quickly, placing his own feet within the footprints.

"Brock!" Liza called. "Let Fel lead. She's a trained tracker."

"I can follow footprints in the snow!" he barked.

"You're following the wrong prints."

Brock paused, considered the trail he was following. It led uphill, back in the direction they'd come from. Fel was already leading the others away at an angle, deeper into the forest, where the skeletal trees stood closer together. He kicked at the prints in frustration, then hurried to catch up.

Liza gripped him by the arm as he caught up. "We'll find him, Brock."

"I was sure he was right behind me," Brock replied as they hurried after Fel. "When he was drafted I told him, I *promised* him, we'd look out for each other, and now—"

Liza's grip tightened, and she pulled him down low. Brock saw that Fel had lifted her fist, signaling that they should stop. If something was wrong, though, he couldn't see what. The world was as silent as ever, the trail they followed showing the only sign of life in a dead forest.

And then he saw the figure standing among the trees.

She was lithe and tall, and so still that Brock had mistaken her for a sapling. Her garments marked her as a stranger. She wore metal and stone and a supple, waxy material that was familiar, but which he couldn't place. Her face was covered with a mask of immaculate white, its chin coming to a point, with simple slits for her eyes and mouth.

"What . . . is that . . . ?" Liza whispered.

Brock shuddered. "Does it remind anyone else of—?"

"The naga," Jett said, his voice husky at the reminder of the monster whose venom had nearly killed him.

Micah scoffed. "It's not a Danger, it's just some kind of scarecrow."

And then the figure tilted its head, turning its black slits on Micah.

"Wedge formation!" Liza shouted, already stepping forward with her shield raised.

The figure lifted its hand, and Brock held his breath. It looked to him like a gesture of greeting, but he was wholly expecting that hand to produce a fireball or a lightning bolt or even a tentacle.

He'd seen far too many tentacles in the last six weeks.

He drew his weapons and saw the others had done the same. Jayna flexed her fingers.

"Liza?" Jett prompted, hefting his hammer. "What's our move?"

The figure stood its ground and said something in a language Brock didn't recognize.

"Anybody catch that?" Micah asked.

"We come in peace," Liza said. "Do you understand?"

The figure ignored her, turning its gaze now on Fel. It spoke again, utterly unintelligible.

"We're wasting time," Brock hissed.

"All right," Liza said. "All right, maybe we just . . . just keep going." She took a sideways step.

And the forest burst into motion.

Suddenly they were everywhere: up in the trees and behind every trunk, and two of them even popped up from within snowdrifts. They all wore those eerie masks, white as their surroundings, and they were all armed. In the time it took Brock to blink, a dozen nocked arrows were pointed directly at them.

"Well," Micah said, dropping his mace into the snow. "*That* I understand."

Brock had gotten used to sorting his enemies into three categories. There were the people, those he could talk to and, in theory at least, reason with. There were the Dangers, beyond reason, with whom communication was impossible. And there was Mousebane, in a category all her own, who seemed at times to understand just what Brock wanted and chose to do the opposite. And who, he noted, had disappeared deep into Fel's pack at the first sign of trouble.

What he wasn't used to were people who just didn't have any idea what he was saying.

"We are looking for our friend, you understand?" he said, enunciating each syllable.

The strangers had taken their weapons and managed to communicate that the group should walk forward. Mostly that was achieved by surrounding them and prodding them with arrows. Other than an initial exchange in their unfamiliar language, they had been as silent as the woods themselves.

"All right, buddy," Jett said to Brock. "You know if they don't speak the trade tongue, talking slowly *in the trade tongue* isn't going to get you anywhere. Besides"—he nodded at the ground—"we're still following the trail. I think it's fairly clear they *are* taking us to Zed."

"So we can all be prisoners together," Micah said. "It'll feel just like being back at the guildhall, I bet. Until they kill us and feed us to the Dangers."

"They won't do that," Jayna said, but she sounded wholly uncertain about it.

"What else would a group of armed weirdos living in the woods want with a bunch of kids? How do you think they survive out here without getting eaten themselves? They've got to be Danger-worshipping cultists sworn into the service of some fiendish abomination." Micah made a face as if the answer were obvious and Jayna were deranged not to have come to the same conclusion.

Brock turned to comfort Jayna, but she didn't look scared— she looked determined. "I'm still good for a spell or two, Liza."

"They are not going to kill and feed us to anything," Fel said.

"Oh yeah?" said Micah. "You figure the Dangers will just eat us alive?"

"Micah . . ." Liza warned.

"Look at what they're wearing," Fel said. "Consider it. Pauldrons of metal and buckles of stone. Their cloaks are woven cotton in a season when animal fur would be preferable. And the rest of it . . . some kind of plant matter."

Brock took a second look at the waxy-looking material on their torsos and arms and legs. She was right. It looked like they'd wrapped themselves in leaves coated in lacquer.

"No animal products at all," Liza said. "Not even Danger skins."

"So what, they live off berries?" Micah made an exaggerated show of scanning their surroundings. "How does that work in the winter, exactly?"

"And who doesn't speak the trade tongue?" Brock put in. "Everyone speaks it. It's the whole point of having a trade language!"

"It's nice to see you two getting along, anyway," Liza said.

Block glared at Micah, and Micah glared back. "We're not getting along," Brock insisted. "We're just . . . annoyed in the same direction."

"Is it getting brighter out?" Jett asked.

He was right, Brock realized. As they'd walked, the forest

had become darker and gloomier, to the point where he'd wondered how their captors could see much of anything through their slitted masks. He'd wholly expected to trip over a clutch of undead elves—according to Jayna, the woods had been *swarming* with them—but as unsettling as their surroundings were, they were clearly moving farther away from where the Lich's forces had lain in ambush. Now, as Jett had indicated, the forest had brightened somewhat. It seemed to grow brighter with each step.

"That isn't sunlight," Liza said. "Does anyone else feel that?"

Brock looked at her. "Feel what?" he asked, but she struggled to explain it.

"Jayna?" Liza prompted.

Jayna shook her head. "I don't feel anything."

Then they crested a hill, and Brock saw the trees. Trees that glowed with their own inner light.

"You think you've seen everything," Jett said. "You flee a horde of reanimated elf corpses and you say, well, that's it, I've seen all there is to see. And then—"

"—glowing trees," Brock finished.

And beyond those trees, the forest was lush and verdant.

Passing between the lit trees was like stepping into another world. After miles and weeks of snow and ice, the greenery all around them was a jarring and welcome change. The air was warm.

"This is some pretty great magic," Jett mused.

"Magic?" Jayna said. "Maybe . . ."

"Maybe? Of course it's magic." Jett removed his gloves and rolled up his sleeves. "Sometimes I forget magic isn't all about setting monsters on fire."

"Not that there's anything wrong with that," Liza said lightly, but she was intently scanning their surroundings. The ground was an uninterrupted expanse of moss, but beneath it was a hard material. Cobblestones. The trees here, thick and heavy with the foliage of high summer, reached far into the air to form a ceiling of leaf and branch. They did not glow from within like those at the perimeter, but daylight filtered through the canopy, lighting the scene in cool shades of green and yellow.

Everywhere there was stone—stone steps, stone wells, stone walls—and everywhere that stone was overrun with algae and weeds and creeping vines.

"It's a dead city," Jayna breathed.

"Are you kidding?" Liza smiled and brushed her fingers across a flower as they walked along the broken cobbles. "This place is very much alive."

"I've never seen anything like it," Jett said, awed.

"Zed has, sort of," Liza replied.

Brock considered the structures as they approached what appeared to be a residential district. The uniform rows of squat stone houses made for a striking study in order and chaos. Despite being of similar size and shape, no two buildings were alike, because nature had left its mark upon each in unique ways.

Some were covered with verdant moss, others with flowering vines that wove unimpeded through open doors and windows. One structure had a tree growing from it, right up through its very roof, but it appeared otherwise intact. He could just make out the movements of the people inside as they snuck glances through darkened windows.

"The shrine we visited last summer," he said. "The druids! Their shrine was like this, the trees and stone all wound together. This is similar, just . . . bigger. Way bigger."

"Druids?" Jayna echoed. "Alive out here all this time? Alone?" She looked around at their silent captors with new interest. "Is it possible?"

"The druids who built that shrine were elves," Jett reasoned. "And these ones were definitely most interested in talking to Fel."

"But I couldn't understand them," Fel said softly.

"So they've got some weird druid language and a secret handshake," Micah said. "We can figure it out. If they're elves, we're on the same side."

Liza's smile faltered. "Probably. But from what we've learned of the divisions in Llethanyl . . ." She glanced at Fel. "Better not let our guard down just yet."

As the druids led them down the avenue, the city grew more cramped, buildings and trees alike crowding in. Eventually they were forced to walk two by two, with half the druids leading the way and the other half following behind. Their silent captors kept their bows drawn, but, strange masks aside, they weren't terribly menacing. Still, Brock was growing nervous once more. He didn't miss the snow, but without it he had no way to know if they were still following Zed's trail. And whatever Liza said about the city, it felt like a dead place to him, a once-great achievement that had been strangled by the green as thoroughly as any Danger could manage. He imagined Freestone's familiar marketplace in a similar state, and the thought made him shudder.

They went down a narrow staircase slick with growth, positioned between two buildings so that the light of the street above was quickly forgotten. If these druids *were* elves, their eyes would be better equipped to handle the darkness. Brock peered ahead, running his hand along the slimy wall to steady himself.

As his eyes adjusted, the staircase bottomed out, and the druids led them through an ancient archway and into an expansive indoor space beyond it.

Indoor wasn't quite right, however. Huge pieces of the structure were missing, allowing shafts of light to illuminate ancient stonework and massive roots. Brock imagined tremendous trees must be high overhead, hidden from view by what remained of the domed ceiling, supported by the roots that wove their way down the walls and deeper still.

He wondered if the vegetation made the ceiling more or less likely to fall on their heads.

There were more druids here, and they parted to reveal Zed standing among them. Brock's heart leaped into his throat, and he held his breath as Zed saw them and rushed forward. If Zed was their prisoner, the druids made no move to stop him, and within a moment he had flung his arms around Brock and Liza and as many of the others as he could reach.

"I'm so glad you're here!" he gushed. "I was afraid I'd never find you and nobody here will speak to me and they *took my scepter*."

One of the druids, the unarmed woman whom they'd first encountered, reached out and poked lightly at the point of Zed's ear as if expecting it to fall off.

Zed suffered the inspection with a small grimace. "Also they keep doing that."

"Yeah, well," Micah said. "We thought they'd have fed you to their sinister woodland overlords by now, so maybe look on the bright side."

Zed's eyes goggled.

Liza huffed. "We didn't—"

"You are bleeding, though," Micah continued. He reached out and, his hand glowing with a honeyed light, touched a small cut on Zed's brow.

The druids all turned to watch, chattering excitedly. Their words echoed about the space like music. And then they bowed their heads to Micah in an unmistakable display of respect.

Liza's jaw dropped. "What . . . the . . ."

"Well," Micah said, puffing out his chest. "All I can say is, it's about time."

"Actually, I think Danger worship might have been easier to wrap my head around," Brock said.

The druids stirred, turning their attention to a grand archway where another of their number appeared. This figure was dressed in the same strange, simple mask, but instead of the lightly armored plant material of their captors, he wore a flowing robe the likes of which Brock had never seen. It shimmered softly in the light, and its color—Brock knew all the dyes available to man and elf, but this garment was a shade he'd never seen before, a rich blue bordering on purple.

This was a regal figure. Someone of authority.

He approached slowly, holding a small object in his upturned palm. He waved his free hand above the object, chanting low and purposefully.

"It's a spell," Zed said, his voice tight.

"I recognize it," Jayna said. "He's holding a parrot's claw."

"Ew," said everyone.

"It's not an *actual* parrot's claw. It's petrified wood—a small tree branch that has hardened to stone over hundreds of years. There isn't a single one in Freestone, but they were used before the Day of Dangers . . . for translation spells."

"That's good news," Liza said.

"Mostly," Jayna said. "But we have to be careful." She cast a look over the group, and her eyes lingered on Brock and Micah. "The charm will translate *everything* we say."

Brock pointed at his chest. "Me? Why are you worried about me? I'm very diplomatic!"

"For the record," Micah said, "I totally get why you're worried about me."

"Sorry," Jayna said. "It's just that the spell will be very, very literal. Some scholars believe that the great war between the dwarves and orcs was ignited over a simple mistranslation of the dwarven word for, um, 'rear end.'"

Jett giggled. Jayna ignored him and continued.

"Once he finishes that spell, we have to avoid idioms, slang . . . Metaphors are totally off the table," she said. "Uh, not literally! I mean—"

Liza sighed wearily. "I get it. Just let me do the talking. Okay?"

The mage came to a stop a few yards from them, and the rest of the druids drifted to the edges of the room, the archers watching them intently. The claw glowed with a soft blue light, and the mage's chanting ended. He turned his eerie gaze upon Fel. This time when he spoke, the claw vibrated in his palm, producing words that Brock understood perfectly.

"Who are you?"

"Greetings, honored host," Liza said, spacing her words out to allow the claw time to sing out in the druid's language. "We are citizens of Freestone. We fight the undead Dangers in the surrounding woods. We require help."

"Not you, Sister of Light," the druid said, and though the words from the claw were spoken neutrally, his tone sounded harsh. He lifted a finger, singling out Fel. "Who are *you*? How is it you do not know our language?"

"M-me?" Fel stammered. "I . . ."

"And what are you?" he asked, turning to consider Zed.

"He is a person and his name is Zed," Brock said hotly.

"Everyone calm down," Liza barked at her team. "Please," she said, returning her attention to the druid. "We are on a crucial mission to liberate Llethanyl from monsters. We must find our friends, or the entire city is doomed."

"Llethanyl?" the druid said. "Llethanyl overburdened its bough long ago."

"Uh, was that a metaphor?" Micah whispered.

"Micah, shush!" cried Jayna.

The druid turned his eyes on Fel once more. "What do we care about Llethanyl? Overrun with monsters, you say? It was ever so." He pulled the mask away from his face, and Fel gasped. He wasn't just an elf—he was a night elf, like her.

"I say let Llethanyl burn."

Chapter Fifteen

Zed

Though the sun waned above them—Zed could just make out the purple haze of dusk through the holes in the dome—the druids' overgrown chamber remained as bright as midday.

Zed sat on the floor, while Liza, Jayna, and Fel spoke haltingly with the druid leader several feet away. Too many voices were confusing the conversation, Liza had said. When Micah piped up that the last bit seemed perfectly clear to him, she banished *all* the boys to the other side of the hall.

Zed didn't mind being left out. He was numb with exhaustion and captivated by the lush beauty of the druids' home. Here, somehow, life still thrived in the dead of winter, plant life twining together with the ruins into a strange new garden.

And elves survived, too, against all odds. Once their leader had removed his mask, many of the others followed suit. Each and every one was a night elf. Half a dozen stood nearby, eyeing Zed and the others curiously, and whispering to one another. They kept their bows raised.

Fel seemed to have been struck dumb by the sight of so many night elves. Though she stood now with Liza and Jayna, the two human girls were doing most of the talking. Fel just watched the druid leader with eyes so large and wide they seemed ready to burst open. It was as if her gaze were too small a container for everything she was seeing.

"You know, I don't think this is going to be so bad," Micah mused. "These backwater elves have probably never met a healing prodigy before. They were falling over themselves when I cleaned up Zed's cut."

Jett shook his head. "Is it too late to feed him to monsters?"

Reclining beside the dwarf, Mousebane yawned, showing off her pointy teeth. The cat had been curled up in Fel's pack, but with the threat behind them and this uncanny warmth bathing down, she'd finally ventured out of hiding. Now she was sprawled out on a patch of moss that had grown over what was once thick carpet. She kept her lazy gaze on Fel across the chamber. Zed nearly reached out to rub her soft belly, but Mousebane turned and hissed at him before he even had a chance to lift his hand.

Finally, the three girls returned. Behind them, the druids' leader raised his palm, and the archers all lowered their bows.

"Well, there's good news and there's bad news," Liza said. "And then there's more bad news. And then finally a little more bad news to top it all off."

"Dessert first," said Brock. "Let's start with the good stuff."

"We're not prisoners," Liza said. "The druids will let us depart safely, but they *strongly* recommend that we wait until morning, when the dead are thinnest. Until then, we're free to explore."

"That's all the news I need, thanks." Micah shot up from the ground with a wide stretch. "I'm off to enjoy some well-deserved praise. Step aside, peons. Ah—sorry, Zed—that was rude. I mean, *pardon me*, peons." Micah winked, then sauntered out of the domed chamber, ducking beneath a curtain of leafy vines. The druids' leader nodded silently to one of the archers, and the night elf followed him out.

"Well, I *was* going give him one of the parrot's claws I enchanted," Jayna said. "But it's probably safer if he doesn't have one." The girl passed around curved petrified tokens, which Zed could smell were pungent with the scent of mint.

"Wait," Jett said. "You enchanted these? During the five breaths you were over there? When did you learn the spell?"

"I just followed the druid's instructions," Jayna murmured.

"Though describing arcane formulas through an omniglot spell really tests the limits of translation magic. The enchantments won't last very long. I needed to conserve my mana. Sorry."

"I didn't understand a word you just said, but this is incredible." Jett turned the pincer over in his hands. "You're even more brilliant than I realized, Jayna. Hexam doesn't appreciate what he has."

Jayna opened her mouth to respond, but no sound actually came out. Instead, her cheeks blushed almost as red as her hair.

"Not that I'm excited to get to the bad news," Brock said, "but I assume there's more to the story here?"

Liza nodded grimly. "The night elves won't help us take back Llethanyl. In fact, as soon as we leave their city, we're on our own. Also, they're not giving back our gear until we go. The conversation was ... tense."

Fel's eyes were on her feet, where Mousebane had padded over and then collapsed again. "The *dro'shea* of Llethanyl always believed the rest of our people were wiped out. That our culture was lost." Her gaze rose from the ground now, cobalt eyes shining. "But that isn't true. These *dro'shea* survived. They've flourished!"

"And as far as they're concerned," Liza said, "the elves are still at war."

"Aren't we?" Fel spun toward Liza, sending Mousebane spilling away. Something had cracked in the young elf's gaze. A container had finally broken. "The Lich attacked the city on his own, but my entire people have been found guilty of the crime. All my life I've been treated like an intruder in my own home, a home my parents gave their lives to protect. Maybe the druids are right. Maybe . . . maybe Llethanyl deserves this!"

"Fel, you don't mean that," Liza said.

"Don't tell me what I mean!" Fel snapped. "You can't understand what it's like. Every day I'm reminded that I'm not just different, but *unwelcome*. I've tried to be a good elf—for the *dro'shea*, and Callum, and the memories of my mother and father—but it never mattered!" Fel waved the parrot's claw, which was gripped so tightly in her palm that Zed worried she'd cut herself. "My parents never knew that our *real* people were alive and waiting for us! And now I've found them, but I can't even speak their language!" She shoved the claw into a pocket and whirled around, her back to the group.

A long, quiet beat passed.

"You're right," Zed said softly. "It's not fair. Why don't we look around together? Like in the market."

"No." Fel let out a shuddering breath. "I'm sorry, Zed, but this isn't a tour I can give you. I've always wondered what was taken from us. What our stories were. I'm going to see what I've missed."

And with that, Fel was gone. Mousebane trotted after her, disappearing into the foliage.

Jett placed a hand on Zed's back as he frowned at the empty

passageway. "Give her space," he said. "She needs to take this in, without an audience."

"So what's next, oh 'Sister of Light'?" Brock asked, turning to Liza.

"For what it's worth," Jayna muttered, "Frond said our next stop was somewhere called Celadon Falls. Not that I have any idea where that is."

Liza gazed up toward the ceiling and closed her eyes. She was standing beside a shaft of light, and the radiance shifted momentarily, covering her olive-brown skin in its glow. "Maybe we could all use a moment to split up and cool off. Figure some stuff out." Then she opened her eyes and gave Brock an impish smile. "Jayna, Jett, want to have a look around?"

Jett was beside her in an instant. "Definitely," he said.

Jayna nodded, following more slowly. The three left the chamber, trailed by two more elven archers, leaving Zed and Brock behind.

"You realize this is the discovery of a lifetime," Brock said. "A lost city of druids survived the Day of Dangers, and we found it. Or, well, I guess they found us. Either way, I expect another sternly worded letter of congratulations from the king."

The two were walking down what had once been a wide city avenue. Every few feet the stone bricks erupted upward, overturned by thick tree trunks or impossibly large roots. Night had fallen, but the canopy of leaves shimmered with a sparkling light that kept the city bright and warm, like lanterns during a festival. A stream ran right through the road ahead of them. Its glittering water was clear and lovely.

"Frond will have to update the guild's flag," Zed agreed. "Five stars won't be enough anymore."

Brock sighed. "Unless we can't save Llethanyl."

A long moment of quiet hung between them.

"Jayna mentioned Callum is your uncle," Brock said. "That's . . . I can't imagine what it must have been like, finding out that way."

"Brock, I . . ." Zed shut his eyes, fighting back a wave of emotions. All the hurt and frustration of the last few days—of the last six weeks—flared up inside him, as fresh as ever. "What did I do . . . to make you hate me?"

Brock grimaced, glancing away. "I don't hate you, Zed. I don't think it's even *possible* to hate you."

Zed thought of Makiva, and his heart bucked. He wondered if that was really true. He'd made a pact with a witch. That made *him* a warlock. Zed couldn't imagine anything Freestoners despised more than elf-blooded warlocks.

"Then why have you been avoiding me?" he asked.

"It's complicated." Brock exhaled. "I know that's not an answer. I promised we'd stick together when we joined the Sea of Stars, and I've let you down. I've got a good reason for it, I swear. Something I've been meaning to talk to you about . . ." Brock glanced over his shoulder. "But it might have to wait just a bit longer."

Behind them, two night elf archers followed a few feet back. They'd lowered their bows, but kept their eyes trained on the boys.

Zed nodded glumly. "I have something to tell you, too. Something important. I should have told you a long time ago, but I was afraid. I still am."

Brock gave Zed a worried glance, but he didn't press him further. "Once this is all over, we both come clean. No more secrets. Deal?"

"Deal," Zed said.

Then Brock took his hand and pulled him in for a stiff, earnest embrace. It felt like a weight had immediately fallen from Zed's shoulders. For the first time in weeks, he and Brock were a team again. Suddenly the prospect of saving Llethanyl didn't feel quite so impossible.

Though it was well past the hour Freestone shuttered its doors, Zed noticed many *dro'shea* were bustling about as he and Brock explored the city. Some carried baskets full of fruits and grains. Others wove fabric outdoors, loitering in the light from the trees. It was like being in Freestone's market again during more prosperous times. The city was full of overgrown structures—stately houses were fused with trees or cloaked in moss—but this didn't feel like a wild place to Zed. It felt like a garden. Flowers grew in neat spirals of color, and many of the trees were pruned into artful silhouettes. Every blade of grass was perfectly level. Zed couldn't help but stare in awe.

And there were plenty of night elves watching *them*, too. Zed noticed a small group of *dro'shea* children peering at him and Brock from behind an enormous tree. When Brock waved, the children shrieked and laughed, disappearing from sight.

"What I don't get is how they've survived the Dangers this long," Zed said. "I didn't notice any wards coming in. Aside from that one mage, there's been no spellcraft to speak of."

"Wait, this seriously isn't magic?" Brock asked, waving upward.

Zed shook his head. "At least not any I can sense. Haven't you noticed the light looks . . . familiar? It's sort of like what Micah does."

"I do my best to forget about what Micah does." Brock searched around, then nodded toward a young elven woman with pale gray skin who was standing over a small sapling. She was dressed in an ornate, flowing robe, similar to the druidic leader's. "Don't look now," he said. "But I think we're about to see some of this nonmagic firsthand."

Indeed, the druid's palms were held carefully over the plant. She took a deep breath, closing her eyes. The sapling shimmered with a glowing amber aureole. Honeyed light dripped from its leaves and trunk, bathing the soil around it in radiance. As Zed and Brock watched, the sapling grew at incredible speed, stretching upward like a dog rising lazily from sleep. It expanded several inches in a moment's time, and pink blossoms flowered along its branches. Then the elven woman let out her breath and the light faded. The sapling dimmed to normal.

The woman opened her eyes, then caught sight of Zed and Brock watching her. She yelped, stumbling backward. The boys both immediately raised their hands.

"Sorry!" Zed said. "We were just watching."

Zed heard his own voice echoed in a foreign tongue, resonating from the parrot's claw in his left hand.

The druid nodded slowly, her eyes flicking to the archers behind them. "Forgive me." Her voice rang out from the claw. "I'd heard there were foreigners in"—the translation spell lapsed as the night elf spoke the name of her city; Zed heard something like *Tascen Ra*, before the magic kicked in again—"Duskhaven, but you're so strange looking. Are all humans so small?"

"Yes," Brock answered, before Zed could respond. "What were you doing there, with the tree?"

The night elf smiled. "This sapling is meek. It sees the towering plants around us and worries that it will never grow tall. I gave it confidence."

"Using magic?" Zed asked.

The woman's brow furrowed as the question was echoed in her tongue. Her head tilted curiously. "Magic? The sapling doesn't need borrowed power from other planes. It must nourish its own anima, or it will never grow strong enough to survive."

"Anima . . ." Zed breathed. "It *is* like Micah's healing. They use anima to make the forest grow! Wait, trees have anima?"

The druid smiled bemusedly. "Everything has it. It fills the living. Before coming here, my people lived in a desert. Only the night offered us any safety from the heat of the sun. But druids can"—the spell lapsed again, and several words echoed out in a rush—"*arguewhisperfamilysingbroker* with the land. We wield the anima of our surroundings to guide and protect the natural world. Always carefully. Always taking only what we need."

"What can you do with it?" Brock asked. He had an inquisitive gleam in his eye. "Does it just make the plants grow?"

"That's one aspect of the art," the druid said, nodding. "We use what's available in the environment around us. We can coax a stubborn tree to action. . . ." She raised her hand, and a tree bough gently lowered from the canopy above, shimmering with light. Zed gasped with delight as it dropped a bright pink fruit right into her palm.

The druid took a bite. As he watched the juice drip down her chin, Zed's stomach quailed with hunger. "And sometimes we can ask natural animals to come to our aid. A swarm of wasps will usually scare off even the most persistent of monsters. And . . . if needed . . . we can even use it to redirect the elemental forces that surround us."

"Elemental?" Zed said.

The elven woman tilted her head again thoughtfully. "How to explain?" She held out the pink fruit, and Zed quickly snatched it up, taking a luxuriously large bite. It was sweeter than any apple he'd had in Freestone.

The druid moved to the edge of the stream that ran through the cobbles. She closed her eyes and held both hands over the clear water. Light shivered from the trees and grass and moss that surrounded her. Strings of brilliance reflected on the surface of the water, until the stream itself seemed to be cascading with brightness. Beneath the druid, the water swelled. It trickled upward, a reverse teardrop, then broke from the stream and ascended into the elf's waiting hands. The bubble floated just above her palms as a perfect sphere.

"Incredible," Zed gasped, forgetting the fruit in his own hand. "It's *just* like magic! I had no idea anima could do this."

The druid turned around, gently revolving her palms. The sphere floated higher still, rotating slowly and smoothly over her head. "Magic breaks the rules," she said. "It creates something from nothing by tearing holes between the *homebarriersacredworlds*. We use it sparingly. Anima bends without breaking, employing what we already have."

"The line between bending and breaking is not always clear, Lanaya." A deep voice echoed out from the parrot's claw in Zed's hand.

The druid yelped, losing her concentration, and the orb of water immediately burst, drenching her. Zed turned around to see the imposing figure of the night elves' leader towering over him and Brock. The leader's mask was back on, obscuring his expression.

"I'm so sorry, *masterfirsthighest* Prime Druid!" Lanaya said. "The foreigners were curious about our arts."

"And you were all too ready to show off your skills, weren't you? Pride is poison, Lanaya. It pollutes the land just as it pollutes us. Learn from the fall of Llethanyl."

The young elf had the good grace not to answer. Instead, she bowed her dripping head.

The Prime Druid—as the parrot's claw had dubbed him—glowered over Zed and Brock. At least Zed assumed he was glowering beneath the mask. "I request the presence of the would-be saviors of Llethanyl. Your Prime, the Sister of Light, has made me a challenge. You will be there to witness her defeat." With that, the Prime Druid stalked away, not bothering to wait and see if the two boys followed.

"Oh, no, Liza," Brock said. "What have you done?"

They arrived at what had once been a massive circular amphitheater. The great stone steps leading down to the center were lined with cushions of moss. Hundreds of small glowing toadstools formed a ring around the space. But the true spectacle was what rose from the stage.

An enormous mushroom grew in the center of the concentric

stone bands. Its cap towered over the amphitheater, resting atop a massive twisting stem. Gazing up, Zed could see swirling, multicolored lights in the gills, which illuminated the space in unearthly hues. Glittering spores fell gently from the mushroom's cap, raining starlight upon the crowds of elves who lounged on the steps.

Zed stopped cold once he caught sight of the enormous toadstool. His mouth fell open.

"Wow." Brock didn't so much say the word as breathe it. The amphitheater had a hushed, serene quality. Fireflies danced around, winking playfully between the clusters of elves.

"This is the *mothersunsetsafetyreaper* Crepuscule." Lanaya spoke from behind them, the words echoing through the parrot's claw. "Our ancestors brought its spores with us from the desert and spread them here. When the spores grew, they knew this place would be a safe home for us."

"It's incredible." Zed shook his head. "Those spores . . . are they safe?"

Lanaya laughed obligingly. "They are to us. The Crepuscule is what protects our people. The spores know us. We're immune to their effects. Monsters and strangers, however, become confused when they approach Duskhaven. The spores cloud their minds. They're gently turned away. If you hadn't been led here by the Prime Druid, you never would have arrived."

"I've never seen anything like it," Zed said. "Hexam would kill to get his hands on a sample."

"Hexam and a few others," Brock muttered. "Lanaya, this isn't a natural mushroom, is it?"

The elf shrugged. "It's protected our people for as long as we can remember. Some believe it first came from the plane of fairies—but many say the same is true of the elves, too. Perhaps we brought it with us." The druid's gaze rose appreciatively up the twirling stalk. "Our sagas don't tell of its beginnings. The Crepuscule's nature is in endings. It comes alive only as the sun sets, shining through the night. And when we die, our bodies are buried here, feeding the mushroom colony."

"It *eats* you?" Zed blurted out.

Lanaya nodded. "Eventually, yes. But only after we've passed. Funguses are the great decomposers. They're vital to the well-being of the land. In giving ourselves to the Crepuscule, we become a part of the power that protects Duskhaven." The elf's blue eyes slowly blinked. "It also wards us against *evilsmokepurple* necromancy. The elves of Llethanyl fear the long night. They refuse to speak of it, and preserve the bodies of their fallen, as if they'd never died. But ignoring something true doesn't make it untrue. Death is not an opinion."

Below them, the Prime Druid strode ahead, his long legs carrying him gracefully over the steps. Zed had been so preoccupied with the enormous toadstool that he'd failed to see his friends were all clustered at the bottom of it until just now. Liza stood with her arms crossed, while Jayna, Jett, and Micah sat nearby on one of the large steps. Zed searched around for Fel, and caught sight of her watching from the amphitheater's edge. Mousebane sniffed a glowing mushroom at her feet and gave it a tentative lick.

When the Prime Druid arrived at the amphitheater's basin, he turned and raised his hands into the air. He didn't acknowledge Liza standing just beside him. The small conversations throughout the space quieted.

The druid spoke in a booming voice, which was repeated from Zed's hand as the enchantment translated.

"These young strangers have wandered into our midst while chasing an impossible task. They wish to revive Llethanyl, a corpse that's long since dead." Murmurs of agreement rose from the night elves. "We have saved their lives and shown them hospitality, and yet still they ask more of us. They beg us to join them in their foolishness, and deliver our enemies from an unnatural fate they brought upon themselves."

Now the crowd began to shout, angry bursts of chatter too jumbled for the parrot's claw to translate. Zed got the general tone, however.

"But despite their foolishness," the Prime Druid boomed, cutting through the talk, "the strangers' Prime is bright. In acknowledgment of a Sister of Light, I have agreed to honor her challenge."

"Sister of Light..." Zed said. "People keep saying that about Liza. What does it mean?"

Lanaya's eyes widened. "You truly can't see it? Your Prime

and her brother are *strongfamilyelf* shining with anima. It dazzles me just to look at them. The boy has already ripened—he reaches inward for his power—but your Prime's anima is still raw. If she were a druid, she'd be exceptional."

Brock was grinning down at the stage. "She's already pretty exceptional, to tell you the truth."

Liza uncrossed her arms, resting her hands on her hips. She scanned the crowd with a resolute expression, unfazed by both the taunts and strange compliments of the Prime Druid.

"If the Sister of Light can answer Afonso's Riddle," the druid said, "we will join the strangers in their futile mission."

Gasps went up from the crowd. Lanaya, too, sucked in a gulp of air. "But that's impossible," the enchanted claw muttered.

"If she fails," the Prime continued, "the humans will relinquish their weapons to us, and leave our home at once."

Brock slapped his palm to his forehead. "Did I say exceptional? Because what I meant was reckless, bullheaded, and suicidal."

The murmurs that rose from the crowd now were less ardent. The elves all turned to regard Zed's friends clustered together at the bottom step of the amphitheater. A voice cried out from the crowd, clear enough that the parrot's claw hummed in Zed's hand.

"But they're just children!" the claw translated.

The Prime Druid was unmoved. "These strangers would

have us fight and die for our enemies," he announced. "If they wish us to risk ourselves, then they must be willing to risk as well."

Liza took a step forward, staring stonily out into the audience. Then Zed saw her gaze find Fel, and Liza's eyes softened. "Llethanyl is not my city," she said, holding her own parrot's claw aloft to translate. "But like Llethanyl, *my* city is also imperfect. Its people can be cruel, its laws unjust."

Liza frowned, perhaps thinking of her own experience with Freestone's ban on female knights. "But it's also filled with goodness," she called. "With acts of kindness and grace. A city isn't just one thing. It contains us—people—and all the many things we are. As long as the elves of Llethanyl survive, the city is not a corpse. That's why we're willing to risk ourselves for it."

She turned to the Prime Druid, squaring her shoulders. "Ask me your riddle."

The druid inclined his head, his mask dramatically blank. "What contains vast distances, hidden in its heart? And has many siblings, more through mishap than by art? Once solved, it dies, but you can resurrect it with a tie."

"Did . . . did the translation spell just *rhyme*?" Zed whispered. "Jayna's magic is starting to intimidate me."

"To be fair, that last one was more of a slant rhyme," Brock whispered back.

Liza's face clouded as she considered the riddle.

253

Zed's mind was doing loops just trying to remember the first line. *Contains vast* what *in its* where?

"This is impossible!" he hissed, just as Liza stepped forward.

"The answer is 'a knot,'" she called.

The Prime Druid inclined his head once again. At the bottom of the amphitheater, Jayna, Jett, and Micah burst into cheers and applause.

But none of the elves stirred. They continued to watch the stage expectantly. Zed turned to find Lanaya was biting her lip.

The Prime nodded to someone waiting at the amphitheater's edge. Two elven druids hustled toward the stage, carrying a large flat shape between them.

The druids set down two wooden stakes, intricately decorated with carved leaves and flowers. Between the stakes was the thickest nest of vines that Zed had ever seen. Even from where he and Brock stood at the outer edges of the arena, he could tell that each vine was covered in sharp-looking thorns. Together they formed an impenetrable knot of vegetation, with a long elliptical shape contained within its center.

"What's happening?" Liza asked. "I answered Afonso's Riddle. Now return our gear and help us stop the Lich."

Deep rumbles of laugher echoed from behind the Prime Druid's mask. "That was not the riddle, human. It was merely an introduction." He turned toward the audience and raised his hands. The long sleeves of his robe billowed down to reveal ropy, muscled arms.

"When our people first came to these lands," the Prime Druid called, "it was to war against the profane *ain'shea* and cowardly *cel'shea*. But then the world tore open, and old conflicts were superseded by the necessities of survival. Our founder, Afonso the Green Knight, led us to the ruins of this city. Together with his druids, he slew the monsters that dwelled within. He spawned the Crepuscule and shielded our people from the unnatural horrors that plagued them, until it was strong enough to protect us on its own. And when the long night finally came for him, as it does for us all, the green knight laid down his sword."

The druid turned, motioning toward the knot of vines. "*This* is Afonso's Riddle. For over two centuries, the blade has been hidden within. Crafted by the cleverest druids, its roots fed by the green knight's own blood, the riddle has remained unsolved since its growth. Only one worthy of Afonso's legacy will be able to untangle the knot." The Prime Druid turned to Liza and nodded in mock respect. "*This* is the question I set before you."

The amphitheater was completely quiet. Liza stepped toward the mass of briars. She reached a hand tentatively forward, then hissed, pulling her finger away.

The Prime Druid chuckled beneath his mask. "I would offer you gloves for the task, but you'd find them little help. The riddle's thorns are sharper than mythril. Even thick cloth will be as water to them."

"It's sort of unfair that he gets to keep using all these metaphors," Brock muttered.

Liza frowned at the druid, then turned back to Afonso's Riddle. She rounded the cluster of vines, searching for a weak spot. She reached in again . . . slowly . . . hesitantly. . . .

"Prime Druid!" Beside Zed, Lanaya stepped forward.

All around the amphitheater, night elves began muttering. The Prime's mask turned, those two slits regarding her coldly.

Lanaya wavered, then took a deep breath. "Please, let these children forfeit!" she called. "The Sister of Light means us no harm. Afonso's Riddle was made to be unsolvable. It's a weapon, not a question. This isn't a fair challenge!"

The Prime Druid stalked to the edge of the stage. "The challenge matches the request!" he boomed.

"The riddle will kill her! Its thorns are poisoned!"

Brock let out a little gasp. Zed's gaze snapped back to the stage, where Liza stood wide-eyed.

The Prime rolled his shoulders, then turned his masked face from Lanaya, back to Liza.

"The challenge stands," he growled.

"Liza!" Fel's voice rang out from the other side of the amphitheater. Zed and Brock both turned in time to see the young ranger snatch a bow fluidly from the hands of one of the elven archers, then aim it toward the stage. She loosed her arrow.

"Zed!" Fel shouted. "Fire!"

Zed wasted precious moments figuring out what Fel meant, then precious more stumbling forward and raising his hand into the air. The missile sailed over the heads of the night elf spectators.

I can't make it, Zed realized. *It's too far!*

Then he felt the chain around his neck grow warm. And suddenly—as if by magic—Zed knew that he *could* make it. He summoned his mana, already boiling with anticipation, and pointed his hand to the arrow. A green streak exploded from Zed's palm, blasting upward. It met the arrow with perfect precision, just as the missile curved downward, then landed with a *thuck* at Liza's feet.

"What is this?" The Prime Druid's voice echoed out from the parrot's claw. "Take that weapon from her!"

There was an uproar as night elves descended upon Fel. Mousebane let out a shrill, then attacked two of the archers as they approached. The cat launched herself up one archer's leg, clawing the poor elf in a blaze of fur and fury, before leaping onto the face of another.

At the bottom of the amphitheater, Liza gazed down at the burning arrow at her feet. Then, before the Prime Druid could stop her, she snatched it up from the ground and lunged forward, positioning the arrowhead as she would a blade. She stabbed it into the vines. There was a great *whoosh!* and a flash of light as the green flames caught, burning quickly through the riddle. Liza waited only half an instant before she plunged her hand into the center of the charred briars, bracing her leg against a wooden stake, and yanked. With a cry, she tore something free of the vines.

All around them, the commotion suddenly quieted. The

archers restraining Fel let their arms drop, now staring wide-eyed at Liza. The entire glittering arena was silent once again.

Liza raised her arm into the air. It was singed and blackened with ash; her skin smoked all the way up to her elbow.

And clutched in her hand was a gleaming green sword.

Chapter Sixteen

Brock

The moment Liza lifted the sword, Brock steeled himself for a fight.

If he'd stopped to think about it, he wouldn't have liked their odds. Seven against a city, unarmed except for an ancient sword and whatever mana Zed and Jayna had left in them. And even if they fought their way free of the city, they'd be lost in a dark forest, knee-deep in snow, surrounded by the undead.

But Brock didn't stop to think about the odds. He clenched his fists and dug his feet in and said to Zed, "Get ready."

No one in the amphitheater moved, though, aside from a few druids leaning in to whisper furiously with their Prime while two others, wary now of provoking Mousebane, cautiously took the bow from Fel. She didn't resist, nor did she do much to suppress the pleased look on her face. Brock was used to seeing her smile, but now she displayed what he could only call a self-satisfied smirk.

He really did have the coolest friends.

Liza lowered the sword and turned toward the Prime. Her expression was placid, showing the respectful poise she would have been forced to learn as a young noble. Brock could see in her body language, though, just how thrilled she was. It must have been all she could do not to pump her fist in the air and whoop in victory.

The Prime Druid, on the other hand, radiated disappointment. Brock had to wonder if the elf had a different mask for less solemn occasions. The eye slits on this one fairly dripped with scorn.

"You have failed our challenge," he said, and Brock found himself gripping his parrot's claw tight enough to hurt.

"Excuse me?" Liza said, her poise dropping in an instant. She kept the sword nonthreateningly at her side, but pointed at it with her free hand. "Riddle solved, I'd say."

"You cheated," the Prime said.

"She didn't," Micah said, rising to his feet. "Among my sister's many shortcomings is that she *never* cheats. She didn't break any rules that were presented to her."

"And she was wise enough to use the greatest tool at her disposal," Jett added.

"Teamwork!" Jayna trilled.

"Right, teamwork," Jett said quickly, rubbing the back of his neck. "I was going to say *teamwork*, not *mystical fire*."

"Maybe this is what Afonso intended to teach you—teach *us*," Fel offered, raising her voice louder than Brock had ever heard it. She opened her hands in a gesture that was part plea, part invitation. "That there are problems you can't solve on your own. That you have to work with others, people who see things differently than you do, in order to overcome life's greatest challenges."

Murmurs swept through the crowd, and Brock saw Lanaya nodding vigorously. He could feel the druids being swayed. They *wanted* to celebrate the riddle being solved.

The Prime quashed those murmurs with a forceful sweep of his hand. "Do not put words into the mouth of our champion," he said hotly. "Afonso gave his life so that we might live free. If he taught us *anything*, it is that we are better off alone." His gaze swept across the amphitheater, trailing past Zed and Brock before returning once more to Fel. "None of you are welcome here. You must leave this place at dawn." He turned to go, but paused, his eye slits turning to Afonso's sword. "And take that tainted relic with you. Consider it the *only* aid you shall receive from Duskhaven."

"Well, the hospitality was nice while it lasted," Brock grumbled.

They had been roughly escorted from the amphitheater,

their parrot's claws had been confiscated, and then they were deposited on a patch of spongy moss beneath a massive oak. Sentries were stationed at a short distance, marking the boundaries of their territory. The message was clear even without the aid of a translation spell: They were to stay put and stay quiet until morning.

Oddly, though the rest of their weapons remained confiscated, the druids had let Liza keep the sword. Brock remembered how the Prime had called it tainted. He wondered if that was how they all saw it—if the druids didn't care to even touch the sword now that she, a human, had pulled it from the thorns.

"I'm sorry, you guys," Liza said, turning the sword in her hand to catch a moonbeam. "I thought I could persuade the Prime to help us. When I pressed him on the issue, he asked if I was challenging his leadership, and I suppose when I said yes it became an actual, formal challenge. Maybe I should have backed down right then, but . . . oh, he just got my blood up."

"Liza, that was totally reckless," Zed said through a huge smile. "It was also amazing and inspiring and a little bit funny. Brock and I loved every minute of it."

"Hey now," Brock said, and Liza looked at him as if daring him to disagree with Zed. Brock faltered. "I'll say *this* much: Frond will be proud."

"It's no wonder Liza was unafraid of the riddle," Jayna said primly. "When she's used to navigating such thorny compliments."

Jett laughed at that—a bit louder than was justified, Brock thought. And then Jayna blushed. And then Brock rolled his eyes back so far he plopped backward onto the moss. It was spongy, and Zed, who was sitting beside him, bounced in place.

"The moss will make a nice bed, at least," Jett said, easing himself down and slowly detaching his mythril leg, which was held in place with a series of leather straps and metal buckles. He sighed in relief, massaging his residual limb. "This will be a far sight better than camping in the snow."

"I can't imagine any of us is going to sleep a wink, though," Liza said. And then Micah's loud snoring came from several yards away, where he was sprawled out on his back and already drooling. "Other than him," she said. "Oh, to be carefree and young again."

"Aren't you, like, five minutes older than him?" Zed asked.

"It was a crucial five minutes," she answered. "I really made the most of them."

"I'll say," said Jett. "When the gods were handing out brains and Micah went for his share, they told him, 'Sorry, that girl who was just here took the last of them.'"

They all chuckled at that, except for Zed, who said, "Aw, he means well."

"Does he, though?" asked Brock from his pillow of moss. He looked over at Fel, who sat apart from the group, stroking Mousebane and apparently lost in thought. "What do you think, Fel? You've got the outsider's perspective."

Fel immediately burst into tears.

Hot panic coursed through Brock. Earlier, he'd been ready to take on dozens of armed druids without a prayer of winning. Now, confronted with a crying girl, he froze in place, utterly perplexed and terrified.

"Brock!" Liza chided.

"Honestly, Brock," Jayna chimed in. The girls went immediately to Fel's side, wrapping her in hugs and whispering soothing words.

Jett replaced his prosthetic, shaking his head sadly and clucking his tongue at Brock as he trailed after the girls.

"Oh, don't *you* start," Brock said. He turned to Zed. "What just happened?"

Zed sidled up close. "I think . . . I think Fel is maybe feeling a little out of place. I think maybe calling her an 'outsider' was the wrong thing to say."

Brock grimaced. "I only meant that she's new to our group."

"I know what you meant," Zed said. "I'm sure she did, too. But she's going to be a little sensitive after all this." He gestured to indicate their surroundings.

Brock studied his friend in silence. He considered himself good at reading people. But he could be careless and miss the important things that Zed often seemed to sense. It had always been that way. Brock could tell what people wanted. But Zed was better at seeing what they needed.

"What about you?" he asked Zed.

"Hmm?" said Zed.

"Are you feeling . . . sensitive? You always wanted to know more about the elves, but the more we learn . . . well. Nothing's really gone the way you must have imagined it would."

"It's strange," Zed said. "I spent so much time feeling like I didn't *fit* and just sort of assuming that meant I was in the wrong place. That it would be different with the elves somehow." He shrugged. "I guess elves are people, too. And people are imperfect."

Micah's snoring crescendoed, seemingly underscoring Zed's point.

"That includes me," Brock said with a sigh. "I'd better go apologize. With all the practice I've had this year, I think I'm getting pretty good at it."

"You're really not! Average at best!" Zed said cheerfully as Brock shuffled toward the phalanx of girls and cat and dwarf. They eyed him as he approached.

"Fel, I'm sorry," he said. "I absolutely didn't mean it. You're part of the team."

"Thank you," Fel said softly, but she didn't meet his eyes.

Liza and Jayna weren't as forgiving.

"We banish you," Jayna said, "to that side of the clearing."

She pointed right at Micah.

Brock turned to Jett for help, and the dwarf only shrugged.

"Get!" said Liza.

Brock sighed. He grabbed his pack and slunk sullenly toward Micah's sleeping form.

But Brock's "banishment" only made it easier for him to sneak away in the night.

Based on everything they'd seen, the guards would expect the adventurers to be loud and conspicuous. It made them careless; Brock slid past them without a problem. Zed even helped without meaning to. He was having some nightmare, and cried out briefly as he tugged at his collar in his sleep, drawing the guards' attention for just a moment.

Brock imagined Zed had experienced a lot of nightmares these past six weeks.

Brock had nightmares, too. A waking nightmare in which the Lady Gray demanded he find items of value in between fighting for his life against an endless parade of horrors. And having to do it all under Lotte's scrutiny.

But Lotte wasn't here now, was she?

He kept to the shadows, creeping as close to the center of town as he dared. Climbing a tree, he settled in on a sturdy branch, took the satchel from his shoulder, and opened it up toward the night sky.

That sky was full of Crepuscule spores. Spores that, through some glorious magic, kept this town and its people safe from their enemies. Safe even from the undead horde that thronged the woods just a half day's march away.

That was the sort of magic Brock could learn to like.

As his satchel filled, Brock smiled to himself. The druids had refused to help Llethanyl, but he could make certain they helped *him*. Whether they wanted to or not.

The Lady Gray would have her treasure.

They were escorted to the edge of the overgrown city at first light. Every one of them hesitated, contemplating the strange threshold where high summer gave way to the dead of winter. They layered on their winter gear under the careful watch of the druids, who finally returned their weapons. Zed hugged his scepter close, and Brock felt a palpable sense of relief to have his daggers back. He'd never have guessed he would grow so fond of them. But then, he'd never have guessed he'd be traipsing through a forest that was haunted by reanimated elf corpses.

"Join the Adventurers Guild," he muttered. "See the world."

Most of the druid escorts were masked sentries with bows, but several townsfolk trailed behind them, apparently interested in seeing the strangers off. Without the parrot's claws, Brock had no idea what any of them were saying to one another, but they looked solemn. Lanaya, the friendly druid who'd been so eager to discuss anima, was among them. She caught Brock's eye, gave a grim smile, and nodded. Her expression said, *Good luck*.

Brock nodded back, and he tried to use his eyes to communicate how certain he was that they were all going to die and then be raised as evil puppet corpses and sent back to Duskhaven and *then* wouldn't the druids be sorry? He wasn't confident she got the message.

"That place was super-boring," Micah said once they were off.

"Which place?" Liza asked. "Do you mean the hidden civilization that is staving off not just countless Dangers but also *all of winter* with the help of a massive glowing toadstool from the realm of the fairies? Is that the place you mean?"

"Got it on your first guess, sis," he said. "And since no one is asking the obvious question, I'll do it: Shouldn't we be heading back to Freestone at this point?"

"No way," Liza said. "Frond and the others will be waiting for us at the wayshelter. We need to regroup."

"And it's not any safer going in the other direction," Jayna said. "Those things were everywhere."

"By now, Lotte will have warned them that the Lich knows their plan," Liza said. "And they'll have come up with a *new* plan. Frond will know what to do."

Jett grunted. "Assuming we can find her."

"Jayna said their next stop was Celadon Falls, and I've been there with the rangers," said Fel. "We're far from any established trail, but I know what direction to go."

"As long as we give the ambush site a wide berth," Liza said, and Zed nodded in vigorous agreement.

As they walked, Brock pulled his cloak tight against the biting cold. The lingering warmth of Duskhaven was leeched away in moments.

He took a small object from his satchel, glancing over his shoulder to be sure no druids remained in view. "Hey, Fel," he said softly, drifting over to her side. "I got you a present."

He opened his hand to reveal a parrot's claw.

Fel's eyes squinted in confusion. "Oh," she said. "Thanks, but why . . . ?"

The parrot's claw translated her words into the *dro'shea* language.

"I woke up early this morning," he said, and he wrinkled up his nose and cast a glare Micah's way. "I know we didn't have time to learn much from the druids, and I thought . . . well, I thought maybe you'd have a use for a tool that can teach you literally any word in the almost-forgotten language of the night elves."

Fel stared at him, stunned.

"Uh, I know," Brock said. "Stealing is bad, but . . . it's the thought that counts?"

"Thank you," Fel said.

And the claw said, "*Savasche.*"

"*Savasche,*" Fel repeated, her eyes glimmering with tears.

Brock smiled. "You're welcome," he said.

And the claw said, *"Davos."*

"Friend," said Zed.

"Tanay."

"Brave," said Liza.

"Seebul."

"Fierce," said Jayna.

"Grishta."

"One of us," said Jett.

"Al de nos."

Micah opened his mouth to speak.

"Micah, please don't ruin the moment," Liza said quickly.

"Micah, *sahv nehro ta.*"

Brock laughed. "That's one we all need to remember."

Fel burst into tears again, but this time the tears were accompanied by a smile—that old familiar smile, returning for the first time in days. She threw her arms around Brock, and he hugged her back.

"See?" he said to Zed over her shoulder. "I told you I was getting the hang of apologizing."

Micah took a deep breath, turned toward the parrot's claw, and before anyone could stop him, he shouted: "POOP!"

The day's journey was difficult. Their brief evening of summer had been a cruel tease, and their bodies reacted poorly to the sudden return to winter, clenching and cramping against the icy wind and the deep drifts. Brock ached all over, and his thoughts had deadened to a low buzz in the back of his skull, when Fel finally pointed ahead and said, "There!"

Brock squinted against the chill, surprised to see a wash of color standing out among the endless white and gray. A hundred paces ahead, the flat stretch of snowy forest ended at a cliff— a tall, craggy outcrop of pearlescent green stone, with a small stream of water trickling down its face. That stream, he knew, would be a waterfall when spring came and melted all the snow.

"Celadon Falls," he said.

There was a door set right into the faint green rock of the cliff. It was unlocked, and opened easily. Unlike the last way-shelter they had visited, this one had been recently accessed.

"Eyes open, everyone," Liza said. "I'll take lead. *Don't* touch any treasure chests."

"And don't let any treasure chests touch you," Brock added. He trailed behind the others, hanging back a moment to check that his satchel was intact and dry.

He'd stolen more than a parrot's claw from the druids, after all, and the contents of his satchel might very well be priceless.

"There's no one here," Liza said. "We didn't beat them here, did we? We couldn't have."

Brock caught up, descending the stairs and stepping into a large room with roughly hewn walls of stone.

"It's empty," he said.

"That's what I *just* said, Brock."

"No, I mean there's *nothing* here." He tapped an empty weapons rack. "We're supposed to keep the wayshelters stocked at all times. This one's been cleared out."

"Frond left a note," Jayna said, returning from an adjacent room with a sheet of paper. Her face was stricken, and she hesitated to say more, casting a furtive and sorrowful look at Fel. Finally she handed the note over to Liza. "It's addressed to you."

"'We've joined up with Lotte,'" Liza read aloud. "'If you see this, you must turn around. Get Zed and the others back to Freestone immediately.'" She let the paper fall from her fingers. "It says, 'The mission is over. Llethanyl is a lost cause.'"

Chapter Seventeen
Zed

The apprentices puttered glumly around the wayshelter, gathering their gear, adjusting their cloaks, and generally delaying their departure. The journey back to Freestone would be long and cold. It would be filled with Dangers of all sorts, though especially with undead ones, and there wasn't a single adult to guide or protect them.

It would also be a journey tinged by defeat. Llethanyl was gone. A new city full of elves had been discovered, and yet it had banished the apprentices within a night. Zed doubted the Sea of Stars would ever find their way there again.

Despite these losses, Fel seemed to be all out of tears. She stood quietly now by the wayshelter's door, staring out into bleak whiteness.

Zed tried not to think about his own disappointment. A knot had clinched inside his chest. His father's city was truly lost to him. Forever.

"I can't believe Frond would just give up," Liza said. She paced the length of the chamber, opening and closing her fists. The green sword gleamed at her hip. "A lost cause? We haven't even tried yet!"

"Something must have happened," Jett said. "They must have gotten some new information." The dwarf sat on a cot, adjusting the linen sock he wore as a liner beneath his prosthetic. Jayna had absconded with the mythril leg some time ago—"to perform a small test," she'd said—retreating into the wayshelter's side room. Zed could sense waves of magic coming from beyond the closed door, thick with the smell of mint.

"Oh, I'll bet they got some new information," Zed muttered. "Like that the queen is lying."

All eyes in the room focused on him, and Zed's ears flared with heat.

"What do you mean?" asked Liza.

Zed sighed. "Callum told me something just before the dead attacked. He said Queen Me'Shala wasn't being honest with us. He didn't have time to say about what."

Liza blinked at him. "And you're just telling us this *now*?"

"A lot's happened, okay?"

"Fel, any ideas?" Liza said, glancing to the doorway.

The night elf shrugged, her eyes thoughtful. "I'm not what you'd call part of the queen's inner circle. Callum never mentioned anything, but he can be a secretive elf."

Zed snorted, and Fel glanced at him.

"Sorry," Zed mumbled. "The cold is getting to my sinuses."

"Frond almost turned us around once already," Micah said. He was lounging in one of the wayshelter's hammocks, arms crossed behind his head. "After we spotted that mountain monster. This plan was always crazy. We should have waited for King Freestone."

"Waited for him to what?" Brock said. "Kick the elves out on their backsides? He was never going to send his precious Stone Sons out beyond the wards. The longer we waited, the worse things got."

"Yeah, and this has improved the situation so much," Micah drawled.

"Well, it's nice to have you two back on opposite sides of an issue, at least." Liza stopped pacing and shook her head. "There's nothing for it, is there? Fel, I . . . I'm so sorry."

"Me too," the night elf said. She closed her eyes, and a frigid breeze crept in from the open doorway, rustling her braids. Mousebane ambled unhappily away from the chill. "Despite what I said in Duskhaven, Llethanyl has always been my home. To be so close and then retreat. It burns."

At the word *burns*, Zed automatically touched the chain around his neck.

He'd had the nightmare again, back in Duskhaven, just before they set off. In his dream the chain became scorching hot, smoldering with an unnatural fever. Once again the clasp had disappeared, so Zed couldn't remove the necklace, no matter how desperately he clawed at it. The fox charm had burned even further than last time. In this dream, it was little more than a smoking lump.

And at the end of the nightmare, Zed was again visited by the watcher. A fiery green fox attended his struggle, observing the scene with burning eyes.

Only this time, before Zed awoke, the fox had spoken.

"*Zed . . .*" Its voice was an echo, delivered from a parched throat. The words were so faint that Zed could barely understand them, but the fox's eyes widened, shining with intensity. It had a message for him and it *would* be heard. "*The fire . . . it burns, Zed. It—*"

Which was when Zed had been booted awake by Micah, and not gently.

Before joining the Sea of Stars, Zed had never been given to eerie or prophetic dreams. In fact, two months before this, his most common dreams had involved eating alarming quantities of candy. But the last time he'd dreamed something this strange, a witch had eventually come to him with an offer to save his city.

Zed had seen enough strangeness by now to trust that these nightmares meant something. And as soon as he and Brock could get a quiet moment, Zed would tell him everything.

Together, they would figure this out.

The door to the side room burst open, and Jayna's alarmed face startled Zed from his worries.

"Jayna, if you're done *testing* my leg," Jett said, "I sort of need it to get back to Freestone."

"We aren't *going* to Freestone!" The girl rushed to Jett, absently handing him the mythril pylon. Then she spun around and held out her other hand toward Liza. "Look what I found balled up and half burned in the back room!"

Liza took a charred slip of paper from Jayna's hand, scrunching her nose in confusion. "This handwriting is terrible," she said. "It's . . . Frond's." She began reading. "'Liza, Celadon wayshelter is not safe. We've joined with Lotte, but the team was forced to move on. Do not tarry here. Bring Zed and the others and join us at Llethanyl.'" Her eyes widened, rising slowly from the page. "'Once you arrive, we'll retake the city. . . .'"

"But if *that* note's from Frond . . . ?" Jett muttered. His dazed expression mirrored Liza's.

"She might have written the second one later." Micah hopped out from the hammock. "*After* she decided to head back to Freestone." But even he looked unsure.

"And then hid her own first note, after trying to burn it?"

Jayna said. "I found it stuffed behind a cot." She grabbed the undamaged paper from the table—the missive telling them to return to Freestone—and rushed it over to Zed. "Smell this," she said.

"No thank you," Zed demurred. "I don't think Frond's washed her hands *once* since we left—"

"Magic!" Jayna said exasperatedly, pushing the note forward. "There are spells to replicate a person's handwriting. Magical plagiarism was a big problem in the Mages Guild."

Zed's eyes brightened and he took the sheet, holding it under his nose. Sure enough, a crisp note of mint wafted up from the page. "There *is* magic!"

"Wait, hold on," Brock said. "What was that bit about the wayshelter being unsafe, though?"

Suddenly, Mousebane shot up, the fur on her tail exploding out into a bludgeon of fluff. She yowled and hissed at the wayshelter's open front door, claws out and scratching at the air.

"Fel . . ." Liza warned, pulling her sword free from her belt. "Maybe you should bolt the door."

But the young elf was already backing away, a look of deep shock on her face. "Oh, no," she whimpered. "No, it can't be."

There was a loud creak as the wayshelter's front door edged open. Purple light spilled into the cramped space, radiating from a tall, ragged figure. The elven ghost was almost transparent, just as the *ban'shea* had been, but gripped within its hand was a very solid-looking longsword, rusted and pitted by use. Its head lolled slightly to one side, and two milky eyes stared blankly forward. The very sight of it seemed to drain the strength from Zed. His arms grew heavy, and his vision blurred.

"A wraith," Fel said. "A spirit of despair, risen to haunt the living. I saw some of them drain the life from their own family members as they fled the city. And this one . . . it looks like . . ."

Once, the male elf's skin had been dark, his long braided hair streaked with silver. Now, the wraith seemed to be fraying at the edges. Its feet floated inches above the floor. The ghost raised its free hand and pointed a thin finger right at Fel.

"My father," Fel finished.

"Zed!" Liza shouted. "Fire!"

Zed could barely hear the order. Something about the presence of the Danger filled him with gloom, sapping him of the will to move. He fought against the torpor. Zed raised his scepter, drawing upon his mana, and sent a gush of green flames pouring out. It billowed uselessly over the wraith, which barely seemed to notice. Its empty eyes just followed Fel as she retreated farther back into the room.

"*Felasege* . . ." A rasping voice issued out from the Danger, though its desiccated mouth never opened. "*Where are you? Do not be afraid. There is no pain.*"

"Father," Fel said, shaking her head. "What has the Lich done to you?"

"*No pain,*" the wraith repeated. "*Felasege . . . Am I here? I feel . . . nothing at all.*" Then it raised its rusted longsword high into the air and lurched forward with shocking speed.

Jayna weakly lifted her hands to conjure a Wizard's Shield, but fell to her knees. All around Zed, the other apprentices were similarly slumping over, suffering from the Danger's sapping presence. With a cry of effort, Jayna threw her hands up again, and a barrier blossomed in front of the ghost, pungent with magic. The wraith's blade careened violently off the shield and ricocheted away, but despite the elf's thin frame and wasted arms, it held firm to the blade. Slowly, with a piercing sound, it dragged the sword back across the floor to its side.

"*Daughter . . . where are you?*"

The ghost jerked forward again. It wavered for a moment at the magic barrier, as if pushing against a great wind. Then the wraith flickered through the shield, passing bodilessly to the other side. The rusted blade clattered to the floor behind it.

"*Why do I feel nothing?*" The wraith raised both hands, its fingers fumbling blindly through the air. It shivered, then jerked toward Fel.

"Stay back!" Jett shouted, somehow finding the strength to step between them. The dwarf swung his hammer in front of him, but it passed right through the figure and pitched Jett into the cots along with it.

Now nothing stood between the ghost and Fel. It hovered inches away from her. Fel sank back against the wall with wide, fearful eyes. The wraith bent forward, its long fingers reaching, as if to caress her face.

"FelasaaaaaaaaHHHHHHH!"

There was an explosive rush of amber light, so dazzling against the purple that for a moment Zed was blinded. He held his hand up against the glare, before thinking to question how he even had the strength to do so. Where the aura of the ghost had drained him, this new light flooded him with vitality. Zed leaped up to his feet, and saw the others were as well. Liza, Brock, Jayna, and Jett. Everyone except . . .

Micah stood behind the ghost, his fist extended and outlined in brilliant gold light. It looked like he'd punched right through the wraith. Where his arm made contact with it, the Danger's shape began to bubble, then fizzle away into purple smoke.

"I feel . . . warm," the wraith rasped. *"Fel, I . . . I can see you. How beautiful you've . . ."*

But before it could finish, the specter dissolved completely away, leaving only an echo and a wisp of vapor.

Slowly, the glow outlining Micah's hand faded, and he slumped forward unsteadily, panting. His hair was slick with sweat, as if he'd just finished a particularly punishing day of Lotte's drills.

"Micah!" Zed rushed to the boy, with Liza just beside him. The two managed to lower him onto a nearby cot, while Jayna hurried to Fel and wrapped a cloak around her shoulders.

"What," exclaimed Brock, "was *that*?"

Jett shook his head in wonder. "Zed's fire couldn't touch the ghost, but Micah . . . Did you destroy it with a *healing punch*?"

"Take a moment," Liza said to her brother. "Catch your breath."

"No time," Micah huffed. "Unfortunately, you dweebs were right again. We have to get to Lletherol."

"Llethanyl," Zed corrected.

"Whatever. I think . . . I think that I might be the best chance we have of saving the city."

They wasted no more time. As soon as Micah could stand, the apprentices gathered their gear and left the wayshelter, edging carefully around the milky green stone. Fel led them forward, her eyes scanning the woods. Even Mousebane insisted on walking on her own four feet, keeping a watchful eye on their surroundings.

Zed had imagined that Fel would lead them back to the Broken Roads, but instead she guided the team through snowy woodlands, saying it would be better to avoid the obvious path. Eventually the trees opened into a sprawling steppe.

The snow was thinner here, and the plain was blanketed with dry grass that came up to Zed's knees. It billowed and whistled in the wind, slowing their progress, but Zed found he could see far into the distance. It was an odd, heady experience—to see so far, with no walls or trees to interrupt the view.

Every now and then, Fel stopped the group to survey the area, ordering the others low while she and Mousebane scanned the horizon. Hours passed without a single undead sighting.

A stark line of mountains loomed in their path, much closer than Zed had realized from the forest. He'd never been so close to anything so colossal. The enormity of those peaks made him feel strangely fragile. Zed remembered the Danger they'd seen— the one that had looked like a mountaintop from far away. The sheer scale of such a creature had nearly drowned him in dread.

The world was *so much* bigger than Zed. Than all of civilization combined, he imagined. These mountains had seen the rise and fall of kingdoms. They had witnessed the Day of Dangers, and any number of calamities before it. Now they watched a train of children marching across the valley, children who hoped that by some miracle they could save one precious city from the same fate that had befallen so many others. That would eventually befall every city, in time. The fact that Zed was here at all, walking this journey and taking this in, seemed itself like a sort of miracle.

The apprentices were all quiet. Liza walked at the rear of the line, with Micah huffing just in front of her. Zed marched behind Fel, watching her long steps and determined gaze. In that moment, she reminded him very much of Callum.

"Fel, are you all right?" Zed ventured, calling over the wind.

"Hmm? Oh yes. Fine." The girl turned and the hardness in her face melted away for a moment, winter flowering into summer. But Fel couldn't sustain the smile for long. It was gone before she'd turned away.

"It's fine if you're not all right, you know," Zed said. "You've had . . . a bad week."

Fel coughed out a laugh that seemed on the verge of caving in.

"Do you want to talk about him?" he pushed on. "About your father?"

Fel's gaze became vague, and her eyebrows scrunched together. "We're almost to Llethanyl. Maybe there will be time to talk when this is all over."

"He really seemed to love you. Even after . . . Well, even now."

"That wasn't really him," Fel said huskily. She breathed out a blossom of steam that blew away as soon as it had formed. "A ghost is just an echo, some strong emotion the person harbored in life that Mort's energy latches on to."

"Then that strong emotion must have been love," Zed said. "Because the ghost seemed to love you a lot."

Fel hesitated, then nodded slowly. "And the Lich used that against us. Against me." She subtly wiped at her eyes.

Zed frowned, his mind whirring. Fel was right. The Lich had known to target her, and right where she'd be.

"What about you, then?" she asked. "Do you want to talk about your father . . . or Callum?"

"You know what?" Zed said. "I think you're right. Let's save the father talk for later."

This time when Fel laughed, it sounded a bit surer. "Let me just say this one thing. . . ." The girl bit her lip nervously, but then sighed and nodded. "Callum can be . . . oh, what's the human word? Locked? Cagey! He feels everything intensely, but he keeps those emotions bottled up. I used to think it was because he's the High Ranger, but I've changed my mind. I think something hurt him a long time ago. Hurt him more than he could handle. And I think he's been running from that hurt ever since."

Zed frowned hard at the grass whipping across his legs, his eyes tracking each step as he took it.

"He volunteered to lead your apprentice journey," Fel continued. "And let me tell you a little secret about Callum: He is *not* the type to babysit. He's been watching out for you in his own way." Fel's eyes flicked back to Zed, then down to the rustling grass that indicated Mousebane prowling below. "You and I both know what it's like to lose family, Zed. To wish we had just one more chance to see them, to hug them . . . to forgive them. If a chance like that presents itself, don't miss it."

In that moment, Zed resolved that he wouldn't.

After a time, Fel raised her hand, making a sharp hissing sound with her teeth. Zed and the others dropped immediately, crouching in the reeds. Fel pointed to a spot in the distance.

Squinting, Zed could just make out a line of about a dozen

figures. He couldn't see many details, but their movements left little doubt as to what they were. The figures lurched and swayed—the same strange, uneven gait Zed had seen among the undead during the attack on camp.

The apprentices waited a long while for the figures to move across the steppe, barely daring to breathe. And they waited even longer after they'd disappeared into the distance.

Finally, Fel rose, signaling forward with two fingers. Zed and the others followed without a word.

Eventually they arrived at the mountainside, where the grass cleared and Zed's feeling of smallness multiplied. Looking up, he found himself awash with vertigo, even with his feet planted firmly on the ground. Fel led the team to a cleft in the mountain, where a single skeletal tree was perched, as if in vigil.

"This is one of the back ways into the city," Fel said, once the team had all gathered around the tree. "We've gotten lucky so far, but once we enter here, Llethanyl will be swarming with the dead."

Micah searched around, taking in the apparently solid mountainside and single tree. "You *want* me to make a snide comment, is what's happening here—before you pull whatever magic branch opens the mountain. I'm not going to fall for it."

Fel *did* look slightly disappointed. "Llethanyl is situated in a valley on the other side of the mountain. There are several entrances in or out, where our mages distorted space to allow groups to slip through. This is one of the lesser known entrances. Callum's tracks lead here."

"I didn't notice any tracks," Brock said.

Fel smiled. "No, you wouldn't have. He left them for *me* to find." She stepped to the tree and placed her palm against the bark. "*Lleth anyl,*" Fel said somberly.

"*Lleth elan,*" a rich elven voice answered. Zed caught a sharp whiff of magic just as the stones behind them began to change. The mountainside warped, like a puzzle where a simple shift in perspective revealed new shapes hidden in the relief. Once, gray crags of rock had attended them, but now an enormous arch towered over the apprentices. Fel turned, eyeing the great door appreciatively. It loomed ten feet tall and was decorated with a tree and a crown of birds.

"He's been here," she said. "And recently. Let's hope we aren't walking into an ambush." She pushed against the door, and it swung open with a ponderous sound. Fel disappeared inside.

Zed glanced back at the others, who were all still staring up at the archway. Then he followed Fel into the dark.

And it was dark. As soon as he'd stepped into the tunnel, or whatever it was, the world went totally black. Zed turned around to find the entrance had disappeared, leaving him immersed alone in the gloom. Panic clenched immediately at his throat.

"Fel?" Zed called.

"I'm right here!" The night elf's voice echoed from up ahead. "It's all part of the enchantment. Just keep moving."

"Where are you guys?" Jett's voice hailed from nearby. "It sounds like you're right next to me."

"We are," Fel said. "We're all here together, but the spell makes us feel alone. Follow the sound of my voice."

Zed took a tentative, terrified step forward. Walking in pure darkness felt unnatural. He waved his arms around him, expecting to encounter walls of some kind—the rocks of the mountain at least—but his fingers passed through empty air.

"Keep moving," Fel said. "It's not very far. It's important not to dawdle on the path. Getting lost *is* possible, and it's not a good idea." Then she began to sing. It was a cheerful little song in the elven language, and though Zed couldn't understand a word of it, it comforted him just to hear Fel's voice.

So Zed moved, though every part of him screamed not to. One foot in front of the other, he trudged through the darkness.

"This is *fascinating* magic," Jayna's voice called out. "I've never seen anything like it."

"It's a very ancient spell, I think," Fel answered, pausing in her singing. "Like Freestone's wards, our mages feed mana into it regularly. It's just *one* of the magical protections my people use."

"The darkness is intense," Micah said. "I can't blast through it."

"Micah!" Liza barked. "Stop. Wasting. Your anima!"

"Sorry, *Mom*."

"We're here, anyway," Fel said. "Just a few more steps."

It didn't take Zed even that long. One step and suddenly the black curtain was pulled away. For a moment, the light was overwhelming. Zed squinted against it. Then, muddy shapes took form. Fel stood in front of him, beaming, and behind her Zed noticed other figures gathered together behind a stone outcropping.

Frond caught sight of him first. She nodded, looking even more ragged than the last time he'd seen her. A dark stain of *something* had caked over her leathers. Hexam was bandaging Lotte, who grimaced and gingerly held her arm aloft.

Behind them, the elven retinue were huddled together: Queen Me'Shala, Selby, Threya, and Callum, all currently engaged in what looked like an intense discussion.

A wide valley glutted with trees expanded into the distance, but above Zed rose the most spectacular skyline he had ever witnessed. Llethanyl was a city cut from glass. Its towers sparkled under the gray sky like multicolored crystals. Silken canopies waved gently in the wind, and an enormous oak tree climbed up from the city's center, a great hand reaching into the air. The tree was bare now in winter, but hundreds of lanterns, intricately folded to look like birds, drifted among its branches.

For all its beauty, however, Llethanyl was empty of life. The lanterns were dark and the city intensely quiet, except for the wind howling through the valley. Squinting into the distance, Zed couldn't spot a single moving figure. It was an exquisite ruin: pale and lovely and totally dead.

Callum glanced distractedly from his conversation, turned back, then whipped around again. His phosphorescent eyes radiated relief. The High Ranger burst away from the queen, and in just a few loping steps had made his way to Zed, wrapping him in an embrace that felt downright familial.

"You're safe," Zed heard him whisper, muffled by his shoulder. "Thank you, thank you, thank you."

"Callum," Fel said. "We have so much to tell you. There's a city of—"

"Just a moment," Callum said. "I want to hear everything, I do, but the situation here is complicated." He pulled away from Zed, his large eyes wet with emotion.

Frond joined them, placing her soiled hand right on Zed's shoulder. He tried not to imagine what the stain was. "Did you all make it?" she said. "Every apprentice?"

Zed nodded, turning around. "We all made it," he said. Behind him, the others were congregated together, staring wide-eyed at the city that rose above them. Liza, Micah, Jayna, and Jett. And . . .

Zed turned, searching the outcropping.

"Brock," he said. "Wh-where's Brock?"

Brock Dunderfel was gone.

Chapter Eighteen

Brock

The darkness spoke to Brock in his father's voice.

It wasn't anything so dramatic as a wraith. But in that dark space, in the utter absence of all light and sound, Brock felt fear blossom in his chest like a flower of ice. The tiny voice in the back of his head, the one that spoke up whenever he doubted himself, was now all he could hear. And that voice just happened to sound an awful lot like his dad.

Over the many years when Brock had been training for a place in the Merchants Guild, his father had been on constant guard against Brock's attempts to cut corners. With summer outside his window and the children of Freestone running free, Brock would do anything he could to get through his assignments faster. But with speed came mistakes, and on more than one occasion Brock's haste had backfired. On those days he was forced to stay at his small desk performing calculations well past the time the sun disappeared below the town wall and lanterns were lit across the city. And his father would say *I hope you learned your lesson, son. There are no shortcuts in life.*

So it figured the one time he tried to take a magical shortcut through a mountain, he would get lost.

What would his father make of Brock's recent choices? Smuggling edible grass and monster guts for a black market shadow broker and her fallen magus was far from the life of stability and security toward which Brock had always been pushed. Then again, looked at another way, it was Brock's father who'd gotten him into this mess, in a transparent attempt to get in good with Lord Quilby.

A transparent and *successful* attempt. Leave it to the elder Dunderfel to get exactly what he wanted, even as the world burned all around him.

"Hello?" Brock called. "Anybody out there?"

Fel's singing had gone silent some time ago. It was difficult to say how long it had been; here, there was no context for time. It felt as if the darkness had somehow rushed in to fill the spot she had left. But the darkness was already everywhere. It was darker than the woods at night. Darker than a dungeon.

He wanted to turn back. Was that the spell influencing his mind, or his own fear? Either way, he would be defiant. He put one foot in front of the other, but had no sense of stepping forward. He thought about touching his face to make sure he was still there in the truest physical sense and not some disembodied consciousness, but he decided he really didn't want to know.

He had to get out of here.

He tried to will himself out of the darkness. Nothing. He focused on shuffling forward, but he no longer felt any ground beneath his feet. He couldn't tell if he was moving anymore, forgot what it felt like to walk. Brock's fear swelled into despair.

And then, there was a light: a slice of pure white in the blackness. And framed in the light was a girl with a sword.

She said his name, and it sounded like music.

Brock lunged for her, heedless of the blade, wrapping his arms around her waist. There was a popping sound, and his stomach lurched, and suddenly Brock's knees found hard stone and his eyes were dazzled with light.

While his eyes adjusted and his vertigo faded, he stayed on his knees and held on to Liza like his life depended on it.

"H-how long was I in there?" he asked. He shivered, his body prickling with gooseflesh where it met cool air.

"Like five seconds," Liza said dismissively, but she patted him affectionately on the head.

"It felt longer," he said, finally releasing her and rising slowly to his feet. "Did you . . . did you *cut* through the darkness?"

"I cut through a *spell*," Liza said excitedly. "The sword just sort of . . . pulled. I swear I could feel it guiding me. It was *amazing*." She stopped to look around her. "This is bad, though." She turned in a circle, and Brock blinked against the torchlight to take in their surroundings. Stone was all around them, but it wasn't the familiar gray stone of home or the cracked, mossy stone of Duskhaven. Everything was white—white, but with swirls of glittering silver where it caught the torchlight. And every surface was etched with intricate detail. There were recesses along the walls, like shallow doorways, just tall and deep enough that an adult could stand within them. But they stood empty, and the overall effect was of a vertical wave of marble, peaks and troughs dipping into shadow and lifting back again to the light in an unbroken pattern.

"It's beautiful," he said.

"It's wrong," Liza responded. "I was just with the others. We were outside. I came back for you . . . I thought we'd end up where I started, but who knows where that spell's brought us."

Brock shivered and held his hands up to a burning torch, but the flame produced no heat. It was no natural fire.

"Don't tell Zed," Brock said. "But I am really starting to hate magic!"

They both flinched as his voice echoed through the large space. They stood in silence as the echo died off, waiting to hear whether anything moved in response. But the place was as silent as a tomb.

And suddenly Brock knew that's exactly where they were.

"This is the mausoleum," he said. "Isn't it? This is where Llethanyl laid their dead to rest."

Liza pointed her sword at the ground, which was littered with broken pieces of white stone. Brock had assumed it was a deliberate choice, given the immaculate state of the walls and ceiling, but now he saw it in a new light. "Those hollows, the recesses all along the walls—they were sealed off once," Liza said. "Something broke in."

"Or broke out," Brock said, and he shuddered. "This is where the Lich got his army. All those dead elves just ... got up and walked out of here."

"Which means we can walk out of here, too." She waved her sword around in the empty air, probing for some sign of the spell that had deposited them here. "I keep hoping that Fel or the others will appear any second, but we have to accept the possibility that we're on our own."

Brock gestured toward a staircase. "I vote we go up."

Liza nodded and led the way upstairs to a nearly identical space. The shattered stone of the floor made their progress awkward; Brock could feel the jagged edges through his boots, and his ankles tilted this way and that with each step. But they crossed the room to another staircase and kept going.

In the next room, something was moving.

Here, one of the hollows still had its lid: an ornate piece of stonework with a carven image of an elf.

"Do you hear—?" Brock whispered, and Liza shushed him.

Suddenly the lid jolted as something on the other side pushed against it. Brock leaped away, reaching out for Liza without thinking. But the lid held.

"I guess that one's stuck," Liza said.

Brock realized he was gripping her arm, which among other things would interfere with her ability to stab their enemies. He reluctantly released her.

"Let's keep moving," he said, and they quickly crossed the room to the sound of the stone lid rattling in place.

The creature in that tomb had to have been there for weeks. It was stuck, but it wouldn't stop trying to escape. Brock considered each hollow they passed in the next room. Row after row of empty tombs in room after room, and each tomb represented an undead soldier in the Lich's army.

That army would not tire. It did not require food or drink or shelter from the cold. And seeing this place, the scale of it, Brock now realized that this unstoppable army numbered in the millions.

"We can't win," he said. "We can't beat this."

"We don't have to beat the army. Only the Lich."

"Right. That sounded only slightly impossible when we had a secret weapon. But Zed's fire didn't work on the wraith. What if it doesn't work on the Lich? What if we get close to it and all Zed manages to do is singe its robe and then we have to fight a newly angry Lich with a cloak of mystical fire?"

"Not to worry." Liza smiled. "I have a plan."

"Please tell me your plan isn't 'Micah walks up to the Lich and punches it with his healing fist.'"

Liza's smile went taut. "Sometimes the best plans are simple."

"And rarely do the best plans rely entirely on Micah."

They kept going. Brock wondered just how deep the elves had built. But whenever they came upon a set of stairs, they went up.

"What's that smell?" Brock asked. "It's familiar."

Liza nodded. "It's myrrh. They used it at the ceremony for the little boy."

"Right," Brock murmured. "To ward off evil, Fel said."

"That's a nice sentiment, but there's a more pragmatic reason for it," Liza said. "It covers the smell of . . . of rot."

Brock grimaced. "This is so wrong in so many ways," he said. "Why bury your dead like this to begin with? It doesn't even seem sanitary."

"It's tradition," Liza said. "Haven't you talked to Fel about it? From their perspective, it's far more natural than fire."

Brock shook his head. "I can't wrap my mind around it."

"That's the root of our problems though, isn't it? Freestone used to draw people from all over Terryn. But we're *all* from Freestone now. And it's like . . . all those different ways of doing things went away, and now we act like there's only one way. The Freestone way." She pursed her lips. "I thought people would be excited to learn from the elves, to consider other viewpoints. But that's not what happened."

"It's not just Freestone, though," Brock pointed out. "Llethanyl's obviously failed to move past a war that ended centuries ago. And those druids weren't exactly open to new ideas."

Liza smirked. "You're almost as protective of Freestone as you are of Zed."

"How could I not be? Freestone is . . . it's fierce. It's been staring down the end of the world for two hundred years and it hasn't blinked. How could you not love it?"

"But you talk about Freestone as if it's alive. As if Freestone itself is fierce, or brave, or ingenious. But cities can't be those things; you're talking about the people who live there. A place is only as good as the individuals who shape it. And when it came to the refugees . . . Freestone failed, Brock. The people and the king of Freestone, we all failed."

Brock couldn't disagree with that. But he chose not to voice his agreement, either, and silence settled over them as they ascended once more.

The room at the top of the stairs was empty, and Liza spoke again as they picked their way across more broken stone.

"And listen," she said. "I wanted to say . . . I know everything has changed recently, and changed fast. And maybe one of those changes is that Zed doesn't lean on you so much. But we *all* rely on you, Brock." She cleared her throat. "Me most of all."

Brock kept his eyes to the floor, as if very concerned with the possibility of tripping. "Okay," he said, knowing it was a completely inadequate response. But he felt emotion swirling in his stomach and his throat and up into his eyes, and he didn't quite trust himself to say more.

"You can lean on us too, sometimes, if you want," she said. "You don't have to fix every problem yourself." She paused. "Anyway, that's all I wanted to say."

Brock nodded.

The next level, at last, was different, the staircase leading them to a small antechamber. The stonework here was less ornate than elsewhere, and there was a single arched doorway. Elven script scrolled across the arch, and Liza pointed out one familiar word: *dro'shea.*

Beyond the threshold was a long stretch of hallway lined with skulls. The low ceiling was of that same familiar white stone, but the walls themselves were nothing but bone, skulls stacked atop one another like bricks, each of them jawless and hollow-eyed.

Brock wanted to ask what this meant. Were all night elves interred this way? Were these the remains of those elves lost in war, or to Dangers beyond the city, their bodies unrecoverable? Did the elves of Llethanyl do this to *punish* the night elves?

That thought was a sour one, and it lingered. If the elves truly believed in resurrection, then this was the cruelest punishment he could imagine.

He wanted to ask Liza what she thought, but the idea of speaking now felt somehow disrespectful. He could scarcely draw breath before those thousand empty stares.

And then a sudden flash of light caught his attention, and he turned to see that one of those stares was not so empty. Within the eye sockets of one skull to his left, small purple flames burned softly.

"Was . . . that like that before?" he asked.

"Here," rasped the skull. It had no jaw, made no movement, but Brock knew it had made the sound.

Across the hall, right at Liza's elbow, another skull's sockets lit with violet fire. "They're here," it said, its voice faint and scratchy.

"Here," said another skull.

"Over here," rasped a fourth.

"Run!" Liza said.

As they ran, the skulls all around them flared to life, the purple fire keeping pace with them. Brock felt that eerie purple light as the weight of countless malevolent eyes. Though each skull's voice was small, their sounds were compounding into a horrid cacophony that he feared would be heard throughout the building.

Liza burst through a set of doors at the end of the hallway, Brock a half step behind her. They entered a dim, dusty room lined with carven panels, the stone worked skillfully to show scenes from elven history. From what Brock saw, most of the scenes were of battle, people fighting atop piles of bodies, and in the low light he could not tell if they were human or elf, *dro'shea* or *ain'shea*, only that they were killing and dying. Aside from the purple hallway at their back, three doors led from the room.

"Which way?" Brock asked.

Running footfalls sounded from beyond the doorway to their right.

"Left!" Liza said.

They ran down a hallway, up another flight of stairs. After a week of marching upon flat terrain, Brock's thighs burned with the effort of so much climbing. Yet he would have given anything for another staircase when they came to a small chamber with no exit.

"There has to be a way out," he insisted. He ran his hands over the stone walls, even tried turning a torch in its sconce. The room was otherwise empty but for two rows of benches and a small altar.

"We'll have to stand and fight," Liza said, and Brock could swear the green sword shone a little brighter when she said it.

But there was a purple light glowing from the doorway, heralding the arrival of a tall armored figure. She did not shamble or lurch into the room; she stepped forward with grace and deadly purpose. Her right hand held a blade with a glittering glass orb for a pommel. In her left, she held a skull, its sockets glowing purple.

The skull hissed. "They are here."

"Who?" said the figure. Her face was shrouded in shadow. "Who defiles this sacred place?"

"Um," Brock said, drawing his daggers, his eyes flitting

between the figure and the jawless skull. "I'm pretty sure this place was defiled before we got here."

"Stay back," Liza snarled, holding her sword between them.

The figure chuckled darkly and took another step forward. "Here," said the skull.

In the low, eerie light, Brock noted the figure's armor, soiled and dented, bore the familiar sigil of a tree and birds.

"It's a sword sister," he breathed.

"I was, once," said the figure. "Now I am a revenant. Doomed by regret. Cursed by failure." With her next step, the light of the room's torches found her angular jawline, her lush lips gone cold and blue. "I killed sages and rangers. Murdered even a minister. I was my queen's blade, but I never knew another guided my hand."

Another step, and the light revealed her fully. She was *ain'shea*, with high cheekbones. Brock saw fine silver in her earlobes.

She had been a lovely elf. But her eyes were gone; in their place, maggots writhed.

Brock and Liza both recoiled.

"He took my eyes, that I would not know him. He took my eyes, and now my world is red!"

She slashed out with the blade, frightfully fast. Liza and Brock dove in separate directions, and the sword struck stone. She lifted it again and chopped at the air, as if feeling around for them—as if guessing where they might have gone. Brock scrabbled farther away, pressing against the wall, and the revenant lowered her sword and raised the skull, pointing it all about the room.

Of course—she had no eyes. Somehow she was using the skull to see.

He held a dagger carefully by the blade, lined up his shot, and sent the dagger flying.

His aim was true. But the blade bounced harmlessly off the skull to clatter upon the ground.

It did, however, get the revenant's attention. She whirled on Brock, sword arm raised.

And Liza thrust forward, slipping her own sword beneath the creature's. The skull shattered in a flash of purple light.

The revenant stumbled back, and while she reeled, Liza stepped lightly across the room to Brock. She gestured for him to be quiet. With their enemy blinded, they would be able to sneak away, but apparently she thought Brock's mouth jeopardized that plan.

I know, he mouthed at her. *It was my plan first!*

She shrugged furiously at him, unable to make sense of his silent bickering.

"I don't need to see you," the revenant said, and the orb upon her sword glowed, patterns swirling on its surface like storm clouds in the summer sky.

A bolt of energy leaped from the orb. The revenant had cast it in the direction Liza had stood before, and Brock hoped for a moment that it would find nothing but empty air and cold stone;

but the bolt turned in midair, careless as a bird of prey, and came straight at Liza. It crossed the room in the time it took Brock to suck in a startled breath.

Liza knocked the magic dart out of the sky with her sword.

The sword sister cast another bolt, and another, and Liza advanced each time, slashing the magical lights from the air as easily as Mousebane swatted at fat houseflies.

"Ha!" Liza cried as the third mote of light snuffed harmlessly against her blade. The way now clear, she advanced on their foe.

"Curse you," the revenant cried. "Curse us all!" And the orb glowed suddenly orange, and the room grew terribly hot.

"Liza!" Brock cried, and he dove for her, knocking her away from the creature as it let forth a massive blast of searing heat.

The noise was incredible, the force shattering the wall at Brock's back, reducing heavy stone to shards and dust. He flinched, squeezing his eyes shut against the dust and covering Liza with his body, fully expecting the ceiling to come crashing down on them. But only silence descended, and as the dust settled, Brock risked a peek at their surroundings.

The crack in the wall stopped short of the ceiling, and the revenant had been hurled back in the blast. Whether dazed or unconscious, she did not stir.

"Look at that," he told Liza. "I guess you really do rely on me."

"Please get off me," she said. "Right now."

"All right, all right," Brock said roughly as he clambered to his feet.

"First things first," Liza said. "This poor woman needs to be put out of her misery."

She looked at him for his agreement, and after a moment he nodded solemnly and turned away. He listened as Liza retrieved her sword, its metal singing upon the stone. And he flinched when the sword struck stone once more.

"You can look now," Liza said. "It's over."

"Only a fool would believe it so," rasped the revenant.

Brock whirled at the sound of the voice, and saw Liza aghast in horror.

The creature had been cleanly decapitated. But she hadn't been silenced. "My service is not yet ended," she said. "Not while the children of Freestone remain free."

"That is . . . that is super-disturbing," Brock said.

"Children?" Liza asked. "You were after us, specifically?"

"I was to deliver you to him, but if not me, then the others will. There is no escape for you."

"Do your worst," Liza said, "because for the record, we don't want to es— Wait. What if we surrender?"

"Surrender?" both Brock and the revenant said at once.

"You're right," Liza said, casting a broad and completely unnecessary wink at Brock. "We're up against unbeatable odds. We see the futility, and wish to submit ourselves to the great Lich himself."

"Well," rasped the head. "In that case, I shall take you to him as my prisoners. And you will know pain and suffering and worse things, the agonies without name or number which await us on the other side of Mort's gray door." The revenant's head chuckled darkly, then came up suddenly short. "I will, of course, require you to carry me there."

Chapter Nineteen
Zed

"It'll snow soon," Frond said. "We don't have time to wait."
She frowned at the sky as the queen and Selby made a series of complicated wizardly gestures in the alcove where Liza had disappeared. For all their finger wriggling, neither Liza nor Brock had materialized from the depths of the spell.

"They're beyond my reach, anyway," Queen Me'Shala announced. She frowned, lowering her hands and wiping a pretty shimmer of perspiration from her pretty face, prettily. "Elderon's Shade is woven throughout the city. It's unlikely, but if they managed to slip between folds in the magic, they could have ended up anywhere in the valley. Even in the heart of Llethanyl."

Frond considered this while tightening a strap on her glove. "Could we use it the same way? To get close to the Lich? The element of surprise could keep Zed safe."

Selby was still working on the spell, but he shook his head before she'd even finished the question. "Not from here. The Shade is meant to have specific entrance and exit points. Without using them, you could end up locked in the crypts."

Zed shuddered at the thought. He was standing with Fel and Callum, keeping a watchful eye on the queen. Brock's vanishing had thrown the team momentarily into panic, but Zed could still feel an accusation bubbling up inside him. For all he knew, Me'Shala had engineered the spell to trap his friends. If she really was betraying the humans, perhaps she wanted as many of them out of the way as possible.

"The good news is," Selby continued, "if your apprentices are merely lost in the Shade, they should be safe for the moment. It won't be pleasant, but there's nothing inside the demiplane that can harm them."

"A demiplane!" Jayna gasped. "Was *that* what we passed through?"

"Oh, gee," Micah gushed with mock enthusiasm. "I hope this means we get another magic lesson!"

"Demiplanes are pocket dimensions separate from our . . ."

Hexam began. He drifted off as Micah's sarcasm finally sank in. Hexam cleared his throat. "Yes, well. At any rate, the creation of one is in violation of several treaties between our cities."

The minister waved away Hexam's pointed look, pausing in his work. "The Shade was created long before such agreements. What's your charming human expression? It's been 'grandparented in.'"

"Grand*fathered*," Hexam muttered.

"Well, that's rather discriminatory, isn't it?" Selby mused cheerfully.

"Enough." Frond pinched the bridge of her nose. "The plan remains the same. Hexam, Zed, and I will head into the city with Callum and the rangers. The remaining group can work on freeing Brock and Liza."

"Wait," said Zed. "There's something else. Micah—"

"There's been a change of plans," Me'Shala interrupted. "My ministers and I will now be leading the siege. Frond, you and your people may wait here in safety. All except for Zed, of course."

The queen spoke casually, as if reminding Frond of a last-minute dinner engagement, but Threya and Selby shifted slightly at the pronouncement, exchanging significant looks. Their postures were suddenly alert. All around Zed, rangers glanced at one another, then toward their queen. The elves' resolved expressions made clear that something was happening. Something they'd been waiting for.

Frond's frown deepened. "No."

"I'm afraid I must insist. This is my city. The rescue of Llethanyl will be won by elves."

"Zed is my apprentice, Your Majesty," Frond said. "His safety is my priority. You placed me in charge, at least let me—"

"Alabasel, you are an exceptional human," the queen said, "and a fine guildmistress. But I am the sovereign leader of a proud and ancient people. *They* are *my* priority—not your rough-neck adventurers. This is not a request. From this moment forward, I am taking control of the mission. The situation is complicated beyond your understanding."

The queen was changing the plan. Thorn, Me'Shala's surviving sword sister, moved her hand slyly toward her blade.

Frond looked around her, absorbing the hostile atmosphere. The adventurers were outmanned two to one, and half were just apprentices. Her shoulders sank. "Me'Shala, don't do this. Not to me."

"Believe me," the queen replied. "It brings me no joy. But we all still want the same thing, Alabasel. We're still allies in this."

"That's a lie!" The words poured from Zed like ambrosia spilling over the lip of a flagon. He pointed an accusing finger at Me'Shala. "You've been working against us from the beginning!"

The queen narrowed her eyes. In her gaze Zed felt something powerful taking aim. A tingling sensation swept over him, and all the hairs on Zed's arm stood on end. "Choose your next words carefully, *half elf*," she drawled. "What exactly do you accuse me of?"

"You . . . well . . ." Zed faltered. His finger drooped. Should he reveal what Callum had told him? What would happen to the High Ranger if he did?

"*Someone* wrote a false note from Frond at the wayshelter," Zed began carefully, "telling us to turn around. Just when we discovered Frond's *real* note, though, Fel's dead father appeared as a wraith and nearly killed her!"

Behind the queen, Selby frowned. "The night elf? What does that prove?"

"Fel was the only one of us who knew the way here," Zed said. "If the Lich could get rid of her, we'd have no way to join you here at Llethanyl."

"Ridiculous," Threya sniped. "The deathling wasn't even part of the expedition! How would the Lich know to target her?"

"Exactly." Zed snapped his fingers. He felt the evidence bolstering him. Something was very wrong with this mission, and he would root it out. Zed threw his shoulders back and met the queen's glare with one of his own. "The only way he'd know was because *Lotte* revealed as much."

On the other side of the clearing, Lotte blanched. "Me?"

"Not on purpose, of course." Zed dipped his head apologetically. "Naturally, she told the rest of you who she'd brought with her while we were separated. I don't know how, but one of *you* warned the Lich. It's the only explanation that makes sense."

Me'Shala's eyes darted from Zed to Fel and back again. She was quiet for a long beat. When she finally spoke, her voice was a terrible whisper. "Felasege, is all of this true? You were targeted?"

"Your Majesty," Threya said, "you cannot trust the word of a deathling—"

"Oh, give it a rest, Threya!" Selby spat. "Your small-mindedness will kill us all."

"The night elves have *always* hated Llethanyl!" Threya continued, speaking over him. "They are death-worshipping zealots who—"

"*Enough!*" The queen's voice boomed, silencing the ministers. "Answer me *now*, night elf." Her russet eyes blazed as she looked to Fel.

The last time Fel had faced the queen's scrutiny, she had shrunk from it. This time, however, the girl squared her shoulders, standing straightbacked. Her own cobalt gaze matched Me'Shala's in its fierceness. "Yes, it's true. The Lich sent my father as a wraith." Then her eyes turned, narrowing upon Threya. "He died for this city, by the way," Fel added. "Fighting for a better Llethanyl. Insult me again, Minister, just one more time, and I'll show you what a zealot I can be."

Threya glowered, but she said nothing else for the moment.

"But why," the queen said, waving past the tension, "do you suspect *me* of betraying my own city?"

"Because I gave him the idea." Callum's voice resonated from behind Zed. Zed felt the High Ranger's hand fall upon his shoulder.

"You?" The queen's eyes widened with surprise.

"Traitor!" Threya hissed. She pulled an enormous sword free of its scabbard.

"I told Zed that you were misleading the adventurers. That we all were. And this was true. The Sea of Stars are our only friends among the humans! They've risked everything to help us, and yet we deceive and betray them!"

"Elves don't need human *friends*," Threya said. "They are not our peers!"

"What exactly were you lying about?" Frond asked Callum. "This? Me'Shala's plan?"

The High Ranger shook his head. "So *many* things. There are . . . weapons. Tools that we've kept secret from Freestone. One of them is Elderon's Shade. As you saw, it can be used to bypass impassable barriers. But the Shade isn't a fixed structure, like a building. It can be moved. Redirected. All one would need is the focus that controls it. And *that* is still hidden in the castle, accessible only to the queen."

Frond's eyes blazed as the implication sank in. She whirled on the queen. "You willfully hid a tool that could be used to invade my city?" Zed had never seen the guildmistress so furious. Real anger boiled behind her eyes. He took an involuntary step backward.

"*Invade?*" The queen laughed mirthlessly. "Your king detained my people in an open-air prison! Don't lecture me about trust, Alabasel! The Shade is a back door. I thought if I could retrieve it here, then even if we failed today, my people *might* have a fighting chance when your knights came with swords drawn." She frowned. "In any case, it's safely locked away. The Lich can't access the focus on his own."

The queen hesitated, her eyes falling to her feet. "But there's a more pressing problem," she said with a resigned sigh. "A weapon that the Lich *does* have access to. When he took the city, Galvino created an . . . abomination. He resurrected an ancient skeleton, a trophy that had been sealed within our crypts. That was the winged shape we saw on the horizon. The 'mountain' that flew away. I knew you would abandon the raid if we told you the truth about it. So I lied."

"What abomination?" Frond pronounced each word with cold deliberateness.

"I think . . ." Hexam's voice faltered. His eyes were on the sky. "I think perhaps I might know."

Shadows began flitting over the ground: small dots of darkness, like scurrying mice. Zed looked upward, toward the branches of the enormous tree that covered the city. Fluttering black shapes were emerging from the lanterns, flocking together into a beating mass.

"Are those . . . bats?" Jayna asked.

"No," rasped the queen. "They are not."

The flock grew as Zed watched, forming into a writhing cloud. And from this murk a figure began to emerge, swimming in the gray sky. A wing. A claw. A lashing tail. The cloud solidified, the individual shapes knitting together in a greater whole. In moments, a long snout had appeared, and two eyes that shone with purple light.

The mountain had arrived.

Zed had never seen a dragon. No one alive in Freestone had, even among the Adventurers Guild. But despite the creature's rarity, it was one of the few Dangers that *everyone* in the city knew well. Giant winged lizards that breathed fire and possessed a wicked intelligence, dragons appeared in countless knightly stories, destroying cities and hoarding mounds of glittering treasure.

The creature that now climbed among the great tree's branches was a dragon, Zed could tell that clearly. And yet it was not. Its scales were formed of some ragged, oily darkness, and its wings fluttered in the rising wind, occasionally smoking away. Its wasted face housed two cavernous hollows, in which purple coals burned from deep within.

"*Dracolich...*" Hexam whispered, his eyes bulging.

Perhaps the creature heard him. Perhaps it had been watching them all along. Whatever the case, the dracolich's purple gaze fell instantly upon the group. It opened its desiccated maw and roared. Zed felt as much as heard it. It was the howl of a once-proud creature brought low.

In the silence that followed, Zed heard a new sound rising all throughout the city. Footsteps—hundreds of them—either summoned by the roar or hidden within it. All across Llethanyl doorways crashed open and a monstrous populace spilled into the streets. The dead made no other sounds as they marched. They didn't moan, or shout, or breathe. They just lurched forward, filling the wide avenues.

Zed realized that there would be no surprise attack on the Lich.

The rangers whipped around, pulling their bows taut. Frond drew her sword, and Thorn echoed her just moments later.

"Hexam," Frond said quietly. "We need a path to the palace."

"Then keep them off me for a moment, please."

"The *palace*?" Lotte exclaimed, rising from her perch and cradling her wounded arm. "It's too late for that! The mission is a failure. We should retreat through the Shade!"

"Hate to say it," Micah piped up, "but I'm with her."

"Yes, back through," Selby readily agreed. "Right this way, everyo—" He took a step into the alcove and slammed into solid stone. Where before there had been a layer of magical muck, now the wall was quite wall-like. "Ah! It appears this entrance is . . . damaged."

"*Hex*-am," Frond called. All around them, the dead were pressing in. Even in the cold, Zed could detect the scent of rot.

"I am *working* on it," the wizard crooned back in an irritable singsong. Hexam's eyes were closed, his fingers weaving into strange patterns. One moment they contorted themselves to look like a beast, and the next a wall of interlocking fingers. Veins of light trailed his movements, forming a circular sigil more complicated than anything Zed had ever seen in the archivist's lessons.

"Mindless, nameless," Hexam chanted, his voice echoing strangely. "A sacred space behind the teeth. The peace which fuels the hunger. The abominable line." The archivist's eyes snapped open. His irises shone with a fierce blue light, and Zed was engulfed by the sharp scent of magic.

"*Back!*" Hexam shouted, stepping forward to meet the approaching horde. The sigil traveled with him, the circle now rotating along an invisible axis. Callum grabbed Zed's and Fel's wrists, falling in behind the wizard, as did the others. Hexam raised his hands, spreading his fingers wide.

The sigil unfolded.

What emerged was a thing of teeth and fire, a great beastly maw that exploded from the seal just as the first wave of enemies reached it. Fiery fangs clamped down upon the undead attackers, obliterating them. Then the grinning mouth stretched forward, transforming from a wolfish muzzle into a tunnel carved from flame. The walls swelled outward, incinerating the dead that crowded against it. In only a few moments a passage had formed, snaking into the city and burning any of the Dangers unlucky enough to touch the outer layer.

"Go . . . *now!*" Hexam cried. And before Zed had time to

realize what was happening, he was pulled *into* the flames.

The inside of the tunnel was surprisingly comfortable for something fashioned entirely of fire. Callum and Frond ran ahead, with Zed and Fel huffing just behind them. Mousebane was perched on Fel's shoulder, warily eyeing the burning border of the tunnel. Zed was too winded to look behind him, but he heard plenty of footsteps following in his wake.

Through the flames, Llethanyl appeared to be set ablaze. Zed couldn't see where they were headed, and just hoped that Hexam's magic knew the path somehow.

There was a rumbling from outside the passage, obscured by the roar of the spell. A shadow fell over them, its darkness distinct even through the flames. Suddenly Zed was knocked from his feet by an enormous black talon as it crashed easily through the fiery barrier. He landed hard on his back, and the world shattered into blinking shards of light.

It had begun to snow. Zed felt the snowflakes before he could see them. They prickled his face with small bites. In the distance, he heard screams of pain and alarm, but he couldn't breathe well enough to call out.

The shadow rose upward, and a squall of wind sent him spilling even farther away. Zed forced himself to roll onto his side, then clawed his way to his hands and knees. Looking up— his vision finally clearing—he saw the fiery tunnel darken where the dracolich's claw had punctured it, hardening into a shell of white-gray ash. The ash spread outward in both directions, extinguishing the flames as it went and collapsing the tunnel upon itself.

But that wasn't the worst of it. Undead elves swarmed from the city's avenues, falling upon the group just as they were recovering. Frond screamed, surging forward and burying her sword into the rib cage of a skeleton. Callum stood with his bow raised, firing arrows into the horde.

Zed searched the chaos for his friends and found Jayna battering a swarm of the undead with mystical darts. Behind her, Jett and Micah nervously gripped their weapons.

The queen and her ministers fought with sword and spell, but Zed caught a glimpse of Thorn, the sword sister, lying prone on the ground. Her body was limp and covered with dots of snow. Was she . . . ?

Thorn's body shivered. An arm struck out, moving stiffly. The sword sister propped herself up, and Zed could see her eyes were wide and vacant. She lurched to her feet, her head lolling to the side.

Then she raised her sword and aimed for the queen's back.

Zed bumbled forward, and the world exploded into mist around him. As he careened out of the fog, his shoulder smashed into Thorn's stomach. Both Zed and the elf went down, sliding away into the snow.

Thorn recovered first. In an instant she was on top of him,

scratching at his face and tearing at his hair, digging her thumb into his cheek. Zed screamed. He tried in vain to grab at her wrists, but she was too strong. The elf's eyes were empty of emotion. The centers of her pupils glowed with pinpricks of violet.

Zed heard a loud *crack*, accompanied by a strobe of light. The weight disappeared from his ribs. Panting, he pushed himself up to find the elf twitching on the ground several feet away. A small line of smoke rose from a singed spot on her chest.

Above him, Me'Shala stood with her hand raised, grimacing at the body of someone who had once been her protector.

"Make for the palace!" Frond's voice bellowed over the tumult.

The queen locked eyes with Zed. Then she swept away without a word.

Zed climbed to his feet, searching for Frond and the others. Snow billowed through the air in heavy white sails. He could no longer see the queen or his guildmates. Zed took a tentative step forward, paused, then turned around.

Which way was the palace?

He spun in a circle, hoping to catch a glimpse of something recognizable. Fear crept through Zed's limbs, a different sort of chill altogether.

"Hello?" Zed called out. "Hey! Is anybody there?" He received no answer.

Until he did.

A horrid keening issued from the storm, shrill and gravelly.

Two shining eyes stalked toward him, beaming with malice, even through the snow. They glared hatefully at Zed.

It was a look that he knew well.

"Mousebane!" he called with relief. He trudged toward the cat, which took several steps back and hissed at his approach. She eyed him distrustfully, perhaps suspecting he might try to pet her.

"Zed! Over here!"

Zed spotted Fel's small shape nearby, waving at him. He huffed after her with Mousebane beside him, just hoping she could still navigate her way through the city in this.

Llethanyl had disappeared behind the curtains of snow. Figures large and small were concealed within the blizzard, their shapes blurred into ominous shadows. Zed kept his eyes on Fel while he walked, afraid to lose sight of her for even a moment.

Which was why he missed the armored skeleton until it leaped out of the din.

"Fel!" Zed shouted, as Mousebane took off like a bolt.

Both were too slow. Fel screamed as the Danger seized her arm, wrenching her to the ground. It lifted a rusted javelin into the air, stabbing downward.

A second figure emerged from the snow, cleaving forward with a scream. Threya plowed into the skeleton with her enormous swords, then hurled it back into the snowfall as two distinct halves.

The minister stood over Fel, breathing raggedly. She looked

down at the young night elf whose life she'd just saved—and then at the blood that began to pour from her own side, where the skeleton's javelin still pierced her.

"Oh," Threya murmured. Her voice was hushed with surprise. "Oh, no . . ." She teetered, then fell into the snow.

"No!" Fel scrambled up, rushing to the minister. "Please, no. Please, please . . ." She ripped off her cloak, wrapping it around the javelin to try and stanch the bleeding. Mousebane trotted to her, watching with wide, curious eyes.

"Help!" Zed cupped his hands and turned around in a circle, searching for any familiar figures. "Callum! *Micah!*" he bellowed into the blizzard. "Anybody . . ."

No response came. The city had gone silent.

"Be quiet," Threya said. "You'll just bring more of those things to us."

"But why?" Fel asked hoarsely. "Why would you save me? I thought you hated night elves. I thought you hated *me*."

"Tell me, deathling . . ." The minister's chest rose and fell with crackling breaths. "Do you really think me such a monster? That I'd let a child die right in front of me?" Her eyes were wide and wet.

"Yes," Fel hissed. "Yes, I did. As a minister, you spoke against the *dro'shea* many times. You took every chance to make our lives harder."

"To be hated by one so young . . ." The minister closed her eyes and grimaced. "Selby was right. I don't expect you to forgive me, but you *must* . . ." Threya's eyes bulged open again, though she now gazed toward some unseeable distance. "Run," she rasped.

"We aren't leaving you!" Fel said. "Just hold on!"

"Go *now.*" Threya's grip tightened. "Before I become . . . one more weapon . . . of *his.* Stop the Lich. . . . I beg you."

Zed remembered how quickly the sword sister had turned on her own queen once she'd fallen. He took Fel's shoulder, pulling her gently away from the minister. Threya released her hand without a fight. "She's right," he whispered. "We have to go, before she—"

"I *know*," Fel snapped, shrugging his hand away.

Mousebane rubbed her face against the girl's leg, mewling. Fel looked down at the cat. She took a deep breath. "I know," she said again, dismally. "I'm sorry, Zed. Let's go."

They went.

Zed couldn't see far through the blizzard, but luckily Fel seemed to know the way. The two trudged side by side, with Mousebane prowling low to the ground. All around them, Llethanyl was hushed, except for the wind and the crunching of their own boots in the snow. They'd had a couple close encounters with crowds of shambling dead, but the blizzard helped to hide *them* just as well from their pursuers.

The closer they came to the palace, however, the fewer

Dangers they saw. The dead seemed to be giving it a wide berth. Zed wasn't sure he wanted to know why. Glancing up, he could just make out the variegated towers spiraling into the clouds. It was a wondrous, dreadful view.

Soon a pillar even larger than the others loomed through the murk, as thick as a city block. It took Zed several moments to realize that this wasn't another tower but the base of the enormous tree he'd seen from the city's outskirts.

"The palace is built into the roots," Fel explained, taking in his wide-eyed gaze.

Zed nodded, frowning. "Do you think the others made it?"

"I don't know," Fel said. "I hope so."

"We need Micah," Zed muttered. "He might be the key to ending this." He cursed himself for not telling Frond when he'd had the chance.

"Frond ordered everyone to the palace." Fel pointed to a shape just beyond. "That's the entrance. And the most likely place they'd all go."

Zed squinted, finally noticing the shrouded white archway hidden within the snow. A great tree decorated the front, wreathed by a halo of soaring birds. The doors were slightly ajar. He nodded, and they began trudging closer.

Before they'd gotten even halfway there, an enormous shadow fell over the square. It appeared without a sound, just a crush of sudden darkness. Zed stumbled back as the shadow descended, and the dracolich landed heavily before the archway.

Its impact shook the ground. Zed had to fight to keep upright against the beating of those great wings.

The gargantuan monster turned its gaze upon them. Even through the snow, its two purple eyes shone brightly.

"*Hasss osss stahvraaaah.*" The creature spoke in a tongue Zed had never heard before. It didn't even sound like something a person could produce—equal parts thunder, rattle, and snake hiss. Zed felt the vibration of its voice in his chest.

"Back!" He reached for his scepter and sent a warning gout of green fire in an arc over their heads. "Don't come any closer!"

"Hmmmm. I smell *Fie*."

Zed's mouth fell open. What had it just said?

"My master has bid me kill the sorcerer without completely destroying its body." The dracolich issued a rattling sound from the back of its throat, then opened its mouth. Inside was a nightmare landscape of tongue and teeth. "He wishes to add it to his army. This will not be easy, I think."

The creature snaked forward with alarming speed for something so huge. Zed was reminded of the lizards that scurried across Freestone's cobblestones in the summer. The dracolich lowered its face and peered at them. Its maw was as large as an outtown home. The smell of decay threatened to overwhelm Zed.

The dragon's burning purple eyes passed from Zed to Fel.

"Any others, I may eat," it rumbled. "Though I do not hunger so much anymore. Perhaps this was meant as an insult. Death has made me slow . . . confused. In my time I was grand."

"Let us pass and we can free you!" Zed said, stepping in front of Fel. Slowly, carefully, he drew upon his mana, pooling it into the scepter. "We're here to stop the Lich."

"I know why you have come," the dragon boomed. "As does he. Your hunt was always misguided. You do not understand your prey." The dragon reared up again, its muzzle rising several stories. It snorted, and a vivid gush of orange flame erupted from its nostrils. "But the time for speaking is over, I think. Perhaps the flames will leave enough of you behind." The dracolich opened its mouth, wide enough for Zed to see something spark within its throat.

He raised his scepter, and threw everything he could at that spark.

The explosion was unlike anything Zed had ever seen before, larger and more awful than even the blast that had destroyed Mother Brenner. There was a sucking sound like a great deep breath, and then silence, as Zed and Fel were blown from their feet and tossed through the air.

When Zed came to he was lying in the snow. His clothes smoked. Fel was beside him, and she was saying something, though Zed couldn't make it out over the high-pitched whine in his ears.

The fire . . .

He followed Fel's finger as it pointed up and away.

It burns, Zed.

The dracolich was on fire. It watched them from the center

of a circle of meltwater, a black skeleton outlined in emerald flames. But even within all that green, two purple lights shone bright and clear from the sockets of its skull.

The flames had eaten the dragon's skin, and eaten it hungrily. The oily mass of shadows that covered it dripped apart, globs burning to ash before they reached the ground. Soon the flames, too, had guttered away, extinguished by the cold.

The skeleton still remained, grinning calmly at Zed.

"Interesting . . ." the dracolich cooed. "But not enough, I think."

It roared, sending snow crashing from the surrounding towers into the streets. Clouds of it washed over Zed and Fel, choking the air.

The dragon's enormous skeletal wings unfolded, the tips disappearing into the mist. It raised a great taloned foot.

Slowly the snow settled, and in the haze Zed could make out figures filling the streets of Llethanyl. An army of the dead was arriving to block their way out. They were surrounded. Beaten.

"*Seebul.*"

Zed snapped around, searching for the voice that had spoken.

"*Grishta.*"

These were words he knew. He'd heard them just recently.

Lights began to ripple out from the surrounding figures, filling the square with an amber radiance. They shimmered prettily against the snow, transforming each flake into a sparkling mote.

The snow suddenly stopped in midair.

Zed gasped. He reached out to touch one of the suspended snowflakes, and it melted against his touch. Then all the snow followed, water cascading to the ground in a wash of warm rain like a summer storm. In moments, the air was clear and bright.

And elves surrounded him. Living, breathing elves. Druids filled the square, clad in their indigo robes and all wearing pristine white masks. The Prime Druid stood ahead of the others, carrying an ornate wooden crook topped with blue toadstools. He stamped the staff against the stone avenue. Light rippled from his feet along the ground, and in its wake bursts of green sprouted from the earth.

Behind the skeletal dragon, the great tree, too, began to shimmer with light. Pink flowers erupted from its branches, filling the air with a sudden, sweet aroma. The tree's bark brightened, until it glowed so white-hot that Zed had to look away.

"This light . . ." The dragon's voice was soft. Covetous.

The branches of the great tree creaked in a jangling chorus. Then, with a huge *crack*, one of the boughs reached out and snagged the dracolich's wing like a grasping hand. The dragon roared. Where the tree's glowing bark touched it, the skeleton began to sizzle and smoke. The dracolich tried to pull away, clawing against the trunk of the tree, but vines lashed out where it made contact, and moss engulfed the talon.

One of the druids approached Zed and Fel, helping them to their feet. *"Cresca dilane,"* the druid said, her voice muffled from behind her mask. She pointed urgently to the archway. Zed recognized the voice of Lanaya, the young druid he'd spoken with at Duskhaven. He didn't understand her words, but figured he got the point.

"Fel, come on," he said. "I think they're going to hold it off for us."

Fel nodded. Her eyes were wide as she took in the assembled elves. "They came...." A huge smile graced her face. "They actually came!" Fel bounded to the young druid. "*Savasche*," she said, with real conviction. "*Savasche, savasche, savasche!*"

Lanaya laughed and took Fel's hands in her own. "*Al de nos*," she answered warmly. Then she pointed to the archway, her tone serious. "*Cresca*," she said again. "*Unlat comini.*"

"Time to go," said Zed.

"Yes," Fel agreed. "Time to go save my city."

Chapter Twenty
Brock

"I really am sorry about this," Brock said. "So, so, so sorry."

"Finally, an apology from the mouth of Brock Dunderfel," Liza said. "And it's addressed to the severed head of an undead assassin. Typical."

"None of this is *typical*," Brock groaned. "Please don't let this be our new normal."

They'd found a shuttered lantern with a circular handle, just big enough, once emptied of wick and oil, to contain the revenant's head. Now Liza held it aloft as if she were holding any other lantern.

The revenant had tried its best to kill them, but Brock still felt guilty carrying its head around like this. It felt like making a mockery out of another being's death, and that sat uneasy with him.

Then again, it eased his guilt a little that the revenant was such a jerk. It kept gloating about their imminent doom, which was no way to make friends.

Several long minutes ago, they'd entered a subterranean tunnel, and the immaculate stonework of the crypts had given way to hard-packed dirt. Brock assumed magic had been used to form the tunnel, for its sides were perfectly flat, and plant roots almost seemed to hold the soil in place like a net. As they walked, the roots grew thicker, until the walls were more wood than soil, and Brock realized they were seeing the root structure of the massive tree at Llethanyl's heart.

"The Lich will cut out your tongues!" cried the revenant. "Oh, could I but see it. Still, I'll savor the silence, oh yes."

"I think your new friend is telling us to shut up," Liza said.

"How is it even talking?" Brock asked. "It doesn't have any lungs."

Liza shrugged. "Magic? All right, the Lich is going to eat our tongues. I guess that means we're still going the right way."

In truth, there was only one way to go.

"Do you feel that?" Liza asked.

"What?"

She paused. "I can't describe it. I feel like something's happened up there. . . . The *sword* is buzzing."

Brock raised an eyebrow. "How hard did you hit your head before?"

"Never mind. Come on."

"Forward," said the revenant. "Forward to doom."

The tunnel began to incline, and the soil gave way entirely to wood. Brock marveled at how gradually, how organically, one setting transitioned to the next. Eventually they were walking a hallway of polished wood—until the hall came to an abrupt end.

"Keep going," rasped the head.

"I guess you can't see through all the maggots," Brock said. "But you led us to a dead end."

"Never the end," said the revenant. "Never dead . . ."

"Brock, here." Liza had set the revenant's lantern down to consider the wall. "I think . . . I think it's a door." She rapped her knuckles lightly against it, and the space behind it sounded hollow. But when she pushed, nothing happened.

"If this actually opens into the palace, it's probably a hidden door," Brock said. "Don't push. Try sliding."

Liza pressed her palms to the wall and pivoted. It slid open without a sound. A curtain hung in the recess beyond, blocking their view, but Brock could tell it was a well-lit interior space. "We made it," he said.

"So eager," said the head. "So eager to die."

Brock stuck his tongue out.

"And what about you?" Liza asked. Her voice was husky. "Do you want to die?"

The head chuckled. "I cannot die. My new lord will not allow it."

"But if it were possible," Liza insisted. "If you had a choice."

The head stilled, though the maggots upon it still writhed. It appeared thoughtful—even sad. "I . . . do not . . . There is no choice. There is only the Lich."

"Brock," Liza said. "Look away."

Brock considered the curtain. There was a flash of green, and the sound of metal piercing metal. Liza had plunged her sword through the lantern.

"Did it work that time?" Brock asked, and when he turned, he saw Liza's stricken face. "Hold on. Are you *crying?*"

"Yes," she said, unashamed of the tears cutting tracks through the grime on her cheeks. "It's awful what the Lich has done. Monstrous. Don't you see it? He's not just a killer or a conqueror. He's . . . *warped* the natural order. He took something sacred and he's dragged it through the mud."

Brock nodded mutely. He knew what she meant. He understood the pity she felt for the sword sister and everyone else the Lich had touched. Most of all, he understood her fury—the rage that was evident in the tightness of her jaw, the squint of her eyes.

"Well," he told her, "I'd say it's time someone dragged *him* through the mud. Wouldn't you?" He pulled a reasonably clean handkerchief from his satchel pocket and handed it to her.

Liza smiled. Instead of wiping her tears away, she wiped the blade of her sword. "Count me in," she said.

"Great." Brock gestured toward the curtain. "Uh, ladies first?"

"Cowards second." She winked. "Come on!"

The palace interior was a marvel. It appeared to have been entirely carved out of the inside of the tree, but the wood of the walls was smooth to the touch and glowed with a soft interior light. Rugs and tapestries and little side tables with silver sculptures furnished the hallways, making it all seem so *normal*—Brock could almost forget he was walking within a living structure.

But a thin layer of dust covered everything, a visible reminder that this grandest of homes had been abandoned by the living. It was a haunted place, and it shuddered occasionally, as if frightened, or determined to uproot itself and flee.

Or maybe Brock was projecting his own feelings.

They wound their way past empty rooms and darkened windows, and soon enough their hallway ended in a grand foyer.

To Brock's continued astonishment, it was filled with familiar faces.

Zed and Fel huffed raggedly at the doorway, their clothes somehow both wet and singed. Jett was bandaging a cut on Jayna's arm while Micah looked on, a bit bruised and battered himself. But they were alive, all of them.

"I'm telling you I can just *heal* her," Micah groused.

Liza recognized her cue. "Save your anima, Micah," she said, and all five of them leaped to their feet upon hearing her voice.

"You're okay!" Jayna said, crossing the foyer to embrace her friend.

"Brock, where were you?" Zed asked, stepping forward more hesitantly.

"I know I have a habit of disappearing," he said. "But that time it was *not* my fault."

"Where's everybody else? Frond? Lotte?" Liza asked.

Zed bit his lip. "We got separated. It all happened so fast. There was a dragon—a *dracolich* . . ."

Micah rolled not just his eyes but his entire head. "Here we go again. Zed and Fel versus the drakle itch."

Fel made a frustrated *harrumph*, and Zed gestured madly at Micah. "It was kind of a big deal!"

Brock patted him on the shoulder, inadvertently producing a puff of ash. "And I want to hear all about it."

"Later," Jett said. "The dragon is restrained for now, but—" The palace trembled. "Well, but *that*."

"We should wait for Frond," Brock said. The entire group looked at him with undisguised surprise. "What?" he said. "It's not a compliment or anything. It's a sound strategy."

"I don't know how long we can wait," Liza said. "Stopping the Lich is the only way to win, and I don't want to lose the element of surprise."

"Dear girl, you sound just like an elf. I think I should like to keep you." A ripple of tension went through the group at the

335

sound of the voice. When Queen Me'Shala stepped from the shadows, not even Fel showed the respect of touching her fingers to her lips.

"Where'd you come from?" Micah asked.

The queen smiled. Her cheeks were flushed from exertion, and Brock thought it made her only more beautiful. "This is my palace. You don't think I come and go through the most obvious door?"

Micah shrugged broadly, eager to convey he'd given the matter very little thought. Whatever charm the queen held for Brock, Micah was apparently immune.

"You're alone, Majesty?" Fel asked. "Your sword sister—"

The queen shook her head, a momentary sadness registering and then just as suddenly gone. "They gave everything to get me here. Now we must honor their sacrifice with action. But where is Frond?" she asked. "Callum?"

"Last time I saw them," Zed answered, "they were with you."

Brock was surprised at the iciness in his friend's voice. "Uh, what he means is—"

"She knows what I mean," Zed said sharply.

The queen was unmoved by any of it. "It's chaos out there. And knowing those two, they've stopped to help every stray kitten along the way." She clucked her tongue. "I know they will be fine. But we cannot wait. Galvino is *here*. In *my* home. And we've brought you all this way, Zed." She lifted her hands toward him as if bestowing a blessing. "My secret weapon."

Brock tried to pass a meaningful look to Micah, but the healer was preoccupied with digging a particularly elusive booger from his nose.

Me'Shala gasped at the state of the throne room, her eyes wide with horror as they swept across the cavernous space. Brock tried to imagine it as it once had been: a huge vaulted ceiling with arches of living wood, and walls draped with ivy that had been braided into lush, elaborate geometries. Branches grew inward into the room, reaching out from ceiling and floor; they might have once held fanciful ornaments and mystical baubles or even living birds.

The wood was dead now, the ivy rotted, and the branches broken and gnarled. If indeed they had held ornaments, those were likely shattered upon the floor, but no floor was visible. The entire room, huge as it was, was shrouded in a swirling lavender miasma that came up to Brock's knees and obscured his view of his own feet.

At the center of the haze was a throne of wet, rotting wood. And upon that throne was the Lich.

He stood, rising to his full and intimidating height. His skin was pale gray, pulled taut and paper-thin across his face; his eyes were a luminous purple above sunken cheeks. His clothing, however, was fine, with gleaming embroidery to match the circlet of silver he wore over his stringy white hair.

"Me'Shhhala," he hissed, lurching forward. Though he was well across the room, Brock flinched at the sudden movement. The Lich paused momentarily, then took another stumbling step. He moved in an ungainly manner, in awkward fits and starts, his body all twisted. He held his arms out at strange angles, his hands hanging limp.

Brock took an involuntary step back. The queen, however, stood her ground. "You shall not address me, traitor. Not until you remove that ridiculous *hat*."

The Lich rasped. Brock couldn't tell if he was laughing or panting. His thin lips, already pulled tight, split open, flesh tearing against yellow teeth. His blood was thick and dark.

"What have you done to yourself, Galvino?" There was more scorn than pity in the queen's voice. "*This* is the power you sought? Mort's energies have ruined you. You are undone." She held out a hand. "Stand down now. Stop this horror."

"Shhhhala," he said, lurching ever closer. Brock was getting truly nervous now.

"I see my orders do not carry the weight they once did here." The queen lowered her hand. "So I'll ask nicely. Zed, would you please end this?"

Zed hesitated only a moment, then he stepped before the queen and held forth his scepter. Its jewel flashed green.

A torrent of flame burst forth, so sudden and intense that Brock, even expecting it as he was, felt his heart leap in awe.

They all stepped back, including the queen, and Brock shielded his face against the heat and the eerie green light.

The Lich, however, was unaffected. He stood, immune and unconcerned, some magic diverting the flames around his broken body. Even his finery remained untouched by the fire.

Zed's flame cut out.

"What—?" said the queen.

"Oh, no," Zed said unconvincingly. "I was sure that would work." He winked at Brock as Micah got into position for their *true* plan. They just needed the Lich to come another step closer. . . .

"Shhhala," the Lich moaned, his torn lips flapping. "Help. Help me."

"*Help* you?" the queen echoed, stunned. Brock tore his eyes from Micah to consider Galvino. There was a look of real pain etched across his features.

At that moment Micah darted forward, right fist aglow, and he punched the Lich squarely in the mouth. Honeyed light flared from the impact, and the loose and rotting flesh of Galvino's jaw exploded away into ash. The creature reeled back, but Micah gripped it by its glittering robe and struck it again, and again, and with a fourth blow nothing remained of the Lich's head but a cloud of gray ash.

Micah dropped the remains of their enemy into the mist at his feet. He took a heaving breath, then he pumped his still-glowing fist into the air. "How about that? Let's hear it for the *secret* secret weapon."

Something brushed against Brock's calf, slithering past him.

In the far corner of the room, the mist swelled. Brock saw faces in the fog, ghostly forms taking shape from nothingness.

"It didn't work," Brock said. "We beat the Lich. Why didn't it work?" He looked wildly from face to face, and saw his own shock and fear mirrored by each of his companions.

And he saw Selby step through the door at their backs.

"Ah, good, we're all here," he said. "Me'Shala, your ministers have a bone to pick with you. In fact, I think I *see* the bone. It's sticking out of that hole in poor Threya." He waved a hand upward, where a hiss drew Brock's attention to the shadows. Threya was there, crouched in the dead branches high above. The left half of her torso was one giant bruise, purple flesh marred with branching veins of black rot. Her eyes were aglow with violet malice.

Selby laughed at his own joke.

"*You're* working with the Lich?" Liza demanded.

"No, child," Selby said. "So close! But no, no, I *am* the Lich."

Brock couldn't believe it. He stood in stunned silence, trying to make sense of Selby's words.

Finally the queen spoke. "That's not possible," Me'Shala said. Her voice trembled with barely contained emotion.

"It's not only possible," Selby said. "It was inevitable. Once, our people strolled the long roads of eternity. We were immortals. The sagas said we had to earn back our right to live forever, but you always lacked the vision and the courage to do what was necessary. How then could any true elf stand by and do nothing?"

"He's lying," Jayna said. "He must be. If he were responsible for this, the power would have consumed him. Turned him into . . ." She waved a hand despairingly at the area where Galvino's corpse had finally fallen to its rest.

Selby nodded sadly. "It's true that with power comes . . . sacrifice, and Mort's assistance isn't free, I'm afraid. The more one pulls from that plane, the more one's body suffers. But I found a way around all that—I only had to use a *little* bit of necromancy, enough to animate *one* corpse, and *that* corpse could act as the focus through which Mort's energies flowed into our plane and raised an army. I suppose it's dear Threya's turn now, but Galvino served the purpose so well, don't you think? He was always the best of us—the most visionary—so I gave him the honor. I controlled the man who controlled the legions." He shrugged. "All great leaders delegate. Of course, he had to die first, but it's not as if he'd have betrayed you willingly."

"Galvino's been dead this whole time," Jett growled. "We were all afraid of the puppet, while we made room at our table for the puppeteer."

"I've been called worse," Selby said. "Though truthfully Freestone's hospitality left something to be desired. I suppose we've *all* suffered a bit."

"Your suffering hasn't yet begun," the queen said. "And it will not soon end, believe me."

"Posture all you want, Me'Shala. It's the only regal thing about you, after all. Well, that and your access to the royal treasury. Couldn't find any way around *that* . . ."

Me'Shala stiffened.

"See your mistake now, do you? Coming all the way back here?" Selby steepled his fingers. "I was content to let you flee to Freestone. That city will fall too, after all. But their wards are better than I expected. I needed another way in. So go on, Me'Shala." He grinned. "Open the door for me."

"Elderon's Shade." Jayna gasped. "The demiplane!" She turned to her friends. "The elves created a way to walk an army right through our wards. The demiplane we traveled through to get here!"

"Its focus is safe within the treasury," Me'Shala explained. "Someplace only one of my blood can reach. Selby needs me alive."

Brock frowned, a memory flaring unbidden at the mention of a treasury. The Lady Gray had expressed her desire for some item from those elven coffers. Had she known Me'Shala had hoarded not riches, but weapons?

"I need *you* alive, yes," Selby said. "But how many of these children are you willing to watch die before you giv—?"

Suddenly, Selby was struck through the heart with an arrow.

His words ended in a bloody cough, and he looked down at his chest in shock.

Brock turned to see that Fel had loosed the arrow. She was already nocking a second in her bow.

Selby gripped the shaft and pulled, tearing the arrow from his chest, heedless of the gore. "Well, anyway, I suppose it's time to take matters into my own hands."

Violet mist roiled where his blood met the air, and Brock knew that the foul energies of Mort were somehow sustaining him.

"I never liked you," Selby said, regarding Me'Shala coldly. "The elves will be better off when you're gone." His eyes flared purple, and the queen was hurled across the room, where Threya fell upon her.

"As for the rest of you," Selby said. Brock shuddered as the minister turned his eyes on them. "I've been paying attention. And I've prepared something special for each of you. The half elf has so much angst about his father, doesn't he?"

Oh, no, Brock thought. He couldn't . . .

Brock turned to look across the room, where the ghostly shapes had roiled within the fog. One of those ghosts had taken ragged form now, and it was drifting slowly toward them.

Toward *Zed*.

Brock felt a wave of hopelessness threaten to overwhelm him. It might have been the wraith's unholy aura, already clawing its way into him at this distance. But he heard Zed's choked sob, and he knew that there was nothing supernatural about what Zed was feeling.

The wraith was hazy, flowing like a tattered banner on a breeze. All the same, Brock could tell it looked a little like Callum. The same jaw, the same flared ears.

But it had Zed's hopelessly messy hair, riddled with cowlicks.

"*Do I have a son?*" the wraith asked in a thin voice, casting about blindly even as it drifted ever closer to Zed. "*I have no son.*"

Brock stepped between Zed and the wraith, turning to grip his friend by the arms. "Zed, listen to me. You have to run. Run!" Zed showed no sign of hearing him, so Brock forcibly turned him around and shoved him. "Don't let that thing touch you!"

Selby chuckled. "Look at you all. The dwarf with his hammer and the wizard with her shield," he said. "You all really should learn some new tricks."

To one side, Jett was surrounded by grasping hands from within the fog. They gripped his hammer with ghostly fingers, trapping the dwarf in a tug-of-war he couldn't win.

Jayna had hurried to the queen's side and thrown her shield up, deflecting the attacks of the other minister, who clawed at the translucent barrier with ragged, bloody fingers. The queen lay unmoving, and Jayna was coughing uncontrollably. Her shield wasn't keeping out the fog, and something in the fog was affecting her. . . .

Micah ran forward, hurling himself at Selby. But the minister caught Micah's punch in one palm.

"Ah, yes," Selby said. "And the obnoxious healer. I'll admit, I was surprised to see the energies of Mort are so vulnerable to that light of yours." Micah's knees buckled, and Selby held fast. "But I'm not fully dead yet. And it just so happens that *I've* got a new trick I've been meaning to try." Brock watched in horror as Selby's ruined chest began to knit itself back together, while purple-black bruises blossomed all along Micah's arm. Micah gasped, writhing in pain, unable to pull away.

Brock rushed forward and slashed at Selby's forearm with his daggers, leaving wicked cuts in his flesh. The minister dropped Micah, but laughed as the new injuries knit themselves closed.

Brock gripped Micah by the arms and pulled him back out of reach, but the boy was heavy. Liza appeared at his side, along with Jett, now hammerless, and they all huddled together. Brock saw that Zed was staying just ahead of the wraith, which pursued him as he elf-stepped blindly across the room; he had to be running out of energy. Fel fought alone against Threya, Jayna and the queen unconscious at her feet.

"The world is dead," Selby said. "It died two hundred years ago. We've tried to deny it, as the elves have long refused to accept death." He grinned. "But death is not the end. Death can be tamed."

Selby began chanting in a low voice, words Brock didn't recognize, but just hearing them filled him with dread. Selby made a furious series of gestures with his fingers, which popped as he forced them into unnatural arrangements. The hair on Brock's arms stood on end as the temperature around them dropped.

A web of purple energy burst forth from Selby's hands. The mass shivered across the chamber, not like light or fire, but like frost upon glass. It was as if the air before them were freezing, cracking, *dying*.

With a splintering lurch, the tangle engulfed them.

Brock shielded his face. It should have been the end, but a sheen of brilliant blue arced suddenly into being, intercepting the attack.

Brock gaped as the energies met. The barrier was a spell he knew well—Jayna's signature Wizard's Shield. But this time, it came from an unexpected source.

Jett's prosthetic leg shone with azure sigils. The dwarf looked down at it in awe as the ethereal bubble shattered into glittering rain all around them.

"What was that?" Brock asked.

"Jayna—she must have enchanted the mythril. Folded the spell right in." Jett grinned. "She really is brilliant."

Selby had evidently put a lot into that blast. He appeared momentarily dazed, staggering backward as his fingers popped back into place. But he wouldn't be down for long.

Brock desperately searched his mind for a solution, some angle that Selby hadn't planned for. Nothing. There was nothing!

Brock shouldn't have even been here. Frond had left him behind for a reason. He wasn't a wizard or a healer. He didn't have any mystical legendary blades. He wasn't a hero.

Brock was a sneak. He was a smuggler and a thief. And all he had left in his useless satchel was a useless pile of . . . a pile of . . .

He gripped Liza by the shoulders. "Follow me. We have to be quick. Hey, *Selby*!" he bellowed.

When the minister looked up, Brock dashed forward and threw his satchel as hard as he could. It slammed into Selby's stomach.

"Run him through!" Brock cried to Liza. "Through the bag!"

Liza did, screaming as she plunged the sword into Selby's stomach. Her momentum carried him back, forcing him against a wall.

The sword flared with golden-green light, making Selby look otherworldly. He laughed as the new wounds they'd inflicted once more knit themselves back together. But soon his laughter stopped. "What?" he said. "What is this?"

Toadstools erupted from the satchel, small and numerous, growing larger as they spread across his abdomen.

Liza hesitated. "Brock, what—?"

"Lanaya said it in Duskhaven: 'Funguses are the great decomposers.' So I . . . took some spores."

Selby shrieked, clawing at Liza's hands now, trying desperately to break her grip on the sword.

"Just don't let up!" Brock cried.

Liza dug her heels in and gritted her teeth, keeping Selby pinned even as he writhed and bucked. His manic movements only made it worse for him; as his wound grew, the Crepuscule filled it with new and hungry life, spurred on by the druidic magic of Liza's shining sword.

The toadstools grew large all around Selby's torso, with smaller tendrils of fungus popping up all along his arms, up his neck. His tongue bubbled and blistered with growths. By the time his eyes and ears were overgrown, his middle section had rotted away entirely, and what was left of the elf slid in pulpy pieces to the floor.

The fog began to thin almost immediately. Brock saw Threya's corpse slump to the floor like a discarded doll beside the unconscious body of the queen she had been forced, in death, to betray. Fel panted with exhaustion, Micah groaned in pain, and Brock's heart thrummed in his chest as he scanned the room for his best friend.

Zed stood eerily still, holding one hand out as the wraith of his lost father frayed apart before him. It looked like he wanted to reach out, to risk touching the phantom, but in the instant before Zed could move, it was gone.

"What—what just *happened*?" Liza said, shaking the rot from her sword, which had grown dim.

Brock fell to his knees. The fear and horror and grief all left him in a rush, but no happiness seeped in to replace it. All he felt now was *tired*. Tired in his limbs, in his bones, and in his heart.

"It doesn't feel like it," he said. "But we won."

Chapter Twenty-One

Zed

I n the days that followed Selby's defeat, Zed watched as winter turned to spring. Not true spring, which was still weeks
away, but a bright and strange likeness of it, courtesy of the
druids.

With the necromancer vanquished, the dracolich had
burned away, exploding into purple fog that drifted apart in the
wind. The rest of the dead who walked Llethanyl fell where they
stood, turning the city itself into a sort of crypt.

Queen Me'Shala and the apprentices had limped from the
palace, exhausted and nearly broken, where they found a small
army of druids waiting in the square. Frond, Hexam, Lotte,
and the surviving rangers had all been herded into a small

circle, with a dozen arrows now pointed their way. The adults looked . . . confused.

As did Me'Shala. Zed had never seen the elven queen so visibly shocked, not even when all three of her own ministers had attacked her.

And so, despite their fatigue, hours of explanation followed, carefully conducted through magicked tokens. All through their talks, Queen Me'Shala watched the druids with naked wonder. And when the story of Duskhaven's survival had finally been told, the queen surprised everyone by bursting into tears.

"*La fael*," Me'Shala said—the elven words for "thank you." "*La fael*, Duskhaven. *La fael*, Frond. *La fael*, apprentices *il* humans *il dro'shea*. *Druids* have returned to the elves!" The queen fell to one knee, her gratitude echoing through the square in three different tongues. She bent low, folding herself into the unmistakable pose for humility.

It seemed elves did bow after all.

After the corpses had been cleared, carried by the rangers into the crypts, the team rested in Llethanyl a few days more. Micah slowly tended to their injuries, careful not to show off too much while Liza was within view. For all their fine control of anima, the druids apparently lacked the ability to heal, a distinction that puzzled the adventurers.

While they recovered, Queen Me'Shala took a needle to one of the city's banners and sewed several small shapes into the design.

Callum and the rangers combed the city. Eventually a hidden cache of ancient-looking manuals on necromancy were discovered in Selby's old rooms, along with a knife carved from solid bone that flickered with ghastly purple gleams. Where Selby had found them remained a mystery. The druids destroyed the knife, and the books were confiscated by Frond, in case there was something useful to be gleaned from them. None of the elves protested.

Zed explored the city during this time, taking in the spiraling towers as they glittered in the sunlight. One afternoon, Callum brought Zed to his childhood home, a strangely lovely house at the edge of the city that was shaped like an onion bulb. The High Ranger ushered his nephew inside, hovering anxiously at the doorway while Zed looked around.

Zed ran his fingers over the unfamiliar furniture. The chairs and dressers were all constructed with looping veins of white wood, lodes that spiraled outward into twirling branches. Light poured in from enormous decorative windows in the ceiling.

It was a home carved from a dream—gorgeous and spacious and absolutely weird. Zed tried to imagine living here—growing up here—but it all felt too strange.

Strange, and *wonderful*.

Then Callum showed him to what had been his father's room. They sat inside, together, talking until the sun fell.

The day before their journey back to Freestone, Zed parked himself against a tree and finished his note to Brock. He wrote it all down, every detail.

He described his vision with Makiva, and their conversation in the otherworldly forest. He wrote of his strange dreams with the watching fox, and the burning chain around his throat.

And Zed told the truth about his green fire. The magic that could mean his execution.

He wasn't sure if he actually had the courage to speak the words aloud to his best friend, but he knew he could hand Brock a note. Then, once Brock had read it, they would decide what to do next. Together.

Once he'd finished, Zed folded the vellum into a neat square and tucked it away into the sorcerous codex. He stood, stretching, enjoying the unnatural warmth provided by the druids.

He decided it would be a good opportunity to try one of the exercises from the codex. At first Zed had been wary of the book, considering it was a gift from Selby, but the elves had assured him its instructions were legitimate.

Zed braced his feet, taking deep, controlled breaths, just as the first exercise described. He closed his eyes, reaching inward, until he felt his mana—the deep, quiet pool. Normally he only skimmed the surface of the pool, taking small sips of magic to better conserve it. But this exercise was about exploration. About learning the depths of his reserves.

With a second breath, Zed plunged himself in magic.

His entire body began to tingle—a pleasant, exhilarating rush. Zed's muscles surged with vitality, and he felt buoyed with confidence. The magic tugged at his hands, a strange yearning sensation. It *wanted* to be used. Wanted to burn.

The instructions for the exercise had said to just test the mana then pull slowly back out again, but they hadn't specifically mentioned *not* casting spells. He would just make a small flame.

Zed raised his right hand into the air. The magic seemed to boil eagerly inside him. It was an itch that demanded scratching.

A curl of green fire unfolded, small and gentle. It weaved between his fingers like a kite in the wind, sailing with lovely precision. Zed grinned, astonished by his own control over the fire. He'd never managed to—

"It burns, Zed."

A sibilant voice hissed loudly in Zed's ears, startling him. He shook his head, alarmed.

"What was—?"

"It burns. It burns. It burns. It burns."

It whispered again. Then again and again.

Zed covered his ear with his left hand. He tried to quash his mana and put out the flame, but the magic was running freely now. He couldn't get a grip on it. Zed felt the mana still tingling throughout his body, growing warm, then hot.

The fire split away from his hand and now began circling around him, growing and changing. It transformed into a blazing chain. Several smaller fires burst into being, hanging in the air like lanterns. Zed remembered these. Makiva had called them will-o-wisps.

"It burns, Zed. It burns. ItburnsZeditburnsITBURNSITBURNS-ZEDITBURNS!!"

Zed opened his mouth to scream, but no noise came out. His head was ringing and the world was spinning. He couldn't breathe. The chain . . . the chain around his throat . . . *was burning.*

"ZED!"

Then, suddenly, the fires all went out. Zed's body went limp, his head and arms lolling forward.

A long moment of quiet passed. A warm breeze stirred the grass around him. Zed rose, blinking into the sun. He glanced around, but the glade was empty. Silent.

He quickly gathered up his scepter and his book, stuffing them both into his bag. Then he turned and marched through the grass, back to the group.

The journey home was long and strenuous. Dangers attacked several times, emboldened by the melting snow, but a large contingent of druids had accompanied the party, and they helped defend against the monsters. There were no casualties, but one of the rangers was bitten by something called a gibbering gab, and she had to be muffled with a wad of cloth when its venom compelled her to recount her most embarrassing secrets.

As the story of Brock's ingenious solution spread among the elves—Smuggling spores from the Crepuscule to combat the undead! Using Liza and her sword to empower their growth!— Zed's friend enjoyed a sort of begrudging admiration from both the rangers and druids.

On the one hand, it was a deceitful act: absconding with a pouch full of Duskhaven's most sacred substance. But ultimately it had worked when nothing else did, and the elves couldn't deny the boy's resourcefulness. Frond, at least, seemed to regard Brock with new esteem.

Though Zed caught Lotte watching the boy suspiciously.

Liza also enjoyed a certain celebrity among the *dro'shea*. For mastering their champion's sword—a feat which hadn't been accomplished in two centuries—the druids had taken to calling her *the green knight*. Zed had never seen her so pleased.

"So what's the title for a female knight?" Brock wondered aloud one evening during camp. "Should we call you Ser Liza now?"

"There was one like a thousand years ago who went by Dame," Micah piped up from the tree where he was reclining. "Rhymes with—"

"You don't want to finish that sentence," Jett said, hefting his hammer from hand to hand. Jayna glared at Micah, seated beside the dwarf.

"Micah, remember what we talked about?" Liza called instructively. "About *killing with kindness*?"

Micah smiled sweetly at his sister. "*Kindness* is a pretty twisted name for a longsword."

"Speaking of," Fel broke in brightly. She was learning to handle the siblings as well as any of them. "Liza should name her new weapon. All the truly legendary blades have names. There's the famous 'bird which dances joyfully in the storm.' Oh, and who could forget 'the last lonely child of the mountain hermit'?"

Jayna shook her head. "My, the elven language is . . . descriptive."

"I already have a name for it," Liza said, holding the sword up against the fire. It glowed prettily in the firelight, almost as if lit by a brightness all its own. "*The Solution*."

The apprentices sat in silence for a moment. Finally, Fel cleared her throat. "That still sounds a little twisted."

Fel, for her part, was treated as no less than the savior of the elves. She was a bridge to the future, the uniter of Llethanyl and Duskhaven, and the restorer of the ancient druids. Her actions in helping Liza to solve the riddle and her final plea for cooperation had been what eventually convinced the druids that Llethanyl might be worth saving.

The queen was effusive in her praise for the girl, often asking Fel to accompany her so that they might speak of the days to come.

On the third day of the journey, Callum joined Zed at the back of the line. He watched the boy for a long beat, but Zed's eyes stayed forward, a casual smile playing across his face. They walked in silence for a time, neither of them speaking.

Finally, the High Ranger broke the quiet. "Zed," Callum started nervously. "I've been thinking about the future. And about you. Thinking perhaps I might—"

Zed laughed. The harsh sound of it brought Callum up short.

"Listen," Zed said. "I can appreciate what you're doing here. It's sweet, really. You feel guilty for abandoning me, but the truth is that I'm fine. I didn't need you then, and I don't now. So if you're entertaining ideas of sticking around and playing the father figure, let me save you the trouble. Your city is saved. Everything worked out. Let's just leave it at that."

Now Zed finally turned. He watched as the ranger's expression tightened in grief.

After a moment, Callum nodded. "Very well," he said thickly.

The ranger's cloak faded from view as he pushed back up the line. Zed's fingers rose, slowly stroking the chain around his neck. A flicker of movement caught his eye and he turned to find Mousebane regarding him from within the trees. The cat's eyes were huge and yellow.

Mousebane hissed at him, the fur along her back standing on end.

Zed's face split into a snarl. He hissed back.

When the Stone Sons caught sight of their party marching up the Broken Roads, the knights' eyes landed first on a banner waving wildly in the breeze.

Horns blared, announcing the team's arrival. By the time the gates had been opened and they finally stepped into the city, a crowd had congregated, whispering curiously.

Queen Me'Shala entered first, with Fel by her side. The young ranger gripped an enormous banner, topped with the emblem of Llethanyl: the great tree wreathed by birds.

But the emblem now featured a new design, an extension that had been added by the queen herself. At the tree's base, a ring of toadstools encircled the roots. It was the ancient symbol of the *dro'shea*, to honor the elves of Duskhaven.

The queen made straight for the city's market, a vision of poise even after her long travels. Zed and the others followed behind, the druids bringing up the rear. Their white masks tilted as they wondered at this strange human city. No knights moved to stop them. Instead, they kept the crowds at bay as their company passed.

When Me'Shala reached the square, the elves erupted from their shanties, pressing around the queen and reaching their hands toward her. Me'Shala extended her left hand, brushing her fingertips with those of her people. Her right arm she kept laid across Fel's shoulders, gently gripping the girl.

The adventurers and druids trailed them, fielding curious looks from both humans and elves.

The market's fountain had been cleared and was now encircled by a phalanx of knights. When Me'Shala and the others arrived, they found King Freestone himself waiting for them beneath the statues of the Champions. His stony expression was markedly *less* adoring than those of the elves who filled the square.

As Me'Shala finally reached him, the monarchs both inclined their heads.

"Your Majesty," the king said gruffly. "Though your people tried to hide it from my Stone Sons, it's come to our attention that you've been missing for a number of days. You *and* the guildmistress of the Adventurers Guild." The king's hard gaze fell to Frond, who looked on silently.

"Not missing, my dear King Freestone," the queen said. "Merely away. We were quite aware of where we were. And I'm pleased to return bearing the most remarkable news. Llethanyl has been restored. The Lich is no more, and my people may return to our home."

The king's mouth fell open.

Whispers broke like waves among the elves as the queen's pronouncement spread through the crowd. They seemed to hardly believe their own monarch. Zed watched as a young wood elf covered his mouth with his hands, tears welling in his eyes.

"How ... ?" the king asked.

"It's a grand story, involving many miraculous turns." The queen shifted, waving her hand to the group of masked elves behind her. "Today marks the beginning of a new era for Llethanyl. It's a moment of transformation, for nothing less will be required of us if we're to avoid repeating the mistakes of our past. But first, my old friend, I would ask you to kindly get these knights *away* from my people."

Things were busy over the next few days, as the elves prepared for their long journey home. Fel was at the guildhall less and less, having become something of a favorite companion of the queen's.

The news that a hidden sect of druids had been discovered sent shock waves through the elves and humans alike. King Freestone called several special councils on the matter, summoning Frond away for hours at a time. Zed and the others weren't privy to these talks, but they got the impression that many questions were asked and only some of them answered. The *dro'shea* of Duskhaven remained aloof, even by elven standards, and they were especially mistrustful of this stone city that had cut itself off from the land.

Still, new ties had been formed. From Freestone's perspective, the small, broken constellation of Terryn's last survivors had grown a bit brighter, and that was a cherished victory.

Zed kept to himself in these days. He ran drills with the others, and was a dutiful student in his lessons with Hexam, but he remained remote. He sat impassively when Jayna finally exploded on Hexam during one of the wizard's more haphazard lectures, berating him for his stinginess in teaching her useful spells for the field.

With Hexam's office in shambles, they'd taken their lessons that day outside in the training yard. A small audience of guild members pretended not to listen while Jayna described how she'd failed her fellow apprentices during the battle against Selby. She used every bad word she knew, and some she didn't but bravely attempted anyway.

"I will never, *ever* find myself unable to protect my friends again—do you hear me? Even if it means I have to go marching into Silverglow Tower itself and demand that *they* provide me with a *real* education. You—you don't appreciate what you have!"

Jayna swallowed, suddenly self-conscious. The nearby adventurers had burst into applause. "In me, I mean."

She left that particular lesson with three new spells to memorize.

And then came the day for farewells.

The adventurers had all gathered just outside the city gates, helping the rangers to oversee the procession of elves as they departed Freestone. Zed stood with the other apprentices, watching Syd wave along a young family of sun elves. The mother cried with joy as she lifted her golden child into her arms and began the long journey homeward.

"I can't believe Fel didn't come to say good-bye," Liza said, wiping away a tear of her own.

"We'll get her on the way out," said Jett. But he, too, seemed glum as his eyes searched through the crowd.

Zed caught sight of Callum leading a troop of clamoring elven children into the center of the procession, where they'd be safest from any monster attacks. In all the time he'd been back, Zed hadn't mentioned Callum once to his mother, much less their family connection.

The High Ranger seemed to sense he was being watched. His gaze rose, and for a moment the two locked eyes, just staring at one another. Then Callum nodded to Zed, his face a mask.

Zed nodded back. An instant later, Callum was gone, ushered away by his duties.

As the morning dwindled, so did the lines of elves exiting the city. Frond joined the apprentices after a time, nodding in a satisfied way at the progress.

Eventually, Me'Shala arrived at the gate, flanked by two new sword sisters in gleaming armor.

"Alabasel, I . . ." The queen seemed to shrink as she reached the guildmistress. Her gaze fell to the ground, then fluttered back up again. "Thank you," she said. "For helping us. For *saving* us."

Frond's face was hard. The edges of her mouth bent into a slight frown. "Freestone and Llethanyl will always be allies," she said blandly. "Remember that as you hoard your illegal magical artifact with the power to infiltrate my city."

The queen pursed her lips. "We're not so different, Alabasel," she murmured. "Is there anything you wouldn't do to protect Freestone? To keep one of those 'last lights' burning?"

The guildmistress remained silent.

Me'Shala sighed, then stood a bit straighter. "Well, in honor of that alliance between our cities, and in thanks for everything you and your people have done for us, at least allow me to leave you with a small gift." The queen held out her hand, where one of the sword sisters placed a crystal flask filled with milky blue liquid. "This is a very rare tincture, a potion whose formula was lost many years ago. Only a few bottles remain among my people. I'd like you to have one." As Me'Shala pressed the flask into Frond's hands she leaned in and whispered something into the guildmistress's ear. Then she kissed her scarred cheek.

Now Frond's stony expression finally melted away. Her eyes widened in shock.

The queen stepped back, smiling slyly. She gazed down at the apprentices. "My thanks to you as well. You children saved my life, and my city. Frond is very lucky to have such a fine team supporting her. You will always be welcome in Llethanyl."

Then Me'Shala glanced to Zed, her eyes lingering, her face unreadable. "Good-bye, Zed. The path of a half elf is a lonely one, and for that you have my pity. But there are good and loyal friends beside you. Treasure them."

Zed nodded. He watched as the queen joined the procession, flanked by her guards, then disappeared into the crowd.

Frond hurried away, leaving the apprentices to attend the last of the rangers as they trailed out of the city. Elves clasped hands with and embraced adventurers, then followed the winding parade as it snaked away into the trees.

Finally, once all of Llethanyl had departed, the Stone Sons closed the city gate.

Jayna wiped her eyes as the apprentices made their way back toward the guildhall's private door. Liza held her friend's shoulder, staring sadly at the ground. Brock and Jett plodded behind, Jett still watching the trees where the elves had disappeared.

"She really didn't say good-bye . . ." he said.

When they arrived at the hatch, Micah reached out to take the handle. But it lurched from his grip, as someone pulled the door open from the other side.

There, Fel gazed out at the apprentices, her eyes bright with cheerful confusion. "Oh, no, you all look so sad! Don't worry—I overheard Frond saying we won't have to wait the full six years until the next visit."

"Fel!" Liza cried, leaping forward and tackling the young elf in a hug. "What are you still doing here? Your people just left!"

Fel laughed, returning the embrace. "Lotte didn't tell you? The queen offered to make me a minister, but I decided to wait. I think she believed that having me around would impress the druids. Or soothe her own conscience." Fel rolled her eyes. "Until Duskhaven revealed themselves, Queen Me'Shala was all too happy to leave my people behind. I'm thrilled that she's committed to change, but she has some hard truths to face about herself, too. I won't be her tool, or her flatterer."

"Wouldn't you be the best choice for a minister, then?" asked Jayna.

"I'm just a kid," Fel said, shaking her head. "And I think that's why she wanted me. The druids will show her what's what. I want to be a *real* minister someday, and I'll make a better one if I have a broader view of other cultures. Maybe you noticed, but elves can be a little exclusive."

"Now that you mention it . . ." Brock said with a grin.

"Anyway, I'm now the official elven liaison to the Adventurers Guild." She beamed at her friends. "Mousebane and I are staying in Freestone!"

Zed watched.

He watched as the adventurers meandered aimlessly around their hall, adrift in the suddenly ample space.

He watched as Frond called Hexam and Lotte urgently into her office, her hand trembling as it gripped the flask Me'Shala had given her. Once they were all inside, the guildmistress slammed the door closed behind them.

He watched as Brock turned to him, his eyebrows raised inquisitively. "She *really* needs to work on the whole subtlety thing," Brock said.

Zed watched. His mouth opened, and words came drifting out: "I guess so."

But Zed hadn't spoken them. *Zed* hadn't spoken once since they'd left Llethanyl. Nor had he moved a muscle. He could only watch as *someone else* manipulated his hands and spoke with his voice. And this presence was now turning him away from his best friend, while Zed screamed silently in his own mind.

"Brock! Brock! Help me! BROCK!"

"Hey, uh, Zed . . . ?" Brock said.

Zed's body stopped. It pivoted, turning back toward the boy.

"In Duskhaven I mentioned there was something I needed to tell you." Brock's voice was soft. Nervous. "And you said there was something you wanted to confess to me, too. Do you . . . Is everything all right?"

"Brock, this isn't me! Can't you tell this isn't me?"

Zed's face smirked. "Yeah, sorry about that. Guess all the excitement just got to me. Honestly, I can't even remember what I meant to tell you. But if there's something *you* need to get off your chest, feel free."

"I . . . what?" Brock faltered. He looked stricken. "It sounded like it might be important, though. Like you were in trouble."

"Obviously it wasn't *that* important, or I'd remember."

A long moment passed, while Brock frowned skeptically at him. "You know what? Forget it. It's fine."

Zed's body turned away without a moment's hesitation. "Forgotten."

Zed howled as his legs carried him away from his bewildered friend and through the guildhall. They marched him up the stairs to the barracks and then into his room. Most of the guild was still downstairs, so the cramped quarters were silent and empty. Zed's hand gently closed the door behind him.

"Nice try, Zed," said the presence who spoke with his voice. It was the first time the presence had ever acknowledged him. Zed was shocked into silence by the strangeness of being addressed by himself. "Sorry, but I can't have you spilling our secrets, can I? Our pact is between *us*."

Zed's body crossed the room and sat down upon his mattress. His hands worked slowly and patiently as they untied his boots. "I've been watching you, you know. Keeping an eye on you from the necklace. Keeping you safe, like any good mentor would. I told you that once you'd made your way in the world, we could speak again of payments. But I never dreamed it would happen this fast. You were more powerful than Foster ever was. The fire burned so *brightly* in your hands."

Makiva.

Zed's mouth curled into a smile. "With my help, you'll accomplish so many great things, my talented pupil. So many great and terrible and *gruesome* things. When we're through, this dreary world will fall away like a dream, and you'll witness horrors unlike anything you can imagine. This time we'll do it right, Zed, *without* any interruptions." Makiva sighed, pulling Zed's boots gently from his feet. "But there are still so many preparations to make. We must be patient, you and I."

As Zed watched helplessly, a pair of burning eyes opened in the far corner of the room. Green flames licked outward from the orbs, forming into the fiery shape of a fox. It was the animal from Zed's dreams, the watcher who'd spoken to him in urgent whispers.

The creature's shape billowed, exploding into smoke as the

flames finally guttered away. The clouds expanded, re-forming into a gaunt man with haunted eyes and pointed ears.

The man seemed almost to be made of the strange smoke. His shape curled and twisted in surprising directions.

"I tried to warn you." Zed heard a wry voice echoing through his thoughts, as if it inhabited the same strange nonspace from which he watched Makiva controlling his body. *"She hides inside the chain. Uses the fire to burn a way into you. You used too much of it, and now she'll take what's owed her."*

"Foster," Zed gasped. *"Foster Pendleton."* His own bodiless voice was laced with disgust.

The smoky figure nodded slightly.

"Welcome to the club, kid."

Chapter Twenty-Two

Brock

After so many days on the Broken Roads, the warrens beneath the streets of Freestone felt cramped. Brock was eager to do his business and get back to the guildhall. Get back *home*, he tried out, and found that the thought fit well enough.

He donned his slender mask, made his way to the Lady Gray's office, and removed the panel in the wall. He paused only when he'd dipped his quill in ink and stood before the ancient map. Was he really prepared to do this?

"There's a hidden village," he said. "Those masked elves—I'm sure you heard about them?"

The Lady inclined her head.

"You should send for Master Curse," Brock said, and then he got to work on the map, starting with Celadon Falls and working his way back along the path. By the time he'd finished, Master Curse had joined them. The magus leaned against a bookshelf and glared.

"There's a whole city hidden in the middle of the forest. Elven druids have been living there, without walls, since the Day of Dangers."

"How is that possible?" asked Curse.

"I can't quite put my finger on it." Brock pulled a small package from his new satchel. It was a tightly wadded handkerchief the size of a pomegranate. "Oh, wait, that doesn't quite work unless you realize—there's a finger wrapped up in here."

Curse recoiled. Brock thought it was funny, but he himself flinched when he realized the Lady was standing at his shoulder. "Explain," she said.

"It's the Lich's finger. It's all that's left of him, and it's riddled with a fungus—the same species that the druids use to protect their city."

"Magic?" she asked. "Like our wards?"

"Something like that, but their version is a huge mushroom in the center of the city. It keeps away the Dangers and even the snow. Their stories claim it originated in Fey."

"Interesting," Curse said. "True or not, it's certainly interesting."

"I had a bag full of spores for you," Brock said. "I . . . lost it. And this is the best I could do."

The Lady fixed her eyes on Curse. "You can work with this?"

Curse wrinkled his nose. "If I must." He held out a hand for the package.

"Careful with it," Brock said, feeling a pang of guilt. "The druids . . . this thing is sacred to them."

"It's a rotting finger," Curse said, snatching it from Brock's hand. "And potentially a great weapon. No more than that."

"Well," Brock said. "It's more like a *shield* than a weapon."

"Of course," the Lady Gray purred. "I'm sure that's what he meant."

When Curse had gone, Brock sighed wearily. "Well, I'd love to say it's been fun, but even *I'm* not that good a liar. Are we done here?"

The Lady took up one of her ledgers and flipped through it. "You may see yourself out."

"I mean are we *done*?" Brock said hotly. "I just betrayed an entire civilization for you. I brought back a kind of magic we didn't even know existed. And I don't want to brag or anything, but in stopping a power-mad Lich before he could tear Freestone down to its foundations, I also *saved your life*. Although that last part was more of an unhappy side effect."

"You're right," she said, bobbing her head. "You've certainly proven your value, Brock Dunderfel! I do believe I'll keep you after all." She put the book down to give him an unobstructed view of her smile. "You didn't think I'd just cut you loose, really? Just like that?"

Brock's fury rose within him, but he knew better than to unleash it, knew from a lifetime's practice how to temper and tame it and—

"Forget it," he said. "I'm done. Forget you, and forget Zed, who clearly doesn't want *my* help. And forget our idiot king and this lousy city full of awful people. I'm done." He ripped the mask from his face and let it flutter to the floor, then he ground it beneath his boot. "I quit."

He didn't even take a moment to savor the look of shock on the Lady's face as he turned his back on her and stormed out of her office.

It had taken longer than he'd expected, but he'd finally managed to wipe that intolerable smirk off her face.

It was late when Brock returned to the Sea of Stars guildhall. He crept silently through the door, hoping he might get to bed for once without having to lie to any of his friends.

Sure enough, the common area was empty of friends. Alabasel Frond sat alone in the dark, leaning her chin into her fists, gazing off into the distance.

For a breathless moment, Brock feared he had been caught.

But he forced himself to stay calm. Whatever Frond knew, he could talk his way out of it.

But when he took a step forward, Frond looked sharply at him and said, "I didn't see you there." Then she returned to her quiet contemplation—gazing not at a distant nothing, Brock realized, but at the statue at the back of the room. The statue that had once been a living boy.

Brock swallowed a dozen jokes. The sight of Frond deep in thought was comical to him and practically begged for comment. But he'd heard the story about how she had dragged that stone-cursed boy back to the guildhall, all alone for days, surrounded by Dangers, her fingers a bloody mess and her back in such pain she'd finally submitted herself to the ministrations of the Golden Way healers she so disliked.

"Do you know the elves have no word for 'regret'?" she asked.

"I might have heard that," Brock said. "It doesn't mean they don't *feel* regret, though."

"I'm not sure," Frond said, keeping her eyes forward. "After everything Me'Shala did, everything her people had been through—everything she had us *risk* for her. She tried to explain her actions, but I know she wouldn't do anything differently if she could change it. Isn't that what *regret* means?" She narrowed her eyes. "A determination to do better. To *be* better."

Brock smirked. Frond managed to make emotions sound like exercise.

"The elves didn't believe in death, not really, and it nearly cost them everything," she said, standing. "Maybe I'm the same. The more I try to save everyone, the more death I see." She strode toward the statue. "You may as well stick around to watch, I suppose."

"Uh, watch what?"

It was then Brock saw she was holding something. It was the gift Me'Shala had given her—a strange blue liquid in a delicate and beautiful flask.

Frond shattered that flask over the statue's head.

"Hey!" Brock said, taking a step back though he was nowhere near the shards of glass. "How about some warning next—"

He stopped, the words failing him as he watched the viscous liquid drip over the stone boy's brow, off his nose, pattering on his shoulders and his outstretched hand. Wherever the liquid touched stone, veins stretched out, a patchwork web of blue upon gray. But those veins were not liquid and they were not webs. They were cracks.

The statue was coming apart.

Brock saw the worry on Frond's face, and he feared that this was some strange mercy—that the boy who'd been turned to stone would now crumble to ash before them. When the stone fell away, though, there was something behind it: Cloth. Flesh. Terrified eyes. The boy was still there, whole beneath the stone, and he was alive.

He collapsed into Frond's outstretched arms, trembling and weak. "Brock, water!" she barked. He snapped out of his trance and brought a pitcher forward.

The boy gaped. "How—? Where?"

"You're safe," Frond said, lowering him gently to the ground, but keeping one hand at the back of his head, the other lightly touching his shoulder. "You're home, Nirav."

Nirav appeared delirious; his hair and skin were covered with powdered stone, but he made no effort to wipe it away. He blinked as if blinded by the low light, and his voice was weak and raw.

"Drink," Frond said, holding the pitcher to his lips.

Nirav drank, and then he fell into sleep. Brock stood there for a long time in silence while Frond held the unconscious boy. When at last he turned to leave, Frond spoke.

"*This* is how we save the world, Brock," she said. "This is how we win it back. One life at a time."

Acknowledgments

I f writing a book is an adventure, then writing a series is an epic quest—one that would be impossible without the support of an extraordinary cast of supernatural helpers. We are immensely grateful to our family and our friends: those who have cheered us on, challenged us, and inspired us—and, we suspect, cast a spell or two to guide us along the way. There's no other explanation for how fortunate we are; it must be magic.

A special round of thank-yous is due to the amazing Disney Hyperion team, the true heroes behind these books. Thanks to editorial warriors Kieran and Mary, design wizard Mary Claire, and that gallery of rogues, Cassie, Seale, Dina, and Kevin. And to the dozens of others across the company, those unsung heroes whose labors get these books into the hands of readers worldwide: Thank you. We couldn't ask for better guildmates.

Thanks once again to Manuel Sumberac and Virginia Allyn

for lending their enormous talents to the creation of the book's cover and map, respectively. These are gorgeous works of art, and we're humbled to see the world we imagined come to life in so stunning a fashion.

Our agents, Ammi-Joan Paquette and Josh & Tracey Adams, possess the wisdom of the ages. We are so very lucky for their guidance and their faith.

We're especially grateful for the insights of our sensitivity readers, Kati Gardner and Natasha Razi, as well as our indispensable early reader (and Frond's #1 fan), Laura Bisberg. And thanks to Damien Mittlefehldt for lending us his video-making skills—and for finding the last quiet corner of New York City.

Our deepest appreciation goes to the teachers, librarians, parents, and booksellers who coordinated our many school visits. Your generosity, positivity, and commitment left an unforgettable impression on us, and we're honored to have joined such a passionate community of book lovers and literacy advocates.

In fact, far and away our favorite part of this entire experience has been the opportunity to interact with our young readers. So a special, wholehearted thanks to all the kids out there who have joined the guild—especially to the self-identified nerds among you. You were our inspiration on days when the writing was difficult—and we *can't wait* to see the stories that you go on to write in the future.

Finally, to Zack and Andrew: You make the entire journey worthwhile. This one's for you.

DON'T MISS THE THRILLING
CONCLUSION TO THE TRILOGY

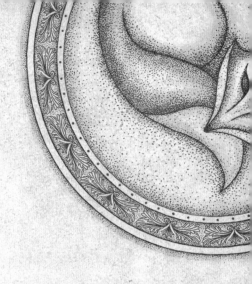

Chapter One

Zed

Makiva stood in the crowded market, gazing across a crush of people. She watched with eyes that were not her own. Thin, tawny fingers—Zed's fingers—brushed the scepter that was sheathed at her side.

People.

She had known so many of them in her long lifetime. All sorts. She'd walked the royal courts of both human and elven capitals. She'd seen the dwarves of Dragnacht forge their rune-enchanted blades—a secret no outsider had ever beheld. She'd hunted wolves with the northern orcs and enjoyed a meal of fragrant cheeses in a halfling hillhouse. She'd even witnessed the "Day of Dangers" firsthand, and the many atrocities that *people* were capable of, after the illusion of civilization had been dispelled from their world.

Makiva had met some of the best and worst people that Terryn had to offer. She'd even taught a few.

She'd despised them all.

How long had she spent among these soft, comfortable cowards, crammed within their walls like maggots inside a—

"Mmmmm, delicious."

Ahead of her, Brock took in an obnoxiously loud sniff of the air, interrupting her thoughts. "I love the scent of the market in the morning," he said. "The freshly baked bread, the crisp sawdust . . . and it's early, so there's only a *hint* of garbage smell." Brock turned to grin at his friend, and Makiva forced Zed's lips into something resembling a smile. There were teeth, at least.

"Indeed," she muttered blandly.

Once Brock had turned back around, the smile coiled into a sneer. Of all the *people* still clinging to this mudball of a world, Makiva especially despised Brock Dunderfel. She could barely get a minute away from the mouthy twerp anymore. No matter how cold she was to him, he seemed determined to repair the boys' fractured friendship.

That, or he'd grown suspicious of Zed, and was keeping an eye on him. Makiva wasn't sure which was more irksome.

"I still think you'd have had better luck at the smithy's," said Liza. "Frond prefers practical gifts to . . . whatever it is you're hoping to find *here*." She frowned at the tailors' stands, and the reams of colorful cloth that festooned the market's garment rows.

"Well, you only have yourself to blame for *practically* buying the Smiths Guild out of stock," Brock said. "How many throwing stars can one woman own before the king starts to worry?"

The three apprentices wandered the market with Lotte, so Brock could retrieve a last-minute birthday present for Alabasel Frond. The guildmistress turned a mere fifty years old that day, but the adventurers acted as if she'd climbed into a dragon's maw and lived to gossip about the cavities.

Frond had said no celebration. She'd demanded it, in fact. But apparently it held some significance to the guild that their leader's age was once again divisible by ten. Enough so that Lotte had disobeyed a direct order and planned a surprise party.

Now Lotte glanced down at Makiva. An expression of concern pursed her brow. "Zed, are you sure you don't want a little silver for a gift? Honestly, I wouldn't mind."

Makiva shrugged, glancing away from the quartermaster and back toward the shoppers and merchants who buzzed about the square. "I've already finished my preparations," she said in Zed's high tenor.

It was almost true. Makiva had so many wonderful plans for Freestone: a garden of horrors that was just on the verge of flowering. Some had been years in the making, but Makiva was very patient.

As she watched the adventurers joke and chat, she brushed Zed's fingers against the mythril chain that was wreathed around his neck. For the first time that morning, a true smile graced Zed's lips.

These people had no idea what was coming for them.

Zed watched his own back as it moved through the market, ambling unhurriedly behind his friends.

Watching was all he—the real Zed—could do anymore.

On a cool, dark morning shortly after his possession, he'd found himself aburptly ejected from his own body, as if Makiva had shouldered him out. He still remembered the shock of suddenly seeing *himself* rise from bed—the cold horror of his lips smiling and his arms stretching lazily upward, all without him. "Finally, a little elbow room," Makiva had sighed with pleasure. It was the last time she'd acknowledged him.

He followed now as a strange sort of spirit—a smoky, invisible bystander, billowing just a few feet away. Though he moved through the crowd, eyes passed over him without notice. No one could see him.

Though not for lack of trying. Zed had spent the last several weeks trying desperately to break through to his friends. He'd screamed in their ears from morning bell 'til night, and made horrible, vulgar faces just inches from their noses. He'd tried pleading and cajoling and calling them names. Nothing had worked.

So far.

"Oh, what about these leather bracers?" Liza said, skipping to a nearby tanner's stand. "Frond's last pair were melted by a spitting multipede."

"Not bad, but I've got something a bit . . . frillier in mind." Brock's eyes twinkled mischievously.

"Oh no," Liza breathed. "Brock, what did you do?"

"I wasn't here," said Lotte, rubbing her temples. "I had no part in this. Frond will be mad enough about the party."

"Brock once bought his dad a silver-plated shoehorn," Zed announced. *"He wrote a note saying he should have 'something nice to wedge his head from his own butt.'"* Zed laughed at the memory. Occasionally it helped just to talk to his friends, to pretend like things were normal.

Though sometimes it made him feel worse. Zed's laughter ebbed. *"I wish you all could hear me,"* he said with a sigh.

He knew the others had no sense that he was there. Maybe he was only torturing himself. But loneliness had been taking its toll.

"Brock, tell me this isn't going to be another silver-plated shoehorn."

Zed's attention snapped to his body, where Makiva was smirking. She flicked *his eyes* to him—the briefest glance—then back toward Brock.

Brock laughed, slapping a hand on the imposter's shoulder. "No prank is worth the punishment I got for that one. Though it was close."

Zed glared as Makiva giggled in his voice, but she didn't spare him another glance.

"Be careful what you wish for around her. She'll use it against you every time."

A second smoky figure stretched lazily into being. Soon a gaunt man with a tired face and pointed ears sat atop one of the booths. Like Zed, this spirit also wore a chain around his neck, but his edges were more frayed. Smoke curled slowly away from the boundaries of his form.

This was Foster Pendleton, also known as the Traitor of Freestone. He was the most famous elf-blooded man in history, and the warlock who had ended the world.

"Not now, Foster," Zed muttered. *"I'm trying to contact my friends. I'm pretty sure I saw Brock's ear twitch in my direction this time."*

Foster was a victim of Makiva's, too, though he hadn't yet offered up any details about how he'd fallen into the witch's power. Or about his role in the Day of Dangers.

Then again, Zed hadn't asked. It wasn't that he didn't have questions for the warlock—Zed had many of them, history books full—but a part of him was scared of what the answers would be.

The other spirit merely rolled his eyes. *"As much as I admire your demented determination,"* he said, *"they're never going to respond. Only Makiva can see or hear us. Give it a rest. You're exhausting to watch."*

"*Well*, you're *welcome to leave*," Zed responded with a glare. "*I'll call you if I need a depressing grump.*"

"*If only I could*," Foster said. "*But, like you, I'm still tethered to the chain.*"

The warlock exploded into a curl of smoke, then twisted through the air, re-forming beside Brock. He peered down at the boy. "*Hey Brock*," he said. "*Liza's way out of your league and your punch lines are adequate at best.*" Then he turned to Zed, shrugging. "*See? If that didn't give him goose bumps, I don't know what will.*"

Foster dissolved again, re-forming several feet away atop the stall of an oblivious haberdasher. He pretended to dust off his eternally undusty sleeves. "*Though it* was *kind of fun. Perhaps you're on to something, after all.*"

"*Please*," Zed hissed. Foster glanced up from his cuff, his smile faltering at Zed's expression. "*She's taken everything from me.... I have to keep trying.*"

The warlock sighed and shook his head. "*Not everything, Zed. Not by a long shot. When this is over, she'll have taken things from you that you didn't even realize you had to lose.*" The spirit extended his arms, and that was when Zed realized where they'd arrived.

Surrounding them was the fountain square. The stage where Zed had undertaken his Guildculling loomed nearby, though today it was bare of flags and frippery. The square's fountain stood at the center of the space, the four Champions of Freestone still watching over the city, immortalized as statues.

Foster's gaze moved between the figures, his lips pressed tightly together. Then he settled on the fifth plinth, the empty one that represented Foster himself. His image was forever unwelcome in Freestone.

"Better not to hope," Foster said softly, *"than have those hopes turned against you."*

For a moment, the warlock's edges became indistinct as he stared at the plinth. His features swam, the smoke churning. Then, with an irritated grunt, he snapped back into focus.

"Oh Brock, no . . ." Liza's voice cut through the noise of the crowd. She began to laugh, a high belly laugh that filled Zed simultaneously with delight and despair.

Brock stood before a tailor's stall, holding a lacy white apron on which the words "World's Best Guildmistress" had been sewn in a loopy script. Both *i*'s in *Guildmistress* were dotted with hearts.

Liza nearly fell over, she was laughing so hard. Even Lotte was working to contain a smile. Only Makiva, watching from within Zed's body, seemed immune to the joke. She glanced distractedly around the square. Zed watched his own eyes as they searched through the crowd.

They alighted on something, Makiva's gaze focusing.

"It cost a small fortune to have it made in time," said Brock, "but I think you'll agree that Frond is worth it."

"I don't know whether I want to be there when she sees it," said Lotte, "or if I want to be very far away."

Zed followed Makiva's glance to a tall, thin man who was

standing in the center of the square. He was dressed in the distinctive robes of a magus—a ranking member of the Mages Guild—though his robes were crimson colored, instead of the usual blue. The mage's hood was pulled up so that it concealed most of his head, but his face was clearly visible. He looked dazed, his eyes far away.

"Help," the man said softly. Mildly. "Please help."

No one in the crowd appeared to hear him. Shoppers passed distractedly.

"Help," the man said again. "Please I . . . seem to have made a terrible mistake. I just wanted—" He tilted, nearly falling into a woman who was carrying a bushel of wheat. She shrieked as she scrambled out of his way.

The cry caught the attention of the others. Zed watched Brock as he glanced toward the man, and saw his friend's eyes brighten with recognition.

"Master . . . Curse?" Brock muttered under his breath.

The mage was stumbling now, tilting back and forth as he moved. His eyes grew vaguer, his pupils rolling slackly. A ropy line of drool fell from his mouth, dribbling onto his robes.

"Oh dear," the man said. "Oh no. Help. I just wanted . . . I just wished to expand my mind."

A low hum began buzzing in the air, so soft that Zed could barely hear it. All around him, shoppers and merchants placed their hands to their ears. Some rubbed at their temples, their faces screwed up in pain.

Zed glanced to Foster. *"What's happening?"*

The other spirit's face was grave. *"Something very bad."*

Lotte touched a finger to her face, just under her nose. It came away bloody. "What in the—?"

The mage's hood slipped, falling to his shoulders. Which was when Zed saw the thing that was clinging to his skull.

It was unlike any creature he'd ever encountered, natural or Danger. Thick tentacles coiled around the magus's head, each pulsing with its own serpentine movements, as if they were separate beings. But the limbs connected at a gelatinous mantle, which clutched his skull like the palm of a large fleshy hand.

Two wide, glassy eyes stared out into the crowd from that mantle, bright with unfathomable intelligence.

The magus's mouth lolled open. "Hel—"

The market exploded with noise. The buzzing sound sharpened, filling the air like a scream. Shoppers grabbed their heads, their faces wild with pain. Those unlucky enough to be closest to the magus fell immediately to the cobbles. Their eyes rolled up so that only the whites showed. Blood dribbled from their noses.

Zed glanced back to his friends, who were similarly affected. Brock pulled at his hair, howling, while Lotte thrashed and fell back into a tent tarp.

Liza sank to her knees, screwing her eyes closed. She tried to reach for her sword, but her hand was trembling so badly she couldn't unsheathe it.

"I've seen this before!" Foster called over the hum. *"It's a type of*

Danger called a mindtooth! It consumes its victims' brains, using them for psychic energy!"

Zed rushed to Brock's side. His friend's eyes were frantic. All around the square, more people were seizing and collapsing. The very air seemed to vibrate. It was all Zed could do to hear anything through the noise.

"Why isn't it affecting us like them?" Zed shouted to Foster.

"We aren't really here!" Foster called back. *"We're both trapped in the chain!"*

Zed glanced at his body as Makiva also took a knee. The imposter placed his hands to his temples, but Zed's mouth was smiling, and his eyes gleamed with stormy satisfaction. Small waxy stoppers had been plugged into his ears. Makiva had . . . protected herself?

"Makiva!" Zed yelled. *"She did this somehow!"*

"Wow, what a bright kid you are! No wonder the Mages Guild wanted you!"

A shadow fell across the cobbles as a single shape rose slowly off the ground. Zed turned to see that Liza had risen unsteadily to her feet. Clutched in her hand was the Solution, the mysterious green sword she'd won that winter from a sect of elven druids.

Liza took a shaky step toward the magus.

Foster arched an eyebrow, still standing by the fountain. *"Your friend has some spunk!"* he called. *"But she'll never make it! The shrill of a mindtooth is overwhelming. Everyone in this square will be dead by the next bell! Except Makiva, of course!"*

Dead by the next bell . . .

Zed surged forward as a cloud of smoke, then re-formed beside Liza. *"Liza!"* he shouted right in her ear. *"Keep going! You can do it!"*

Liza gritted her teeth. She took another step forward.

Zed glanced to the magus, a good ten feet away. He was still standing, but his body hung limply—a coat dangling from a peg. The mindtooth's grip had expanded; its tentacles now covered most of the man's head. Those awful eyes continued to stare outward, wide and emotionless.

Liza took two more clumsy steps, then nearly pitched over. Zed followed just beside her. He tried to put his hand on her shoulder, to help steady her, but it dissolved on contact, puffing into a brume of vapor. It re-formed only after he'd pulled away.

Liza shrieked. Blood dripped from her nose and veins pulsed in her temples.

"Liza, don't you dare give up!" Zed shouted. *"You are the strongest person I know! Take another step! Take it* now!*"*

She did. Her foot lurched forward and the rest of Liza followed slowly behind.

"Another!"

She took another.

"And another!"

"I can't!" Liza screamed.

From the hat stand, Foster leaned forward in surprise. *"Wait, did she . . . ?"*

"*You can, Liza, and by Fie you will!*" Zed boomed. "*Take. Another. Step. NOW!*"

With a warrior's bellow Liza surged onward, making three long strides toward the mindtooth and raising her sword.

Zed gasped as the waves of pressure emanating from the Danger appeared to break over the blade, just like ripples of parting water. One more grueling step, and Liza stood within a foot of the creature. She held her sword high, a lantern guiding her through the dark.

"*I can't believe it . . .*" Foster said with earnest wonder. "*Keep going, muscular little girl! Keep going!*"

The wide eyes of the mindtooth rolled toward Liza, spinning loosely in their sockets. Suddenly a tentacle snapped free from the magus's head, shooting toward her raised blade. It slithered around the sword and tried to pry it from Liza's hand.

The girl held firm, bracing her boots into the cobblestones.

Another tentacle shot out, then a third. They pulled together, nearly tugging Liza off her feet.

"*Liza, you've got it!*" Zed shouted from beside her. "*Now do what you do best!*"

"*I . . . protect . . . my . . . city!*" Liza howled and pulled at her blade. The mindtooth's eyes spun wildly as it scrabbled to cling to the mage's head, but too many of its tentacles were wrapped around the sword. She tore the Danger away from the magus with a ferocious scream.

The buzzing noise cut off suddenly, and every person in the

square seemed to slump as one, the tension leaving their bodies.

Every person except Liza. The girl raised her sword over her head and brought the mindtooth down hard against the cobbles—once, twice, three times—each with a viscous, wet *plop*.

"*Shining Lux, she did it!*" Foster hooted, billowing just beside Zed. "*Your friend slew a mindtooth! Wow!*"

All around them, people were beginning to cry and scream. Zed saw that many were rising with dazed expressions, but some—too many—stayed collapsed against the stones.

The body of the magus lay limp in the center of the square, totally still.

Zed rushed to find Brock, but his friend was already standing, helping Lotte to her feet. The quartermaster's face was pale as ash.

Only Zed's own face was calm. Serene, even.

Zed watched as Makiva rose and discreetly removed her earplugs. His own brown eyes were sparkling with amusement. She glanced right at Zed—at the real Zed—and winked.

"*That doesn't seem good,*" Foster muttered.

"*No,*" Zed croaked. Dread gripped his throat. It felt just like a burning chain. "*No, I think things are about to get much worse.*"